My Friend Smith
A Story of School and City Life

by
Talbot Baines Reed

My Friend Smith
A Story of School and City Life
by Talbot Baines Reed

Copyright © 2024

All Rights reserved.

No part of this publication may be reproduced, stored in a retrieval system, or transmitted in any form or by any means, electronic, mechanical, photocopying or Otherwise, without the written permission of the publisher.
The author/editor asserts the moral right to be identified as the author/editor of this work.

ISBN: 978-93-63053-96-0

Published by
DOUBLE 9 BOOKS
2/13-B, Ansari Road
Daryaganj, New Delhi – 110002
info@double9books.com
www.double9books.com
Tel. 011-40042856

This book is under public domain

ABOUT THE AUTHOR

Talbot Baines Reed was an English author of boys' fiction who lived from April 3, 1852, to November 28, 1893. He created a type of school stories that lasted until the middle of the 20th century. The Fifth Form at St. Dominic's is one of his most well-known works. He often and regularly wrote for The Boy's Own Paper (B.O.P.). Most of his writing was first published there. Reed became a well-known typefounder through his family's business. He also wrote the standard work on the subject, History of the Old English Letter Foundries. John Reed was a colonel in Oliver Cromwell's army during the English Civil War. The Reed family came from him. Their home was in Maiden Newton, which is in the county of Dorset. They moved to London at the end of the 18th century. Andrew Reed (1787–1862), Talbot Reed's grandpa, was a minister in the Congregational Church and the founder of many charitable organizations, such as the London Orphan Asylum and a hospital for people who could not get better. He was also a well-known hymn writer. His "Spirit Divine, attend our prayers" can still be found in many hymnals today. Talbot Baines Reed grew up in a happy family where Charles Reed was very religious and thought that tough outdoor games were the best way to raise boys.

CONTENTS

Chapter One
 How I came to be sent to Stonebridge House 9

Chapter Two
 How I made my First Acquaintance with Stonebridge House 16

Chapter Three
 How a Mysterious New Boy came to Stonebridge House 24

Chapter Four
 How Smith and I took a breath of Fresh Air and Paid for it 33

Chapter Five
 How a Chapter of Misfortunes befel My Friend Smith and Me 43

Chapter Six
 How things came to a Crisis at Stonebridge House 52

Chapter Seven
 How there arose a Notable Rebellion at Stonebridge House 60

Chapter Eight
 How the Rebellion collapsed, and we left Stonebridge House 69

Chapter Nine
 How I replied to an Advertisement and waited for the Answer 79

Chapter Ten
 How I ran against my Friend Smith in an Unexpected Quarter 89

Chapter Eleven
 How my Friend Smith and I entered on New Duties in New Company 100

Chapter Twelve
 How my Friend Smith and I knocked about a Bit in our New Quarters 109

Chapter Thirteen
    How my Friend Smith and I caught a Young Tartar 118

Chapter Fourteen
    How Smith went Home and I took Part in an Evening Party 128

Chapter Fifteen
    How I got rather the Worst of it in a Certain Encounter 138

Chapter Sixteen
    How I experienced some of the Downs and Ups of Fortune 148

Chapter Seventeen
    How I gave a Little Supper to some of my Friends 157

Chapter Eighteen
    How my Friend Smith came back, and told me a Great Secret 166

Chapter Nineteen
    How Hawkesbury put in an Appearance at Hawk Street 176

Chapter Twenty
    How I served my Friend Smith anything but a Good Turn 184

Chapter Twenty One
    How a Door closed between my Friend Smith and me 193

Chapter Twenty Two
    How I tried to forget my Friend Smith, and failed 201

Chapter Twenty Three
    How I began to discover that I was not a very
    Nice Boy after all 210

Chapter Twenty Four
    How I found that Hope deferred makes the Heart sick 219

Chapter Twenty Five
    How I took part in a not very successful Holiday Party 229

Chapter Twenty Six
    How I fell badly, and was picked up in a way
    I little expected 238

Chapter Twenty Seven
    How I suffered a Relapse, which did me good 247

Chapter Twenty Eight
   How I found myself once more at Hawk Street 256

Chapter Twenty Nine
   How I began to see Daylight through my Troubles 265

Chapter Thirty
   How I paid off a Score, and made a rather
   Awkward Discovery 275

Chapter Thirty One
   How I made a still more Important Discovery 284

Chapter Thirty Two
   How I came to have several Important Cares upon me 293

Chapter Thirty Three
   How Several Visitors Called at our Lodgings 302

Chapter Thirty Four
   How I got rid of the Petty-Cash, and of Mr Smith's Secret 311

Chapter Thirty Five
   How Jack and I talked louder than we need have done 320

Chapter Thirty Six
   How Hawkesbury and I came across one another
   rather seriously 328

Chapter Thirty Seven
   How Hawkesbury and I spent a Morning in
   the Partners' Room 338

Chapter Thirty Eight
   How I ended the Day more comfortably than
   I had expected 348

Chapter Thirty Nine
   Which parts me from the Reader, but not from my
   Friend Smith 355

Chapter One
How I came to be sent to Stonebridge House

"It was perfectly plain, Hudson, the boy could not be allowed to remain any longer a disgrace to the neighbourhood," said my uncle.

"But, sir," began my poor old nurse.

"That will do, Hudson," said my uncle, decisively; "the matter is settled—Frederick is going to Stonebridge House on Monday."

And my uncle stood up, and taking a coat-tail under each arm, established himself upon the hearthrug, with his back to Mrs Hudson. That was always a sign there was no more to be said; and off I was trotted out of the dreaded presence, not very sure whether to be elated or depressed by the conversation I had overheard.

And indeed I never was quite clear as to why, at the tender and guileless age of twelve, I was abruptly sent away from my native village of Brownstroke, to that select and popular "Academy for Backward and Troublesome Young Gentlemen," (so the advertisement ran), known as Stonebridge House, in the neighbourhood of Cliffshire.

Other people appeared to divine the reason, and Mrs Hudson shook her head and wiped her eyes when I consulted her on the subject. It was queer. "I must be a very backward boy," thought I to myself, "for try as I will, I don't see it."

You must know I was an orphan. I never could recollect my mother—nor could Mrs Hudson. As to my father, all I could recall of him was that he had bushy eyebrows, and used to tell me some most wonderful stories about lions and tigers and other beasts of prey, and used now and then to show me my mother's likeness in a locket that hung on his watch-chain. They were both dead, and so I came to live with my uncle. Now, I could hardly tell why, but it never seemed to me as if my uncle appeared to regard it as a privilege to have me to take care of. He didn't whack me as some fellows' uncles do, nor did he particularly interfere with my concerns, as the manner of other uncles (so I am told), is. He just took as little notice as possible of me, and as long as I went regularly to Mrs Wren's grammar-school in the village, and as long as Mrs Hudson kept my garments in proper order, and as long as I showed up duly on state occasions, and didn't bring more than a square inch of clay on each heel (there was a natural affinity between clay and my heels), into his drawing-room, he scarcely seemed to be aware that his house possessed such a treasure as an only nephew.

The part of my life I liked least was the grammar-school. That was a horrid place. Mrs Wren was a good old soul, who spent one half of her time looking over her spectacles, and the other half under them, for something she never found. We big boys—for twelve is a good age for a dame's grammar-school—we didn't exactly get on at old Jenny Wren's, as she was called. For we gradually discovered we knew almost as much as she did herself, and it dawned on us by degrees that somehow she didn't know how to keep us in order. The consequence was, one or two boys, especially Jimmy Bates, the parish clerk's son, and Joe Bobbins, the Italian oil and colourman's son, didn't behave very well. I was sorry to see it, and always told them so.

They got us other boys into all sorts of scrapes and trouble. One day they would hide poor Jenny's spectacles, and then when search was made the lost treasure would be found in some one else's desk. Or they would tie cotton reels on the four feet and tail of the old tabby cat, and launch her, with a horrid clatter, right into the middle of the room, just as I or one of the others happened to be scampering out. Or they would turn the little boys' forms upside down, and compel them with terrible threats to sit on the iron feet, and then in the middle of the class "sneak" about them.

Poor Jenny couldn't manage the school at all, with such boys as Jimmy Bates and Joe Bobbins in it. Up to boys of ten she was all right; but over ten she was all at sea.

However, she worked patiently on, and taught us all she could, and once or twice gave us a horrible fright by calling up at our houses, and reporting progress there (Mrs Hudson always received her when she came up to my uncle's). And for all I know I might be at Jenny Wren's school still if a tremendous event hadn't happened in our village, which utterly upset the oldest established customs of Brownstroke.

We grammar-school boys never "hit" it exactly with the other town boys. Either they were jealous of us or we were jealous of them. I don't know, but we hated the town boys, and they hated us.

Once or twice we had come into collision, though they always got the best of it. One winter they snowballed us to such a pitch that as long as the snow was on the ground a lot of the little kids would no more venture to school alone than a sane man would step over the side of a balloon.

Another time they lined the street down both sides, and laughed and pointed at us as we walked to school. That was far worse than snowballs, even with stones in them. You should have seen us, with pale faces and hurried steps, making our way amid the jeers and gibes of our tormentors—some of the little ones blubbering, one or two of the bigger ones looking hardly comfortable, and a few of the biggest inwardly ruminating when and how it would best be possible to kill that Runnit the news-boy, or Hodge the cow-boy!

These and many other torments and terrors we "Jenny Wrenites" had endured at the hands of our enemies the town boys, on the whole patiently. In process of time they got tired of one sort of torment, and before their learned heads had had time to invent a new one, we had had time to muster up courage and tell one another we didn't care what they did.

Such a period had occurred just before my story opens. It was a whole month since the town boys had made our lives unhappy by calling, and howling, and yelling, and squeaking on every occasion they met us the following apparently inoffensive couplet:—

"A, B, C, Look at the baby!"

How we hated that cry, and quailed when we heard it! However, after about a fortnight's diligent use of this terrible weapon the town boys subsided for a season, and we plucked up heart again. Four whole weeks passed, and we were never once molested! Something must be wrong in the village! Of course we all came to the conclusion that the town boys had at last seen the error of their ways, and were turning over new leaves.

Rash dream! One day when we were least expecting it, the "Philistines were upon us" again, and this time their device was to snatch off our caps! It was too terrible to think of! We could endure to be hooted at, and pelted, and said "A, B, C" to, but to have our little Scotch caps snatched off our heads and tossed over pailings and into puddles, was too much even for the meek disciples of Jenny Wren. The poor little boys got their mothers to fasten elastics to go under their chins, and even so walked nearly half a mile round to avoid the market cross. It was no use, the manoeuvre was discovered, and not only did the youngsters have their caps taken, but were flipped violently by the elastics in the face and about the ears in doing so. As for us older ones, some ran, other walked with their caps under their tunics, others held them on with both hands. The result was the same; our caps were captured!

Then did Jimmy Bates, and Joe Bobbins, and Harry Rasper, and I, meet one day, and declare to one another, that this sort of thing was not to be stood.

"Let's tell Mother Wren," said one.

"Or the policeman," said another.

"Let's write and tell Fred Batchelor's uncle," said another. That referred to my relative, who was always counted a "nob" in the village.

"I say, don't do any," said the redoubtable Bobbins. "The next time they do it to me *I* mean to kick!"

The sentiment was loudly applauded, and a regular council of war was held, with the following decision. We four were to go home together that afternoon, and without waiting to be chased, would ourselves give chase to the first bully we saw, and take *his* cap! The consequences of course might be fearful—fatal; but the blood of the "Jenny Wrenites" was up. Do it we would, or perish in the attempt.

I think we all got a little nervous as the afternoon school wore on and the hour for departing approached. Indeed, when we were about to start, Bates looked very like deserting straight away.

"Oh, you three go on," he said, "I'll catch you up; I just want to speak to Jenny."

"No we don't," we all protested; "we'll wait here, if it takes you till midnight to say what you've got to say to Jenny."

This valiant determination put an end to Bates's wavering, and with a rueful face he joined us.

"Now, mind," said Rasper, "the first you see!"

"Well," exclaimed I, starting suddenly to run, "that's Cad Prog, the butcher-boy, there; come along."

So it was! Of all our enemies Cad Prog was the most truculent, and most feared. The sight of his red head coming round the corner was always enough to strike panic into a score of youngsters, and even we bigger boys always looked meek when Prog came out to defy us.

He was strolling guilelessly along, and didn't see us at first. Then suddenly he caught sight of us approaching, and next moment the blue apron and red head disappeared with a bolt round the corner.

"Come on!" shouted Rasper, who led.

"So we are!" cried we, and hue and cry was made for Cad Prog forthwith.

We sighted him as we turned the corner. He was making straight for the market. Perhaps to get an axe, I thought, or to hide, or to tell my uncle!

"Come on!" was the shout.

It's wonderful how a short sharp chase warms up the blood even of a small boy of twelve. Before we were half down the street, even Bates had no thought left of deserting, and we all four pressed on, each determined not to be last.

The fugitive Prog kept his course to the market, but there doubled suddenly and bolted down Side Street. That was where he lived; he was going to run into his hole then, like a rabbit.

We gained no end on him in the turn, and were nearly up to him as he reached the door of his humble home.

He bolted in—so did we. He bolted up stairs—so did we. He plunged headlong into a room where was a little girl rocking a cradle—so did we. Then began a wild scuffle.

"Catch him! Take his cap off!" cried Bobbins.

"He hasn't got a cap!" cried Rasper—"butcher-boys never have!"

"Then pull off his apron!" was the cry.

In the scuffle the little girl was trodden on, and the cradle clean upset. A crowd collected in the street. Cad Prog roared as loud as he could, so did his little sister, so did the baby, so did Jimmy Bates, so did Joe Bobbins, so did Harry Rasper, so did I. *I* did not care what happened; I went for Cad Prog, and have a vague idea of my hand and his nose being near together, and louder yells still.

Then all of a sudden there was a tramp of heavy footsteps on the stairs, and all I can remember after that was receiving a heavy cuff on my head, being dragged down into the street, where—so it seemed to me for the moment—at least a million people must have been congregated; and, finally, I know not how, I was standing in the middle of my uncle's study floor, with my coat gone, my mouth bleeding, and my cap, after all, clean vanished!

It was a queer plight to be in. I heard a dinning in my ears of loud voices, and when I looked at the bust on the top of the bookcase it seemed to be toppling about anyhow. Some people were talking in the room, but the only voice I could recognise was my uncle's. He was saying something about "not wanting to shield me," and "locking-up," the drift of which I afterwards slowly gathered, when the village policeman—we only had one at Brownstroke—addressing my uncle as "your honour," said he would look in in the morning for further orders.

At this interesting juncture the bust began to wobble about again, and I saw and heard no more till I woke next morning, and found Mrs Hudson mopping my forehead with something, and saying, "There now, Master Freddy, lie quite still, there's a good boy."

"What's the matter?" said I, putting up my hand to the place she was washing.

It was something like a bump!

"It's only a bruise, Master Freddy—no bones broken, thank God!" said she, motioning me to be silent.

But I was in no mood to be silent. Slowly the recollection of yesterday's events dawned on me.

"Did they get off Cad Prog's apron," I inquired, "after all?"

Of course, the good old soul thought this was sheer wandering of the mind, and she looked very frightened, and implored me to lie still.

It was a long time before I perceived any connection between our chase of the redoubtable Cad Prog up Side Street yesterday and my lying here bruised and in a darkened room to-day. At last I supposed Mr Prog must have conquered me; whereat I fired up again, and said, "Did the other fellows finish him up?"

"Oh, dear me, yes," said the terrified nurse; "all up, every bit—there now—and asked for more!"

This consoled me. Presently a doctor came and looked at my forehead, and left some powders, which I heard him say I was to take in jam three times a day. I felt still more consoled.

In fact, reader, as you will have judged, I was a little damaged by the adventure in Side Street, and the noble exploit of my companions and myself had not ended all in glory.

A day or two after, when I got better, I found out more about it, and rather painfully too, because my uncle landed one day in my bedroom and commenced strongly to arraign me before him.

He bade me tell him what had happened, which I did as well as I could. At the end of it he said, "I suppose you are not aware that for a day or two it was uncertain whether you had not killed that child that was in the room?"

"I?" I exclaimed. "I never touched her! Indeed I didn't, uncle!"

"You knocked over the cradle," said my uncle, "and that's much the same thing."

I was silent. My uncle proceeded.

"And I suppose you are not aware that the barber who tried to take you down the stairs is now in the hospital with an abscess on his leg, the result of the kick you gave him?"

"Oh, I can't have done it, uncle—oh, uncle!"

And here I was so overwhelmed with the vision of my enormities and their possible consequences that I became hysterical, and Mrs Hudson was summoned to the rescue.

The fact was, in the account of the fray I appear to have got credit for all the terrible deeds that were there done; and I, Master Freddy Batchelor, was, it appeared, notorious in the village as having been guilty of a savage and felonious assault upon one C. Prog, of having also assaulted and almost "manslaughtered" Miss Prog the younger, and further of having dealt with my feet against the shin of one Moppleton, a barber, in such manner as to render him incapable of pursuing his ordinary avocations, and being chargeable on the parish infirmary; besides sundry and divers damage to carpets, crockery, glass, doorposts, kerb-stones, and the jacket of the aforesaid C. Prog. On the whole, when I arose from my bed and stepped once more into the outer world, I found myself a very atrocious character indeed.

At home I was in disgrace, and abroad I was not allowed to wander beyond my uncle's garden, except to church on Sunday under a heavy escort. So on the whole I had not a very good time of it. My uncle was terrifically glum, and appeared to think it most audacious if ever I chanced to laugh or sing or express any sentiment but deep grief and contrition in his presence. Mrs Hudson read me long lectures about the evil of slaying small children and laming barbers, and I was occasionally moved to tears at the thought of my own iniquities. But at the age of twelve it is hard to take upon oneself the settled gloom of an habitual criminal, and I was forced to let out at times and think of other things besides my wicked ways. I got let off school—that was one alleviation to my woe—and being free of the garden I had plenty of opportunity of letting off the steam. But it was slow work, as I have said; and I was really relieved when, a week or two afterwards, my uncle made the announcement with which this chapter begins.

How I fared, first at Stonebridge House, and subsequently in the City Life for which it was meant to train me, will be the theme of this particular veracious history.

Chapter Two
How I made my First Acquaintance with Stonebridge House

The eventful Monday came at last, and with my little box corded up, with Mrs Hudson as an escort, and a pair of brand-new knickerbockers upon my manly person, I started off from my uncle's house in the coach for Stonebridge, with all the world before me.

I had taken a rather gloomy farewell of my affectionate relative in his study. He had cautioned me as to my conduct, and given me to understand that at Stonebridge House I should be a good deal more strictly looked after than I had ever been with him. Saying which he had bestowed on me a threepenny-bit as "pocket-money" for the term, and wished me good-bye. Under the circumstances I was not greatly overcome by this leave-taking, and settled down to make myself comfortable for my long drive with Mrs Hudson to Stonebridge.

Mrs Hudson had been my nurse ever since I could remember, and now the poor old soul and I were to part for good. For she was to see me safely inside the doors of Stonebridge House, and then go back, not to my uncle's (where she would no longer be needed), but to her own home. Of course she was very much depressed by the prospect, and so indeed was I. For a good while we neither of us said much. Then, by way of changing the subject and beguiling the way, she began to address to me long and solemn exhortations as to my conduct at the new school. She knew as much about "schools for backward and troublesome boys" as I did; but that was no matter.

She made me promise, for one thing, that I would make a point of wearing a clean collar three times a week; and, for another, of calling the housekeeper's attention to the very first sign of a hole in my socks. (As my socks, by the way, usually showed the daylight in upon six out of the ten toes, and one out of the two heels every time I took off my boots, I was promising a lot when I made this bargain!) Further, I was to see my Sunday clothes were always *hung* on pegs, and not *laid* in drawers; and my blue necktie, mind, was not to be touched till my black-and-pink was past work.

From these matters she passed on to my conduct towards my new masters and companions.

"Mind and always tell them the truth straight out, Freddy," she said, "and say 'sir' whenever you speak to Mr Ladislaw—and say your prayers regularly night and day, won't you? and be very careful to use your own comb and brush, and not lend them about to the other young gentlemen."

Mrs Hudson, you see, had an easy way of flying from one topic to another. Her exhortations were crowded with pieces of good advice, which may have sounded funny when all strung together, but were each of them admirable taken separately. I of course promised her everything.

The journey was a long one, but the day was bright, and we had a good basketful of provender, so it was not tedious. At length the driver turned round, and said we should come in sight of Stonebridge at the next turn of the road.

My spirits began to sink for the first time. Dismal and all as Brownstroke had been, how did I know I should not be happier there, after all, than at this strange new place, where I knew no one? I wished the driver wouldn't go so fast. Mrs Hudson saw my emotion, I think, for she once more opened fire, and, so to speak, gathered up the last crumbs of her good counsel.

"Oh, and Freddy dear," fumbling nervously in her pocket, and letting down her veil, "write and tell me what they give you to eat; remember, pork's bad for you, and leave your cuffs behind when you go out bird's-nesting and all that. Mind, I'll expect to hear about everything, especially about whether you get warm baths pretty regularly, and if Mr Ladislaw is a good Christian man—and look here, dear," she continued hurriedly, producing a little parcel from the depths of her pocket, "you're not to open this till I'm away, and be sure to take care of it, and don't—"

"That there chimbley," interrupted the driver at this stage, "is the fust 'ouse in Stonebridge."

Five minutes later we were standing in the hall of Stonebridge House.

It didn't look much like a school, I remember thinking. It was a large straggling building, rather like a farmhouse, with low ceilings and rickety stairs. The outside was neat, but not very picturesque, and the front garden seemed to have about as much grass in it as the stairs had carpets. As we stood waiting for some one to answer our ring, I listened nervously, I remember, for any sound or trace of my fellow "backward and troublesome boys," but the school appeared to be confined to one of the long straggling wings behind, and not to encroach on the state portion of the house.

After a second vigorous pull at the bell by our coachman, a stern and scraggy female put in her appearance.

"Is this Frederick Batchelor?" she inquired, in tones which put my juvenile back up instantly.

"Yes, this is Master Freddy," put in the nervous Mrs Hudson, anxious to conciliate every one on my behalf. "Freddy, dear, say—"

"Is that his box?" continued the stern dame.

"Yes," said Mrs Hudson, feeling rather chilled; "that's his box."

"Nothing else?"

"No, except his umbrella, and a few—"

"Take the box up to my room," said the lady to a boy who appeared at this moment. "Where is the key?"

"I've got that, marm," replied Mrs Hudson, warming up a little, "and I should like to go over his things myself as they are unpacked."

"Wholly unnecessary," replied the female, holding out her hand for the key. "I see to everything of that kind here."

"But I *mean* to open the box!" cried Mrs Hudson, breaking out into a passion quite unusual with her.

I, too, had been getting the steam up privately during the last few minutes, and the sight of Mrs Hudson's agitation was enough to start the train.

"Yes," said I, swelling out with indignation, "Mrs Hudson and I are going to open the box. You sha'n't touch it!"

The female appeared to be not in the least put out by this little display of feeling. In fact, she seemed used to it, for she stood quietly with her arms folded, apparently waiting till we both of us thought fit to subside.

Poor Mrs Hudson was no match for this sort of battle. She lost her control, and expressed herself of things in general, and the female in particular, with a fluency which quite astonished me, and I did my little best to back her up. In the midst of our joint address a gentleman appeared on the scene, whom I correctly divined to be Mr Ladislaw himself.

Mr Ladislaw was a short, dapper man, in rather seedy clothes, with long sandy hair brushed right back over the top of his head, and no hair at all on his face. He might have been thirty, or he might have been fifty. His eyes were very small and close together; his brow was stern, and his mouth a good deal pulled down at the corners. Altogether, I didn't take to him at first glance, still less when he broke into the conversation and distinctly took the part of Mrs Hudson's adversary.

"What is all this, Miss Henniker?" he said in a quick, sharp voice, which made me very uncomfortable.

"This is Mr Jakeman's servant," answered the female. "She was talking a little rudely about Frederick Batchelor's luggage here."

"And so was I!" I shouted valiantly. "It's not *your* luggage, and you sha'n't have it, you old—beast!"

The last word came out half-involuntarily, and I was terribly frightened as soon as it had escaped my lips.

I do not know how Mr Ladislaw or Miss Henniker took it, for I dare not look up. I heard Mrs Hudson utter a mild protest, and next moment was conscious of being taken firmly by the hand by Mr Ladislaw and led to the door from which he had just emerged.

"Remain here, Batchelor," said he, sternly, "till I come back."

There was something in his voice and manner which took the spirit out of me, and he might have spared himself the trouble of locking the door behind him. I found myself in a small study, with shelves on the walls and a writing-table in the window, which looked out on to a playground, where, in the distance, I could catch sight of three boys swinging.

This first prospect of my future companions so interested me that I had actually nearly forgotten all about poor Mrs Hudson, when Mr Ladislaw entered the study and said—"The person is going now, Batchelor. If you like you can say good-bye."

I flew out into the hall. Mrs Hudson was there crying, alone. What we said, and how we hugged one another, and how desperately we tried to be cheerful, I need not relate. I was utterly miserable. My only friend, the only friend I had, was going from me, leaving me in this cheerless place all alone. I would have given worlds to return with her. Mr Ladislaw stood by as we uttered our last farewells.

"Be a good boy, Freddy, dear; be a good boy," was all she could say.

"So I will, so I will," was all I could reply. Then she turned to where the coach was waiting. But once more she paused, and drew from her pocket another parcel, this time a box, of the nature of whose contents I could readily guess.

"It's only a few sweets, dear. There, be a good boy. Good-bye, Freddy!"

And in another minute the coach was grating away over the gravel drive, and I stood utterly disconsolate in Stonebridge House, with my box of sweets in one hand and Mr Ladislaw at the other.

Some of my readers may have stood in a similar situation. If they have, I dare say they can remember it as vividly as any incident in their life. I know I can. I remember instinctively ramming the box into one of my side trousers pockets, and at the same time wondering whether both the hats hanging on the pegs were Mr Ladislaw's, or whether one of them belonged to some one else.

Then suddenly it came over me that the former gentleman stood at my side, and all my misery returned as he said—

"I will take you to Miss Henniker, Batchelor; follow me."

The sound of the wheels of Mrs Hudson's coach were still audible down the road, and as I turned my back on them and followed Mr Ladislaw up the carpetless stairs, it seemed as if I was leaving all hope behind me.

I found Miss Henniker in the middle of a large parlour, with my box lying open on the ground beside her, and some of my vestments already spread out on the table. A half inclination to renew the rebellion came over me, as I thought how poor dear Mrs Hudson had been triumphed over; and all these tokens of her kindly soul, folded so neatly, inventoried so precisely, and all so white and well aired, had here fallen into strange hands, who reverenced them no more than—than the shirts and collars and cuffs of I do not know how many more "backward or troublesome" boys like myself. But I restrained my feelings.

"I will leave Batchelor in your charge for the present," said Mr Ladislaw. At the same time he added something in an undertone to Miss Henniker which I did not catch, but which I was positive had reference to the dear departed Mrs Hudson, whereat I fumed inwardly, and vowed that somehow or other I would pay Miss Henniker out.

When Mr Ladislaw was gone Miss Henniker continued her work in silence, leaving me standing before her. She examined all my clothes, looked at the mark on every collar, every sock, and scrutinised the condition of every shirt-front and "dicky." At last she came to my Sunday suit, at the sight of which I remembered all of a sudden my nurse's injunction, and said, as meekly as possible, "Oh, if you please, Mrs Hudson says those are to be hung up, and not laid flat!"

Miss Henniker stared at me as if I had asked her her age!

"Silence!" she said, when she could sufficiently recover herself; "and—"

"And," continued I, carried away with my subject, and really not hearing her remonstrance—"and, if you please, I'm to have three clean collars a week, and you're to darn—"

"Frederick Batchelor!" exclaimed Miss Henniker, letting drop what she had in her hand, and stamping her foot with most unwonted animation; "did you hear me order you to hold your tongue? Don't dare to speak again, sir, till you're spoken to, or you will be punished."

This tirade greatly surprised me. I had been quite pleased with myself for remembering all Mrs Hudson's directions, and so intent on relieving my mind of them, that I had not noticed the growing rage of the middle-aged Henniker. In after years, when this story was told of me, I got the credit of being the only human being, who all by himself, had succeeded in "fetching" the Stonebridge housekeeper. At present, however, I was taken aback by her evident rage, and considered it prudent to give heed to her admonition. The unpacking was presently finished, and the scarlet in the Henniker's face had gradually toned down to its normal tint, when, turning to me, she silently motioned me to follow her. I did so, along a long passage, in which there were at least two turnings. At the end of this was a door leading into a room containing half a dozen beds. Not a very cheerful room—long and low and badly lighted, with only two washstands, and a rather fusty flavour about the bedclothes. Don't suppose, at my age, I was critical on such points; but when I take my boy to school, I do not think, with what I know now, I shall put him anywhere where the dormitory is like that of Stonebridge House.

"That," said Miss Henniker, pointing to one of the beds, "is your bed, and you wash at this washstand."

"Oh," said I, again forgetting myself; "you are to be sure my brush and comb—"

"Silence, Batchelor!" once more reiterated Miss Henniker.

From the dormitory I was conducted to the schoolroom, and from the schoolroom to the dining-room, and from the dining-room to the boot-room, and my duties were explained in each.

It was in the latter apartment that I first made the acquaintance of one of my fellow "troublesome or backwards."

A biggish boy was adopting the novel expedient for getting on a tight boot of turning his back to the wall and kicking out at it like a horse when I and my conductress entered.

The latter very nearly came in for one of the kicks.

"Flanagan," said she, "that is not allowed. I shall give you a bad mark for it."

Flanagan went on kicking till the end of the sentence, and then subsided ruefully, and said, "The bothering thing won't come on or off, please, ma'am. It won't come on with shoving."

"If your boots are too small," replied the lady, solemnly, begging the question, "you must write home for new ones."

"But the bothering things—"

"Batchelor," said Miss Henniker, turning to me, "this is the boot-room, where you will have to put on and take off your boots whenever you go out or come in. This boy is going out, and will take you into the playground with him," and away she went, leaving me in the hands of the volatile Flanagan.

"Who are you?" he demanded.

It was a horribly dark place, this boot-room, and I could scarcely see who it was who was questioning me. He seemed to be a big boy, a year or two older than myself, with a face which, as far as I could make it out, was not altogether unpleasant. He continued stamping with his refractory boots all the time he was talking to me, letting out occasionally behind, in spite of Miss Henniker.

"Who are you? What's your name?" he said.

"Fred Batchelor," I replied, deferentially.

"Batchelor, eh? Are you a backward or a troublesome, eh?"

This was a poser. I had never put the question to myself, and was wholly at a loss how to answer. I told Flanagan so.

"Oh, but you're *bound* to know!" he exclaimed. "What did they send you here for, eh?"

Whereupon I was drawn out to narrate, greatly to Flanagan's satisfaction, the affair of Cad Prog and his baby sister.

"Hurrah!" said he, when I had done. "Hurrah, you're a troublesome! That makes seven troublesomes, and only two backwards!" and in his jubilation he gave a specially vigorous kick out behind, and finally drove the obstinate boot home.

"Yes," said he, "there was no end of discussion about it. I was afraid you were a backward, that I was! If the other new fellow's only a troublesome too, we shall have it all to ourselves. Philpot, you know," added he confidentially, "is a backward by rights, but he calls himself one of us because of the Tuesday night jams."

"Is there another new boy too?" I inquired, plucking up heart with this friendly comrade.

"Oh! he's coming to-morrow. Never mind! Even if he's a 'back' it don't matter, except for the glory of the thing! The 'troubs' were always ahead all Ladislaw's time, and he's no chicken. I say, come in the playground, can't you?"

I followed rather nervously. A new boy never takes all at once to his first walk in the playground; but with Flanagan as my protector—who was "Hail fellow, well met," with every one, even the backwards—I got through the ordeal pretty easily.

There were eight boys altogether at Stonebridge House, and I was introduced—or rather exhibited—to most of them that afternoon. Some received me roughly and others indifferently. The verdict, on the whole, seemed to be that there was plenty of time to see what sort of a fellow I was, and for the present the less I was made to think of myself the better. So they all talked rather loud in my presence, and showed off, as boys will do; and each expected—or, at any rate, attempted—to impress me with a sense of his particular importance.

This treatment gave me time to make observations as well as them, and before the afternoon ended I had a pretty good idea whom I liked and whom I did not like at Stonebridge House.

Presently we were summoned in to a bread-and-cheese supper, with cold water, and shortly afterwards ordered off to bed. I said my prayers before I went to sleep, as I had promised good Mrs Hudson, and, except for being shouted at to mind I did not snore or talk in my sleep—the punishment for which crimes was something terrific—I was allowed to go to sleep in peace, very lonely at heart, and with a good deal of secret trepidation as I looked forward and wondered what would be my lot at Stonebridge House.

Chapter Three
How a Mysterious New Boy came to Stonebridge House

When I rose next morning, and proceeded to take my turn at the washstand, and array my person in the travel-stained garments of the previous day, it seemed ages since I had parted with Brownstroke and entered the gloomy precincts of Stonebridge House.

Everything and everybody around me was gloomy. Even Flanagan seemed not yet to have got up the steam; and as for the other boys—they skulked morosely through the process of dressing, and hardly uttered a word. It was a beautiful day outside; the sun was lighting up the fields, and the birds were singing merrily in the trees; but somehow or other the good cheer didn't seem to penetrate inside the walls of Stonebridge House.

I tried to get up a conversation with Flanagan, but he looked half-frightened and half guilty as I did so.

"I say," said I, "couldn't we open the window and let some fresh air in?"

(Mrs Hudson had always been strong on fresh air.)

"Look-out, I say," said Flanagan, in a frightened whisper; "you'll get us all in a row!"

"In a row?" I replied. "Who with?"

"Why, old Hen; but shut up, do you hear?" and here he dipped his face in the basin, and so effectually ended the talk.

This was quite a revelation to me. Get in a row with Miss Henniker for speaking to one of my schoolfellows in the dormitory! A lively prospect and no mistake.

Presently a bell rang, and we all wended our way down stairs into the parlour where I had yesterday enjoyed my *tête-à-tête* with Miss Henniker. Here we found that lady standing majestically in the middle of the room, like a general about to review a regiment.

"Show nails!" she ejaculated, as soon as all were assembled.

This mysterious mandate was the signal for each boy passing before her, exhibiting, as he did so, his hands.

As I was last in the procession I had time to watch the effect of this proceeding. "Showing nails," as I afterwards found out, was a very old-established rule at Stonebridge House, and one under which every generation of "backward and troublesome boys" who resided there had groaned. If any boy's hands or nails were, in the opinion of Miss Henniker, unclean or untidy, he received a bad mark, and was at once dismissed to the dormitory to remedy the defect.

One or two in front of me suffered thus, and a glance down at my own extremities made me a little doubtful as to my fate. I did what I could with them privately, but their appearance was not much improved.

At last I stood for inspection before the dreadful Henniker.

"Your hands are dirty, Batchelor. A bad mark. Go and wash them."

The bad mark, whatever it might mean, appeared to me very unjust. Had I known the rule, it would have been different, but how was I to know, when no one had told me?

"Please, ma'am, I didn't—"

"Two bad marks for talking!" was my only reply, and off I slunk, feeling rather crushed, to the dormitory.

I found Flanagan scrubbing at our basin.

"Ah," said he, "I thought you'd get potted."

"I think it's a shame," said I.

"Look-out, I say," exclaimed Flanagan, skipping away as if he'd been shot, and resuming his wash at the other basin.

Presently he came back on tip-toe, and whispered, "Why can't you talk lower, you young muff?"

"Surely she can't hear, here up stairs?"

"Can't she? That's all you know! She hears every word you say all over the place, I tell you."

I went on "hard all" at the nail-brush for a minute or so in much perplexity.

"Keep what you've got to say till you get outside. Thank goodness, she's rheumatic or something, and we can open our mouths there. I say," added he, looking critically at my hands, "you'd better give those nails of yours a cut, or you'll get potted again."

I was grateful for this hint, and felt in my pocket for my knife. In doing so I encountered the box of sweets Mrs Hudson had left in my hand yesterday, and which, amid other distractions, I had positively forgotten. "Oh, look here," said I, producing the box, delighted to be able to do a good turn to my friendly schoolfellow. "Have some of these, will you?"

Flanagan's face, instead of breaking out into grateful smiles, as I anticipated, assumed a sudden scowl, and at the same moment Miss Henniker entered the dormitory!

Quick as thought I plunged the box back into my pocket, and looked as unconcerned as it was possible to do under the trying circumstances.

"Flanagan and Batchelor, a bad mark each for talking," said the now painfully familiar voice. "What have you there, Batchelor?" added she, holding out her hand. "Something Mrs Hudson gave me," I replied.

"I wish to see it."

I was prepared to resist. I could stand a good deal, but sheer robbery was a thing I never fancied. However, a knowing look on Flanagan's face warned me to submit, and I produced the box.

The lady took it and opened it. Then closing it, she put it in her own pocket, saying—

"This is confiscated till the end of the term. Flanagan and Batchelor, 'Show nails.'"

We did show nails. Mine still needed some trimming before they were satisfactory, and then I was bidden descend to the parlour for prayers.

Prayers at Stonebridge House consisted of a few sentences somewhat quickly uttered by Mr Ladislaw, who put in an appearance for the occasion, followed by a loud "Amen" from Miss Henniker, and in almost the same breath, on this occasion, the award of a bad mark to Philpot for having opened his eyes twice during the ceremony.

After this we partook of a silent breakfast, and adjourned for study. Miss Henniker dogged us wherever we went and whatever we did. She sat and glared at us all breakfast time; she sat and glared at us while Mr Ladislaw, or Mr Hashford, the usher, were drilling Latin grammar and arithmetic into us. She sat and glared while we ate our dinner, and she stood and glared when after school we assembled in the boot-room and prepared to escape to the playground. Even there, if we ventured to lift our voices too near the house, a bad mark was shot at us from a window, and if an unlucky ball should come within range of her claws it was almost certainly "confiscated."

I don't suppose Stonebridge House, except for Miss Henniker, was much worse than most schools for "backward and troublesome boys." We were fairly well fed, and fairly well taught, and fairly well quartered. I even think we might have enjoyed ourselves now and then, had we been left to ourselves. But we never *were* left to ourselves. From morning to night, and, for all we could tell, from night till morning, we were looked after by the lady housekeeper, and that one fact made Stonebridge House almost intolerable.

We were lounging about in the so-called "playground" that afternoon, and I was beginning to discover a little more about some of my new schoolfellows, when there appeared walking towards us down the gravel path a boy about my own age.

He was slender and delicate-looking, I remember, and his pale face contrasted strangely with his almost black clustering hair and his dark big eyes. He wasn't a handsome boy, I remember thinking; but there was something striking about him, for all that. It may have been his solemn expression, or his square jaw, or his eyes, or his brow, or his hair, or the whole of them put together. All I know is, that the sight of him as he appeared that afternoon walking towards us in the playground, has lived in my memory ever since, and will probably live there till I die.

"Here comes the new boy," said Philpot. Of course we all knew it must be he.

"And a queer fish, too, by all appearances," responded Flanagan.

"Very queer indeed," said Hawkesbury. Hawkesbury was one of the two "backwards,"—but for all that he was the cleverest boy, so the others told me, in the whole school.

"He doesn't seem very bashful," said another.

Nor indeed did he. He sauntered slowly down the path, looking solemnly now on one side, now on the other, and now at us all, until presently he stood in our midst, and gazed half inquiringly, half doubtfully, from one to the other.

I know I felt a good deal more uncomfortable than he did himself, and was quite glad when Flanagan broke the solemn silence.

"Hullo, youngster, who are you, eh?"

"Smith," laconically replied the new boy, looking his questioner in the face.

There was nothing impudent in the way he spoke or looked; but somehow or other his tone didn't seem quite as humble and abject as old boys are wont to expect from new. Flanagan's next inquiry therefore was a little more roughly uttered.

"What's your Christian name, you young donkey? You don't suppose you're the only Smith in the world, do you?"

We laughed at this. It wasn't half bad for Flanagan.

The new boy, however, remained quite solemn as he replied, briefly, "John Smith."

"And where do you come from?" said Philpot, taking up the questioning, and determining to get more out of the new-comer than Flanagan had; "and who's your father, do you hear? and how many sisters have you got? and why are you sent here? and are you a backward or a troublesome, eh?"

The new boy gazed in grave bewilderment at the questioner during this speech. When it was ended, he quietly proceeded to move off to another part of the playground without vouchsafing any reply.

But Philpot, who was on his mettle, prevented this manoeuvre by a sudden and dexterous grip of the arm, and drew him back into the circle.

"Do you hear what I say to you?" said he, roughly, emphasising his question with a shake. "What on earth do you mean by going off without answering?"

"It's no business of yours, is it?" said the new boy, mildly.

"Yes," exclaimed Philpot, "it is. You don't suppose we fellows are going to be humbugged by a young sneak like you, do you?"

"I sha'n't tell you, then!" quietly replied Smith.

This astounding reply, quietly as it was uttered, quite took away Philpot's breath, and the breath of all of us. We were so astonished, indeed, that for some time no one could utter a word or make up his mind what to do next.

Then gradually it dawned on the company generally that this defiant, stuck-up youngster must immediately be put down.

"Come here!" said Philpot, as majestically as he could.

Smith remained where he was, as solemn as ever. But I, who stood near, could detect a queer light in his black eyes that looked rather ominous.

When one fellow, in the presence of an admiring audience, grandly orders a junior to "Come here!" and when that junior coolly declines to move, it is a very critical situation both for the boy who orders and the boy who disobeys. For the one, unless he follows up his brag, will pretty certainly be laughed at; and the other, unless he shows the white feather and runs away, will generally come in for a little rough usage. This seemed likely to happen now. As Smith would not come to Philpot for a thrashing, Philpot must go to Smith and thrash him where he stood. And so doubtless he would have done, had not Mr Hashford appeared at that very moment on the gravel walk and summoned us in to preparation.

This interruption was most unsatisfactory. Those who wanted to see what the new boy was made of were disappointed, and those whose dignity wanted putting to-rights were still more disappointed.

But there was no helping it. We trailed slowly indoors, Philpot vowing he would be quits with the young cub some day, and Hawkesbury, in his usual smiling way, suggesting that "the new boy didn't seem a very nice boy."

"I know what *I* should do," said Flanagan, "if I—"

"A bad mark to Flanagan for not coming in quietly," said the voice of Miss Henniker; and at the sound the spirit went out from us, and we remembered we were once more in Stonebridge House.

"Preparation" was a dreadful time. I knew perfectly well, though I could not see her, that Miss Henniker's eyes were upon me all the time. I could feel them on the back of my head and the small of my back. You never saw such an abject spectacle as we nine spiritless youths appeared bending over our books, hardly daring to turn over a leaf or dip a pen, for fear of hearing that hateful voice. I could not help, however, turning my eyes to where the new boy sat, to see how he was faring. He, too, seemed infected with the depressing air of the place, and was furtively looking round among his new schoolfellows. I felt half fascinated by his black eyes, and when presently they turned and met mine, I almost thought I liked the new boy. My face must somehow have expressed what was passing through my mind, for as our eyes met there was a very faint smile on his lips, which I could not help returning.

"Batchelor and Smith, a bad mark each for inattention. That makes four bad marks to Batchelor in one day. No playground for half a week!"

Cheerful! I was getting used to the lady by this time, and remember sitting for the rest of the time calculating that if I got four bad marks every day of the week, that would be twenty-eight a week, or a hundred and twelve a month; and that if four bad marks deprived me of half a week's playground, one month's bad marks would involve an absence of precisely fourteen weeks from that peaceful retreat; whereat I bit my pen, and marvelled inwardly.

The dreary day seemed as if it would never come to an end. My spirits sank when, after "preparation," we were ordered up stairs to tea. How *could* one enjoy tea poured out by Miss Henniker? Some people call it the "cup that cheers." Let them take tea one afternoon at Stonebridge House, and they will soon be cured of that notion! I got another bad mark during the meal for scooping up the sugar at the bottom of my cup with my spoon.

"Surely," thought I, "they'll let us read or play, or do as we like, after tea for a bit?"

Vain hope! The meal ended, we again went down to our desks, where sheets of paper were distributed to each, and we were ordered to "write home"! Write home under Miss Henniker's eye! That was worse than anything!

I began, however, as best I could. Of course, my letter was to Mrs Hudson. Where she was, was the only home I knew. I was pretty certain, of course, the letter would be looked over, but for all that I tried not to let the fact make any difference, and, as I warmed up to my task, I found my whole soul going out into my letter. I forgot all about its contents being perused, and was actually betrayed into shedding a few tears at the thought of my dear absent protectress.

"I wish I was back with you," I wrote. "It's *miserable* here. The sweets you gave me have been stolen by that horrid old—"

At this interesting juncture I was conscious of somebody standing behind me and looking over my shoulder. It was Miss Henniker!

"Give me that," she said.

I snatched the letter up and tore it into pieces. I could stand a good deal, as I have said, but even a boy of twelve must draw the line somewhere.

Miss Henniker stood motionless as I destroyed my letter, and then said, in icy tones—

"Follow me, Batchelor."

I rose meekly, and followed her—I cared not if it was to the gallows! She led me to her parlour, and ordered me to stand in the corner. Then she rang her bell.

"Tell Mr Ladislaw I should like to see him," said she to the servant.

In due time Mr Ladislaw appeared, and the case for the prosecution forthwith opened. My misdemeanours for the entire day were narrated, culminating with this last heinous offence.

"Batchelor," said Miss Henniker, "repeat to Mr Ladislaw word for word what you were writing when I came to you."

I know not what spirit of meekness came over me. I did as I was told, and repeated the sentence verbatim down to the words, "The sweets you gave me have been stolen by that horrid old—"

"Old what?" said Mr Ladislaw.

"Old what?" said Miss Henniker, I hesitated.

"Come, now, say what you were going to write," demanded Mr Ladislaw.

"Old what, Batchelor?" reiterated the Henniker, keeping her eyes on me.

I must be honest!

"Old beast," I said in a low tone.

"I thought so," said the lady. "Batchelor has called me a beast twice since he came here, Mr Ladislaw."

"Batchelor must be punished," said Mr Ladislaw, who, I could not help privately thinking, was a little afraid of Miss Henniker himself. "Come to my study, sir."

I came, followed of course by the Henniker; and in Mr Ladislaw's study I was caned on both hands. Miss Henniker would, I fancy, have laid it on a little harder than the master did. Still, it was enough to make me smart.

But the smart within was far worse than that without.

"Return to the class-room now, and write at once to your uncle, Mr Jakeman," said Miss Henniker, "and to no one else."

I returned to the room, where I found an eager whispered discussion going on. When a boy was taken off for punishment by the Henniker, those who were left always had a brief opportunity for conversation.

The subject of discussion, I found, was Smith, who sat apart, with no paper before him, apparently exempt from the general task. As usual, he was looking solemnly round him, but in no way to explain the mystery. At last Hawkesbury, the "pet" of the school—in other words, the only boy who seemed to get on with Miss Henniker and Mr Ladislaw—had walked up to Mr Hashford's desk, where the usher sat in temporary authority, and had said, "Oh, Smith, the new boy, hasn't any paper, Mr Hashford."

"No, I was told not to give him any," said the usher, terrified lest the Henniker should return.

"I wonder why?" said Hawkesbury.

"Yes, it is strange," replied Mr Hashford; "but please go to your place, Hawkesbury; Miss Henniker will return."

Hawkesbury had reported this brief conversation to his fellows, and this was what had given rise to the discussion I found going on when I returned from my caning. It was soon cut short by the Henniker's reappearance; but the mystery became all the greater when it was seen that no notice was taken of the new boy's idleness, and that at the close of the exercise, when we were all called upon to bring up our letters, his name was distinctly omitted.

My effusion to my uncle was brief and to the point.

Dear Uncle Jakeman,—Miss Henniker wishes me to say that I have had five bad marks to-day. I have also been caned hard on both hands for writing to dear Mrs Hudson, and for calling Miss Henniker bad names. I hope you are very well. Believe me, dear uncle, your affectionate nephew,—

Fred. Batchelor.

With the exception of striking out the "dear" before Mrs Hudson this letter was allowed to pass.

In due time and to my great relief the bell rang for bed, and glad of any chance of forgetting the hateful place, I went up stairs to the dormitory.

The new boy, I found, was to occupy the bed next mine, at which I was rather pleased than otherwise. I could not make out why I should take a fancy to Smith, but somehow I did; and when once during the night I happened to wake, and heard what sounded very much like a smothered sob in the bed next mine, I at least had the consolation of being sure I was not the only miserable boy at Stonebridge House.

Chapter Four
How Smith and I took a breath of Fresh Air and Paid for it

As "circumstances over which I had no control" prevented my joining my fellow troublesome and backward boys in their daily retreat to the playground for the next few days, I had only a limited opportunity of seeing how the new boy settled down to his new surroundings.

Inside Stonebridge House we were all alike, all equally subdued and "Henpecked." The playground was really the only place where any display of character could be made; and as for three days I was a prisoner, Smith remained as much a mystery to me at the end of the week as he had been on the day of his arrival.

I could, however, guess from his looks and the looks of the others that he was having rather a bad time of it out there. Hawkesbury used to come in with such a gracious smile every afternoon that I was certain something was wrong; and Philpot's flushed face, and Rathbone's scowl, and Flanagan's unusual gravity, all went to corroborate the suspicion. But Smith's face and manner were the most tell-tale. The first day he had seemed a little doubtful, but gradually the lines of his mouth pulled tighter at the corners, and his eyes flashed oftener, and I could guess easily enough that he at least had not found his heart's content at Stonebridge House.

My term of penal servitude expired on Sunday; and in some respects I came out of it better than I had gone in. For Mr Hashford had the charge of all detained boys, and he, good-hearted, Henniker-dreading usher that he was, had spent the three days in drilling me hard in decimal fractions; and so well too, that I actually came to enjoy the exercise, and looked upon the "repeating dot" as a positive pastime. Even Miss Henniker could not rob me of that pleasure.

"Batchelor," whispered Flanagan to me, as we walked two and two to church behind the Henniker that Sunday, "that new fellow's an awfully queer cove. I can't make him out."

"Nor can I. But how's he been getting on the last day or two?"

"Getting on! You never knew such scenes as we've had. He's afraid of nobody. He licked Philpot to fits on Thursday—smashed him, I tell you. You never saw such a demon as he is when his dander's up. Then he walked into Rathbone; and if Rathbone hadn't been a foot taller than him, with arms as long as windmills, he'd have smashed Rathbone."

"Did he try it on you?" I inquired.

"No—why should he?" said the sturdy Flanagan; "time enough for that when I make a brute of myself to him. But I dare say he'd smash me too. It's as good as a play, I tell you. That time he did for Philpot he was as quick with his right, and walked in under his man's guard, and drove up at him, and took him on the flank just like—"

"A bad mark to Flanagan for talking, and to Batchelor for listening," rose the voice of Miss Henniker in the street.

This public award made us both jump, and colour up too, for there were a lot of ladies and gentlemen and young ladies close at hand, all of whom must have distinctly heard the Henniker's genial observation. However, I was most curious to hear more of Smith. Flanagan and I both had colds the rest of the way and finished our conversation behind our handkerchiefs.

"Have you heard any more about him?" asked I. "Not a word. He's as close as an owl. Hawkesbury says Hashford told him he came here straight from another school. By the way—keep your handkerchief up, man!—by the way, when I said he's afraid of no one, he *is* afraid of Hawkesbury, I fancy. I don't know why—"

"I don't think I like Hawkesbury, either. He's got such an everlasting grin."

"So will you have if you don't talk lower, you young idiot," said Flanagan. "Yes, it's the grin that fetches Smith, I fancy. I grinned at him one day, meaning to be friendly, but he didn't half like it."

I laughed at this, greatly to Flanagan's wrath. Luckily, however, no evil consequences happened, and we reached church without any more bad marks.

Of all days, Sunday at Stonebridge House was the most miserable and desperate. We had not even the occupation of lessons, still less the escape to the playground. After church, we were marched back to the school, and there set to read some dry task book till dinner.

And after dinner we were set to copy out a chapter of Jeremiah or some other equally suitable passage from beginning to end on ruled paper, getting bad marks as on week days for all faults. After this came tea, and after tea another dreary march forth to church. But the culminating horror of the day was yet to come. After evening church—and there really was a sense of escape and peace in the old church, even though we could not make out the sermon—after evening church, we were all taken up to Miss Henniker's parlour, and there doomed to sit perfectly still for a whole hour, while she read aloud something by one of the very old masters. Oh, the agony of those Sunday evenings!

I have sat fascinated by that awful voice, with a cramp in my leg that I dared not stir to relieve, or a tickling in the small of my back from which there was no escape, or a cobweb on my face I had not the courage to brush away. I have felt sleep taking possession of me, yet daring neither to yawn, nor nod my head, nor wink my eyes. I have stared fixedly at the gas, or the old china ornament on the mantelpiece, till my eyes became watery with the effort and I have suffered all the tortures of a cold in the head without the possibility either of sniffing or clearing my throat!

It made no difference to Miss Henniker that she was reading aloud. She had her eye on every one of us the whole time, nay, more than ever; and many a bad mark was sprinkled up with her readings.

"Once more, dearly beloved—Batchelor, a bad mark," became to me quite a familiar sound before I had been many Sundays at Stonebridge House.

This particular Sunday evening I thought I should go mad, at least, during the first part of the performance. I *couldn't* sit still, and the more I tried the more restless I became. At last, however, some chance directed my eyes to where the new boy was sitting in a distant corner of the room, and from that moment, I can't tell why, I became a model of quiet sitting. I found myself forgetting all about the cobwebs, and Mrs Hudson, and the china ornament, and the small of my back, and thinking of nothing but this solemn, queer boy, with his big eyes, and black hair, and troubled face. The more I looked at him the more sorry I felt for him, and the more I wished to be his friend. I would—

"Batchelor, repeat the last words I read," broke in Miss Henniker.

She thought she had me, but no! Far away as my thoughts had been, my ears had mechanically retained those last melodious strains, and I answered, promptly, "Latitudinarianism of an unintelligent emotionalism!"

One to me! And I returned to my brown study triumphant, and pretty secure against further molestation.

I made up my mind, come what would, I would speak to the new boy and let him see *I* was not against him.

Some one will smile, of course, and say, sarcastically, "What a treat for the new boy!" But if he only knew with what fear and trembling I made that resolution, he would acquit Fred Batchelor of any very great self-importance in the matter.

Bedtime came at last, and, thankful to have the day over, we crawled away to our roosts. The new boy's bed, as I have said, was next mine, and I conceived the determination, if I could only keep awake, of speaking to him after every one was asleep.

It was hard work that keeping awake; but I managed it. Gradually, one after another dropped off, and the padding footsteps overhead and the voices below died away till nothing was heard but the angry tick of the clock outside and the regular breathing of the sleepers on every hand.

Then I softly slid out of bed and crawled on my hands and knees to Smith's bed. It was an anxious moment for me. He might be asleep, and wake up in a fright to find some one near him; or he might be awake and resent my intrusion. Still I determined I *would* go to him, and I was rewarded.

"Is that Batchelor?" I heard him whisper as I approached his bed.

"Yes," I answered, joyfully, and feeling half the battle over.

"Come in," said he, moving to make room for me.

"Oh no!" I said, in terror at the very idea. "Suppose I fell asleep. I'll kneel here, and then if any one comes I can crawl back."

"What is it?" Smith said, presently, after a long and awkward pause.

I was thankful that he broke the ice.

"Oh," I whispered, "aren't you jolly miserable here, I say?"

"Pretty!" said he. "Aren't you?"

"Oh, yes! But the fellows are all so unkind to you."

Smith gave a little bitter laugh. "That doesn't matter," he said.

"Doesn't it? I wish I was bigger, I'd back you up — and so will Flanagan, if you let him."

"Thanks, old man!" said the new boy, putting his hand on my arm. "It's not the fellows I mind, it's —" and here he pulled up.

"Old Henniker," I put in, in accents of smothered rage.

"Ugh!" said Smith; "she's awful!"

But somehow it occurred to me the Henniker was not what Smith was going to say when he pulled up so suddenly just before. I felt certain there was something mysterious about him, and of course, being a boy, I burned to know.

However, he showed no signs of getting back to that subject, and we talked about a lot of things, thankful to have scope for once for our pent-up feelings. It was one of the happiest times I had known for years, as I knelt there on the hard carpetless floor and found my heart going out to the heart of a friend. What we talked about was of little moment; it was probably merely about boys' trifles, such as any boy might tell another. What was of moment was that there, in dreary, cheerless Stonebridge House, we had found some interest in common, and some object for our spiritless lives.

I told him all about home and my uncle, in hopes that he would be equally communicative, but here he disappointed me.

"Are your father and mother dead too?" I said.

"Not both," he replied.

It was spoken in a tone half nervous, half vexed, so I did not try to pursue the subject.

Presently he changed the subject and said, "How do you like that fellow Hawkesbury?"

"Not much; though I don't know why."

Smith put out his hand and pulled my face close to his as he whispered, "I hate him!"

"Has he been bullying you?" I inquired.

"No," said Smith. "But he's—ugh—I don't know any more than you do why I hate him. I say, shall you be out in the playground to-morrow?"

"Yes, unless I get four bad marks before. I've two against me already."

"Oh, don't get any more. I want to go for a walk."

"A walk!" I exclaimed. "You'll never be allowed!"

"But we might slip out just for a few minutes; it's awful never to get out."

It *was* awful; but the risk. However, I had promised to back him up, and so I said where he went I would go.

"If it was only to climb one tree, or see just one bird on the bushes," he said, almost pathetically. "But I say, ain't you getting cold?"

I was not, I protested, and for a long time more we continued talking. Then at last the creaking of a board, or the noise of a mouse, startled us in earnest, and in a moment I had darted back to my bed. All was quiet again.

"Good-night, old boy," I whispered.

"Good-night, old man. Awfully good of you," he replied. "I'll come to you to-morrow."

And not long after we were both sound asleep.

I managed to keep down my bad marks below four next day, so that I was able once more to take my walks abroad in the playground.

It was with a little feeling of misgiving that I sallied forth, for Smith was at my side, reminding me of our resolution to escape, if only for a few minutes, to the free country outside. I would greatly have preferred not trying it, but Smith was set on it, and I had not the face to leave him in the lurch.

The far end of the playground, beyond the swings, broke into a patch of tangled thicket, beyond which again a little ditch separated the grounds of Stonebridge House from the country outside.

To this thicket, therefore, we wandered, after "showing ourselves" on the swings for a few minutes, for the sake of allaying suspicions. The other fellows were most of them loafing about on the far side of the gravel yard, where the marble holes were; so we managed to make our escape pretty easily, and found ourselves at length standing on the breezy heath. Once there, Smith's whole manner changed to one of wild delight. The sense of freedom seemed to intoxicate him, and the infection seized me too. We scampered about in a perfectly ridiculous manner; up hills and down hollows, leaping over bushes, chasing one another, and, in fact, behaving exactly like two kids (as we were), suddenly let loose from confinement.

"I say," said I, all out of breath, "suppose we run clean away, Smith?"

Smith pulled up in the middle of a scamper, and looked up and down on every side. Then the old solemn look came as he replied, "Where to, that's it?"

"Oh, Brownstroke, if you like; or your home. Let's turn up, you know, and give them a jolly surprise."

Smith's face clouded over as he said, hurriedly, "I say, it's time to be going back, or we shall get caught."

This was an effectual damper to any idea of flight, and we quickly turned back once more to Stonebridge House.

We found our gap all right, and strolled back past the swings and up the gravel walk as unconcernedly as possible, fully believing no one had been witness of our escapade. We were wrong.

Hawkesbury came up to us as we neared the house, with the usual smile on his face.

"Didn't you hear me calling?" he said. "You know it's against rules to go out of bounds, and I thought—"

"What! who's been out of bounds?" said the voice of the Henniker at that moment.

Hawkesbury looked dejected.

"Who did you say, Hawkesbury, had been out of bounds?"

"I'd rather not tell tales," said Hawkesbury, sweetly.

"I've been out of bounds," blurted out Smith, "and so has Batchelor. I asked him to come, and Hawkesbury has been spying and—"

"Silence," cried Miss Henniker. "Smith and Batchelor, follow me."

We followed duly to Mr Ladislaw's study, where we were arraigned. Hawkesbury was sent for as evidence. He came smiling, and declared he may have been mistaken, perhaps it was two other boys; he hoped we should not be punished, etcetera. Smith was nearly breaking out once or twice during this, and it was all I could do to keep him in. Hawkesbury was thanked and dismissed, and then, with the assistance of Miss Henniker, Mr Hashford, and Mr Ladislaw, Smith and I were birched, and forbidden the playground for a fortnight, during which period we were required to observe absolute silence.

So ended our little adventure out for a puff of free air! Among our fellows we gained little enough sympathy for our misfortunes. Flanagan was the only fellow who seemed really sorry. The rest of the ill-conditioned lot saw in the affair only a good opportunity of crowing over their ill-starred adversary, and telling me it served me right for chumming up to such a one.

One day, greatly to my surprise, when the Henniker was away superintending the flogging of Flanagan for some offence or other, Hawkesbury came over and sat beside me.

"Oh," said he, softly, "Batchelor, I've been wanting to tell you how sorry I am I helped get you into your scrape. I didn't mean—I was only anxious for you to know the rule. I hope you'll forgive me?" and he held out his hand.

What could I do? Perhaps he was telling the truth after all, and we had thought too badly of him. And when a big boy comes and asks pardon of a small one, it is always embarrassing for the latter. So I gave him my hand, and told him I was sure he did not mean it, and that it did not matter at all.

"Thanks, Batchelor," he said, smiling quite gratefully. "It's a relief to me."

Then I watched him go on what I knew was a similar errand to Smith, but, as I expected, his reception in that quarter was not quite so flattering as it had been in my case. I could see my chum's eyes fire up as he saw the elder boy approach, and a flush come over his pale cheeks. I watched Hawkesbury blandly repeating his apology, and then suddenly, to my astonishment and consternation, I saw Smith rise in his seat and throw himself furiously upon his enemy. Hawkesbury was standing near a low form, and in the sudden surprise caused by this attack he tripped over it and fell prone on the floor, just as Miss Henniker re-entered.

There was a brief pause of universal astonishment, then the Henniker demanded, "What is this? Tell me. What is all this, Hawkesbury?"

Hawkesbury had risen to his feet, smiling as ever, and brushing the dust from his coat, replied softly, "Nothing, really nothing, ma'am. I fell down, that's all."

"I knocked you down!" shouted Smith, panting like a steam-engine, and trembling with excitement.

"Oh," said Hawkesbury, kindly, though not quite liking the downright way in which the adventure had been summed up. "It was only play, Miss Henniker. My fault as much as Smith's. He never meant to be so rough. Really."

"Silence, both!" said Miss Henniker. "Smith, follow me!"

"Oh, Miss Henniker, please don't punish him," said Hawkesbury.

"Silence," replied the Henniker, icily. "Come, Smith."

Miss Henniker had the wonderful art of knowing by instinct who was the culprit in cases like this. She was never troubled with a doubt as to her verdict being a right one; and really it saved her a great deal of trouble.

Smith was haled away to justice, where, in addition to a flogging and further term of imprisonment, he was reduced for a given period to a bread-and-water diet, and required publicly to beg Hawkesbury's pardon.

That there might be no delay about the execution of the last part of the sentence, the culprit was conducted back forthwith to the schoolroom, accompanied by Miss Henniker and Mr Ladislaw.

"Hawkesbury," said the latter, addressing the injured boy, "I have desired Smith to beg your pardon here and now for his conduct to you. Smith, do as you have been told."

Smith remained silent, and I who watched him could see that his mind was made up.

"Do you hear Mr Ladislaw, Smith?" demanded the Henniker; "do as you are bid, at once."

"Please, sir," began Hawkesbury, with his pleasant smile.

"Silence, Hawkesbury," said the Henniker. "Now, Smith."

But she might have been addressing a log of wood.

"Do you hear what I say to you?" once more she exclaimed.

Smith only glared at her with his big eyes, and resolutely held his tongue.

"Then," said Mr Ladislaw, "Smith must be publicly punished."

Smith was punished publicly; and a more repulsive spectacle I never wish to witness. A public punishment at Stonebridge House meant a flogging administered to one helpless boy by the whole body of his schoolfellows, two of whom firmly held the victim, while each of the others in turn flogged him. In the case of an unpopular boy like Smith, this punishment was specially severe, and I turned actually sick as each of the cowardly louts stepped up and vented their baffled wrath upon him. Hawkesbury, of course, only made the slightest pretence of touching him; but this of all his punishment seemed to be the part Smith could bear least. At last, when it was all over, the bruised boy slunk back to his desk, and class proceeded.

That night, as I knelt beside my poor chum's bed, he said, "We've paid pretty dear for our run on the heath, Fred."

"*You* have, old man," I replied.

Smith lay still for some time musing, then he said, "Whatever do they mean by forgiving enemies, Fred?"

Smith didn't often get on these topics, and I was a little nervous as I replied, "What it says, I suppose."

"Does it mean fellows like Hawkesbury?"

"I should say so," said I, almost doubtful, from the way in which he spoke, whether after all I might not be mistaken.

"Queer," was all he replied, musingly.

I tried hard to change the subject.

"Are you awfully sore, Jack?" I said. "Have one of my pillows."

"Oh no, thanks. But I say, Fred, don't you think it's queer?"

"What, about forgiving your enemies? Well, yes it is, rather. But, I say, it's time I cut back. Good-night, old man."

And I crept back to bed, and lay awake half the night listening to him as he turned from side to side in his sleep, and feeling that everything and everybody was queer, especially my friend Smith.

Chapter Five
How a Chapter of Misfortunes befel My Friend Smith and Me

The summer wore on, and with it the gloom of Stonebridge House sunk deeper and deeper into our spirits. After a week or two even the sense of novelty wore off, and we settled down to our drudges' doom as if we were destined all our lives never to see any place outside the Henniker's domain.

If it hadn't been for Smith I don't know how I should have endured it. Not that we ever had much chance of enjoying one another's society. In school it was wholly impossible. In the playground (particularly after our recent escapade), we had very little opportunity given us; and at night, when secretly we did contrive to talk, it was with the constant dread of detection hanging over us.

What concerned me most of all, though, was the bad way in which Smith seemed to get on with every one of his schoolfellows except me, and—perhaps Flanagan. With the bullies, like Philpot and Rathbone, he was at daggers drawn; towards the others he never took the trouble to conceal his dislike, while with Hawkesbury an explosion seemed always, imminent.

I could not understand why he got on so badly, especially with Hawkesbury, who certainly never made himself disagreeable, but, on the contrary, always appeared desirous to be friendly. I sometimes thought Smith was unreasonable to foster his instinctive dislike as he did.

"Jack," said I one night as he was "paying a call" to my bedside—"Jack, I'm half beginning to think Hawkesbury isn't so bad a fellow after all."

"Why?" demanded Smith.

"Oh, I don't know. He's done me one or two good turns lately."

"What sort?"

"Well, he helped me in the Latin the other day, of his own accord, and—"

"Go on," said Smith, impatiently.

"And he gave me a knife to-day. You know I lost mine, and he said he'd got two."

Smith grunted.

"I'd like to catch him doing a good turn to me, that's all," said he. "I'd cure him of that!"

I didn't like to hear Smith talk like this. For one thing, it sounded as if he must be a great deal less foolish than I was, which nobody likes to admit; and for another thing, it seemed wrong and unreasonable, unless for a very good cause, to persist in believing nothing good about anybody else.

So I changed the subject.

"I say," said I, "what are you going to do these holidays?"

"Stay here," said he. "Are you going home?"

"What!" I exclaimed. "Stay here for four weeks with the old Hen? Why ever, Jack?"

"Don't know—but that's what I've got to do. Are you going home?"

"I suppose so," said I, with an inward groan. "But, Jack, what *will* you do with yourself?"

"Much as usual, I expect. Sha'n't get much practice in talking till you come back!" added he, with a low laugh.

"Jack, why don't you go home?" I exclaimed. "Are you in a row there, or what? You never tell me a word about it."

"Look-out, I hear some one moving!" cried Smith, and next moment he was back in his bed.

I was vexed. For I half guessed this alarm had been only an excuse for not talking about home, and I didn't like being silenced in that way. Altogether that night I was a good deal put out with Smith, and when presently he whispered across "Good-night," I pretended to be asleep, and did not answer.

But I was not asleep, and could not sleep. I worked myself first into a rage, then into an injured state, and finally into a miserable condition over my friend Smith.

Why should he keep secrets from me, when I kept none from him? No, when I came to think over it, I did not keep a single secret from him! Did he think I was not to be trusted, or was too selfish to care? He might have known me better by this time. It was true I had told him my secrets without his asking for them; in fact, all along he had not seemed nearly as anxious as I had been for this friendship of ours. My conscience stung me at this last reflection; and there came upon me all of a sudden a sense of the utter desolation of this awful place without a single friend! No, I determined it should take more than a little pique to make me cast away my only friend.

And with the thought, though it must have been far on in the night, I slipped from my bed and crawled to his.

He was fast asleep, but at the first touch of my hand he started up and said, "What's the row?"

"I'm sorry, Jack; but I was in a temper to-night, and couldn't go to sleep till I made it up."

"A temper! what about?" said he. "I didn't know you were."

"I fancied you wouldn't—that is, that you thought—you didn't trust me, Jack."

"You're the only fellow I do trust, Fred, there," said he, taking my arm. Then, with a sigh, he added, "Why shouldn't I?"

"What a beast I was, Jack!" cried I, quite repentant. "I don't—"

"Hush!" said Jack. Then, whispering very close to my ear, he added, "There are some things, you know, I *can't* tell even you—about home—"

There was a sound in the room, as of a boy, suddenly aroused, starting up in his bed. Our blood turned cold, and we remained motionless, hardly daring to breathe, straining our ears in the darkness.

Suddenly the boy, whoever he was, sprang from his bed, and seizing the lucifers, struck a light.

It was Hawkesbury! I had almost guessed it. I felt Jack's hand tighten on my arm as the sudden glare fell full upon us, and Hawkesbury's voice cried, "Oh, you fellows, what a start you gave me! I couldn't make out what the talking was. I thought it must be thieves!"

At the same moment the dormitory door opened, and a new glare lit up the scene. It was Miss Henniker in her dressing-gown, with a candle.

"What, talking? Who was talking?" she said, overhearing Hawkesbury's last exclamation.

It was a queer picture that moment, and I can recall it even now. Hawkesbury standing in his night-shirt in the middle of the room. I, as lightly clad, crouching transfixed beside my friend's bed, who was sitting up with his hand on my arm. And the Henniker there at the door, in her yellow-and-black dressing-gown and curl-papers, holding her candle above her head, and looking from one to the other.

"Who was talking?" she demanded again, turning to Hawkesbury.

Hawkesbury, smiling, returned to his bed, as he replied, "Oh, nothing. I think I must have been dreaming, and woke in a fright."

But as he spoke his eyes turned to us two, and Miss Henniker's followed naturally. Then the whole truth dawned upon her.

I rose from my knees and walked sheepishly back to my bed.

"What are you doing out of your bed, sir?" demanded she.

It was little use delaying matters by a parley, so I replied, bluntly, "Talking to Smith."

"And I," added the loyal Smith, "was talking to Batchelor!"

"Silence!" cried the Griffin. "Batchelor, dress immediately, and follow me!"

I did as I was bid, mechanically—that is, I slipped on my knickerbockers and slippers—and found myself in a couple of minutes, thus airily attired, following Miss Henniker, like a ghost, down the long passage. She led the way, not, as I expected, to the parlour, or to Mr Ladislaw's room, but conducted me upstairs and ushered me into a small and perfectly empty garret.

"Remain here, Batchelor!" said she, sternly.

The next moment she was gone, locking the door behind her, and I was left shivering, and in total darkness, to spend the remainder of the night in these unexpected quarters.

My first sensation was one of utter and uncontrollable rage. I was tempted to fling myself against the door, to shout, to roar until some one should come to release me. Then as suddenly came over me the miserable certainty that I was helpless, and that anything I did would be but labour lost, and injure no one but myself. And, Smith, too! It was all up with our precious secret parleys; perhaps we should not even be allowed to see one another any more. In my misery I sat down on the floor in a corner of my dungeon and felt as if I would not much care if the house were to fall about my ears and bury me in the ruins. Cheerful reflection this for a youth of my tender years!

As I sat, shivering and brooding over my hard fate, I heard footsteps ascending the stairs. When you are sitting alone in an empty room, at the dead of night, this is never a very fascinating sound, and I did not much enjoy it.

And as I listened I could make out that the footsteps belonged to two people. Perhaps I was going to be murdered, I reflected, like Prince Arthur, or the two boys in the Tower! At the same moment a streak of light glimmered through the crack of the door, and I heard a voice say, "Come this way, Smith."

So Smith, too, was going to be locked up for the night. My heart bounded as for an instant it occurred to me it would be in my dungeon! No such good fortune! They passed my door. At any rate, my chum should know where I was, so I proceeded to make a demonstration against my door and beseech, in the most piteous way, to be released. Of course, it was no use, but that did not matter; I never expected it would.

I listened hard to the retreating footsteps, which stopped at the end of the passage. Then a door opened and shut again, a key turned, one pair of steps again returned past my door, and as I peeped through the keyhole I had a vague idea of a yellow-and-black gown, and knew that the Henniker had gone back to her place.

If only Smith had been shut up next door to me I might have been able to shout to him so that he could hear, but what chance was there when three or four rooms at least divided us? After all, except that he was near me, and knew where I was, things were not much better than they had been before. So I sat down again in my corner and sulkily watched the first glimmers of dawn peep in at the little window. It must be about 3 a.m., I thought. And that meant four good hours before any chance of a release came. And as it was, my feet were pretty nearly dead with cold, and a thin nightgown is not much covering for a fellow's body and arms. It rather pleased me to think the adventure might end fatally, and that at my inquest Miss Henniker might be brought in guilty of manslaughter.

It must be breezy, for those leaves have been tapping away at my window the last minute or so pretty hard. Bother the leaves! And yet, when you come to think of it, you do not often hear leaves tap as hard as that! My window will be smashed in if they keep it up at that rate. So I get up lazily and approach the scene of action.

I nearly screamed as I did so, for there, close up against the window, was a face! I was so taken aback that it took me a good minute to recover my wits and perceive that the apparition was none other than my faithful friend Jack Smith, and that the tapping I had been giving the leaves such credit for had been his eager attempts to attract my attention.

I sprang to the window, jubilant, and opened it.

"Oh, Jack! hurrah! However did you get here?"

"Oh, you have *spotted* me at last, have you?" said he, with a grim smile. "I've been here five or ten minutes."

"You have!" exclaimed I.

"Yes. My window opened on to this ledge, too; so I didn't see why I shouldn't come."

"You might have fallen and killed yourself. But I say, Jack, won't you come in? Even if we do get caught things can't be much worse than they are."

"I know that—so I think you'd better come out."

"What for?" exclaimed I, in astonishment.

"To get away—anywhere," said he.

In a moment I was up on the window-sill, scrambling out on to the ledge beside him. The fresh morning breeze blew on my face as I did so, and a glorious sense of freedom took hold of both our drooping spirits. We needed no words. Only let us get free!

"Come along," said Jack, crawling along the narrow ledge which ran round the top of the house.

"How shall we get down?" I asked.

"That's what I want to find out," said Jack. "Isn't there a water-pipe or something in front?"

Carefully we made our perilous journey round the side of the house towards the front. Smith leaned over and peered down.

"Yes," said he, "there's a water-pipe we could easily slide down, if we could only get at it. Look!"

He couldn't get his hands round, much less his feet.
It was nervous work watching him.

I looked over too. The ground seemed a long way below, and I felt a trifle nervous at the prospect of trying to reach it by such unorthodox means as a water-pipe, even could we get at that pipe. But the ledge on which we were overhung the side of the house, and the pipe began under it, just below where we stood.

"We must try, anyhow," said Jack, desperately. "I'll go first; catch hold of my hands, Fred."

And he was actually going to attempt to scramble over and round under the ledge, when he suddenly paused, and cried, "Hold hard. I do believe this bit of ledge is loose!"

So it was. It shook as we stood upon it.

"We might be able to move it," said Jack.

So we knelt down and with all our might tugged away at the stone that divided us from our water-pipe. It was obstinate at first, but by dint of perseverance it yielded to pressure at last, and we were able triumphantly to lift it from its place.

It was easy enough now reaching the pipe. But here a new peril arose. Sliding down water-pipes is an acquired art, and not nearly as easy as it seems. Jack, who volunteered to make the first descent, looked a little blue as he found the pipe was so close to the wall that he couldn't get his hands round, much less his feet.

"You'll have to grip it hard with your ankles and elbows," he said, beginning to slide down an inch or two; "and go slow, whatever you do."

It was nervous work watching him, and still more nervous work when at length I braced myself up to the effort and proceeded to embrace the slender pipe. How I ever managed to get to the bottom I can't say. I remember reflecting about half way down that this would be good daily exercise for the Henniker, and the mere thought of her almost sent me headlong to the bottom.

At last, however, I stood safe beside my chum on the gravel walk.

"Now!" said he.

"Now," I replied, "where shall we go?"

"London, I think," said he, solemnly as ever, "All right—how many miles?"

"Eighty or ninety, I fancy—but where's your coat?"

"In the dormitory. I was too much flurried to put it on."

"Never mind, we can use mine turn about. But I wish we'd got boots instead of slippers."

"So do I," replied I, who even as I stood felt the sharp gravel cutting my feet; "ninety miles in slippers will be rather rough."

"Never mind," said Jack, "come on."

"Come on," said I.

At that moment, to our dismay and misery, we heard a window above us stealthily opened, close to the water-pipe, and looking up beheld the Henniker's head and yellow-and-black body suddenly thrust out.

"Batchelor and Smith—Mr Ladislaw," (here her voice rose to pretty nearly a shriek)—"Mr Ladislaw! come at once, please—Batchelor and Smith, running away. Mr Ladislaw, quick! Batchelor and Smith!"

We stood motionless, with no spirit left to fly, until the door was opened, and Mr Ladislaw, Miss Henniker, and Mr Hashford, all three, sallied out to capture us.

Among them we were dragged back, faint and exhausted, into Stonebridge House, all thoughts of freedom, and London, effectually banished from our heads, and still worse, with the bitter sense of disappointment added to our other miseries.

Mr Hashford was set to watch us for the rest of the night in the empty schoolroom. And he had an easy task. For even though he fell asleep over it, we had no notion of returning to our old scheme. Indeed, I was shivering so, I had no notion of anything but the cold. Jack made me put on his coat, but it made very little difference. The form I was on actually shook with my shivering. Mr Hashford, good soul that he was, lent me his own waistcoat, and suggested that if we all three sat close together—I in the middle—I might get warmer. We tried it, and when at six o'clock that same eventful morning the servant came to sweep the room she found us all three huddled together—two of us asleep and one in a fever.

I have only a dim recollection of what happened during the next week or so. I was during that time the most comfortable boy in all Stonebridge House. For the doctor came every day, ordered me all sorts of good things, and insisted on a fire being kept in my room, and no lessons. And if I wished to see any of my friends I might do so, and on no account was I to be allowed to fret or be disturbed in mind. I couldn't help feeling half sorry for Miss Henniker being charged with all these uncongenial tasks; but Stonebridge House depended a great deal on what the doctor said of it, and so she had to obey his orders.

I took advantage of the permission to see my friends by requesting the presence of Smith very frequently. But as the Henniker generally thought fit to sit in my room at the same time, I didn't get as much good out of my chum as I might have done. I heard he had had a very smart flogging for his share of that eventful night's proceedings, and that another was being saved up for me when I got well.

It was quite a melancholy day for me when the doctor pronounced me convalescent, and said I might resume my ordinary duties. It was announced to me at my first appearance in school, that on account of my delinquencies I was on the "strict silence" rule for the rest of the term, that my bed was removed to the other dormitory, and that I was absolutely forbidden to hold any further communication, either by word or gesture, with my friend Smith.

Thus cheerfully ended my first term at Stonebridge House.

Chapter Six
How things came to a Crisis at Stonebridge House

A year passed, and found us at the end of it the same wretched, spiritless boys as ever. Stonebridge House had become no more tolerable, the Henniker had grown no less terrible, and our fellow "backward and troublesome boys" were just as unpleasant as they had been. No new boys had come to give us a variety, and no old boys had left. Except for the one fact that we were all of us a year older, everything was precisely the same as it had been at the time of the adventure related in my last chapter. But that one year makes a good deal of difference. When Smith and I slid down the water-pipe a year ago we were comparatively new friends, now we had grown to love one another like brothers. When the Henniker, on the same occasion, put an end to our scheme of escape, we had endured her persecutions but three months, now we had endured them for fifteen. A great deal of secret working may go on in a fellow's mind during a year, and in that way the interval *had* wrought a change, for we were a good deal more to one another, Smith and I, and a good deal more desperate at our hard lot, both of us, than we had been a year ago.

It had been a miserable time. My holidays alone with my uncle had been almost as cheerless as my schooldays at Stonebridge House with Miss Henniker. If it hadn't been for Smith I do believe I should have lost every vestige of spirit. But happily he gave me no chance of falling into that condition. He seemed always on the verge of some explosion. Now it was against Hawkesbury, now against the Henniker, now against Mr Ladislaw, and now against the whole world generally, myself included. I had a busy time of it holding him in.

He still showed aversion to Hawkesbury, although I differed from him on this point, and insisted that Hawkesbury was not such a bad fellow. Luckily, however, no outbreak happened. How could it, when Hawkesbury was always so amiable and forgiving and friendly? It was a wonder to me how Jack *would* persist in disliking this fellow. Sometimes I used to be quite ashamed to see the scornful way in which he repulsed his favours and offers of friendship. On the whole I rather liked Hawkesbury.

The summer term was again drawing to a close, and for fear, I suppose, lest the fact should convey any idea of pleasure to our minds, the Henniker was down on us more than ever. The cane was in constant requisition, and Mr Ladislaw was always being summoned up to administer chastisement.

Even Hawkesbury, who generally managed to escape reproach, came in for her persecution now and then.

One day, I remember, we were all in class, and she for some reason quitted the room, leaving Mr Hashford in charge.

Now, no one minded Mr Hashford very much. He was a good-natured fellow, who did his best to please both us and his mistress; but he was "Henpecked," we could see, like all the rest of us, and we looked upon him more as a big schoolfellow than as a master, and minded him accordingly. We therefore accepted the Henniker's departure as a signal for leaving off work and seizing the opportunity to loosen our tongues and look about us. Hawkesbury happened to be sitting next to me. He put down his pen, and, leaning back against the desk behind him, yawned and said, "I say, Batchelor, I hope you and Smith haven't been quarrelling?"

"Quarrelling!" exclaimed I, astounded at the bare notion. "Why, whatever puts that into your head?"

"Oh," said he, with his usual smile, "only fancy. But I'm glad it isn't the case."

"Of course it isn't," said I, warmly.

"I haven't seen you talking to him so often lately; that's why," said Hawkesbury; "and it always seems a pity when good friends fall out."

I smiled and said, "How can I talk to him, except on the sly, in this place? Never fear, Jack Smith and I know one another too well to fall out."

"Ah, he is a mysterious fellow, and he lets so few people into his secrets."

"Yes," said I, colouring a little. "He doesn't even let me into them."

Hawkesbury looked surprised. "Of course you know where he came from first of all, and all that?"

"No, I don't," I said.

"What, not know about— But I'd better not talk about it. It's not honourable to talk about another boy's affairs."

"Hawkesbury," said Mr Hashford at this moment, "don't talk."

This was quite a remarkable utterance for the meek and mild Mr Hashford to make in the Henniker's absence, and we all started and looked up in a concerned way, as if he must be unwell.

But no, he seemed all right, and having said what he had to say, went on with his work.

Hawkesbury took no notice of the interruption, and went on. "And, on the whole, I think it would be kinder not to say anything about it, as he has kept it a secret himself. You see—"

"Hawkesbury," again said Mr Hashford, "you must not talk."

Hawkesbury smiled in a pitiful sort of way at Mr Hashford, and again turned towards me to resume the conversation. "You see—" began he.

"Hawkesbury," again said Mr Hashford, "this is the third time I have told you not to talk."

"Who was talking?" cried the Henniker, entering at that moment.

"Hawkesbury, I'm sorry to say, Miss Henniker."

"Hawkesbury—a bad mark for—"

"Oh!" said I, starting up, "I was talking—"

"A bad mark to you, Batchelor, for interrupting me, and another for talking. Hawkesbury, a bad mark for talking in class."

We were all astonished. We had hitherto looked upon Hawkesbury as a privileged person who might do as he liked, and upon Mr Hashford as a person who had not a soul of his own. Here was the phenomenon not only of our schoolfellow getting publicly censured, but of Mr Hashford backing up Miss Henniker, and Miss Henniker backing up Mr Hashford.

Flanagan afterwards confided to me his theory of this unwonted event. "I expect," said he, "Hashford's just got his screw raised, and wants to show off a bit before the Hen, and she wants to encourage him to be rather more down on us, you know. She's got the toothache, too, I know, and that accounts for her not being particular who she drops on, though I am surprised she pitched on Hawkesbury. How pleased your chum Smith will be!"

But my friend Smith, when I had a chance of speaking to him, seemed indifferent about the whole affair, being taken up with troubles of his own. A letter had come for him that day, he told me, in tones of fierce anger. It had been opened and read as usual, before being handed to him. He did not complain of that; that was an indignity we had to submit to every time we received a letter. But what he did complain of, and what had roused his temper, was that the last half-sheet of the letter had been deliberately torn off and not given to him.

Directly after class he had marched boldly to the Henniker's parlour and knocked at the door.

"Come in!" snapped she.

Smith did come in, and proceeded to business at once.

"You haven't given me all my letter, ma'am," he said.

Miss Henniker looked at him with some of the same astonishment with which she had regarded me when I once told her she was to see my socks were regularly darned.

Then she pulled herself up, in her usual chilly manner, and replied, "I am aware of that, Smith."

"I want it, please, ma'am," said Smith.

Again the Henniker glared at this audacious youth, and again she replied, "You will not have it, Smith!"

"Why not?"

"Leave the room instantly, sir, for daring to speak like that to me, and write out one hundred lines of Caesar before you get your dinner!" cried the Henniker, indignantly. "You've no right to keep—"

"Smith, follow me!" interrupted Miss Henniker, in her most irresistible voice, as she led the way to Mr Ladislaw's study.

Smith did follow her, and was flogged, of course.

I was as indignant as he was at this tale of injustice; it reminded me of my box of sweets last year, which I had never seen back.

Smith's rage was beyond all bounds. "I won't stand it!" said he; "that's all about it, Fred!"

"What can we do?" asked I.

That was the question. And there was no answering it. So we slunk back to our places, nursing our wrath in our bosoms, and vowing all sorts of vengeance on the Henniker.

Nor were we the only boys in this condition of mind. Whether it was the Henniker was thoroughly upset by her toothache, or by Hawkesbury's bad conduct and Smith's impertinence, I cannot say, but for the next day or two she even excelled herself in the way she went on.

There was nothing we could do, or think, or devise, that she did not pounce upon and punish us for. Some were detained, some were set to impositions, some were flogged, some were reduced to bread and water, some had most if not all of their worldly goods confiscated. Even

Hawkesbury shared the general fate, and for a whole week all Stonebridge House groaned as it had never groaned before.

Then we could stand it no longer. We all felt that; and we all found out that everybody else felt it. But as usual the question was, what to do?

It was almost impossible to speak to one another, so closely were we watched, and even when we did, we discovered that we were all at sixes and sevens, and agreed only on one thing, which was that we *could not* stand it.

At length one day, to our infinite jubilation, as we were dismally walking from the schoolroom to the parlour, we saw the front door open. A fly was standing at it, and as we passed, the Henniker in her Sunday get-up was stepping into it!

What had we done to deserve such a mercy? She was going to pay a state call somewhere, and for one blessed hour at any rate we should be at peace!

A council of war was immediately held. For once in a way Stonebridge House was unanimous. We sunk all minor differences for a time in the grand question, what should we do?

A great many wild suggestions were immediately made.

Rathbone undertook, with the aid of any two other fellows, to inflict personal chastisement on the public enemy.

This was rejected peremptorily. It would be no use, we should catch it all the worse afterwards; besides, bad as she was, the Henniker was a woman, and it would be cowardly to thrash her.

"Tie up her hands and feet and gag her," suggested Philpot.

Wouldn't do again. She'd get Ladislaw to help her out.

"Tie up Ladislaw and Hashford too."

We weren't numerous or strong enough to do it.

"Let's all bolt," suggested Flanagan.

They'd send the police after us. Or if they didn't, how were we to get on, without money or shelter or anywhere to go?

"Suppose," said I, "we shut them out of the schoolroom and barricade the door, and don't let them in till they accept our terms."

"That's more like it," said some one; "but then what about food? We can't store enough, even if we emptied the larder, to stand a long siege."

"Well, then," said Smith, "suppose we screw them up, and don't let them out till they give in."

"That's it," said every one, "the very thing."

"What do you say, Hawkesbury?" inquired I.

"Well," said he, smiling pleasantly, "it's not a nice thing to turn against one's master and mistress; but really Miss Henniker has been very vexing lately."

"Hurrah! then you agree?" And the question was put all round, every one assenting. At least so I thought. But Smith as usual was doubtful of Hawkesbury.

"You agree, Hawkesbury?" said he.

"Really," said the other, with a smile, "it isn't nice to be suspected, Smith. Isn't it enough to say a thing once?"

"Oh yes, yes," cried out every one, impatiently, and most anxious to keep the meeting harmonious. "He said he did, Smith; what more do you want? Do let's pull all together."

"Just what I want," said Smith.

"Well," said Philpot, "I propose we lock them up in the big schoolroom."

"Wouldn't it be better," said Flanagan, "to lock the Henniker up in her own room, and let Ladislaw and Hashford have the parlour? It will be more comfortable for them. There's a sofa there and a carpet. Besides, the window's a worse one to get out of."

"How about feeding them?" some one asked.

"That'll be easy enough," said Smith. "There's a ventilator over all the doors, you know. We can hand the things in there."

"I vote the old Hen gets precious little," interposed Rathbone. "I wouldn't give her any."

This idea was scouted, and it was resolved that all the prisoners should have a sufficient, though, at the same time, a limited amount of provisions. That being arranged, the next question was, when should we begin? We had to take a good many things into account in fixing the important date. To-day was Friday. The butcher, some one said, always brought the meat for the week on Monday; but the baker never came till the Wednesday. So if we began operations on Monday we should have a good supply of meat but very little bread to start with; and it was possible, of course, the baker might smell a rat, and get up a rescue. It would be better, on that account, to defer action till after the baker's visit on Wednesday. But then the washerwoman generally came on the Thursday. We all voted the washerwoman a nuisance. We must either take her a prisoner and keep her in the house, or run the risk of her finding out that something was wrong and going back to the village and telling of us.

"If we could only keep it up a week," said Smith, "I think we could bring them to terms."

"Suppose we drop a line to the washerwoman the day before not to call," suggested I.

The motion met with universal applause, and I was deputed to carry it out at the proper time. The good lady's address I knew was on a slate in Miss Henniker's pantry.

"And I tell you what," said Smith, starting up with the brilliancy of the suggestion; "let's hide away all the bread we can find, except just what will last over to-morrow. Then most likely she'll tell the baker to call on Monday, and we can begin then!"

It was a brilliant suggestion. Two of the company departed forthwith to the larder, and unobserved hid away a few loaves in one of the empty trunks in the box-room.

Our plans were ripening wonderfully. But the most difficult business was yet to come. What terms should we require of our prisoners as the price of their release? And on this point, after long discussion, we found we could not agree. Some were for the immediate dismissal of the Henniker; others demanded that she should not be allowed to speak without special permission; and others that she should remain in her parlour all day long, and come out only for prayers and to give orders to the tradesmen.

These proposals were too absurd to take seriously; and as presently the company began to grow a little quarrelsome over the matter, it was decided for peace' sake that the question should be deferred, and terms arranged when the prisoners themselves offered to give in.

"If I may make a suggestion," said Hawkesbury, who had taken no part in the previous discussion, "it is that you should appoint one fellow captain, and agree to obey his orders. You'll never manage it if you don't."

"Not at all a bad idea," said one or two. "You be the captain, Hawkesbury."

"No, thank you," said he, smiling gratefully. "I really am not used to this sort of thing; but I think Smith, now, would be just the fellow."

I considered this beautiful of Hawkesbury, coming so soon after Smith's rather uncomplimentary behaviour to him.

The proposition was generally approved. Smith was not a favourite, but he had made the only suggestions of any real use in the present case, and appeared to have entered into the scheme so warmly that it was evident no one would make a better captain.

He received his new dignity with great complacency.

"I'll do my best," said he, "if you fellows will back me up and stick to the engagement."

Our time was now getting brief, so after a few more hurried suggestions and discussions we separated and returned to our ordinary duties.

That evening the Henniker was no better than she had been during the day. Her brief sojourn in society that afternoon had not improved her a bit, Flanagan, as usual, suggested a plausible reason.

"I expect," whispered he, "she went after a new pupil and didn't hook him; that's why she's in such a precious tantrum."

"Flanagan!" cried the well-known voice—"Flanagan, come here!"

Flanagan obeyed, and stood meekly before the tyrant.

"This is the eighth time to-day, Flanagan, I have rebuked you for talking. You are detained for the rest of the term. Hold out your hand, Flanagan!"

It was not often the Henniker inflicted corporal punishment herself; when she did it was pretty smart, as Flanagan found. In the absence of a cane she had used the ruler, and as Flanagan—who unsuspectingly supposed she was merely seized with a desire to inspect his nails—held out his hand knuckles upwards, the ruler descended on his knuckles with such force that the luckless youth howled for astonishment, and performed a dance *solo* in the middle of the floor.

We were sorry for him, yet we inwardly smiled to think how soon the tables would be turned.

That night, just before we went to bed, as I was in the shoe-room looking for my slippers, I had the satisfaction of hearing the Henniker say to the kitchen-maid, "Matilda, we're getting short of bread. Let the baker know to call on Monday next week."

Things could not have promised better for our desperate scheme!

Chapter Seven
How there arose a Notable Rebellion at Stonebridge House

Of course we were wrong; of course we were foolish.

But then, reader, please remember we were only boys goaded up to the last pitch, and quite unable, as I have narrated, to stand the Henniker any longer.

It was no game we were embarked on. If you had seen the seriousness of our faces as we inspected the parlour and reconnoitred the Henniker's future prison, that Saturday; if you had heard the seriousness of our voices as we solemnly deliberated whether nails or screws would be best to use in fastening up the doors—you would have found out that, "backward and troublesome" boys as we were, we could be in earnest sometimes.

"Screwing's quieter," said Rathbone.

"Nailing's quicker," said Philpot.

"Isn't that a thing the captain had better decide?" softly suggested Hawkesbury, turning to Smith.

I always got fidgety when the senior boy and my chum got near each other. Smith had such a way of firing up instinctively at whatever the other might say, even when it meant no harm.

He flared up now with his eyes, and then turning to the two boys, said, shortly, "Screws of course; that's been settled long ago."

Hawkesbury smiled gratefully, and said he was sure a matter like that would not be overlooked.

Well, the Henniker went on having her fling that Saturday and Sunday. We caught it right and left, and took it all meekly. Nay, some of us took it so meekly that I was once or twice afraid our secret would be suspected.

The regulation-reading in the parlour on Sunday evening was a shocking time for me. I had no intention of being bad, but somehow, what with the excitement of our scheme, and the dreariness of the reader's voice, and the closeness of the room, I fell asleep and nearly rolled off my form.

The Henniker put down her book.

"Batchelor," said she, "you shall be punished. Stand on the form and read aloud."

And so saying, she handed me the book and pointed to the place.

This was the very refinement of torture, and I draw a veil over the sad spectacle which followed. Nor was I the only victim standing there struggling and perspiring through the long sentences, turned back whenever I made a mistake, to begin the page over again, till the end of the chapter seemed to get farther and farther away; the other boys, too, came in for part of the tragedy, for the Henniker, being now free of her book, had no occupation for her eyes but to glare at them, and no occupation for her tongue but to level bad marks and rebukes and punishments at the head of every offender.

"Reading" lasted that evening until ten o'clock, and to this day I cannot imagine how it ever came to an end even then. I know I never got to the end. This sad experience gave a considerable additional zest to our hopes of freedom on the following day.

Smith was not the sort of fellow to undertake what he did not mean to carry through, and I was astonished to see how carefully his plans were laid, and how precisely he had allotted to every one of us our respective duties.

Monday dawned at length, and we rose from our beds like patriots on the morning of a battle which is to decide their freedom or slavery.

I had two minutes' whisper with Smith as we went down to breakfast.

"Tell the fellows," said he, "that the signal to begin will be just when morning school is over. The Hen goes to get ready for dinner, and Shankley and Philpot are to follow and screw her up. The holes are already bored, so it won't take long."

"Suppose she yells," suggested I.

"Not likely, but if she does—her room's far enough away. Oh! by the way, I've screwed her window already. I thought we can one of us easily smash a pane for her if she wants more ventilation."

"And how about Ladislaw and Hashford?"

"I'm going down, when the Henniker's safe, to ask them both to step up into the parlour. They'll probably think something's wrong, and hurry up. (I've screwed that window, too, by the way.) Then you and Rathbone are to screw their door when they are safe in—I've put the key outside, too—and I've told the other fellows to be ready to bring a lot of desks and things out of the schoolroom and pile them up, in case they kick too hard."

"Upon my word, Jack, you're a regular general. But I say, we've forgotten the two servants."

"No, we haven't. I've told them what's up, and they won't interfere; but—shut up now."

During the morning we continued to pass round word what the arrangements were, and waited feverishly for the close of morning school. As we sat in the class-room we had the satisfaction of seeing first the butcher's pony and then the baker's cart drive up the front garden and drive back again. We were all right for the "sinews of war" for a day or two, anyhow!

The Henniker kept it up till the last, and distributed her favours lavishly and impartially all round. But we heeded it not; we even enjoyed it, for were not we to have our innings next?

It seemed as if morning school would never end. At last a fluttering at our hearts, more convincing even than the clock, told us the hour was come. We rose from our seats. The rebellion at Stonebridge House had begun.

The Henniker marched with stately tread from the room, and up the stairs to her own apartment. It seemed a long journey to us, who sat listening in breathless silence, and at last the closing of her door seemed to resound all over the house.

"Now then," said Smith to Shankley and Philpot, who, with their shoes off and their tools in their hands, stood ready, like two trained assassins, for the word of command. "Now then, and keep quiet, whatever you do!"

They went. There was nothing stately about their march. They darted up the stairs two steps at a time, and the last we saw of them was as they turned the corner into the passage, at the end of which was situate the enemy's fortress.

It seemed a year before they returned!

At last Shankley, with beaming face, burst into our midst.

"It's all right!" said he, in an excited whisper. "She sounded a little like kicking, so Philpot's keeping guard. We had one screw half in before she even heard us."

"What did she say then?" asked three or four eager questioners.

"She wanted to know who was there, and if we wanted to speak to her we must wait till she came down, and a bad mark to whoever it was for coming and disturbing her."

There was a general laugh at this, which Smith hurriedly checked.

"The thing's only half done yet," he said. "Time enough to laugh when the other two are safe."

This was a wise rebuke, and we became serious in an instant.

"Now," said Smith, "have you got the screwdriver and screws all right, Batchelor? The rest of you be ready if I call;" and off he went to summon the two masters to the parlour.

It was a critical moment, for every thing depended on our getting both into the room together.

Smith, so he told us afterwards, found both Mr Ladislaw and Mr Hashford talking together in the study of the former. He entered the room suddenly, and crying, in an agitated voice, "Oh, will you both please step up to Miss Henniker's parlour at once? Please be quick!" as suddenly vanished.

Of course both the masters, making sure Miss Henniker must be in a fit, or else that the house must be on fire, rushed upstairs, gallantly side by side, to the rescue. Rathbone and I, who were in hiding behind the door next to that of the parlour, could hear them scuttling towards us along the passage, and making straight for their trap. They rushed wildly into the room. In a moment we were out after them, the door was slammed to, the key was turned, and the first screw was well on its way home before they even found out that the beloved Henniker was not there!

Then, after a moment's pause (during which screw number two had started on its way), the handle of the door was shaken, and Mr Hashford's voice cried out, "Who is there? What are you doing there, you boys?"

His only answer was a mighty cheer from the assembled pupils of Stonebridge House, which must have been quite as explicit as the longest explanation.

"Now then," cried Smith, as once more the handle of the door was violently agitated; "look sharp, you fellows, with the desks—"

"Smith," cried the voice of Mr Ladislaw, from within; "you shall answer for this, Smith. Undo the door at once, sir."

But it had been agreed no parley should be held with the besieged, and Smith's only answer was to help to drag up the first desk and plant it firmly against the door. The blockade was soon made, but until it was, the fellows kept steadily and seriously to work.

Then ensued a scene I shall never forget, and which told significantly as the most thrilling story what had been our privations and persecutions and unhappiness at Stonebridge House.

The fellows yelled and rushed through the school as if they were mad. They shouted, and sung, and halloed, and laughed. They flung books and rulers and ink-pots to the four winds of heaven. They put the cane in the fire, and one of the Henniker's reading books, which was lying in the study, they tore into a thousand pieces. They burst into every forbidden nook and cranny of the house. They rushed down to the kitchen and up to the attics. They bawled down the speaking-tube, and danced on the dining-room table. Nothing was omitted which could testify to their glee at the new emancipation, or their hatred of the old *régime*. They held a mock school outside the Henniker's door, and gave one another bad marks and canings with infinite laughter, by way of cheering up their prisoner.

Finally the calls of hunger put an end to this strange demonstration, and with a mighty stampede we made for the kitchen. To our surprise, it was empty.

"Why, where's the cook and housemaid?" cried one and another to Smith.

"Oh," said Smith, who with the cares of generalship upon him had taken only a small part in the jubilation which had just been celebrated, "the servants have gone home. They both live at Felwick, so I said they might take a week's holiday."

The coolness of this announcement was received with much laughter, in the midst of which, however, Hawkesbury was heard to say, "I hope Smith is a good cook, for really I can't eat my food raw."

This was certainly a matter we had not reckoned on, and the idea of raw meat did cast a temporary shadow on our happiness. But Smith replied, "Oh, of course we do the cooking by turns. By the way, Hawkesbury, you and Flanagan have to see to that to-day."

Hawkesbury's smile left him for an instant.

"Nonsense; I'm not going to do anything of the sort."

"Then you'd better be the captain," said Smith glumly, "if you aren't going to obey orders."

Hawkesbury's smile returned.

"Oh, if it's the captain's orders, of course. Come along, Flanagan."

"Come along," said the jovial Flanagan; "I think we'll make a hash of it with a vengeance!"

Whereat this little breeze blew over. As a matter of fact, we all assisted at the cooking of this celebrated meal, and made a terrific hash of it, which, nevertheless, we relished greatly, and declared we had never tasted such a dinner since we came to Stonebridge House. No more we had!

But amid our own feasting it would never do to forget our prisoners. Three parcels were made, containing each a liberal helping of bread and meat, with little parcels of salt and butter thoughtfully added.

"Write on them 'For two days,'" said Smith, "and bring them up."

"How about water?" asked some one.

"There's enough in each room for a day or two," said Smith, who seemed to have taken note of everything.

"I don't see the fun of feeding them up this way," said Rathbone. "You'll never get them to give in as long as you make them so jolly comfortable."

"I'd like to see how you liked it for two days," said Smith. "I don't suppose you'd think yourself overfed or jolly comfortable either. But come on; have you got the string?"

Each parcel was attached to a long piece of string, and conveyed in state by the entire school to its respective destination. The Henniker was first fed. Amid shouts of "Cheer, boys, cheer," and "Rule Britannia," we marched up to her door and halted, while Smith, with the aid of a rake, lifted the parcel on to the small ventilator above the door, and gave it a little shove over the other side.

"Now lower away," said he to the boy who held the string.

"Smith, I hear your voice," cried the Henniker. "Smith, open my door, *please*."

Except for the last extraordinary expression the Henniker's voice sounded much as usual. No answer, of course, was given, and we waited until the parcel should be detached from the string.

For about five minutes it remained untouched, during which period the holder tried to attract the attention of the prisoner by sundry spasmodic jerkings of the string. At length the fish did bite. Without a word the parcel was detached from the string. We turned to go.

"Plate, knife, and fork in the cupboard," cried out Smith, as we did so.

"You don't mean to say," said Rathbone, as we went along, "that you've put a knife and fork for her?"

"Yes, I have," said Smith, in a manner which did not encourage the truculent Rathbone to pursue the subject.

The feeding of the two masters was a longer process. For to reach their door it was necessary to climb over a perfect jungle of desks and chairs piled up against it; and when reached it was discovered that the glass ventilator, which usually stood open, had been shut and fastened inside. But Smith was not to be baulked by a trifle. He coolly broke the glass with his rake, till he had made a hole big enough to admit the parcels, which, one after the other, were lifted over the opening, and lowered within reach of their respective owners. In the present case the string to which they were attached was double, so, when it was found that neither was taken, Smith gave the order to "run" the string, and let them drop the parcels off on to the floor. This was done, and we were turning to go, when Mr Ladislaw's voice rose in angry tones.

"Listen to me, boys," he cried, authoritatively.

A general yell was the only answer to this, mingled with loud laughter, as Mr Hashford's head suddenly appeared at the broken ventilator. The apparition was the signal for a general fusillade of paper balls, in the midst of which the usher modestly retired from observation.

The evening was spent in the same rollicking manner as the afternoon. We held mock school in Mr Ladislaw's study, and got Flanagan to dress up in an old gown of the Henniker's, which was found in the boot-room, and enact that favourite character's part, which he did to the life. We also made out our own "reports" for home, and played a most spirited game of croquet in the hall, with potatoes for balls and brooms for mallets, besides treating our prisoners to a ravishing concert by an orchestra of one dinner-bell, two dish-covers, two combs and paper, and one iron tray.

We kept it up till rather late, and, indeed, it was not till Smith summoned us to a council of war that the problem of how and where to spend the night occurred to us.

"Some of us ought to stay up as sentinels," said our captain.

"Well, I can't, for one," said Philpot, "for I was never so sleepy in my life."

"I should think," said Hawkesbury, sweetly, "if the captain stayed up we should be quite safe."

Why *should* Smith glare so whenever Hawkesbury spoke? I wondered. I'm sure there did not seem to be anything offensive in this.

"I'll stay up, Jack," said I, more with a desire to avert a row than because I felt particularly "spry."

"So will I," said Shankley, "if you'll dig me in the ribs when I get sleepy."

"I'll tell you what," said Smith, after having recovered himself. "Suppose we bring all the beds down and camp out on the landing."

This was carried with acclamation, and every one forthwith proceeded to his dormitory, and reappeared staggering under the weight of his bedclothes. One monstrous bed was made in which we all "camped out" in turn, one fellow only remaining awake as sentinel for an hour at a time.

"We shall have to settle to-morrow," said Smith, when he had returned to "camp," after having gone the round and seen that all lights were out, and all doors and bolts fastened—"we shall have to settle to-morrow what to say to them about coming out, you fellows."

"I thought that was left to the captain," said Hawkesbury.

"I vote we stick out against the Henniker having anything to do with us," said Philpot, "in or out of school."

"Yes, and do away with afternoon school and preparation too," said Rathbone; "they are both nuisances."

"And get a holiday to go out of bounds once a week," said Flanagan in the act of dropping asleep.

These sweeping schemes of reform, however, agreeable as they sounded, seemed none of them likely to receive the assent of our prisoners.

Smith's idea was a good deal more moderate. "I don't see that we can stick out for more than leave to talk when we are not in class, and do away with 'detentions.'"

"That really seems hardly worth all the trouble," said Hawkesbury, "does it?"

"It's left to the captain," said Smith, shortly, "and that's my idea, if you agree."

"We ought to bargain they don't take any more notice of this affair, or write home about it," suggested Shankley.

"Who cares what they write home?" scornfully inquired Smith.

"Ah, it may not matter to *you*," said Hawkesbury, smiling very sweetly, "but to all the rest of us it does."

Smith glared at the speaker, and looked as if he was about to fly at his throat; but he controlled himself, and merely replied, "Very well, then, they are to promise not to say anything about it at home, as well as give in on the other things. Is that settled?"

Everybody said "yes," and shortly afterwards most of the mutineers were peacefully asleep.

"Fred," said Smith to me that night, as we kept watch together, "unless that fellow Hawkesbury lets me alone I shall give the thing up."

"Don't do that," said I. "Really, I don't think that Hawkesbury means it. I'll speak to him if you like." It cost me a great effort to say this.

Smith fired up unwontedly at the suggestion.

"If you do, you and I will never be friends again," he said, passionately. Then recovering himself, he added, repentantly, "Fred, I'm awfully sorry I lost my temper. I know I'm a brute; but please don't think of speaking to any one about it."

"All right, old man," said I.

And so the night wore on, and when presently it came to be our turn to lie down and sleep in the big bed, I, at any rate, did so a good deal disturbed in my spirit, and not altogether sure whether in our present escapade we Stonebridge House boys were not making rather fools of ourselves.

Chapter Eight
How the Rebellion collapsed, and we left Stonebridge House

I was roused next morning early by the sound of voices, and found that a fresh council of war was being held in the big bed on the question of the ultimatum. Smith was away at the time.

"I mean to say," said Rathbone, "Smith's far too mild to suit me."

I felt called upon to stick up for my chum.

"Why did you make him captain?" I said. I had long got past the stage of being afraid either of Rathbone or Philpot at Stonebridge House.

"Well," retorted the malcontent, "why doesn't he go the whole hog?"

"Depends on what you call the whole hog," I replied.

"Why, instead of feeding them up like fighting-cocks I'd starve them—I would. And I'd have locked them all together in an empty garret, and not in rooms with sofas and beds and all that nonsense. And I wouldn't let them out till they came out on their knees and promised to do whatever they were ordered. That's what I'd do, and I'll tell—"

"Now then, Rathbone," cried Smith, entering at that moment, "it's your turn to look after the grub, remember. Look alive, or we shall have no breakfast."

It was a curious indication of the power that was in my friend Smith, that Rathbone—though the words of mutiny were even then on his lips—quietly got up and went off to his allotted duties without saying a word.

"Look here," said Smith, presently, pulling two papers from his pocket, "I've written out the terms we agreed to. How will this do?

"'To Mr Ladislaw, Miss Henniker, and Mr Hashford,—We, the undersigned boys of Stonebridge House, are willing to release you on the following conditions:

"'1. That leave be given to the boys to talk to one another when not in class.

"'2. That detention for bad marks given by Miss Henniker be abolished.

"'3. That you say nothing to any one about all this.

"'As long as you stick to these conditions, and Miss Henniker doesn't plague us, we agree to be steady and not mutiny any more.' That's about all we need say, isn't it?"

"I don't see," said Philpot, "the use of the last clause. We don't want to bind ourselves down."

"There's no harm, though, in saying we won't kick up a row if they treat us properly."

"I don't know," said Philpot, doubtfully. "I don't want to sign away my right to kick up a row."

We laughed at this ingenuous admission, and Smith said, "Well, I think we've a better chance of bringing them to book if we keep it in. What do you say, Flanagan?"

"Oh yes, keep it in. You know I like rows as well as anybody, but what's the use of them when there's nothing to make them about?"

"I think it had better stay in," said I. "What do you say, Hawkesbury?"

Hawkesbury smiled in an amused way, as if it was a joke.

This appeared to incense Smith greatly, as usual.

"Why ever don't you say what you think instead of grinning?" he blurted out.

"Why, you know, my dear fellow, we leave it all to you. I agree to anything!"

I verily believe if Smith had had a boot in his hand it would have found its way in the direction of his enemy's smile. Happily he hadn't; so he turned his back on the speaker, and proceeded, "Very well, then we'd better sign these at once. I've got a pen and ink here. Look sharp, you fellows."

"Don't you think," said Hawkesbury, blandly, once more, "as it's all been left to the captain, he had better sign the paper in the name of the school? You don't mind, Smith, I'm sure?"

Smith snatched up the pen hastily, and signed his name at the foot of each document.

"I'm not afraid, if that's what you mean."

I could watch the working of his face as he hurriedly folded each paper up into the form of a note, and knew the storm that was going on in his own breast. Certainly Hawkesbury, however good his intentions, was a little aggravating.

"Perhaps you'll throw that in over the Henniker's door?" said Smith, handing one of the notes to Hawkesbury.

Again Hawkesbury smiled as he replied, "Really, I'm such a bad shot; I'd much rather you did it."

"Give it me," I cried, interposing before my friend could retort. "I'll throw it in."

Saying which I took the missive, and after one or two bad shots, succeeded in getting it through the ventilator and hearing it drop in the middle of the Henniker's floor.

"A letter for you," I cried by way of explanation. "You've an hour to give an answer."

"Batchelor," replied Miss Henniker from within, in what seemed rather a subdued voice, "you are doing very wrong. Let me out immediately, Batchelor."

"Not till you promise what's written in the note," replied I, quitting the place.

A similar ceremony was enacted by Smith in delivering the "ultimatum" to the two masters, and we then adjourned for breakfast.

"What shall we do to-day?" asked Flanagan, who was quite fresh again after yesterday's hard work.

"Oh, any mortal thing you like," said Shankley. "I mean to go and have a rare walk over the roof."

"I vote we make up a party and go down to the village," said another.

"No, no," said Smith, looking up, "we must stay indoors, or the thing will soon get known. You can do anything you like indoors."

There was a little growling at this, although we knew there was reason in the prohibition.

"I don't see any harm in going out on the heath," said Rathbone; "you did that yourself once."

"Yes, and some one saw me do it," replied Smith. "I say, stay in doors."

His tone was peremptory, and as usual it had its due effect. The fellows ate their breakfast quietly and said no more about it.

The meal was rather a protracted one, owing to Rathbone having forgotten to put the bag in the coffee-pot before he inserted the coffee, and thus spoiling the beverage altogether. He was sent back to make it over again—a circumstance which by no means had the effect of soothing his spirits.

By the time breakfast was done the hour had nearly arrived when our prisoners were to give their answers to our manifesto.

As we were preparing to march up stairs, with a view to ascertain their decision, Hawkesbury met us, coming down with his hat on.

"Where are you going?" demanded Smith.

Hawkesbury looked very pleasant indeed as he replied, "Oh, please don't mind me. I'm going out for a walk. I've got a headache, and really I don't see much use playing about indoors."

Smith's face darkened. "Didn't you hear me say there was no going out?" he said.

Hawkesbury smiled and seemed much amused. Smith's wrath was rising apace. "What I said I'll stick to!" cried he, standing across the step. "You sha'n't go out!"

"Hawkesbury," I interposed, anxious to avert a row, "we've all promised to obey the captain, you know."

"Really," replied Hawkesbury, "I didn't. Please let me pass, Smith."

"Then you were speaking false," exclaimed the irate Smith, "when you said you did promise?"

"Really, Smith, I didn't say I did promise—"

"Wretched liar!" replied Smith.

"That's not a nice name to call a fellow," mildly replied Hawkesbury. "I hope I'm a gentleman, and don't deserve it."

"Bah," said Smith, in tones of utter disgust, standing aside and letting his enemy pass. "Go where you like, we want no sneaks here!"

Hawkesbury walked on, smiling pleasantly.

"Good-bye for the present," said he. "Mind you obey your captain, you fellows. We all know *he's* a gentleman, don't we?"

And he went out, leaving us all in a state of utter astonishment.

A babel of voices at once arose. Some declared Hawkesbury was quite right not to stand being ordered about; others said he ought to have been stopped going out, and others said, "Who cared if he did go?"

In the midst of this my eyes turned to Jack Smith. His face, which had been flushed and excited, was now pale and solemn. He either did not hear or did not heed the discussion that was going on; and I must confess I felt half-frightened as my eyes suddenly met his. Not that he looked dangerous. He had a strange look—half of baffled rage and half of shame—which was quite new to me, and I waited anxiously to discover what he meant.

As his eye met mine, however, he seemed to recover himself and to make up his mind.

"Batchelor," said he, "get the screwdriver."

"What are you going to do?" asked some one. "Are you going to lock Hawkesbury out?"

"No," said Smith, quietly; "but I'm going to let out the others."

"What!" cried the fellows at this astounding announcement: "without waiting for their answer? We shall all get expelled!"

"No, you won't!" said Smith, doggedly, and rather scornfully.

"You don't mean to say you're going to show the white feather?" said Rathbone.

"I mean to say I'm going to let them out."

"Yes, and get all the credit of it, and leave us to get into the row," said Philpot.

Smith turned round short on the speaker and held out the screwdriver. "Here," said he, "if you want the credit, go and do it yourself!"

Of course, Philpot declined the tempting offer, and, without another word, Smith walked up to the passage and began pulling away the desks from the parlour door.

Flanagan and one or two of us, sorely perplexed, helped him; the others stood aloof and grumbled or sneered.

The two masters within heard the noise, but neither of them spoke.

At last all was clear, and Smith said, "Now then, you'd better go, you fellows!"

We obeyed him, though reluctantly. Our curiosity as well as our anxiety prompted us to stay. We retired to the end of the passage, where from a distant door we nervously watched Smith turn the key and draw out first one screw then the other from the door that divided him and us from our masters.

At last we saw it open. Smith walked into the room and shut the door behind him. What happened inside we never exactly knew. After half an hour, which seemed to us as long as a day, the three emerged, and walked straight down the passage and up the stairs that led to Miss Henniker's room. Smith, with the screwdriver, walked in the middle, very solemn and very pale.

Stealthily we crawled up after them, and hid where we could observe what was to follow.

Mr Ladislaw knocked at the Henniker's door.

"Well?" said a voice within.

The word was mildly spoken, and very unlike the snap to which we had been accustomed in former days.

"It is I," said Mr Ladislaw, "and Mr Hashford."

"I shall be glad if you will immediately have my door opened," was the reply.

"Smith, unscrew the door at once," said Mr Ladislaw.

Smith solemnly proceeded to do as he was bid, and presently the screws were both dislodged.

"Is it done?" said the Henniker when the sound ceased.

"Yes, Miss Henniker; the door is quite free."

"Then," said the Henniker—and there positively seemed to be a tremor in the voice—"please go; I will be down presently."

So the little procession turned and once more walked down the stairs, Smith, with his screwdriver, still walking solemnly in the middle. We who were in hiding were torn by conflicting desires. Our first impulse was to remain and enjoy the spectacle of the crestfallen Henniker marching forth from her late prison. But somehow, rough boys as we were, and not much given to chivalric scruples, the sound of that tremble in the Henniker's voice, and with it the recollection of the part we had taken in her punishment, made us feel as if, after all, the best thing we could do was not to remain, but to follow the others down stairs.

As we were doing so the ten o'clock bell rang for morning classes, and we naturally sought the schoolroom, where, with Mr Hashford in the desk, school was assembled just as if nothing had happened. Hawkesbury was the only absentee.

I certainly admired Mr Hashford on this occasion. He appeared to be the only person in the room who was not thoroughly uncomfortable. Indeed, as we went on with our work, and he, almost pleasantly, entered into it with us, we felt ourselves getting comfortable too, and could hardly believe that the usher now instructing us had, an hour ago, been our prisoner, and that we so recently had been shouting words of mutiny and defiance all over the school. It was like a dream—and, after all, not a very nice dream.

But we were recalled to ourselves when presently, along the passage outside our door, there resounded a footstep which instinct told us belonged to the Henniker. Not much chance of feeling comfortable with that sound in one's ears!

But to our surprise and comfort it passed on and descended the stairs. It was like a reprieve to convicted felons.

Class went on, and the clock was getting on to twelve—the usual hour for a break—when the door opened, and Mr Ladislaw put in his head and said, "Smith, will you step down to my study? Mr Hashford, the mid-day bell will not ring till one to-day."

Smith solemnly followed the master from the room, and for another hour we worked in class—one of us, at any rate—feeling very anxious and not a little uneasy.

When the bell did ring, and we went down stairs, not knowing exactly what was to become of us, my first thought was, what had become of Smith? He was not in the playground, where we wandered about listlessly for a quarter of an hour before dinner, nor was he to be seen when presently we assembled in the memorable parlour for our mid-day repast.

It was not a very grand meal, that dinner. We partook of the cold remains of a joint which one of ourselves had made a woeful attempt to cook the day before, and which now tasted anything but delicious. Miss Henniker was in her usual place, and as we sat with our eyes rigidly fixed on the plates before us, we were conscious of her glancing once or twice towards one and another of us, and then turning away to speak to Mr Ladislaw, who was also present. Except for the whispered conversation of these two not a word was uttered during the meal. Even Flanagan, when, in reaching the salt, he knocked over his water, did not receive the expected bad mark, but was left silently to mop up the spill as best he could.

It was a terrible meal, and my anxiety about my friend Smith made it all the worse.

Dinner was over, and we were descending to afternoon class in Mr Ladislaw's study, when the front door opened and Hawkesbury entered.

We could see he was taken aback and utterly astonished to see Mr Ladislaw and Miss Henniker at liberty and us once more at our old tasks. For a moment his face looked concerned and doubtful, then, suddenly changing, it broke out into smiles as he ran up to Mr Ladislaw.

"Oh, Mr Ladislaw," cried he, "and Miss Henniker, I am so glad! I really couldn't bear to be in the school while they were treating you so shamefully!"

"Where have you been, Hawkesbury?" said Mr Ladislaw.

"Oh! I went out in hopes of being able to—"

"You have told no one of what has occurred?" said Mr Ladislaw, sternly.

"Oh, no!" said the smiling Hawkesbury; "I really went out because I couldn't bear to be in the school and be unable to do anything for you and Miss Henniker. I *am* so glad you have got out!"

None of us had the spirit to protest. We could see that Hawkesbury's statement, and his expressed joy at their liberation, had gone down both with Mr Ladislaw and Miss Henniker—and at our expense, too; and yet we dared not expostulate or do ourselves justice.

Afternoon school went on, and still no Smith appeared. Was he locked up in the coal-hole or in one of the attics up stairs? I wondered; or had he been given into custody, or what? No solution came to the mystery all that afternoon or evening. We worked silently on, conscious that the Henniker's eyes were upon us, but aware that she neither spoke nor interfered with us.

Bedtime came at last, and, in strange trouble and anxiety, I went up. I almost made up my mind to ask Mr Hashford or Mr Ladislaw what had become of Smith, but I could not screw my courage up to the pitch.

As I was undressing, Hawkesbury came near me and whispered, "Where is Smith?"

I vouchsafed no reply. I had been used to give Hawkesbury credit for good intentions, but I had had my confidence shaken by that day's events.

"Don't be cross with me, Batchelor," said he; "I really don't deserve it."

"Why did you desert and leave us all in the lurch?" growled I.

"I did not mean to do it," said he, very meekly; "but really, when I woke this morning I felt I was doing wrong, Batchelor, and could not bear to stay in and stand by while Mr Ladislaw and Miss Henniker were kept shut up. That's really the reason, and I thought it would be kinder of me to keep out of the way and not spoil your fun. Smith quite misunderstood me, he did really."

"Why didn't you say you wouldn't join before we began?" I asked.

"Why, because you know, Batchelor, I was in a bad frame of mind then, and was angry. But I tried hard to forgive, and I blame myself very much that I even seemed to agree. You mustn't think too hardly of me, Batchelor."

I said nothing, but went on undressing, more perplexed than ever to know what to think. Hawkesbury, after a warm "Good-night," left me, and I was thankful, at any rate, for the prospect of a few hours' sleep and forgetfulness.

I was just getting into bed, and had turned back the clothes to do so, when I suddenly caught sight of a scrap of paper appearing from under my pillow.

I first supposed it must be some remnant of last night's sports, but, on taking it out, found that it was a note carefully rolled up and addressed to me in Smith's well-known hand.

With eager haste I unfolded it and read, "I'm expelled. Good-bye. Write 'J.,' Post-Office, Packworth."

Expelled! sent off at an hour's notice, without even a word of good-bye! My first sensations were selfish, and as I curled myself up in bed, with his note fast in my hand, I felt utterly wretched, to know that my only friend, the only comfort I had at Stonebridge House, had been taken away. What should I do without him?

Expelled! Where had he gone to, then? Packworth, I knew, was a large town about ten miles from Brownstroke, where my uncle now and then went on business. Did Jack live there, then? And if he did, why had he never told me? At any rate, I could get over and see him in the holidays. "Write to me." How was that possible here? unless, indeed—unless I could smuggle the letter into the post. Poor Jack expelled! Why should he be expelled more than any of us, except Hawkesbury? What a fury he had been in with Hawkesbury that very morning! Certainly Hawkesbury was aggravating. Strange that my friend Smith and Hawkesbury—that my friend Jack—that Jack and Hawk—

And here, in a piteous muddle of mind and spirit, I fell asleep.

I remained another year at Stonebridge House after Jack Smith had been expelled. We did not get a single holiday during that period, so that my scheme of walking over from Brownstroke, and finding him out at Packworth, never came off. And I only contrived to write to him once. That was the first time, the Sunday after he had left, when the Henniker saw me dropping my letter into the post. After that I was closely watched, and I need hardly say, if Jack ever wrote to me, I never got his letter. Still I cherished the memory of my friend, and even when Stonebridge House was most desolate, found some consolation in feeling pretty sure I had a friend somewhere, which is more than every one can say.

I made steady progress with my arithmetic and other studies during the year, thanks to Mr Hashford, who, good fellow that he was, took special pains with me, so that at the end of the year I was pronounced competent to take a situation as an office-boy or junior clerk, or any like post to which my amiable uncle might destine me.

I was not sorry to leave Stonebridge House, as you may guess. During the last year, certainly, things were better than they had been. No reference was made on any occasion, either in public or in private, to the great rebellion of that summer. The Henniker never quite got over the shake she had had when we rose in arms against her, and Mr Ladislaw appeared proportionately subdued, so on the whole things were rather more tolerable. And for lack of my lost friend, I managed to improve the acquaintance of the good-natured Flanagan, besides retaining the favour of the smiling Hawkesbury.

So passed another year, at the end of which I found myself a wiser and a sadder boy, with my back turned at length on Stonebridge House, and my face towards the wide, wide world.

Chapter Nine
How I replied to an Advertisement and waited for the Answer

The day that witnessed my departure from Stonebridge House found me, I am bound to confess, very little improved by my year or two's residence under that dull roof. I do not blame it all on the school, or even on Miss Henniker, depressing as both were.

There is no reason why, even at a school for backward and troublesome boys, a fellow shouldn't improve, if he gave his mind to it. But that is just where I failed. I didn't give my mind to it. In fact, I made up my mind it was no use trying to improve, and therefore didn't try. The consequence was, that after Jack Smith left, I cast in my lot with the rest of the backward and troublesome boys, and lost all ambition to be much better than the rest of them.

Flanagan, the fellow I liked best, was always good-humoured and lively, but I'm not sure that he would have been called a boy of good principles. At any rate, he never professed to be particularly ambitious in any such way, and in that respect was very different from Hawkesbury, who, by the time he left Stonebridge House, six months before me, to go to a big public school, had quite impressed me with the worth of his character.

But this is a digression. As I was saying, I left Stonebridge House a good deal wilder, and more rackety, and more sophisticated, than I had entered it two years before. However, I left it also with considerably more knowledge of addition, subtraction, multiplication, and division; and that in my uncle's eye appeared to be of far more moment than my moral condition.

"Fred," he said to me the day after I had got home, and after I had returned from a triumphant march through Brownstroke, to show myself off to my old comrades generally, and Cad Prog in particular—"Fred," said my uncle, "I am going to send you to London."

"To London!" cried I, not knowing exactly whether to be delighted, or astonished, or alarmed, or all three—"to London."

"Yes. You must get a situation, and do something to earn your living."

I ruminated over this announcement, and my uncle continued, "You are old enough to provide for yourself, and I expect you to do so."

There was a pause, at the end of which, for lack of any better remark, I said, "Yes."

"The sooner you start the better," continued my uncle. "I have marked a few advertisements in that pile of newspapers," added he, pointing to a dozen or so of papers on his table. "You had better take them and look through them, and tell me if you see anything that would suit you."

Whereat my uncle resumed his writing, and I, with the papers in my arms, walked off in rather a muddled state of mind to my bedroom.

Half way up stairs a sudden thought occurred to me, which caused me to drop my burden and hurry back to my uncle's room.

"Uncle, do you know the Smiths of Packworth?"

My uncle looked up crossly.

"Haven't you learned more sense at school, sir, than that? Don't you know there are hundreds of Smiths at Packworth?"

This was a crusher. I meekly departed, and picking up my papers where I had dropped them, completed the journey to my room.

It had been a cherished idea of mine, the first day I got home to make inquiries about my friend Smith. It had never occurred to me before that Smith was such a very common name; but it now dawned slowly on me that to find a Smith in Packworth would be about as simple as to find a needle in a bottle of hay.

Anyhow, I could write to him now without fear—that was a comfort. So I turned to my newspapers and began to read through a few of the advertisements my uncle had considerately marked.

The result was not absolutely exhilarating. My uncle evidently was not ambitious on my account.

"Sharp lad wanted to look after a shop." That was the first I caught sight of. And the next was equally promising.

"Page wanted by a professional gentleman. Must be clean, well-behaved, and make himself useful in house. Attend to boots, coals, windows, etcetera. Good character indispensable."

I was almost grateful to feel that no one could give me a good character by any stretch of imagination, so that at any rate I was safe from this fastidious professional gentleman. Then came another:

"News-boy wanted. Must have good voice. Apply Clerk, Great Central Railway Station."

Even this did not tempt me. It might be a noble sphere of life to strive to make my voice heard above a dozen shrieking engines all day long, but I didn't quite fancy the idea.

In fact, as I read on and on, I became more and more convinced that my splendid talents would be simply wasted in London. Nothing my uncle had marked tempted me. A "muffin boy's" work might be pleasant for a week, till the noise of the bell had lost its novelty; a "boy to learn the art of making button-holes in braces" might perhaps be a promising opening; and a printer's boy might be all very well, but they none of them accorded with my own ideas, still less with my opinion of my own value.

I was getting rather hopeless, and wondering what on earth I should say to my uncle, when the brilliant idea occurred to me of looking at some of the other advertisements which my uncle hadn't marked. Some of these were most tempting.

"A junior partner wanted in an old-established firm whose profits are £10,000 a year. Must bring £15,000 capital into the concern."

There! If I only had £15,000, my fortune would be made at once!

"Wanted a companion for a nobleman's son about to travel abroad."

There again, why shouldn't I try for that? What could a nobleman's son require more in a companion than was to be found in me?

And so I travelled on, beginning at the top of the ladder and sliding gently down, gradually losing not only the hope of finding a situation to suit me, but also relinquishing my previous strong faith in my own wonderful merits. I was ready to give it up as a bad job, and go and tell my uncle I must decline all his kind suggestions, when, in an obscure corner of one paper, my eye caught the following:

"Junior clerkship. An intelligent lad, respectable, and quick at figures, wanted in a merchant's office. Wages 8 shillings a week to commence. Apply by letter to Merrett, Barnacle, and Company, Hawk Street, London."

I jumped up as if I had been shot, and rushed headlong with the paper to my uncle's study.

"Look at this, uncle! This will do, I say! Read it, please."

My uncle read it gravely, and then pushed the paper from him.

"Absurd. You would not do at all. That is not one of those I marked, is it?"

"No. But they were all awful. I say, uncle, let's try for this."

My uncle stared at me, and I looked anxiously at my uncle.

"Fred," said he sternly, "I'm sorry to see you making a fool of yourself. However, it's your affair, not mine."

"But, uncle, I'm pretty quick at figures," said I.

"And intelligent and respectable too, I suppose?" added my uncle, looking at me over his glasses. "Well, do as you choose."

"Will you be angry?" I inquired.

"Tut, tut!" said my uncle, rising, "that will do. You had better write by the next post, if you are bent on doing it. You can write at my desk."

So saying he departed, leaving me very perplexed and a good deal out of humour with my wonderful advertisement.

However, I sat down and answered it. Six of my uncle's sheets of paper were torn up before I got the first sentence to my satisfaction, and six more before the letter was done. I never wrote a letter that cost me such an agony of labour. How feverishly I read and re-read what I had written! What panics I got into about the spelling of "situation," and the number of l's in "ability"! How carefully I rubbed out the pencil-lines I had ruled, and how many times I repented I had not put a "most" before the "obediently"! Many letters like that, thought I, would shorten my life perceptibly. At last it was done, and when my uncle came in I showed it to him with fear and trembling, and watched his face anxiously as he read it.

"Humph!" said he, looking at me, "and suppose you do get the place, you won't stick to it."

"Oh yes, I will," said I; "I'll work hard and get on."

"You'd better," said my uncle, "for you'll have only yourself to depend on."

I posted my letter, and the next few days seemed interminable. Whenever I spoke about the subject to my uncle he took care not to encourage me over much. And yet I fancied, gruff as he was, he was not wholly displeased at my "cheek" in answering Merrett, Barnacle, and Company's advertisement.

"Successful!" growled he. "Why, there'll be scores of other boys after the place. You don't expect your letter's the best of the lot, do you? Besides, they'd never have a boy up from the country when there are so many in London ready for the place, who are used to the work. Mark my word, you'll hear no more about it."

And so it seemed likely to be. Day after day went by and the post brought no letter; I was beginning to think I should have to settle down as a newspaper-boy or a page after all.

At the end of the week I was so disheartened that I could stay in the house no longer, but sallied out, I cared not whither, for a day in the fresh air.

As I was sauntering along the road, a cart overtook me, a covered baker's cart with the name painted outside, "Walker, Baker, Packworth."

A brilliant idea seized me as I read the legend. Making a sign to the youth in charge to stop, I ran up and asked, "I say, what would you give me a lift for to Packworth?"

"What for? S'pose we say a fifty-pun' note," was the facetious reply. "I could do with a fifty-pun' note pretty comfortable."

"Oh, but really, how much? I want to go to Packworth awfully, but it's such a long way to walk."

"What do you weigh, eh?"

"I don't know; about seven stone, I think."

"If you was eight stun I wouldn't take you, there! But hop up!"

And next moment I found myself bowling merrily along in the baker's cart all among the loaves and flour-bags to Packworth.

My jovial driver seemed glad of a companion, and we soon got on very good terms, and conversed on a great variety of topics.

Presently, as we seemed to be nearing the town, I ventured to inquire, "I say, do you know Jack Smith at Packworth?"

The Jehu laughed.

"Know him—old Jack Smith? Should think I do."

"You do?" cried I, delighted, springing to my feet and knocking over a whole pyramid of loaves. "Oh, I *am* glad. It's him I want to see."

"Is it now?" said the fellow, "and what little game have you got on with him? Going a grave-diggin', eh?"

"Grave-digging, no!" I cried. "Jack Smith and I were at school together—"

The driver interrupted me with a loud laugh.

"Oh, my eye, that's a good 'un; you at school with old Jack Smith! Oh, that'll do, that'll do!" and he roared with laughter.

"But I really was," repeated I, "at Stonebridge House."

"You was? How long before you was born was it; oh my eye, eh?"

"It was only last year."

"Last year, and old Jack lost the last tooth out of his head last year too."

"What! has he had his teeth out?" cried I, greatly concerned.

"Yes, and all his hair off since you was at school with him," cried my companion, nearly rolling off the box with laughter.

"What do you mean?" I cried, in utter bewilderment at this catalogue of my friend's misfortunes.

"Oh, don't ask me. Old Jack Smith!"

"He's not old," said I, "not very, only about sixteen."

This was too much for my driver, who clapped me on the back, and as soon as he could recover his utterance cried, "My eyes, you *will* find him growed!"

"Has he?" said I, half envious, for I wasn't growing very quickly.

"Ain't he! He's growed a lump since you was at school together," roared my eccentric friend.

"What is he doing?" I asked, anxious to hear something more definite of poor Jack.

"Oh, the same old game, on'y he goes at it quieter nor he used. Last Sunday that there bell-ringing regular blowed him out, the old covey."

A light suddenly dawned upon me.

"Bell-ringing; old covey. That's not the Jack Smith I mean!"

"What!" roared my companion, "you don't mean him?"

"No, who?" cried I, utterly bewildered.

"Why, old Jack Smith, the sexton, what was eighty-two last Christmas! You wasn't at school with him! Oh, I say; here, take the reins: I can't drive straight no longer!" and he fairly collapsed into the bottom of the cart.

This little diversion, amusing as it was, did not have the effect of allaying my anxiety to hear something about my old schoolfellow.

My driver, however, although he knew plenty of Smiths in the town, knew no one answering to Jack's description; and, now that Packworth was in sight, I began to feel rather foolish to have come so far on such a wild-goose chase.

Packworth is a large town with about 40,000 inhabitants; and when, having bidden farewell to the good-natured baker, I found myself in its crowded bustling streets, any chance of running against my old chum seemed very remote indeed.

I went to the post-office where my two letters had been addressed, the one I wrote a year ago, just after Jack's expulsion, and the other written last week from Brownstroke.

"Have you any letters addressed to 'J'?" I asked.

The clerk fumbled over the contents of a pigeon-hole, from which he presently drew out my last letter and gave it to me.

"Wait a bit," said he, as I was taking it up, and turning to leave the office. "Wait a bit."

He went back to the pigeon-hole, and after another sorting produced, very dusty and dirty, my first letter. "That's for 'J' too," said he.

Then Jack had never been to Packworth, or got my letter, posted at such risk. He must have given me a false address. Surely, if he lived here, he would have called for the letter. Why did he tell me to write to Post-Office, Packworth, if he never meant to call for my letters?

A feeling of vexation crossed my mind, and mingled with the disappointment I felt at now being sure my journey here was a hopeless one.

I wandered about the town a bit, in the vague hope of something turning up. But nothing did. Nothing ever does when a fellow wants it. So I turned tail, and faced the prospect of a solitary ten-mile walk back to Brownstroke.

I felt decidedly down. This expedition to Packworth had been a favourite dream of mine for many months past, and somehow I had never anticipated there would be much difficulty, could I once get there, in discovering my friend Smith. But now he seemed more out of reach than ever. There were my two neglected letters, never called for, and not a word from him since the day I left Stonebridge House. I might as well give up the idea of ever seeing him again, and certainly spare myself the trouble of further search after him.

I was walking on, letters in hand, engaged in this sombre train of thought, when suddenly, on the road before me, I heard a clatter of hoofs accompanied by a child's shriek. At the same moment round a corner appeared a small pony galloping straight towards where I was, with a little girl clinging wildly round its neck, and uttering the cries I had heard.

The animal had evidently taken fright and become quite beyond control, for the reins hung loose, and the little stirrup was flying about in all directions.

Fortunately, the part of the road where we were was walled on one side, while the other bank was sloping. I had not had much practice in stopping runaway horses, but it occurred to me that if I stood right in the pony's way, and shouted at him as he came up, he might, what with me in front and the wall and slope on either side, possibly give himself a moment for reflection, and so enable me to make a grab at his bridle.

And so it turned out. I spread out my arms and yelled at him at the top of my voice, with a vehemence which quite took him aback. He pulled up dead just as he reached me, so suddenly, indeed, that the poor child slipped clean off his back, and then, before he could fling himself round and continue his bolt in another direction, I had him firmly by the snaffle.

The little girl, who may have been twelve or thirteen, was not hurt, I think, by her fall. But she was dreadfully frightened, and sat crying so piteously that I began to get quite alarmed. I tied the pony up to the nearest tree, and did what I could to relieve the young lady's tribulation, a task in which I was succeeding very fairly when a female, the child's nurse, arrived on the scene in a panic. Of course my little patient broke out afresh for the benefit of her protectress, and an affecting scene ensued, in the midst of which, finding I was not wanted, and feeling a little foolish to be standing by when so much crying and kissing was going on, I proceeded on my way, half wishing it had been my luck to secure that lively little pony for my journey home.

However, ten miles come to an end at last, and in due time I turned up at Brownstroke pretty tired, and generally feeling somewhat down in the mouth by my day's adventures.

But those adventures, or rather events, were not yet over; for that same evening brought a letter with the London postmark and the initials M., B., and Company on the seal of the envelope!

You may fancy how eagerly I opened it. It ran as follows:

"Messrs Merrett, Barnacle, and Company are in receipt of Frederick Batchelor's application for junior clerkship, and in reply—"

"What?" I gasped to myself, as I turned over the leaf.

"—would like to see Batchelor at their office on Saturday next at 10:15."

I could hardly believe my eyes. I rushed to my uncle and showed him the letter.

"Isn't it splendid?" I cried.

"Not at all," replied he. "Don't be too fast, you have not got the place yet."

"Ah, I know," said I, "but I've a chance at least."

"You have a chance against a dozen others," said my uncle, "who most likely have got each of them a letter just like this."

"Well, but, of course, I must go on Saturday?"

"You still mean to try?" said my uncle.

"Why yes," said I resolutely. "I do."

"Then you had better go to town on Saturday."

"Won't you go with me?" I inquired nervously.

"No," said my uncle; "Merrett, Barnacle, and Company want to see you, not me."

"But—" began I. But I didn't say what I was going to say. Why should I tell my uncle I was afraid to go to London alone?

"Where am I to live if I do *get* the place? London's such a big place to be in."

"Oh, we'll see to that," said my uncle, "in due time. Time enough for that when you get your place."

This was true; and half elated, half alarmed by the prospect before me, I took to my bed and went to sleep.

My dreams that night were a strange mixture of Merrett, Barnacle, and Company, the little girl who fell from the pony, Jack Smith, and the jovial baker; but among them all I slept very soundly, and woke like a giant refreshed the next day.

If only I had been easy in my mind about Jack Smith, I should have been positively cheerful. But the thought of him, and the fact of his never having called for my letters, sorely perplexed and troubled me. Had he forgotten all about me, then? How I had pictured his delight in getting that first letter of mine, when I wrote it surreptitiously in the playground at Stonebridge House a year ago! And I had meant it to be such a jolly comforting letter, too; and after all here it was in my pocket unopened. I must just read it over again myself. And I put my hand in my pocket to get it. To my surprise, however, only the last of the two letters was there, and high or low I could not find the other. It was very strange, for I distinctly remembered no having it in my hand after leaving Packworth. Then suddenly it occurred to me I must have had it in my hand when I met the runaway pony, and in the confusion of that adventure have dropped it. So I had not even the satisfaction of reading over my own touching effusion, which deprived me of a great intellectual treat.

However, I had other things to think of, for to-morrow was Saturday, the day on which I was to make my solitary excursion to London in quest of the junior clerkship at Merrett, Barnacle, and Company's.

Chapter Ten
How I ran against my Friend Smith in an Unexpected Quarter

I suppose my uncle thought it good discipline to turn a young fellow like me adrift for a whole day in London to shift for myself, and wrestle single-handed with the crisis that was to decide my destiny.

He may have been right, but when, after an hour's excited journey in the train, I found myself along with several hundred fellow-mortals standing in a street which seemed to be literally alive with people, I, at any rate, neither admired his wisdom nor blessed him for his good intentions.

Every one but myself seemed to be in a desperate hurry. Had I not been sure it was the way of the place, I should have been tempted to suppose some tremendous fire, or some extraordinary event was taking place at the other end of the street, and that every one was rushing to get a glimpse of it. I stood a minute or two outside the station, hoping to be left behind; but behold, no sooner had the tail of the race passed me, when another, indeed two other train-loads of humanity swarmed down upon me, and, hustling me as they swept by, fairly carried me along with them.

One thing alarmed me prodigiously. It was not the crowd, or the noise, or the cabs, or the omnibuses, or the newspaper-boys, or the shops, or the policemen, or the chimney-pot hats. These all astonished me, as well they might. But what terrified me was the number of boys like myself who formed part of the procession, and who, every one of them as I imagined, were hurrying towards Hawk Street.

My uncle had told me that I should find Hawk Street turning out at the end of the street in which the station stood, and this was precisely the direction in which these terrible boys were all going.

How knowing they all looked, and how confident! There was not one of them, I was certain, but was more intelligent than I, and quicker at figures. How I hated them as they swaggered along, laughing and joking with one another, looking familiarly on the scene around them, crossing the road in the very teeth of the cab-horses, and not one of them caring or thinking a bit about me. What chance had I among all these?

There was not much conceit left in me, I assure you, as I followed meekly in their wake towards Hawk Street that morning.

My uncle's directions had been so simple that I had never calculated on having any difficulty in finding my destination. But it's all very well in a quiet country town to find one street that turns out of another, but in London, between nine and ten in the morning, it's quite a different matter. At least so I found it. Half a dozen streets turned out of the one which I and the stream descended, and though I carefully studied the name of each in turn, no Hawk Street was there.

"Can you tell me where Hawk Street is?" I inquired at last of a fellow-passenger after a great inward struggle.

"Hawk Street? Yes. Go through Popman's Alley, and up the second court to the left—that'll bring you to Hawk Street."

"But uncle said it turned—" My guide had vanished!

I diligently sought for Popman's Alley, which I found to be a long paved passage between two high blocks of buildings, and leading apparently nowhere; at least I could discover no outlet, either at the end or either side. Every one was in such a hurry that I dared not "pop the question" as to the whereabouts of Hawk Street again, but made my way back once more to the entrance. By this time I was so muddled that for the life of me I could not tell which was the street I had come down, still less how I could get back to it.

Ask my way I must, if I died for it! Ten o'clock had struck ten minutes ago, and I was due at Merrett, Barnacle, and Company's at 10:15.

I noticed a boy ahead of me walking rather more slowly than the rest. I would ask him, and stick to him till he put me right. So I made up to him boldly.

"Will you show me the way to Hawk Street, please?" I said, as I came up.

He turned round suddenly as I spoke. Was it possible? Here, in London, where one might as soon expect to meet a body one knows as meet the man in the moon!

It was my friend Smith!

"Jack!" I exclaimed.

"Fred!" exclaimed Smith, seizing my hand.

There was no doubt about it, and no doubt about all my foolish suspicions as to his having forgotten me or ceased to care for me being groundless. His solemn face lit up almost to a look of jubilation as he grasped my hand and said, "Why, Fred, old man, whatever are you doing here?"

"What are *you* doing?" cried I. "Whoever would have thought of running up against you in this place? But I say," said I, suddenly remembering the time. "I have got to be in Hawk Street in two minutes, Jack. For goodness' sake, show us the way, if you know it."

Smith opened his black eyes very wide.

"You have to be somewhere in Hawk Street?" he asked.

"Yes. Merrett, Barnacle, and Company's the name. I'm after a place they have got there."

Smith's face passed through a variety of expressions, ending in the old solemn look as he quietly said, "So am I."

"You!" I exclaimed. "You after the same place? Oh, Jack!"

"I'm awfully sorry," said he. "I didn't know—"

"Oh, it's not that," I interrupted, "at all. I wish they had two places, though."

"So do I. Perhaps they have. But I say, you'd better look sharp."

"Aren't you coming too?" I said.

"I haven't to be there till 10:30. They'll see you first."

At that moment a clock chimed the quarter, and startled me nearly out of my wits.

"That's the time," cried I. "Where *ever* is Hawk Street, Jack?"

"This is it we're in, and that's the place over the way. Merrett's is on the first-floor."

"Be sure you wait outside for me," said I, preparing to dart over.

"Yes," said he. "But, Fred, promise me one thing."

"What?" said I, hurriedly.

"Not to show off badly because I'm after the place too."

Old Jack! He gave me credit, I fear, for a good deal more nobleness than I had a right to claim.

"All serene," said I, "if you'll promise the same."

"Yes," said he. "Mind, honour bright, Fred."

And so we parted, he to pace up and down the street for a long quarter of an hour, and I to present myself before the awful presence of Messrs Merrett, Barnacle, and Company.

If all the youths who had flocked with me from the station in the direction of Hawk Street had been bound (as my fears had suggested), for this place, they would have found themselves rather cramped for room by the time they were all assembled; for the first-floor offices which I entered were decidedly limited in their capacity. I, who had been expecting at least a place capable of holding several scores of clerks, was somewhat taken aback to find myself in a counting-house which accommodated only half a score, and even that at rather close quarters. In fact, I was so much taken aback that, although I had seen the name plainly inscribed on the door, I was constrained to inquire on entering, "Is this Messrs Merrett, Barnacle, and Company's office, please?"

"Yes," said one of the clerks, shortly, "what about it?"

"Oh, if you please," I began, "I've come to—that is I've—"

"Come, out with it, can't you?" said the clerk.

"It's the situation," said I, feeling very uncomfortable.

"Well, what about it?" said the clerk, who, evidently cheered by the smiles of his fellow-clerks, thought it a good joke to browbeat a poor green country boy.

"Only I've come after it," faltered I.

"Have you, though? And who told you to do that, I'd like to know?"

"My uncle—that is I had a letter—" but here a general laugh interrupted my confession, and I felt very foolish indeed.

"So you've got an uncle, have you? Do you ever lend him your gold watch?"

This witticism was lost on me. I didn't see the connection between my uncle borrowing my gold watch (if I had had one), and the situation at Messrs Merrett, Barnacle, and Company's. But it would never do to make myself disagreeable.

"I've not got a gold watch, or a silver one either," I said.

This seemed to occasion fresh merriment among my catechist and his fellows.

"Why don't you say who told you to come?" demanded the clerk.

"I did say," mildly replied I. "I got a letter."

"What's that to do with it? I got a letter to-day, didn't I, Wallop, to tell me my washerwoman had changed her address. But that's no reason for my coming here."

This was perfectly sound reasoning. So I amended my explanation.

"I got a letter from Merrett, Barnacle, and Company.—"

"*Messrs*. Merrett, Barnacle, and Company, if you please," put in the clerk.

"I beg your pardon," said I, "from Messrs Merrett, Barnacle, and Company, telling me to be here at 10:15."

"Oh. Why didn't you say that before? What's the use of prevaricating when it's just as easy to tell the truth straight out, eh? What's the time now?"

"Twenty past," said I, looking at the clock.

"And you call that punctual? That's a nice beginning, anyhow. What's your name?"

"Batchelor," said I.

This again appeared to afford amusement to the company in general; and one or two jokes at the expense of my name were forthcoming, which I bore with as good a grace as I could.

At length it pleased the clerk who had cross-examined me to get off his stool, and after poking the fire and consulting the directory, and skirmishing pleasantly with a fellow-clerk for a minute or two, to go to the door of the inner-room and knock there.

"Come in," I heard a voice answer, and the clerk entered.

He emerged again in a moment and beckoned to me. Now was the time! I braced myself up to the ordeal, and not heeding the facetious dig in the ribs which the clerk gave me in passing, I put on my best face, and entered the awful presence.

Two gentlemen sat facing one another at the table, one of them old, the other middle-aged. These I instantly guessed to be Messrs Merrett and Barnacle. Mr Barnacle, the junior partner, who had a sharp voice and a stern face, undertook my examination, Mr Merrett only coming in occasionally with some mild observation.

"You are Batchelor," said Mr Barnacle, when I had entered and carefully closed the door behind me. I noticed he held in his hand my original letter of application. "You are Frederick Batchelor. How is it you are late?"

"I'm sorry, sir," faltered I, at this rather discouraging beginning, "but—"

And here I stuck. What was the use of trying to explain what still remained the fact?

Mr Barnacle eyed me keenly, and continued, "You are fourteen, you say, have just left school, and are good at arithmetic. What school were you at?"

"Stonebridge House, sir."

"Where is that?"

"In Cliffshire."

"And you think you would suit us?"

"I'd try, sir," said I.

"Do you know what our work is?" said Mr Barnacle.

"No, sir, not exactly," I replied.

"Generally speaking," mildly put in Mr Merrett, "you've a sort of idea."

"Yes," said I, not quite sure whether I was telling the truth or not.

Mr Barnacle touched his bell, and the clerk appeared.

"Bring me the invoice-book, Doubleday."

Mr Doubleday returned directly with a large account-book, which he deposited on the table before the junior partner.

Mr Barnacle pushed it towards me.

"I want a list made out of all the goods sent to Mr Walker, of Bombay, since the beginning of the year. Let me see you make it out." Then touching his bell again, he said to Mr Doubleday, the clerk, "Here, Doubleday, give this boy some invoice paper and a pen, and let him write at your desk. He is to make a copy of all Walker's invoices since the beginning of this year."

"Yes, sir," said Doubleday.

"Be particular that he receives no assistance, and bring me the sheets when completed. Batchelor, take this book and follow Mr Doubleday to the counting-house."

"Do it as well as you can, without any help," mildly put in Mr Merrett, by way of encouragement.

I followed my conductor in a state of terrible trepidation, feeling that all this wasn't a bit like what I had expected my interview with Messrs Merrett, Barnacle, and Company to be.

"Here, hop up, young fellow," said Mr Doubleday, pointing to a high stool at one of the desks, "and pull up your boot."

I concluded this last expression meant make haste, and I accordingly pulled up my boot, and lost no time in setting myself to my task.

I was to make out a list of all that Walker of Bombay had had since the beginning of the year. I opened the big account-book; it contained a great many accounts, some long, some short. I began at the beginning, and searched through for any belonging to Walker of Bombay.

At length, after about twenty pages, I found an entry dated December 30th last year. That would not do; I was only to make a list of what had been sent this year; and yet, on looking again, I saw it noted that these goods, though entered on the 30th of December, had not been shipped till the 2nd of January. Here was a poser to begin with. I looked up and caught the eye of Doubleday, who, evidently enjoying my perplexity, was watching me.

"I say," I ventured to say, "does he mean—"

"Hold your tongue, sir," broke out the virtuous Doubleday. "Didn't you hear Mr Barnacle say you were to get no assistance? What do you mean by it? I'm ashamed of you; so's Wallop."

"I shall mention the matter to the governor," observed Wallop, with a grin at his ally.

"Oh, don't," I said. "I beg your pardon!" It was evidently hopeless to expect any light from without on the problem, so I decided for myself I would include the account in question. I was just beginning to copy it out, and to shut my ears to the chaff that was going on around me, when the counting-house door opened, and the solemn face of my friend Smith appeared, asking if Messrs Merrett, Barnacle, and Company were at home.

His quick eye detected me at once, and I felt very uncomfortable, lest he should misunderstand the state of affairs and jump to the conclusion that I had been already engaged by the firm. At all risks I determined to put him right on this point.

"I'm not taken on, Jack," I said, before his question had been answered. "They've given me—"

"I'll give you a box on the ears, young gentleman," broke out the amazed Doubleday. "You're forgetting yourself. Go on with your work. Now then, young hop-o'-my-thumb," said he, addressing himself to Smith, "what do you want?"

Smith solemnly produced a letter, which he exhibited to the senior clerk.

"Oh, you're after the place too, are you, young bull's-eye?"

"Yes," said Smith, solemnly, and apparently not aware that the last expression had been intended as a joke.

"Why don't you laugh, eh?" cried Wallop; "we all laugh here when Doubles makes a joke; don't we, Crow?"

Mr Crow, thus appealed to, replied, "Oh, of course. We don't get much laughing, though."

Mr Doubleday waxed red in the face at this, and rounded on Smith.

"Don't go staring at me, do you hear? Look in the fireplace, can't you? and then you won't set alight to anything. Do you know this kid here?" added he, pointing at me over his shoulder.

"Yes," replied Smith.

"Do you know he's after the place?"

"Yes," said Smith.

"Then what do you want to come after it for? One of you's enough, ain't it?"

Smith stared solemnly at the speaker, whereat that virtuous individual waxed once more very wroth.

"Look here, if you can't cast your eyes somewhere else, young fellow, I'll cast them for you, so now. Why don't you answer my question?"

"I was told to be here at half-past ten," replied Jack.

"Then what do you mean by coming at twenty-eight past, eh, you young ruffian? Stay outside the door till the right time."

Smith obeyed solemnly, and for exactly two minutes remained outside. At the end of that period he returned.

Mr Doubleday, evidently perplexed for the moment how to get a rise out of him, announced him to the partners, and I saw him vanish into the inner-room.

"I say, Wallop," said Doubleday, when he had disappeared, "I hope they're not going to take on a couple of them."

My heart bounded as I listened. The bare suggestion was delightful.

"I hope not," said Wallop. "I don't see what they want *one* for."

"Oh, I do," said Crow (who I supposed had hitherto been the junior), "he'll be jolly useful, you know, running errands, and all that."

"All I can say is, unless he does it better than you, he'll be very little use."

"There you go," said Crow, in a sulk. "The more a fellow does for you the more you growl. You see if I get you any more cheap neckties. I'm always ashamed, as it is, to ask for ninepenny sailor's knots and one-and-twopenny kid gloves at the shop."

"Tell the truth—they're one-and-three. I suppose you get one-and-twopenny and pocket the odd penny!"

This pleasant recrimination might have proceeded I know not how long, greatly to the detriment of my task, had not some one at the other desk changed the subject.

"Don't you fret, you there," said he, "the junior's not for you at all. He's for the imports. I told the governor we wanted a boy in our department last week."

"You did!" exclaimed Doubleday. "Why, I told him we couldn't possibly do without more help here in the exports a fortnight ago."

I don't know if any one saw my face when this glorious announcement was made. I could have danced on my desk for joy! Just suppose—suppose it should turn out that Jack Smith should be taken on in the export department and I in the import—or the other way round! I could hardly contain myself at the bare idea. Wouldn't I be glad! I would get Wallop one-and-fourpenny gloves and only charge him one-and-three for them, to signalise the joyous event. I would let myself out as a slave to the entire office, if only Jack Smith and I were both taken on! How was he getting on in the partners' room? I wondered. I hoped—

"I suppose you've done," said Doubleday, looking round at this point; "if so you can hook it."

"I haven't quite," said I, dashing back to my work.

I finished at last, and before Jack had come out of the inner-room too.

I handed my papers to Doubleday, who looked at them critically.

"Well," he said, "that's a pretty show. Have a look at this, Wallop, I say. Your youngest grandchild could make his sevens nearly as well as that!"

As Mr Wallop was about eighteen years old, I ventured to regard this language as figurative on the part of Mr Doubleday, and trusted the sevens were not quite as bad as he made out.

"All right," said Doubleday, "you can cut home to your mother-in-law. You'll probably hear no more about it. There's millions of other loafers after the berth."

"When will I know?" I faltered.

"Let's see, this is the nineteenth century, ain't it? Call again about the year two thousand. February the thirty-first's the most convenient day for us, we're all at home then. Ta-ta."

I departed rather disconsolately, and waited half an hour outside in the street for Smith.

"Well," said I, when presently he appeared, "how did you get on?"

"Not very grand," said he. "I had to do some accounts like you. I heard one of the partners say yours were pretty good when the clerk brought them in."

"Really?" cried I, with pleasure I could hardly disguise. "But, I say, Jack, unless you get on too, it'll be an awful sell."

"We can't both get on," said Jack.

"I don't know," said I. And I related what I had overheard in the counting-house.

Smith brightened up at this. A very little encouragement was enough to set us building castles in the air. And we did build castles in the air that morning as we paced the crowded city streets.

By the time these architectural exercises were over it was time for me to go back to the station and catch my train; but not before I had tried to extract from Jack what he had been doing with himself since he was expelled from Stonebridge House.

As before, he was very uncommunicative. All I heard was that the reason he didn't get my letters at Packworth was that he had told me, or thought he had told me, to address my letters to "T," and I had always addressed them to "J." But even had I addressed them correctly, he would only have received the first, as a fortnight after he left Stonebridge he went to London, where he had hitherto been working as a grocer's shop-boy. You should have seen the look of disgust with which he referred to this part of his life! But now, having seen Merrett, Barnacle, and Company's advertisement, he was applying for their situation.

But in all his story he would tell me nothing about his home, or his relatives, so that as to knowing who my friend Smith was, or where he came from, I went back that afternoon to Brownstroke as much in the dark as ever. But I had found *him*!

Chapter Eleven
How my Friend Smith and I entered on New Duties in New Company

The two days which followed my eventful expedition to London were among the most anxious I ever spent. Young and unsophisticated as I was, I knew quite enough of my own affairs to feel that a crisis in my life had been reached, and that a great deal, nay, everything, depended on how my application for Merrett, Barnacle, and Company's situation turned out. If I succeeded there, I should have made a start in life—modest enough, truly, but a start all the same—and who was to say whether from the bottom of the ladder I might not some day and somehow get to the top? But if I missed, I knew full well my uncle would take my affairs into his own hands, and probably put me to work which would be distasteful, and in which I should be miserable. So you see, reader, I had a good deal staked on my little venture.

The miserable thing was that I might never hear at all from the firm, but go on hoping against hope, day after day, in a suspense which would be worse than knowing straight off that I had failed. However, I kept up appearances before my uncle, for I didn't want him to think it was no use waiting a little before he took me in hand himself. I spent several hours a day working up my arithmetic, making out imaginary invoices against every imaginable person, and generally preparing myself for office work. And the rest of my time I spent in cogitation and speculation as to my future destiny, and the merits and demerits of those enviable mortals, Doubleday, Wallop, and Crow, of the Export Department of Messrs Merrett, Barnacle, and Company.

On Tuesday morning two letters came for me with the London postmark, one in Jack Smith's well-remembered handwriting, the other with the awful initials, "M., B., and Company," on the seal.

I opened Smith's letter first. It was very short.

"Dear Fred,—I hear to-day I have got the situation. I'm afraid that means you have missed it. I'm awfully sorry, old boy, that's all I can say. I hope in any case you will come to London. I'll write again. Ever yours,—Jack."

I flung down the letter in a whirl of mingled feelings. That Jack Smith had got the situation I could not help being glad. But that I had lost it was simply crushing. Although I had kept reminding myself all along in words that the chances were very remote, I yet discovered how I had at heart been reckoning on my success almost to a certainty. And now I was utterly floored.

All this was the first hurried impression caused on my mind by my friend Smith's letter; and for a minute I quite forgot, in my mortification, that I had in my hand another letter—a letter from Merrett, Barnacle, and Company themselves. Then suddenly remembering it, I called to mind also the vague rumour of two clerks being wanted in the office, and with new hope and wild anxiety I tore open the envelope.

Could I believe my eyes?

"Frederick Batchelor is informed that his application for junior clerkship is successful. He will be required to begin work on Monday next at 9 a.m."

For the space of two minutes, reader, I knew not if I was standing on my head or my feet. I will pass over the excited day or two which followed. My uncle, of course, did what he could to check my glee. He said Merrett, Barnacle, and Company must be easily pleased, but they would soon find out their mistake, and that I might as well make up my mind to be dismissed after the first fortnight, and so on. I didn't take it much to heart; and after the first gush did not trouble my relative much with my prospects.

I was, however, a little curious to know what proposal he would make about my board and lodging in the great metropolis, which, after all, was a matter of some little consequence to me.

He did not see fit to relieve my anxiety on this point until the very eve of my departure from Brownstroke, when he said, abruptly, "You will be gone before I'm down to-morrow, Frederick. Don't forget the train starts at two minutes before six. I have arranged for you to lodge with Mrs Nash, whose address is on this card. There will be time to take your trunk round there before you go to your work. For the present I shall pay for your lodging."

"Shall I get my meals there?" I ventured to ask.

"Eh! You must arrange about that sort of thing yourself; and take my advice, and don't be extravagant."

As my salary was to be eight shillings a week, there wasn't much chance of my eating my head off, in addition to providing myself decently with the ordinary necessaries of life.

"I say I shall pay your lodging for the present, but before long I expect you to support yourself entirely. I cannot afford it, Frederick."

It had never occurred to me before that I cost anything to keep, but the fact was slowly beginning to dawn on me, and the prospect of having shortly to support myself cast rather a damper over the pictures I had drawn to myself of my pleasant life in London.

"Good-bye," said my uncle. "Here is half-a-sovereign for you, which remember is on no account to be spent. Keep it by you, and don't part with it. Good-night."

And so my uncle and I parted.

It was with rather subdued feelings that next morning I set out betimes for the station, lugging my small trunk along with me. That trunk and the half-sovereign I was not to spend comprised, along with the money which was to pay my fare, and the clothes I wore, the sum of my worldly goods. The future lay all unknown before me. My work at Hawk Street, my residence at Mrs Nash's, my eight shillings a week, I had yet to find out what they all meant; at present all was blank—all, that is, except one spot, and that was the spot occupied by my friend Smith. I could reckon on him, I knew, whatever else failed me.

I caught my train without much difficulty, as I was at the station at least half an hour before it was due, and had a third-class carriage to myself all the way to London. There were not many people travelling at that early hour, and when I reached the great metropolis at seven o'clock the station and streets looked almost as deserted as on the former occasion they had been crowded.

Mrs Nash's residence, so the card said, was in Beadle Square, wherever that might be. I was, however, spared the anxiety of hunting the place up, for my uncle had authorised me to spend a shilling in a cab for the occasion; and thus conveyed, after twistings and turnings which positively made my head ache, I arrived in state at my future lodging.

The "square" was, like many other City squares, a collection of tumbledown dingy houses built round an open space which might once have contained nothing but green grass and trees, but was now utterly destitute of either. There was indeed an enclosure within rusty and broken iron palings, but it contained nothing but mud, a few old beer-cans, and a lot of waste-paper, and one dead cat and one or two half-starved living ones. A miserable look-out, truly, as I stood on Mrs Nash's doorstep with my trunk waiting to be let in.

A slatternly female, whom I supposed to be the servant, admitted me.

"Is Mrs Nash in?" said I.

"Yes, that's me," said the lady. "I suppose you're young Batchelor."

She spoke gruffly and like a person who was not very fond of boys.

"Yes," said I.

"All right," said she; "come in and bring your trunk."

I obeyed. The place looked very dark and grimy, far worse than ever Stonebridge House had been. I followed her, struggling with my trunk, up the rickety staircase of a house which a hundred years ago might have been a stylish town residence, but which now was one of the forlornest ghosts of a house you ever saw.

I found myself at last in a big room containing several beds.

"Here's where you'll sleep," said the female.

"Are there other boys here, then?" I asked, who had expected a solitary lodging.

"Yes, lots of 'em; and a bad lot too."

"Are they Merrett, Barnacle, and Company's boys?" I inquired.

"Who?" inquired Mrs Nash, rather bewildered.

I saw my mistake in time. Of course this was a regular lodging-house for office-boys generally.

"Leave your box there," said Mrs Nash, "and come along."

Leading to the floor below the dormitory, I was shown a room with a long table down the middle, with a lot of dirty pictures stuck on the wall, and one or two dirty books piled up in the corner.

"This is the parlour," said she. "Are you going to board, young man?"

I looked at her inquiringly.

"Are you going to get your grub here or out of doors?" she said.

"Do the other boys get it here?" I asked.

"Some do, some don't. What I say is, Are you going to or not?"

"What does it cost?" I said.

"Threepence breakfast and threepence supper," said Mrs Nash.

I longed to ask her what was included in the bill of fare for these meals, but was too bashful.

"I think," said I, "I had better have them, then."

"All right," said she, shortly. "Can't have breakfast to-day; too late! Supper's at nine, and lock-up at ten, there. Now you'd better cut, or you'll be late at work."

Yes, indeed! It would be no joke to be late my first morning.

"Please," said I, "can you tell me the way to Hawk Street?"

"Where's that?" said Mrs Nash. "I don't know. Follow the tram lines when you get out of the square, they'll take you to the City, and then—"

At this moment a youth appeared in the passage about my age with a hat on one side of his head, a cane in his hand, and a pipe, the bowl as big as an egg-cup, in his mouth.

"I say, look here, Mrs Nash," said he, in a sleepy sort of voice; "why wasn't I called this morning?"

"So you was," said Mrs Nash.

"No, I wasn't," drawled the youth.

"That's what you say," observed the landlady. "I say you was; I called you myself."

"Then you ought to have knocked louder. How do you suppose a fellow who was out at a party overnight is to hear you unless you knock hard? I shall be late at the office, all through you."

Mrs Nash said "Shut up!" and the youth said "Shan't shut up!" and Mrs Nash inquired why, if he was late, he did not go off instead of dawdling about there, like a gentleman?

This taunt seemed to incense the youth, who put his nose in the air and walked out without another word.

"There," said Mrs Nash, pointing to his retreating form, "you'd best follow him; he's going to the City, the beauty."

I took the hint, and keeping "the beauty" at a respectful distance, followed in his lordly wake for about twenty minutes, until the rapidly-crowding streets told me I was in the City. Then, uncertain how to direct my steps, I quickened my pace and overtook him.

"Please can you tell me the way to Hawk Street?"

He took two or three good puffs out of his big pipe, and blew the smoke gracefully out of the corners of his mouth, and, by way of variety, out of his nose, and then said, in a condescending voice, "Yes, my man; first to the left and second to the right."

He certainly was a very self-assured young man, and struck me as quite grand in his manners. I had positively to screw up my courage to ask him, "I say, you are one of Mrs Nash's lodgers, aren't you?"

He stared at me, not quite sure what to make of me.

"Only," said I, by way of explanation, "I saw you there just now, and Mrs Nash said I'd better follow you."

"Mrs Nash is a jolly sight too familiar. So are you."

With which the stately youth marched on, his nose higher in the air than ever.

I was not greatly reassured by this first introduction, but for the time being I was too intent on reaching Merrett, Barnacle, and Company's in good time to think of much beside. Fortunately my fellow-lodger's direction was correct, and in a few minutes I found myself standing on familiar ground in Hawk Street.

When I entered the office the youth who rejoiced in the name of Crow was the only representative of the firm present. He was engaged in the intellectual task of filling up the ink-pots out of a big stone jar, and doing it very badly too, as the small puddles of ink on nearly every desk testified. He knew me at once, and greeted me with great alacrity.

"Hullo! young 'un, here you are. Look sharp and fill up the rest of these, do you hear? and mind you don't make any spills!"

I proceeded to obey, while Mr Crow, quite a grandee now that there was some one in the office junior to himself, stood, with his legs apart, before the fireplace and read the *Times*, giving an occasional glance at my proceedings.

"Hold hard!" he cried, presently, in an excited manner, when, having filled all the ink-pots along one of the desks, I was proceeding to attack on the other side of the screen; "hold hard! you don't want to fill up for the Imports, I say. They can do that themselves!"

Of course I agreed with him in this, and was just about restoring the jar to Mr Crow's custody, when Jack Smith entered the office.

"Hullo! Jack," I cried, feeling quite an old hand; "here you are. Isn't it fine?"

"Rather," said Jack, solemnly, returning my grasp. "I *am* glad."

"So am I. I was in such a fright when—"

"Now then, you young 'un there," said Crow, looking up from his paper, "don't go dawdling, I say. Just stick fresh nibs in all the Export pens, and look sharp about it, too."

"I'll help you, Fred," said Jack Smith, as I proceeded to obey.

"No, you won't!" said Crow; "we don't want you messing about in our department. You stick to your Imports."

It was evident Exports and Imports at Messrs Merrett, Barnacle, and Company's were not on absolutely brotherly terms. Anyhow I had to stick in the nibs unassisted.

Presently the other clerks began to drop in, among them Mr Doubleday, who was very witty on the subject of my appointment, and told Wallop he understood I was to be admitted into partnership next week, and would then sign all the cheques.

"All right!" said Wallop; "I'll put off asking for a rise till next week."

I was presumptuous enough to laugh at this, which greatly offended both the magnates. Doubleday ordered me to my desk instantly.

"Get on with your work, do you hear? and don't stand grinning there!"

"What had I better do?" I inquired, mildly.

"Do?" said Mr Doubleday, proceeding to take up his pen and settle himself to work; "I'll let you know what to— Look here. Crow," he broke off, in a rage, pointing to one of the ink puddles which that hero had made, "here's the same beastly mess again! Every Monday it's the same—ink all over the place! Why on earth don't you keep your messes to yourself?"

"That young 'un filled up to-day," said Crow, coolly pointing to me.

I was so astounded by this false charge that I could hardly speak. At last I retorted, "I didn't; you know I didn't!"

"Yes, you did!" said Crow.

"I didn't fill up that pot; it was done before I got here."

"Don't tell lies!" said Crow.

"I'm not telling lies!" cried I.

"Yes, you are!" said Crow. "I'm ashamed of you!"

"Oh, it was you, was it?" demanded Mr Doubleday, turning to me; "then just come and wipe it up. Look sharp!"

I was disposed to resist this piece of injustice to the utmost, but somehow the morning of my arrival it would hardly look well to figure in a row.

"I didn't do it," said I, in an agitated voice, "but I'll wipe it up."

"Look sharp about it, then!" said Doubleday, grinning at Wallop.

It is one thing to offer to wipe up an ink puddle, and quite another to do it.

"Now then!" said Doubleday, as I stood doubtfully in front of the scene of operation.

"I don't know," I faltered,—"I, that is—I haven't got anything I can do it with."

"What! not got a handkerchief!" exclaimed the head clerk, in apparent consternation.

"Yes; but I can't do it with that. Wouldn't some blotting—"

"Blotting-paper!—the firm's blotting-paper to wipe up his messes! What do you think of that, all of you? Come, out with your handkerchief!"

Things looked threatening. I saw it was no use resisting. Even the Imports were standing on their stools and looking over the screen. So I took out my handkerchief and, with a groan, plunged it into the spilt ink.

Doubleday and the clerks evidently appreciated this act of devotion, and encouraged me with considerable laughter. My handkerchief and my hand were soon both the colour of the fluid they were wiping up, and my frame of mind was nearly as black.

"Now then," said Doubleday, "aren't you nearly done? See if there's any gone down the crack there. Is there?"

I stooped down to inspect the crack in question, and as I did so Mr Doubleday adroitly slipped his pen under my soaking handkerchief, and, by a sudden jerk, lifted it right into my face.

At the same moment the door opened and Mr Barnacle entered! He looked round for a moment sharply, and then, passing on to the inner-room, said, "Doubleday, bring the two new office-boys into my room."

If I had heard just the sentence of death pronounced on me I could hardly have been more horrified. My face and hand were like the face and hand of a negro, my collar and shirt were spotted and smeared all over with ink, and even my light hair was decorated with black patches. And in this guise I was to make my first appearance before my masters! Jack Smith's expression of amazement and horror as he caught sight of me only intensified my own distress, and Doubleday's stern "Now you're in for it!" sounded hopelessly prophetic.

I could do nothing. To wipe my face with my clean hand, with the tail of my jacket, with my shirt-sleeve, could do no good. No; I was in for it and must meet my doom!

But I determined to make one expiring effort to escape it.

"Please, sir," I cried, as we came to the door and before we entered, "I'm very sorry, but my face is all over ink. May I wash it before I come in?"

I was vaguely conscious of the titters of the clerks behind me, of the angry grip of Doubleday on one side of me, and of Smith's solemn and horrified face on the other, and the next moment I was standing with my friend in front of Mr Barnacle's awful desk.

He regarded me sternly for a moment or two, during which I suffered indescribable anguish of mind.

"What is the meaning of this?" said he. "I don't understand it."

"Oh, please, sir," cried I, almost beseechingly, "I'm so sorry. I was wiping up some ink, and got some on my face. I couldn't help."

Mr Barnacle looked angry and impatient.

"This is no place for nonsense," said he.

"Really I couldn't help," I pleaded.

There must have been some traces of earnestness visible, I fancy, on my inky face, for I saw Mr Barnacle look at me curiously as I spoke, while there was the faintest perceptible twitch at the corners of his lips.

"Go and wash at once," he said, sternly.

I fled from his presence as if I had been a leper, and amid the merriment of my fellow-clerks sought the sink at the other end of the office and washed there as I had never washed before.

After much exertion, my countenance resumed something like its natural complexion, and the white skin faintly dawned once more on my fingers. My collar and shirt-front were beyond cleaning, but at the end of my ablutions I was, at any rate, rather more presentable than I had been.

Then I returned refreshed in body and mind to Mr Barnacle, whom I found explaining to Smith his duties in the Import Department. He briefly recapitulated the lecture for my benefit, and then dismissed us both under the charge of Mr Doubleday to our duties, and by the time one o'clock was reached that day, and I was informed I might go out for twenty minutes for my dinner, I was quite settled down as junior clerk in the Export Department of Merrett, Barnacle, and Company.

Chapter Twelve
How my Friend Smith and I knocked about a Bit in our New Quarters

Smith and I had a good deal more than dinner to discuss that morning as we rested for twenty minutes from our office labours.

He was very much in earnest about his new work, I could see; and I felt, as I listened to him, that my own aspirations for success were not nearly as deep-seated as his. He didn't brag, or build absurd castles in the air; but he made no secret of the fact that now he was once in the business he meant to get on, and expected pretty confidently that he would do so.

I wished I could feel half as sure of myself. At any rate, I was encouraged by Jack Smith's enthusiasm, and returned at the end of my twenty minutes to my desk with every intention of distinguishing myself at my work.

But somehow everything was so novel, and I was so curiously disposed, that I could not prevent my thoughts wandering a good deal, or listening to the constant running fire of small talk that was going on among my fellow-clerks. And this was all the less to be wondered at, since I myself was a prominent topic of conversation.

Mr Doubleday was a most curious mixture of humour, pomposity, and business, which made it very hard to know how exactly to take him. If I dared to laugh at a joke, he fired up, and ordered me angrily to get on with my work. And if I did become engrossed in the figures and entries before me, he was sure to trip me up with some act or speech of pleasantry.

"Why don't you stick a nib on the end of your nose and write with it?" he inquired, as I was poring over an account-book in front of me, trying to make out the rather minute hieroglyphics contained therein.

I withdrew my nose, blushingly, to a more moderate distance, a motion which appeared greatly to entertain my fellow-clerks, whose amusement only added to my confusion.

"Hullo! I say," said Doubleday, "no blushing allowed here, is there, Wallop?"

"Rather not. No one ever saw *you* blush," replied Mr Wallop.

This turned the laugh against Doubleday, and I, despite my bashfulness, was indiscreet enough to join in it.

Mr Doubleday was greatly incensed.

"Get on with your work, do you hear? you young cad!" he cried. "Do you suppose we pay you eight bob a week to sit there and grin? How many accounts have you checked, I'd like to know?"

"Six," I said, nervously, quite uneasy at Mr Doubleday's sudden seriousness.

"Six in two hours—that's three an hour."

"Quite right; not bad for Dubbs, that, is it, Crow?" put in Wallop.

"No. He's reckoned it up right this time."

"I wish *you'd* reckon it up right now and then," retorted Doubleday. "How about the change out of those two handkerchiefs?"

"There is no change," said Crow, sulkily; "they were sixpence each."

"What's the use of saying that, when they are stuck up fourpence-halfpenny each in the window, you young thief?"

"You can get them yourself, then," replied the injured Crow. "I'll go no more jobs for you—there! I'm not the junior now, and I'm hanged if I'll put up with it."

"You'll probably be hanged, whether you put up with it or not," was Mr Doubleday's retort, who, apparently desirous to change the conversation, suddenly rounded on me, as I was looking up and listening to the edifying dialogue.

"Now then, young Batchelor, dawdling again. Upon my word I'll speak to Mr Barnacle about you. Mind, I mean what I say."

"You'd better look-out, young turnip-top, I can tell you," growled Crow; "when Dubbs means what he says, it's no joke, I can tell you."

On the whole my first afternoon's work at Merrett, Barnacle, and Company's was somewhat distracting, and by the time half-past six arrived I felt I had not accomplished quite as much as I had intended.

My first care on rejoining Jack was to sound him as to the possibility of his coming to lodge at Mrs Nash's. To my delight he anticipated me by inquiring, "Have you got any place to lodge, Fred?"

"Yes," said I, "and I only wish you'd come there too, Jack."

"Whereabouts is it?" he asked.

"Mrs Nash's, at Beadle Square. But you will come, won't you?"

"Perhaps there's not room."

"Oh yes," said I, taking upon myself to assert what I did not know, "there is. Come along, old man, it'll make all the difference if we get together."

"How much is it?" asked Jack, doubtfully.

"Come along, and we'll ask," said I, dragging him along.

He came, and together we bearded Mrs Nash in her den.

"I say, Mrs Nash," said I, "my friend's coming to lodge here, please."

Mrs Nash eyed Jack suspiciously, and then said abruptly, "No room."

"Oh, bother! Can't he sleep with me, then?" I inquired.

"No," replied she, "he can't. It's not allowed."

"When will there be room?" Jack asked.

"Next week, may be."

"Oh, how jolly!" I exclaimed. "Then you will come, Jack, won't you?"

"How much is it?" inquired Jack of Mrs Nash.

"Three-and-six a week—in advance," said Mrs Nash; "no tick."

Jack pulled rather a long face.

"It'll be a tight fit," said he to me, "out of eight shillings a week."

"Oh, I can pay part," said I, too delighted at the prospect of Jack's company to admit of any obstacle. "My uncle pays my lodging, you know, so I have the eight shillings all to myself."

Jack, however, scouted the idea. After a little more parleying, to my unspeakable joy he told Mrs Nash he would come next week. I begged hard for him to be allowed to share my quarters in the meanwhile. The landlady was inexorable, so we had to submit.

Jack took me a long stroll through the London streets that evening, entertaining me with a description of his life as a grocer's shop-boy, now happily at an end. I forbore to ask him any questions on the mysterious subject of his home, and he of course never referred to it. Our walk ended again at Beadle Square, where we parted for the night; he to return to some poor lodging in a distant part of the town, I to take part in the nine o'clock supper at Mrs Nash's.

I was rather nervous as I approached the parlour where were congregated my fellow-lodgers, and heard the sound of their noisy voices and laughter. I half repented that I had committed myself to sup on the premises; it would have been so much less embarrassing to slip in just at ten o'clock and go straight to bed. However, I was in for it now.

I opened the door and entered the room. The parlour was full of boys — two dozen or more — of all ages, and engaged in all sorts of occupations. Some lounged lazily in front of the fireplace, some were indulging in rough horse-play in the corners, some were reading novels, some were writing, some were talking, some were laughing.

As I entered, however, everybody suddenly ceased his occupation and stared at me — everybody, that is, except the small group who were skirmishing in the corner nearest the door. These, with the most laudable presence of mind, took in my situation at once, and next moment I was one of the skirmishing party and having rather a lively time of it.

By this time the rest of the company had taken in the state of affairs.

"Pass him on there," some one called, and I was accordingly passed on in rather a lively way to another party of skirmishers, who in turn, after buffeting me up and down a bit among themselves, passed me on to another group, and so on, till, with back and limbs and head all rather the worse for wear, I had performed the tour of the room and found myself finally pitched head-first into the embrace of the lordly youth who that morning had condescended to point out to me the way to Hawk Street.

"Look here," cried he, kicking out somewhat savagely at my shins; "don't you be so jolly familiar, do you hear? Look what you have done to my shirt-front!"

"I beg your pardon," said I, rubbing my poor shin. "I couldn't help—"

"Yes, you could, you young cad!" cried he, kicking again.

"No, I couldn't, and—oh! I say, stop kicking, please!"

By this time most of the company had gathered round, some calling on the youth to "let me have it" others encouraging me "to go in and win." I felt very greatly tempted, especially after the receipt of the third kick, to act on the suggestion given, and might have done so, had not Mrs Nash at that moment entered the room with the supper.

This interruption created a new diversion.

"I say, Mrs Nash," cried my adversary, "who's this kid? We don't want him here."

"You'll have to have him whether you want him or not," replied Mrs Nash, in her usual gracious way. "He's a lodger here."

"What do you want to shove another lodger in for when you know we're chock-full?" demanded the youth.

"You hold your tongue, Mr Jackanapes," replied Mrs Nash.

"I say, don't you be so familiar," cried the young gentleman, greatly offended. "My name's Horncastle, not Jackanapes."

"Very well, then, Mr Horncastle, you'd better hold your tongue."

"I sha'n't hold my tongue. You've got a spite against us, that's what it is, or you wouldn't go crowding us out with kids like this."

"Crowding you out!" retorted Mrs Nash, scornfully. "You've got another kid coming next week, my beauty, so you'd better not talk of crowding out till then."

"What! another besides this young cad? Oh, that's too much! We won't stand it. That's all about that," cried Mr Horncastle, in tones of utter disgust.

"Won't you? Then you can cook your own sausages for supper, my man, and shell out what you owe on the nail. We'll see who won't stand it or not!"

This threat had the desired effect: Horncastle knuckled down as if by magic.

"Oh, don't be a brute, Mrs Nash," he said, in tones of agitation. "Do us those sausages, there's a good body, and you can cram in half a dozen kids if you like."

And so the question of my admission was settled satisfactorily, if not flatteringly, for me, and the fellows, the novelty of my appearance being once over, took no more notice of me than of any of the rest of their fellow-lodgers.

Mrs Nash's establishment appeared to be one to which fond parents in the country, whose darlings were about to launch out on the sea of life in London, were invited to confide their sons, under the promise of a comfortable, respectable, and economical home.

As to the comfortable, we who were best able to judge did not admit the description a true one. As to the respectable, that was a matter of opinion. If each of us had been the only lodger there, the place would have been undoubtedly respectable, but with all the rest there, we each of us considered the society rather "mixed." As to the economical, we were all agreed on that point. The place was fearfully and wonderfully economical!

By the time my first week in London was ended I had shaken down fairly well, both to my work at Merrett, Barnacle, and Company's and my quarters at Mrs Nash's. I still found the fellowship of Messrs Doubleday and Wallop and Crow rather distracting, and more than once envied Jack his berth among the Imports where, as a rule, silence reigned supreme. And yet I could hardly bring myself to dislike my fellow-clerks, who, all of them, as far as I had found out, were good-natured, and certainly very entertaining, and who, when they perceived that I was amused by their proceedings, relaxed a good deal in their attitude to me.

I gradually came to be on talking, if not on chaffing terms with several of the fellows, and found myself, I never exactly knew how, installed in the position, lately vacated by Mr Crow, of messenger and confidential commission agent to the company. Most of my twenty minutes in the middle of the day was thus taken up in buying articles of comfort or decoration for one and another of my seniors, or else changing books at the library, taking messages to other clerks in other offices, and otherwise laying myself out for the general good—a self-denial which brought me more kicks than halfpence, but which, all the same, served to establish my footing as a regular member of the Export fraternity at Merrett, Barnacle, and Company's.

Smith, I discovered, was let in for something of the same work with the Imports, but to a much smaller extent. Indeed, he had so much less of it than me that I one day questioned him on the subject.

"I say, Jack, it seems to me the Exports want a jolly lot more things done for them than the Imports. To-day I've got to go to Mudie's to change a book, then I've to get a scarf-pin mended for Crow, and buy a pair of flannel drawers for Wallop, and go and offer two shillings for a five-shilling mariner's compass at the stores for Doubleday. I shall have to get my grub when I can to-day, I expect."

"Oh!" said Jack, "the Imports wanted to let me in for that sort of thing, but I didn't see the use of it, and told them so."

"What did they say?" asked I, astonished at his boldness.

"They didn't like it, of course," said Jack; "but I don't see why they shouldn't do their own jobs."

"Well," said I, "I wouldn't mind if I could stick out too, but somehow I'm in for it now."

And off I started on my round of errands.

I was, however, greatly impressed with Jack's cool treatment of the whole affair. I would as soon have dreamed of refusing to go an errand for

Doubleday or Wallop as of flying. The office, I knew full well, would soon be made pretty hot for me if I did, and it was a marvel how Jack apparently got over the difficulty so easily. He was one of those fellows, you know, who seem to care absolutely nothing about what others think of them. It's all one if fellows hate them or love them, and as for being influenced by any desire to cultivate the good graces of one's neighbours, you might as well expect a bear to cultivate the good graces of a porpoise.

I soon began to suspect that Jack was not altogether comfortable in his new quarters, although he never hinted to the contrary. There were vague rumours which came across the partition of uncomfortableness which silently went on, and in which Jack took a prominent part; and an event which happened just a week after our arrival made the thing certain.

One morning, Mr Barnacle, apparently in a great hurry, looked in at the Import door and called out, "Smith, make me three copies of Elmore's last consignment, at once, on foreign paper."

"Yes, sir," said Jack.

After a pause, I heard him say, "Will you lend me that entry-book, please, Harris, to make the copies from?"

"No," curtly replied Harris; "I'm using it."

"But Mr Barnacle says he must have it at once."

"I can't help that," said Harris.

"That's right, Harris!" said another voice; "pay him out for his beastly, selfish ill-nature!"

"Will you lend me the book, Harris?" again demanded Jack, in tones which I could tell were fast losing their calmness.

"No, I won't! and what's more, shut up your row!" replied Harris.

There was a pause, then I heard Jack get off his stool and march boldly to the door. He came out and passed solemnly through our office to the door of Mr Barnacle's room, which he entered.

Next moment Mr Barnacle came out, very red in the face, and demanded, in a loud voice, "Who is it using the entry-book? Didn't you hear me say the copies were to be made at once, sir? Let Smith have the book."

"It's on his desk," replied Harris, meekly. "I was only ruling off the last line, to show where the account ended."

"Copy it at once," said Mr Barnacle, sharply; "the papers have to be down before twelve, and here's five minutes wasted already."

Smith silently went to work, and Mr Barnacle withdrew.

"Vile young sneak!" I heard Harris say; "I'll pay you out for that!"

"I didn't want to sneak. You should have given me the book," replied Jack solemnly.

"I'll give you *something*, see if I don't!" was the reply.

I believe Jack did receive this promised something. He did not come out at mid-day till late, and then he was pale and flurried.

"Has Harris been bullying you?" I said.

"Been doing his best," replied Jack, gloomily. "I don't much care for him."

This was quite enough. I could guess what it meant.

"I suppose you think I was a fearful sneak?" said Jack.

"No I don't, old man!" said I.

I had, I must confess, felt a little doubtful on the subject; but, then, what else could he have done?

"I'm sorry I did it now," said Jack solemnly; "I sha'n't do it again."

"What else could you do?" I asked.

"I shall have to knock Harris down, I suppose," said Jack, so seriously that I stared at him in bewilderment.

Without doubt my poor chum was preparing a warm time for himself with the Imports at Merrett, Barnacle, and Company's!

That same evening he entered on his new quarters at Mrs Nash's, greatly to my joy, and greatly to the disgust of everybody else.

Horncastle, who had recovered from his temporary fright for the cooling of his sausages, was specially loud in his remonstrances.

"It's no use your coming here," he said, advancing in a menacing way towards Jack on his arrival. "We aren't going to have you—there!"

And with that, as in my case, he emphasised his remark with a smart kick on Jack's shins.

Jack was not a short-tempered fellow, but this unprovoked assault startled him out of his usual composure.

"You'd better not do that again," said he, glaring at his adversary.

Horncastle did *not* do it again. I don't know what it was, but at those words, and the glare that accompanied them, his foot, already raised for further action, dropped quietly beside the other.

"I shall do it again if I choose," he said surlily.

"Then you'd better not choose," quietly said Jack.

"You've got no business here, that's what I say," exclaimed Horncastle, falling back upon a safer line of attack.

"Why haven't I?" said Jack. "I'm a clerk like you."

"And you call yourself a gentleman too, I suppose?" sneered the other.

Jack always fired up when any reference of this kind was made.

"I don't want *you* to tell me whether I am," he retorted.

"Why, he's a regular cad," cried some one. "I know him well; I saw him selling penn'orths of nuts a week or two ago in the Borough."

"You hear that," said Horncastle, turning to Jack. "Was it so?"

"I don't see what it's got to do with you," replied Jack; "but if you want to know, I was."

"I thought so! I thought so!" exclaimed Horncastle; "a wretched shop-boy! Ugh! get away from me."

And by one consent the company followed the example of their leader and left poor Jack isolated in a corner of the room, with only me to stand by him.

But he was not greatly afflicted by the incident, and made no attempt to assert his rights further. And after all we got on very well and had a very jolly evening without the help of Mr Horncastle and his friends, and slept quite as soundly after our day's excitement as if we had been in the wholesale line all our lives.

Chapter Thirteen
How my Friend Smith and I caught a Young Tartar

The novelty of our life in London soon began to wear off. For the first week or so I thought I never should grow weary of the wonderful streets and shops and crowds of people. And the work at the office, while it was fresh, appeared—especially when enlivened by the pranks of my fellow-clerks—more of a game than downright earnest. My eight shillings a week, too, seemed a princely allowance to begin with, and even the lodging-house in Beadle Square was tolerable.

But after a month or so a fellow gets wonderfully toned down in his notions. I soon began to pine inwardly for an occasional escape from the murky city to the fresh air of the country. The same routine of work hour after hour, day after day, week after week, grew tame and wearisome. And I began to find out that even the lordly income of eight shillings a week didn't make the happy possessor, who had to clothe and feed himself, actually a rich man; while as for Mrs Nash's, the place before long became detestable. The fact is, that I, with no cheerier home than Brownstroke to look back on, became desperately homesick before three months in London were over; and but for my friend Smith, I might have deserted entirely.

However, Smith, solemn as he was, wouldn't let me get quite desperate. He was one of those even-tempered sort of fellows who never gush either with joy or sorrow, but take things as they come, and because they never let themselves get elated, rarely let themselves get down.

"Fred," he said to me one day, when I was in the dumps, "what's wrong?"

"Oh, I don't know," said I, "I'm getting rather sick of London, I think."

"Not much use getting sick of it yet," said he. "Time enough in fifty years."

"Jack," said I, "if I thought I had all my life to live here, I should run away."

"You're a duffer, old man. Aren't you getting on at Hawk Street, then?"

"Oh yes, well enough, but it's most fearfully slow. The same thing every day."

Jack smiled. "They can't alter the programme just to suit you."

"Of course not," I cried, feeling very miserable; "of course I'm an ass, but I'd sooner be back at Stonebridge House than here."

"By the way," said Smith, suddenly, "talking of Stonebridge House, who did you think I ran against to-day at dinner-time?"

"Who, old Henniker?" I inquired.

"Rather not. If I had, I think I should have been game for running away along with you. No, it was Flanagan."

"Was it? I should like to have seen him. What's he doing?"

"Not much, I fancy. He says his brother's a solicitor, and he's come up to loaf about in his office and pick up a little law."

"Oh, I like that," I cried, laughing. "Think of old Flanagan a lawyer. But didn't he say where he was living?"

"Yes, Cabbage Street, in Hackney. I forget the number. I say, Fred, suppose we take a stroll this evening and try to find him out. It'll do you good, a walk."

I gladly consented. We gave Mrs Nash due notice that we should not be home to supper, and might possibly be out after ten, and then sallied forth. Hackney was a good four miles from Beadle Square, and by the time we had discovered Cabbage Street it was almost time to be returning. But having come so far we were resolved we would at least make an effort to find out our old schoolfellow. But the fates were against us. Cabbage Street was a new street of small houses, about a third of a mile long. Even if we had known the number it would have taken some time to discover the house; but without that information it was simply impossible. We did try. Jack took the left of the street and began knocking at the odd numbers, starting from 229; while I attacked the even numbers on the right side. But as far as we went no one knew of a Flanagan, and we had to give it up.

It was half-past nine when we finally abandoned the search and turned our faces Citywards once more.

"Horrid sell," said Jack. "We shall have to find out where his brother's office is from the Directory, and get at him that way."

We walked back hard. Mrs Nash's temper was never to be relied on, and it was ten to one she might lock us out for the night.

Luckily Jack was up to all the short cuts, and he piloted me through more than one queer-looking slum on the way.

At last we were getting near our journey's end, and the prospect of a "lock-out" from our lodgings was looming unpleasantly near, when Jack took me by the arm and turned up a dark narrow passage.

"I'm nearly certain it's got a way out at the other end," he said, "and if so it will take us right close to the square."

I followed him, trusting he was right, and inwardly marvelling at his knowledge of the ins and outs of the great city.

But what a fearful "skeery"-looking hole that passage was!

There were wretched tumbledown houses on either side, so wretched and tumbledown that it seemed impossible any one could live in them. But the houses were nothing to the people. The court was simply swarming with people. Drunken and swearing men; drunken and swearing women; half-naked children who swore too. It was through such a company that we had to thread our way down my friend Smith's "short cut." As we went on it became worse, and what was most serious was that everybody seemed to come out to their doors to stare at us. Supposing there were no way through, and we had to turn back, it would be no joke, thought I, to face all these disreputable-looking loungers who already were making themselves offensive as we passed, by words and gesture.

I could tell by the way Smith strode on that he felt no more comfortable than I did.

"You're sure there's a way through?" I said.

"Almost sure," he answered.

At the same moment a stone struck me on the cheek. It was not a hard blow, and the blood which mounted to my face was quite as much brought there by anger as by pain.

"Come on!" said Smith, who had seen what happened.

Coming on meant threading our way through a knot of young roughs, who evidently considered our appearance in the court an intrusion and were disposed to resent it. One of them put out his foot as Smith came up with a view to trip him, but Jack saw the manoeuvre in time and walked round. Another hustled me as I brushed past and sent me knocking up against Jack, who, if he hadn't stood steady, would have knocked up against some one else, and so pretty certainly have provoked an assault. How we ever got past these fellows I can't imagine; but we did, and for a yard or two ahead the passage was clear.

"Shall we make a rush for it?" I asked of Jack.

"Better not," said he. "If there is a way through, we must be nearly out now."

He spoke so doubtfully that my heart sunk quite as much as if he had said there was no way through and we must turn back.

However, what lay immediately before us was obscured by a suddenly collected crowd of inhabitants, shouting and yelling with more than ordinary clamour. This time the centre of attraction was not ourselves, but a drunken woman, who had got a little ragged boy by the collar, and was beating him savagely on the head with her by no means puny fist.

"There!—take that, you young—! I'll do for you this time!"

And without doubt it looked as if we were to witness the accomplishment of the threat. The little fellow, unable even to howl, reeled and staggered under her brutal blows. His pale, squalid face was covered with blood, and his little form crouching in her grip was convulsed with terror and exhaustion. It was a sickening spectacle.

The crowd pressed round, and yelled and laughed and hooted. The woman, savage enough as she was, seemed to derive fresh vehemence from the cries around her, and redoubled her cruel blows.

One half-smothered moan escaped the little boy's lips as she swung him off his feet, and flung him down on the pavement.

Then Jack and I could stand it no longer.

"Let the child alone!" cried Jack, at the top of his voice.

I shall never forget the sudden weird hush which followed that unexpected sound. The woman released her grasp of her victim as if she had been shot, and the crowd, with a shout on their lips, stopped short in amazement.

"Quick, Fred!" cried Jack, flying past me.

He dashed straight to where the little boy lay, swept him up in his arms, and then, with me close at his heels, was rushing straight for the outlet of the court, which, thank Heaven! was there, close at hand. Next moment we were standing in the street which led to Beadle Square.

It all took less time to accomplish than it takes to write, and once out of that awful court we could hardly tell whether we were awake or dreaming.

The boy, however, in Jack's arms settled that question.

"Come on, quick!" said Smith, starting to run again. "They'll be out after us."

We hurried on until we were in Beadle Square.

"What's to be done?" I asked.

"We must take him in with us," said Jack. "Look at the state he's in."

I did look. The little fellow, who seemed about eight years old, was either stunned by his last blow or had fainted. His face, save where the blood trickled down, was deadly pale, and as his head with its shock of black hair lay back on Jack's arm, it seemed as if he could not look in worse plight were he dead.

"We must take him with us," said Jack.

"What will Mrs Nash say?" was my inward ejaculation, as we reached the door.

All the lights were out. We knocked twice, and no one came. Here was a plight! Locked out at this hour of night, with a half-dead child in our charge!

"Knock again," said Jack.

I *did* knock again, a wonderful knock, that must have startled the cats for a mile round, and this time it called up the spirit we wished for.

There was a flicker of a candle through the keyhole, and a slipshod footstep in the hall, which gave us great satisfaction. Mrs Nash opened the door.

At the sight of our burden, the abuse with which she was about to favour us faded from her lips as she gazed at us in utter amazement.

"Why, what's all this? eh, you two? What's this?" she demanded.

"I'll tell you," said Jack, entering with his burden; "but I say, Mrs Nash, can't you do something for him? Look at him!"

Mrs Nash was a woman, and whatever her private opinion on the matter generally may have been; she could not resist this appeal. She took the little fellow out of Jack's arms, and carried him away to her own kitchen, where, after sponging his bruised face and forehead, and giving him a drop of something in a teaspoon, and brushing back his matted hair and loosing his ragged jacket at the neck, she succeeded in restoring him to his senses. It was with a thrill of relief that we saw his eyes open and a shade of colour come into his grimy cheeks.

"What have you been doing to him?" said Mrs Nash.

"He was being knocked about," said Jack, modestly, "and Batchelor and I got him away."

"And what are you going to do with him?" inquired Mrs Nash, who, now that her feminine offices were at an end, was fast regaining her old crabbedness.

"He'd better go to bed," said Smith. "I'll have him in my bed."

"No, you won't!" said Mrs Nash, decisively.

"We can't turn him out at this time of night," said I.

"Can't help that. He don't sleep here, the dirty little wretch."

"He'll be murdered if he goes back," said Jack.

"That's no reason I should have my house made not fit to live in," said Mrs Nash.

"He won't do any harm, I'll see to that," said Smith, rising and taking the boy up in his arms.

"I tell you I ain't going to allow it," said Mrs Nash.

But Jack without another word carried off his burden, and we heard his footsteps go slowly up the stairs to the bedroom. I stayed for some little time endeavouring to appease Mrs Nash, but without much effect. She abandoned her first idea of rushing out and defending the cleanliness of her house by force of arms, but in place of that relieved herself in very strong language on the subject of Jack Smith generally, and of me in aiding and abetting him, and ended by announcing that she gave us both warning, and we might look-out for somebody else to stand our impudence (she called it "imperence"), for *she* wouldn't.

When I went up stairs Jack and his small *protégé* were in bed and asleep. I was quite startled when I caught sight of their two heads side by side on the pillow. It looked for all the world like a big Jack and a little Jack.

"Wouldn't Jack be flattered if I told him so!" thought I.

I was not long in following their example. All night long I dreamt of Flanagan and that dreadful court, and of those two heads lying there side by side in the next bed.

When I awoke in the morning it was very early and not yet light. I soon discovered that what had aroused me was a conversation going on in the next bed.

"Go on! you let me be!" I heard a shrill voice say.

"Hush! don't make a noise," said Jack. "I'll take you home in the morning all right."

"I ain't done nothink to you," whined the boy.

"I know. No one's going to hurt you."

"You let me be, then; do you 'ear?" repeated the boy. "What did you fetch me 'ere for?"

"You were nearly being killed last night," said Jack.

"You're a lie, I worn't," was the polite answer.

"Yes you were," said Jack. "A woman was nearly murdering you."

"That was my old gal—'tain't no concern of yourn."

Evidently there was little use expecting gratitude out of this queer specimen of mortality; and Jack didn't try.

"You stay quiet and go to sleep, and I'll give you some breakfast in the morning," he said to his graceless little bed-fellow.

"You ain't a-going to take me to the station, then?" demanded the latter.

"No."

"Or the workus?"

"No."

"Or old shiny-togs?"

"Who?"

"Shiny-togs—you know—the bloke with the choker."

"I don't know who you mean."

"Go on!—you know 'im—'im as jaws in the church with 'is nightgown on."

"Oh, the clergyman," said Jack, hardly able to repress a smile. "No. I'll take you back to your home."

"To my old gal?"

"Yes, to your mother."

"You ain't a 'avin' a lark with me, then?"

"No," said Jack, pitifully.

With this assurance the small boy was apparently satisfied, for he pursued the conversation no longer, and shortly afterwards I fell off to sleep again.

When next I woke it was broad daylight, and Jack Smith was standing by my bed.

"Fred, I say, he's bolted!" he exclaimed, in an agitated voice, as I sat up and rubbed my eyes.

"Who—the kid?" I asked.

"Yes."

"He's a nice amiable young specimen," replied I. "When did he go?"

"I don't know. When I woke up he was gone."

"Well, it's a good riddance," said I, who really did not see why Jack should be so afflicted about such a graceless young ragamuffin. "Do you know Mrs Nash has given us both warning over this business?"

"I don't care. But, I say, I wonder if he's hiding anywhere."

"Not he. He's safe away, depend upon it, and if Mrs Nash had had any silver spoons they'd be safe away too."

Jack began to dress thoughtfully, and then said, "I'm sorry he's gone."

"I don't see why you should be," I said. "The ungrateful young cad! If it hadn't been for you he might have been killed."

Jack smiled. "He doesn't think so himself," he said. "He told me I'd no business to interfere between him and his 'gal,' as he politely styles his mother. Poor little beggar! I dare say he'll catch it all the worse now. Hullo! I say!" exclaimed Jack, feeling in his pockets. "I'm positive I had a shilling and two pennies in my pocket yesterday evening. I must have been robbed in that court!"

The money had evidently gone, and what was more, I made the pleasant discovery that a sixpence which I had in my pocket, as well as my penknife, were both missing!

Jack and I looked at one another.

"The young thief!" I exclaimed.

"Perhaps it was done in the court," said Jack. "There was an awful crowd, you know."

"All very well," I replied; "but, as it happens, I had my knife out before I went to bed, to cut one of my bootlaces, and when I put it back in my pocket I distinctly remember feeling the sixpence there. No; our young hopeful's done this bit of business."

"I'm awfully sorry, Fred," said Jack; "it was my fault bringing him here."

We went down to breakfast in a somewhat perturbed state of mind. Here we found the assembled company in a state of great excitement. Mr Horncastle, who occupied a bed in the next dormitory to that where Jack and I slept, had missed his collar-stud, which he described as "red coral," and complaining thereof to Mrs Nash, had been told by that lady that Smith and Batchelor had brought a young pickpocket into the house with them last night, and that being so, she was only surprised Mr Horncastle had not lost all the jewellery he possessed. Whereat, of course, Mr Horncastle was in a mighty state of wrath, and quite ready for poor Jack and me when we appeared.

"Oh, here you are. Perhaps you'll hand me out half a sov., you two."

"What for?" demanded I.

"Never you mind, but you'd better look sharp, or I'll give you in charge!" said Horncastle, pompously.

"You're funny this morning," said I, utterly at a loss to guess what he was driving at.

"So will you be funny when you get transported for stealing!"

"What do you mean?" asked Smith, solemnly.

"Mean; why, I mean my collar-stud."

A general laugh interrupted the speaker at this point, which did not tend to improve his spirits.

"What's your collar-stud to do with me, or Batchelor?" demanded Smith, who evidently saw nothing to laugh at.

"Why, you've stolen it!" shouted Horncastle.

Smith gazed solemnly at the speaker.

"You're a fool," he said, quietly.

This cool remark drove the irate Horncastle nearly frantic. He advanced up to Smith with a face as red as the collar-stud he had lost, and cried, "Say that again, and I'll knock you down."

"You're a fool," quietly repeated Jack.

Horncastle didn't knock him down, or attempt to do so. He turned on his heel and said, "We'll see if we're to be robbed by shop-boy cads, or any of your young thieving friends. I'll complain to the police, and let them know you know all about it, you two."

"I don't know anything about it," said I, feeling it incumbent on me to make a remark, "except that I don't think a red bone collar-stud costs ten shillings." This occasioned another laugh at the expense of Mr Horncastle, who retorted, "You're a companion of thieves and blackguards, that's what you are. I'll have you kicked out of the house."

And as if to suit the action to the word, he advanced towards me and aimed a vehement kick at my person.

I had just time to dodge the blow, but as I did so something knocked against my hand. Fancy my astonishment when, stooping to pick it up, I found that it was the missing red bone collar-stud, which had dropped into the leg of its stately owner's trousers, and which this kick had unearthed from its hiding-place!

The laugh was now all against the discomfited Horncastle. Even those who had at first been disposed to side with him against Jack and me could not resist the merriment which this revelation occasioned, particularly when the stud, which Horncastle at once identified, was discovered to be an ordinary painted bone article, with a good deal of the red worn off, of the kind usually sold in the streets for a penny.

Jack and I had at least the relief of feeling that so far we ourselves were the only sufferers by our hospitality to our little ragamuffin acquaintance.

But more was to come of this adventure, as the reader will see.

Chapter Fourteen
How Smith went Home and I took Part in an Evening Party

Two days after the events recorded in the last chapter something happened which materially affected the course of my life in London.

Smith and I were just starting off to the office, after having finally made our submission to Mrs Nash, and induced her, with a promise "never to do it again," to withdraw her threat to turn us out, when the postman appeared coming round the corner.

It was a comparatively rare sight in Beadle Square, and Jack and I naturally felt our curiosity excited.

"May as well see if there's anything for me," said I, who had only once heard from my affectionate relative in six months.

Jack laughed. "I never saw such a fellow," said he, "for expecting things. It's just as likely there's a letter for me as for you."

At this moment the postman came up with a letter in his hand in apparent perplexity.

"Anything for me?" I said.

"Not unless your name's Smith," said the postman. "Smith of Beadle Square, that's the party—might as well send a letter to a straw in a haystack."

"My name's Smith," said Jack.

"Is it?" said the postman, evidently relieved. "Then I suppose it's all right."

So saying he placed the letter in Jack's hand and walked on, evidently quite proud to have found out a Smith at first shot.

Jack's colour changed as he took the letter and looked at it.

He evidently recognised the cramped, ill-formed hand in which it was addressed.

"It's from Packworth!" he exclaimed, as he eagerly tore open the envelope.

I don't think he intended the remark for me, for we had never once referred either to his home or his relatives since the first day we were together in London. In fact, I had almost come to forget that my friend Smith had a home anywhere but in Beadle Square.

He glanced rapidly over the short scrawl, and as he did so his face turned pale and a quick exclamation escaped his lips.

"Anything wrong, old man?" I asked.

"Yes," said he, looking up with a face full of trouble. "Here, you can see it," he added, putting the letter into my hand.

It was a very short letter, and ran thus:—

"Dear Mister Johnny,—Mary is very very ill. Could you come and seen her? Do come—from Jane Shield."

"Mary is my sister," said Jack, nearly breaking down. "I must go, whether Barnacle lets me or no."

Our walk to the office that morning was quicker than usual, and more silent. Poor Jack was in no mood for conversation, and I fancied it would be kinder not to worry him. We reached Hawk Street before any of the partners had come, and Smith's patience was sorely tried by the waiting.

"I say," said he presently to me, "I must go, Fred. Will you tell them?"

"Yes, if you like, only—"

"Now then, you two," cried Mr Doubleday, looking round; "there you are, larking about as usual. Go off to your work, young Import, do you hear? and don't stand grinning there!"

Poor Jack looked like anything but grinning at that moment.

"I'll do the best I can," I said, "but I'm afraid Barnacle will be in a wax unless you ask him yourself."

"I can't help it," said Jack, "I must go."

"Eh? what's that?" said Doubleday, who was near enough to hear this conversation; "who must go?"

"Smith has just heard that his sister's ill," I said, by way of explanation, and hoping to enlist the chief clerk's sympathy, "and he must go to her, that's all."

"Hullo!" interposed Crow, "you don't mean to say he's got a sister. My eyes, what a caution! Fancy a female bull's-eye, Wallop, eh?"

"So you may say," said Wallop the cad, laughing. "I guess I wouldn't fancy her, if she's like brother Johnny."

"And he's got to go to her, poor dear thing, because she's got a cold in her nose or something of the sort. Jolly excuse to get off work. I wish *I'd* got a sister to be ill too."

"Never mind," said Wallop; "if you'd been brought up in gaol you'd be subject to colds. It's a rare draughty place is Newgate."

No one but myself had noticed Jack during this brief conversation. His face, already pale and troubled, grew livid as the dialogue proceeded, and finally he could restrain himself no longer.

Dashing from his desk, he flew at Wallop like a young wolf, and before that facetious young gentleman knew where he was he was lying at full length on the floor, and Jack standing over him, trembling with fury from head to foot.

It was the work of an instant, and before more mischief could be done Doubleday had interposed.

"Look here," said he, catching Jack by the arm and drawing him away from his adversary, "we aren't used to that here, I can tell you! Go to your desk! Do you hear? There's the governor coming up! A nice row you'll get us into with your temper! Come, you Wallop, up you get, I say — you beast! I'm jolly glad the young 'un walked into you. Serves you right! Look alive, or you'll be nobbled!"

The result of these exertions was that when the door opened half a minute later the office was, to all appearance, as quiet as usual.

To our surprise, the comer was not Mr Barnacle, who usually arrived first, but Mr Merrett, who on other days hardly ever put in an appearance till an hour later.

What was the reason of this reversal of the order of things we could not say, and did not much care. Indeed, it was rather a relief to see the mild senior partner instead of the sharp-eyed junior, who was, some of us thought, far too quick to perceive anything amiss. Jack's face brightened as much as any one's at the circumstance. For a moment he forgot all his wrath, and thought only of his poor sister.

He followed Mr Merrett quickly to the door of the partners' room and said eagerly, "May I speak to you a moment, sir?"

"Yes, my man; come in," was the encouraging reply.

"Gone to tell tales, I suppose," said Crow, as the door closed on the two.

"No, he's not," said I, ready to take up the gauntlet for my friend; "and you'd better not say it again!"

"Oh, I say! Look here," said Doubleday, "don't *you* begin at that game, young shaver! We're used to it from your chum bull's-eye, but I'm not going to let you start at it. Besides, Crow wouldn't like it. Get on with your work, do you hear?"

Jack reappeared in a minute with a grateful face, which showed at once that his application had been successful.

"Good-bye," said he, coming to my desk; "I'll send you a line;" and without another word to any one he was gone.

"He's a cool fish, that friend of yours!" said Doubleday, that afternoon to me. "He seems to get on pretty much as he likes."

"He's awfully cut up about his sister," I said. "Poor Jack!"

"No harm in that!" said Doubleday, condescendingly. "I thought he was quite right to walk into that cad Wallop myself. But he'll find it rather hot for him when he gets back, I fancy. When's he coming back?"

"In a day or two, I suppose," said I.

"And you'll be mighty disconsolate, I suppose," said Doubleday, "till he returns? What do you say to coming up to my lodgings to-night, eh, young 'un, to see me?"

I felt very grateful for this unlooked-for honour, and said I would be delighted to come.

"All serene! I've asked one or two of the fellows up, so we'll have a jolly evening. By the way, when you go out get me a couple of boxes of sardines, will you, and a dozen twopenny cigars?"

I executed these commissions, and in due time, business being ended, Doubleday and I and Crow, and the sardines and the cigars, started in a body for Cork Place, where, in a first-floor front, the estimable Mr Doubleday was wont to pitch his daily tent.

They were cosy quarters, and contrasted in a marked manner with Beadle Square. Doubleday knew how to make himself comfortable, evidently. There were one or two good prints on his walls, a cheerful fire in the hearth, a sofa and an easy-chair, and quite an array of pickle-jars and beer-bottles and jam-pots in his cupboard. And, to my thinking, who had been used to the plain, unappetising fare of Mrs Nash, the spread on his table was simply sumptuous.

I felt quite shy at being introduced to such an entertainment, and inwardly wondered how long it would be before I, with my eight shillings a week, would be able to afford the like.

We were a little early, and Doubleday therefore pressed us into the service to help him, as he called it, "get all snug and ship-shape," which meant boiling some eggs, emptying the jam-pots into glass dishes, and cutting up a perfect stack of bread.

"Who's coming to-night?" said Crow, with whom, by the way, I had become speedily reconciled in our mutual occupation.

"Oh, the usual lot," said Doubleday, with the air of a man who gives "feeds" every day of his life. "The two Wickhams, and Joe Whipcord, and the Field-Marshal, and an Irish fellow who is lodging with him. We ought to have a jolly evening."

In due time the guests arrived, Mr Joseph Whipcord being the earliest. He was a freckled youth of a most horsey get up, in clothes so tight that it seemed a marvel how he could ever sit down, and a straw in his mouth which appeared to grow there. Close on his heels came the two Wickhams, whose chief attractiveness seemed to be that they were twins, and as like as two peas.

"Hullo! here you are," was Doubleday's greeting. "Which is which of you to-night, eh?"

"I'm Adam," replied one of the two, meekly.

"All serene, Adam. Stick this piece of paper in your button-hole, and then we'll know you from Abel. By the way, Whipcord, I suppose you never heard my last joke, did you?"

"Never heard your first yet," replied Whipcord, shifting his straw to the other corner of his mouth.

"Oh, yes you did," retorted Doubleday, who as usual always preferred the laugh when it was on his own side. "Don't you remember me telling Crow last time you came that you were a fellow who knew a thing or two? That was a joke, eh, twins?"

"Rather," said both the twins, warmly.

"But my last wasn't about Whipcord at all: it was about you two. I got muddled up among you somehow and said, 'For the life of me I am not able to tell one of you from Adam!'"

"Well?" said Whipcord.

"Well, what!" said Doubleday, savagely "The joke?"

"Why, that *was* the joke, you blockhead! But we can't expect a poor fellow like you to see it. I say, the Field-Marshal's behind time. I'll give him two minutes, and then we'll start without him."

Just then there was a knock at the door, and two fellows entered. One was a tall, thin, cadaverous-looking boy a little my senior, and the other—his exact contrast, a thick-set, burly youth, with a merry twinkle in his eye and a chronic grin on his lips.

"Late again, Field-Marshal," said Doubleday, clapping the cadaverous one on the back with a blow that nearly doubled him up. "Is this your chum? How are you, Patrick?"

The youth addressed as Patrick, but whose real name subsequently was announced as Daly, said he was "rightly," and that it was his fault the Field-Marshal was late, as he had to shave.

This announcement caused great amusement, for Master Daly was as innocent of a hair on his face as he was of being tattooed, and by the manner in which he joined in the laughter he seemed to be quite aware of the fact.

We sat down to supper in great good spirits. I was perhaps the least cheerful, for all the others being friends, and I knowing only my two fellow-clerks, I felt rather out of it. However, Doubleday, who seemed to have an eye for everybody, soon put me at my ease with myself and the rest.

What a meal it was! I hadn't tasted such a one since I came to London. Eggs and sardines, lobster and potted meat; coffee and tea, toast, cake, bread-and-butter—it was positively bewildering. And the laughing, and talking, and chaffing that went on, too. Doubleday perfectly astonished me by his talents as a host. He never ceased talking, and yet everybody else talked too; he never ceased partaking, and took care that no one else should either. He seemed to know by the outside of a cup whether it was full or empty, and to be able to see through loaves and dish-covers into everybody's plate. It would be impossible to say what was not talked about during that wonderful meal. The private affairs of Hawk Street were freely canvassed, and the private affairs of every one of the company were discussed with the most charming frankness. I found myself giving an account of my uncle to the Field-marshal, which confidence he reciprocated by telling me that he was a private in the volunteers (that was why the fellows called him Field-Marshal), and an accountant's clerk, that his income was fifty pounds a year, that he had saved seven pounds, that he was engaged to a most charming person named Felicia, whom at the present rate of his progress he hoped to marry in about twenty years. Whipcord was discoursing on the points of every racehorse in the calendar to the twins, who had evidently never seen a racehorse; and Daly was telling stories which half choked Crow, and kept us all in fits of laughter. It was a new life to me, this, and no mistake.

"Now then, young Batchelor, walk into those sardines, do you hear?" said our host. "Any more coffee, twins? Pass up those tea-cakes when you've helped yourself, Crow. I got them for twopence apiece—not bad, eh? I say, I suppose you've heard what's up in Hawk Street, eh?—jam to the Field-Marshal there. Yes, Harris of the Imports told me: he heard it from Morgan, who knows a fellow who knows old Merrett. Plenty more potted meat in the cupboard; get out some, Batchelor, that's a good fellow. The fact is—sugar enough in yours, Paddy?—the fact is, the old boy is going to put in a nephew—pass up your cup, Adam, Abel, what's your name, you with the paper in your button-hole?—what was your mother about when she gave you such idiotic names, both of you? I'd like to give her a piece of my mind!—a nephew or something of the sort—that'll be the third kid in the last half-year landed in on us—don't you call that lobster a good one for eighteen pence, Paddy, my boy? Never mind, I'll let them know I'm not going to train up all their young asses for nothing—hullo! Batchelor, beg pardon, old man; I forgot you were one of them!"

This occasioned a laugh, which made me look very self-conscious; which Doubleday saw, and tried to help me out.

"If they were all like you," he said, with a patronising smile, "it wouldn't hurt; but that bull's-eye chum of yours is a drop too much for an office like ours. Do you know, I believe it's a fact he's been in gaol, or something of the sort—try a little vinegar with it, Field-Marshal—capital thing for keeping down the fat. Never saw such a temper, upon my word, did you, Crow? Why, he was nearly going to eat *you* up this very morning. And the best of it is, he thinks he's the only fellow in the office who does a stroke of work. Never mind, he's safe at home for a bit; but, my eye! won't he be astonished to find Merrett, Barnacle, and Company can get on without him!"

I was beginning to feel very uncomfortable. It was rank treason to sit by and listen to all this without putting in a word for my friend; and yet in this company I could not for the life of me make the venture. Indeed, to my shame be it said, with the eyes of my companions upon me, and their laughter in my ears, I even faintly joined in the smile at poor Jack's expense.

"Is this pleasant chap a friend of yours?" said the Field-Marshal.

"Yes," said I, rather hesitatingly, "we were at school together, you know."

I despised myself heart and soul for my cowardice, and for me the rest of the meal passed with little enjoyment.

And when the cloth was cleared away fresh difficulties presented themselves.

"Are you a good hand at whist?" asked Adam, as we stood in front of the fire.

"No," said I; "I don't play."

"Don't you? We'll give you a lesson, then."

Now my bringing-up had been peculiar, as the reader knows. In many ways it had been strict, and in many ways lax; but one of the scruples I had always carried about with me was on the subject of gambling.

Consequently I felt particularly uncomfortable at the twin's offer, and at a loss how to respond to it; and before I could resolve the chance was gone.

"Now then," said Doubleday, "make up your fours there, but for goodness' sake don't let both the patriarchs get at the same table! You with the paper and Crow, and Paddy and I—we'll have this table, and you other four take the other;" and before I knew where I was I found myself seated at a table, opposite Whipcord, with thirteen cards in my hand.

I did not know what to do. Had my partner been any one but Whipcord, with the straw in his mouth, I do believe I should have made a mild protest. Had Doubleday or Crow been one of our party, I might have screwed up my courage. But Whipcord had impressed me as a particularly knowing and important personage, and I felt quite abashed in his presence, and would not for anything have him think I considered anything that he did not correct.

"I'm afraid I don't know the way to play," said I, apologetically, when the game began.

"You don't!" said he. "Why, where were you at school? Never mind, you'll soon get into it."

This last prophecy was fulfilled. Somehow or other I picked up the game pretty quickly, and earned a great deal of applause from my partner by my play. Indeed, despite my being a new hand, our side won, and the Field-Marshal and Abel had to hand over sixpence after sixpence as the evening went on. The sight of the money renewed my discomforts; it was bad enough, so I felt, to play cards at all, but to play for money was a thing I had always regarded with a sort of horror. Alas! how easy it is, in the company of one's fancied superiors, to forget one's own poor scruples!

The game at our table came to rather an abrupt end, brought on by a difference of opinion between the Field-marshal and Mr Whipcord on some point connected with a deal. It was a slight matter, but in the sharp words that ensued my companions came out in a strangely new light. Whipcord, especially, gave vent to language which utterly horrified me, and the Field-Marshal was not backward to reply in a similar strain.

How long this interchange of language might have gone on I cannot say, had not Doubleday opportunely interposed. "There you are, at it again, you two, just like a couple of bargees! You ought to be ashamed of yourselves! Look how you've shocked the young 'un there! You really shouldn't!"

I coloured up at this speech. From the bantering tone in which Doubleday spoke it seemed as if he half despised any one who was not used to the sound of profanity; and I began to be angry with myself for having looked so horrified.

The quarrel was soon made up with the help of some of the twopenny cigars, which were now produced along with the beer-bottles. By this time I had been sufficiently impressed by my company not to decline anything, and I partook of both of these luxuries—that is, I made believe to smoke a cigar, and kept a glass of beer in front of me, from which I took a very occasional sip.

My mind was thoroughly uncomfortable. I had known all along I was not a hero; but it had never occurred to me before that I was a coward. In the course of one short evening I had forsaken more than one old principle, merely because others did the same. I had joined in a laugh against my best friend, because I had not the courage to stand up for him behind his back, and I had tried to appear as if bad language and drinking and gambling were familiar things to me, because I dared not make a stand and confess I thought them loathsome.

We sat for a long time that night talking and cracking jokes, and telling stories. Many of the latter were clever and amusing, but others—those that raised the loudest laugh—were of a kind I had never heard before, and which I blush now to recall. Any one who had seen me would have supposed that talk like this was what I most relished. Had they but heard another voice within reproaching me, they might have pitied rather than blamed me.

And yet with all the loose talk was mixed up so much of real jollity and good-humour that it was impossible to feel wholly miserable.

Doubleday kept up his hospitality to the last. He would stop the best story to make a guest comfortable, and seemed to guess by instinct what everybody wanted.

At last the time came for separating, and I rose to go with feelings partly of relief, partly of regret. The evening had been a jolly one, and I had enjoyed it; but then, had I done well to enjoy it? That was the question.

"Oh, I say," said Daly, as we said good-night on the doorstep, "were you ever at a school called Stonebridge House?"

"Yes," said I, startled to hear the name once more. "You weren't there, were you?"

"No; but a fellow I know, called Flanagan, was, and—"

"Do you know Flanagan?" I exclaimed; "he's the very fellow I've been trying to find out. I *would* like to see him again."

"Yes, he lives near us. I say, suppose you come up to the Field-Marshal and me on Tuesday; we live together, you know. We'll have Flanagan and a fellow or two in."

I gladly accepted this delightful invitation, and went back to Mrs Nash's feeling myself a good deal more a "man of the world," and a good deal less of a hero, than I had left it that morning.

Chapter Fifteen
How I got rather the Worst of it in a Certain Encounter

My evening at Doubleday's lodgings was the first of a course of small dissipations which, however pleasant while they lasted, did not altogether tend to my profit.

Of course, I had no intention of going in for that sort of thing regularly; but, I thought, while Jack Smith was away for a few days, there would be no harm in relieving the dulness of my life at Beadle Square by occasionally accepting the hospitality of such decent, good-natured fellows as Doubleday and his friends. There was nothing wrong, surely, in one fellow going and having supper with another fellow now and then! How easy the process, when one wishes to deceive oneself!

But two days after Smith had gone home I received a letter which somewhat upset my calculations. It had the Packworth postmark, and was addressed in the same cramped hand in which the momentous letter which had summoned Jack from London had been written.

I was surprised that it was not in Jack's own hand. It ran as follows:—

"Sir,—I am sorry to say Master Johnny has took ill since he came down. The doctor thinks it is smallpox; so please excuse him to the gentlemen, and say we hope it will make no difference, as he cannot come for a many weeks. Your humble—Jane Shield."

John ill—with smallpox! This was a blow! My first impulse was, at all risks, to go down and look after him. But I reflected that this would be, after all, foolish. I should certainly not be allowed to see him, and even if I were, I could not of course return to the office with the infection about me. Poor Jack! At least it was a comfort that he had some one to look after him.

My first care, after the receipt of the letter, was to seek an interview with the partners and explain matters to them. And this I found not a very formidable business. Mr Barnacle, indeed, did say something about its being awkward just when they were so busy to do without a clerk. But Mr Merrett overruled this by reminding his partner that in a week or two his nephew would be coming to the office, and that, to begin with, he could fill up the vacant place.

"Besides," said he, with a warmth which made me feel quite proud of my friend—"besides, Smith is too promising a lad to spare."

So I was able to write a very reassuring letter to good Mrs Shield, and tell her it would be all right about Jack's place when he came back. Meanwhile, I entreated her to let me know regularly how he was getting on, and to tell me if his sister was better, and, in short, to keep me posted up in all the Smith news that was going.

This done, I set myself to face the prospect of a month or so of life in London without my chum.

I didn't like the prospect. The only thing that had made Beadle Square tolerable was his company, and how I should get on now with Mr Horncastle and his set I did not care to anticipate.

I confided my misgivings to Doubleday, who laughed at them.

"Oh," said he, "you must turn that place up. I know it. One of our fellows was there once. It's an awfully seedy place to belong to."

"The worst of it is," said I—who, since my evening at Doubleday's, had come to treat him as a confidant—"that my uncle pays my lodging there; and if I went anywhere else he'd tell me to pay for myself."

"That's awkward," said Doubleday, meditatively; "pity he should stick you in such a cheap hole."

"I don't think, you know," said I, feeling rather extinguished by Doubleday's pitying tone, "it's such a very cheap place. It's three-and-six a week."

Doubleday gazed at me in astonishment, and then broke out into a loud laugh.

"Three-and-six a week! Why, my dear fellow, you could do it cheaper in a workhouse. Oh, good gracious! your uncle must be in precious low water to stick you up in a hole like that at three-and-six a week. Do you know what my lodgings cost, eh, young 'un?"

"No," said I, very crestfallen; "how much?"

"Fifteen bob, upon my honour, and none too grand. Three-and-six a week, why—I say, Crow!"

"Oh, don't go telling everybody!" cried I, feeling quite ashamed of myself.

"Oh, all serene. But it is rather rich, that. Good job you don't get your grub there."

I did not tell Doubleday that I did get my "grub" there, and left him to infer what he pleased by my silence.

"Anyhow," said he, "if you must hang on there, there's nothing to prevent your knocking about a bit of an evening. What do you generally go in for when your friend Bull's-eye's at home? I mean what do you do with yourselves of an evening?"

"Oh," said I, "they've got a parlour at Mrs Nash's, and books—"

Once more Doubleday laughed loud, "What! a parlour and books included for three-and-six a week! My eye! young 'un, you're in luck; and you mean to say you—oh, I say, what a treat!—do you hear, Crow?"

"Please!" I exclaimed, "what's the use of telling any one?"

"Eh—oh, all right, I won't tell any one; but think of you and Bull's-eye sitting in a three-and-six parlour without carpets or wall-papers reading *Tim Goodyboy's Sunday Picture-book*, and all that."

I smiled faintly, vexed though I was. "They've novels there," I said, grandly.

"No! and all for three-and-six too! No wonder you're snug. Well, no accounting for tastes. I wonder you don't ask me to come and spend an evening with you. It *would* be a treat!"

The result of this conversation and a good many of a similar character was to make me thoroughly discontented with, and more than half ashamed of, my lot. And the more I mixed with Doubleday and his set, the more I felt this. They all had the appearance of such well-to-do fellows, to whom expense seemed no object. They talked in such a scoffing way of the "poor beggars" who couldn't "stand" the luxuries they indulged in, or dress in the fashionable style they affected.

After six months, the clothes with which I had come to London were beginning to look the worse for wear, and this afflicted me greatly just at a time when I found myself constantly in the society of these grandees. I remember one entire evening at Doubleday's sitting with my left arm close in to my side because of a hole under the armpit; and on another occasion borrowing Mrs Nash's scissors to trim the ends of my trousers before going to spend the evening at Daly's.

That occasion, by the way, was the Tuesday when, according to invitation, I was to go up to the lodgings of Daly and the Field-Marshal, there to meet my old schoolfellow Flanagan.

I had looked forward not a little to this meeting, and was secretly glad that he would find me one of a set represented by such respectable and flourishing persons as Doubleday and Daly. When, a fortnight before, Smith and I had hunted up and down his street to find him, I knew nothing of "what was what" compared with what I did now. I was determined to make an impression on my old schoolfellow; and therefore, as I have said, trimmed up the ends of my trousers with Mrs Nash's scissors, invested in a new (cheap), necktie, and carefully doctored the seam under my armpit with ink and blacking.

Thus decorated I hurried off to my host's lodgings. The first thing I saw as I entered the door filled me with mortification. It was Flanagan, dressed in a loud check suit, with a stick-up collar and a horseshoe scarf-pin—with cloth "spats" over his boots, and cuffs that projected at least two inches from the ends of his coat sleeves.

I felt so shabby and disreputable that I was tempted to turn tail and escape. I had all along hoped that Flanagan would be got up in a style which would keep me in countenance, and make me feel rather more at home than I did among the other stylish fellows of the set. But so far from that being the case, here he was the most howling swell of them all.

Before I could recover from the surprise and disappointment I felt he had seen me, and advanced with all his old noisy frankness.

"Hullo! here he is. How are you, Batchelor? Here we are again, eh? Rather better than the Henniker's parlour, eh?"

I forgot all my disappointment for a moment in the pleasure of meeting him. In voice and manner at least he was the Flanagan of old days. Why couldn't he dress rather more quietly?

Daly was there in all his glory, and the Field-Marshal as lank and cadaverous as ever; and besides ourselves there was Whipcord with the straw in his mouth, and one or two other fellows belonging to our host's particular set. The supper was quite as elaborate and a good deal more noisy than that at Doubleday's. I sat next to Flanagan, and hoped to be able to get some talk with him about old days; but I found he was far too much taken up with the fun that was going on to be a very attentive listener. And so I felt more than ever extinguished and out of it, and all my fond hopes of making an impression on my old schoolfellow speedily vanished.

"What are you going to do?" said Whipcord, when the meal was over.

"I don't care," said Daly; "cards if you like."

"Oh, bother cards," was the reply; "let's have a ramble out of doors for a change."

"Hullo! Whip, how is it you're down on cards?" said the Field-Marshal. "I thought you always won."

There was something not very nice in the tone of the cadaverous man of war which roused the ire of the virtuous Whipcord.

"What do you mean, you—who says I always win at cards?"

"You generally win when I'm playing against you," said the Field-Marshal.

"Look here," said Whipcord, very red in the face, and chewing his straw in an agitated manner, "do you mean to insinuate I cheat at cards, eh, you—?"

"I never said anything of the kind," replied the Field-marshal; "I said you generally won, that's all. What's the use of making an ass of yourself?"

I began to perceive by this time that Mr Whipcord was excited by something more than the Field-Marshal's talk. The fact was, he had drunk too much, and that being so, it was worse than useless to reason with him.

"Who says I generally win at cards?" shouted he. "I'll fight any one that says so: if you like, I'll take the lot of you."

The laugh which greeted this valiant challenge only enraged the excited youth the more.

He broke out into language which seemed to be only too ready to his lips, and again shouted, "I'll teach you to call me a cheat, I will! I'll teach you to call me a blackleg, so I will! I'll teach you to call me—"

"A howling jackass," put in the Field-Marshal, whose chief vocation it seemed to be to goad on his irate guest.

"Yes, I'll teach you to call me a howling jackass!" cried Whipcord, turning short round on me, and catching me by the throat.

"Me! I never called you a howling jackass!" cried I, in astonishment and alarm.

"Yes, you did, you young liar; I heard you. Wasn't it him?" he cried, appealing to the company in general.

"Sounded precious like his voice," said one of the fellows, who, as I had scarcely opened my mouth the whole evening, must have had a rather vivid imagination.

"Yes, I know it was you. I knew it all along," said Whipcord, shifting his straw from side to side of his mouth, and glaring at me, half-stupidly, half-ferociously.

"It wasn't, indeed," said I, feeling very uncomfortable. "I never said a word."

Whipcord laughed as he let go my throat and began to take off his coat. I watched him in amazement. Surely he was not going to make me fight! I looked round beseechingly on the company, but could get no comfort out of their laughter and merriment.

Whipcord divested himself of his coat, then of his waistcoat, then he took off his necktie and collar, then he let down his braces and tied his handkerchief round his waist in the manner of a belt, and finally proceeded to roll up his shirt-sleeves above the elbows.

"Now then," said he, advancing towards me in a boxing attitude, "I'll teach you to call me a thief!"

I was so utterly taken aback by all this, that I could scarcely believe I was not dreaming.

"I really didn't call you a thief," I said.

"You mean to say you won't fight?" cried my adversary, sparring up at me.

"Hold hard!" cried Daly, before I could answer. "Of course he's going to fight; but give him time to peel, man. Look alive, Batchelor, off with your coat."

"I'm not going to fight, indeed," said I, in utter bewilderment.

"Yes you are," said Flanagan, "and it won't be your first go in either, old man. I'll back you!"

One or two of the fellows pulled off my coat—my poor seedy coat. I remember even then feeling ashamed of the worn flannel shirt, out at elbows, that was below it, and which I had little expected any one that evening to see.

"Will you have your waistcoat off?" said Daly.

"No," replied I.

"Better," said Flanagan, "and your collar too."

This was awful! My collar was a paper one, and pinned on to the shirt in two places!

"No!" I cried, in desperation at these officious offers; "let me alone, please."

"Oh, all serene! But he's got the pull of you."

Perhaps if I had had a clean linen shirt on, with studs down the front, I might have been more tractable in the matter of peeling.

It had by this time gradually dawned on me that I was in for a fight, and that there was no getting out of it. My adversary was bigger than I was, and evidently far more at home with the customs of the prize-ring. I would fain have escaped, but what could I do?

Meanwhile the table was hurriedly pushed into a corner of the room and the chairs piled up in a heap.

"Now then!" cried the Field-Marshal, who, in some miraculous manner, now appeared as backer to the fellow with whom a few minutes ago he had been quarrelling—"now then, aren't you ready there?"

"Yes," said Flanagan, rolling up my shirt-sleeves; "all ready! Now then, old man, straight out from the shoulder, you know. Keep your toes straight, and guard forward. Now then—there!"

I was in for it then; and, being in for it, the only thing was to go through with it, and that I determined to do.

My adversary advanced towards me, half prancing, with his hands high, his elbows out, his face red, and his straw jerking about like a steam-engine. It might be showy form, I thought, but from the very little I knew of boxing it was not good. And the closer we approached the more convinced of this I was, and the more hope I seemed to have of coming out of the affair creditably.

Now, reader, whoever you are, before I go further I ask you to remember that I am recording in this book not what I ought to have done, but what I did do. You will very likely have your own opinions as to what I should have done under the circumstances. You may think that I should, at all costs, have declined to fight; you may think I should have summoned the police; you may think I should have stood with my hands behind my back till my face was the size of a football, and about the same colour; or you may think I was right in standing up to hit my man, and doing all I knew to demolish him. Do not let me embarrass your judgment; my duty just now is merely to tell you what did happen.

As I expected, Whipcord's idea seemed to be to knock me out of time at the very beginning of the encounter, and therefore during the first round I found it needed all my efforts to frustrate this little design, without attempting on my part to take the offensive.

As it was, I did not altogether succeed, for, Whipcord being taller than I, I could not help coming in for one or two downward blows, which, however, thanks to my hard head, seemed more formidable to the spectators than they really were.

"Not half bad," was Flanagan's encouraging comment when in due time I retired to his side for a short breathing space. "I never thought you'd be so well up to him. Are you much damaged?"

"No," said I.

"Well, you'd best play steady this next round too," said my second. "He can't hold out long with his elbows that height. If you like you can have a quiet shot or two at his breastplate, just to get your hand in for the next round."

This advice I, now quite warmed up to the emergency, adopted.

Whipcord returned to his sledge-hammer tactics, and as carelessly as ever, too; for more than once I got in under his guard, and once, amid terrific plaudits, got "home"—so Flanagan called it—on his chin, in a manner which, I flattered myself, fairly astonished him.

"Now then, Whip, what are you thinking about?" cried the Field-Marshal; "you aren't going to let the young 'un lick you, surely?"

"Time!" cried Daly, before the bruised one could reply; and so ended round two, from which I retired covered with dust and glory.

I felt very elated, and was quite pleased with myself now that I had, stood up to my man. It seemed perfectly plain I had the battle in my own hands, so I inwardly resolved if possible to bring the affair to an end in the next round, and let my man off easy.

Conceited ass that I was! To my amazement and consternation, Whipcord came up to the scratch on time being called in an entirely new light. Instead of being the careless slogger I had taken him for, he went to work now in a most deliberate and scientific manner. It gradually dawned on me that I had been played with so far, and that my man was only now beginning to give his mind to the business. Ass that I had been! Poor wretch that I was!

Before the round had well begun I was reeling about like a ninepin. The little knowledge of pugilism I had, or thought I had, was like child's play against the deliberate downright assault of this practised hand. I did what I could, but it was very little. The laughter of my opponents and the gibes of my backers all tended to flurry me and lose me my head.

Let me draw a veil over that scene.

My opponent was not one of the sort to give quarter. He had had a blow of mine on his chin in the last round, and he had heard the laughter and cheers which greeted it. It was his turn now, and he took his turn as long as I could stand up before him. It seemed as if "time!" would never be called. I was faint and sick, and my face—

Ah! that last was a finishing stroke. I could keep my feet no longer, and fell back into Flanagan's arms amidst a perfect roar of laughter and applause.

At that moment the shame was almost more bitter to me than the pain. This then was the result of my high living! This was what I had got by turning up my nose at my lot in Beadle Square, and aspiring to associate with my betters! This was the manner in which I was to make an impression on my old schoolfellow, and improve my footing with my new friends! No wonder I felt ashamed.

"You'd better invest in a little raw beefsteak," said Flanagan; "that's what will do you most good."

This was all the comfort I got. The fight being over, everybody lost his interest in me and my opponent, and, as if nothing had happened, proceeded to re-discuss the question of playing cards or taking a walk.

I was left to put on my poor shabby coat without help, and no one noticed me as I slunk from the room. Even Flanagan, from whom I had at least expected some sympathy, was too much taken up with the others to heed me; and as I walked slowly and unsteadily that night along the London streets, I felt for the first time since I came to the great city utterly friendless and miserable.

When I returned to Beadle Square every one had gone to bed except one boy, who was sitting up, whistling merrily over a postage-stamp album, into which he was delightedly sticking some recent acquisition. I could not help thinking bitterly how his frame of mind contrasted at that moment with mine. He was a nice boy, lately come. He kept a diary of everything he did, and wrote and heard from home every week. The fellows all despised him, and called him a pious young prig, because he said his prayers at night, and went to a chapel on Sundays. But, prig or not, he was as happy as a king over his stamps, and the sight made me (I knew not why), tenfold more miserable.

"Hullo!" said he, stopping whistling as I came in, "there's a letter for you. I say, if you get any foreign stamps at your office I wish you'd save them for me, will you? Look, here's a jolly Brazil one; I got it—what's the matter?"

I heard not a word of his chatter, for the letter was from Packworth.

"Sir,—We're afraid poor Master Johnny is very bad—he's been taken to the hospital. He said, when he took ill, that it must have been a boy he took out of the streets and let sleep in his bed. Oh, sir, we are so sad! The young lady is better; but if Johnny dies—"

I could read no more. The excitement and injuries of the evening, added to this sudden and terrible news of my only friend, were too much for me. I don't exactly know what happened to me, but I have an idea young Larkins was not able to get on with his postage-stamps much more that evening.

Chapter Sixteen
How I experienced some of the Downs and Ups of Fortune

My reader will hardly accuse me of painting myself in too flattering colours. I only wish I could promise him that the record of my folly should end here. But, alas! if he has patience to read my story to the end he will find that Frederick Batchelor's folly was too inveterate to be chased away by two black eyes and a piece of bad news.

But for the time being I was fairly cowed. As I lay awake that next morning, after a night of feverish tossing and dreaming, I could think of nothing but my friend Smith—ill, perhaps dying, in the hospital at Packworth. I could do nothing to help him; I might not even go near him. Who could tell if ever I should see him again? And then came the memory of my cowardly refusal to stand up for him in his absence when he was being insulted and mocked behind his back. No wonder I despised myself and hated my life in London without him!

I got out of bed, determined at all costs to turn over a new leaf, and show every one that I *was* ashamed of what I had done. But as I did so I became faint and sick, and was obliged to crawl back to bed. I had all this time nearly forgotten my bruises and injuries of the previous evening, but I was painfully reminded of them now, and gradually all the misery of that exploit returned, and along with it a new alarm.

If Smith had caught smallpox from that wretched little street boy, was it not possible—nay, probable—I might be beginning with it too? It was not a pleasant thought, and the bare suggestion was enough to convince me I was really becoming ill.

"I say, aren't you going to get up?" said young Larkins, at my bedside, presently, evidently having come to see how I was getting on after last night's sensation: "or are you queer still?"

"I'm very queer," said I, "and can't get up. I think I'm going to be ill, Larkins. Would you mind calling at Hawk Street, and telling them there?"

"All right!" said Larkins. "But what's the matter with you?"

"I'm not quite sure, but I'm afraid—have I got any spots coming out on my face?"

"Eh? No; but your face is all black and blue, and there's a big bump on one cheek."

"Is there? Then it must be so. Larkins, you'd better not stand too near, I'm afraid I've smallpox!"

Larkins's face grew alarmed, and his jaw dropped. "What! Smallpox? Oh, I say, Batchelor, I hope not. It looks more like as if you'd been fighting."

"That's the smallpox coming on," I said, mournfully; "I'm sure!"

"Perhaps I'd better go," said Larkins, making for the door. "I'll tell them at your office," and with that he bolted suddenly.

It rather pleased me to imagine the sensation which his news would occasion not only down stairs among Mrs Nash's lodgers, but also at the office. I could hear the sound of eager voices below, followed by what I fancied was the hurried stampede of the company from the house. Then presently Mrs Nash's foot sounded on the stairs, and she opened the door.

"Have you had it, Mrs Nash?" I cried, as she appeared.

She made no answer, but walked up straight to my bed. "What's all this nonsense about?" she demanded.

"I'm afraid it's smallpox. I'm so sorry on your account," I said, quite meekly. "I sort of felt it coming on some days," I added, quite convinced in my own mind it had been so.

To my astonishment, the good lady expressed neither surprise nor sympathy. "Fiddlesticks!" said she. "Come, get up!"

"Get up?" I cried, in astonishment. "I can't possibly, Mrs Nash. I tried just now, and couldn't stand!"

"Stuff and nonsense! You ought to be ashamed of yourself going and fighting with a parcel of young roughs over night, and then shamming illness in the morning because you daren't show your black eyes to the governors! Come, you don't get round me with any of your nonsense! Up you get, or I'll start and sweep out the room before you're dressed!"

It was in vain I protested and pleaded. I had to rise, and, dizzy and sick as I felt, to huddle on my clothes and go down stairs, utterly horrified at such inhuman treatment. Mrs Nash even expected, now I was up, I should go to the office; but this I positively declared I could not do, and was therefore permitted to make myself as comfortable as I could in the cheerless parlour, and there wait for the further development of my malady.

Towards mid-day I began to feel hungry, but dared not ask Mrs Nash for anything; it would be so unlike an invalid. But I rang the bell and implored her to send for a doctor, which she finally promised to do.

In the interval I began to feel more and more like myself. It was very aggravating, to be sure! Unless he came quickly the doctor would hardly think me ill at all. And yet I *must* be ill, even though it cost an effort!

When the doctor did arrive I did my best, by putting on a pained expression of countenance, by breathing rather hard and closing my eyes occasionally, to make him feel he had not come for nothing. But somehow I didn't quite succeed. He smiled pleasantly as he just touched my pulse, and gave a single glance at my protruded tongue.

"There's nothing wrong with him, except a black eye or so. Fighting, I suppose. Boys will be boys. Send him to bed early to-night, Mrs Nash, and he'll be all right in the morning."

"But what about—about the smallpox?" I inquired, forgetting that during the last speech I had been lying with my eyes closed, apparently unconscious.

The doctor laughed noisily, and Mrs Nash joined in the chorus.

"We'll see about him when we catch him, my young fighting-cock," replied he, and then went.

Then I hadn't really got it! A nice fool I had made of myself! Larkins had, of course, announced it to all the lodgers at Mrs Nash's, to my employers and fellow-clerks, and here was I all the while as right as a trivet, with nothing but a bruised face and an empty stomach afflicting me. Was ever luck like mine?

I took care to be in bed before the fellows got home that evening, but as I lay awake I could hear their laughter down stairs, and it was not hard to guess what it was about. Larkins came up to my room.

"You're a nice fellow, Batchelor," said he, laughing, "telling me it was smallpox! You gave me such a fright. I told all the fellows, and at your office, and you should have seen how blue they all looked. What a sell it will be when you turn up all serene." This was pleasant.

"You'd better not be too sure," I said, still clinging to my ailment. "It may be it after all. The doctor said I was to go to bed early to-night and keep quite quiet. I'd advise you not to stay in the room, Larkins."

"Oh, all right, good-night," said Larkins, going to the door.

I heard him whistling merrily down the stairs, and felt still more uncomfortable. However, merciful sleep ended my troubles for a season. I slept like a top all that night, and woke next morning as fresh and well as I had ever been in all my life. The only thing wrong with me was the colour of my face. That was certainly rather brilliant. I had to endure a regular broadside of quizzing from my fellow-lodgers that morning at breakfast, which certainly did not tend to cheer me up in the prospect of presenting myself shortly at Hawk Street. I would fain have been spared that ceremony!

There arrived, as I was starting out, a hurried line from Mrs Shield, announcing that Jack was "much the same," which of course meant he was still very ill.

Poor Jack! I had been so taken up with my own fancied ailment that I had scarcely thought of him. As it was I could hardly realise that he was so very ill.

Little had we imagined that evening when he caught up the half-murdered urchin in his arms and carried him to our lodgings what the result of that act would be to one of us! And yet, if it were to do again, I fancied my friend Smith would do it again, whatever it cost. But to think of his being so ill, possibly losing his life, all for a graceless young vagabond who—

"Clean 'e boots, do y' hear, clean 'e boots, sir?"

Looking towards the sound, I saw the very object of my thoughts in front of me. He was clad in a tattered old tail coat, and trousers twice the size of his little legs. His head and feet were bare, and there seemed little enough semblance of a shirt. Altogether it was the most "scarecrowy" apparition I ever came across.

"Shine 'e boots, master?" he cried, flourishing a blacking-brush in either hand, and standing across my path.

I stopped short, and answered solemnly, "Where's that sixpence you stole out of my pocket, you young thief?"

I expected he would be overawed and conscience-stricken by the sudden accusation. But instead of that he fired up with the most virtuous indignation.

"What do yer mean, young thief? I ain't a-goin'—Oh, my Jemimer, it's one of them two flats. Oh, here's a go! Shine 'e boots, mister?"

There were certainly very few signs of penitence about this queer boy. This was pleasant, certainly. Not only robbed, but laughed at by the thief, a little mite of a fellow like this!

"I've a great mind to call a policeman and give you in charge," said I.

He must have seen that I was not in earnest, for he replied, gaily, "No, yer don't. Ef yer do, I'll run yer in for prize-fightin', so now."

"How much do you earn by blacking boots?" I asked, feeling an involuntary interest in this strange gutter lad.

"Some days I gets a tanner. But, bless you, I ain't a brigade bloke. I say, though, where's t'other flat; 'im with the eyes?"

"He's away ill," I said. "He's got smallpox, and says he believes he caught it from you."

"Get 'long!" replied the boy.

"Well, most likely it was in the court where you live."

"You can take your davy of that," replied the boy; "there's plenty of 'im there."

"Have you had it?"

"In corse I 'ave. I say, 'ave yer seen the old gal about?"

"Your mother? No. Why?"

"On'y she's a-missin', that's all; but there, she allers turns up, she does, and wipes me to-rights, too."

"She was nearly killing you the night we saw you," said I.

"'Taint no concern of yourn. Shine 'e boots, sir? 'ere yer are, sir. Not that bloke, sir. Do yer 'ear? Shine 'e boots, mister?"

This last spirited call was addressed to an elderly gentleman who was passing. He yielded eventually to the youth's solicitation, and I therefore resumed my walk to the office with a good deal more to think of than I had when I started.

If I had desired to make a sensation at Hawk Street, I could hardly have done better than turn up that morning as usual. It was a picture to see the fellows' faces of alarm, bewilderment, astonishment, and finally of merriment.

They had all heard that I was laid up with smallpox, which, as my friend Smith was also ill of the same malady, they all considered as natural on my part, and highly proper. They had, in fact, faced the prospect of getting on without me, and were quite prepared to exist accordingly. The partners, too, had talked the matter over, and come to the decision of advertising again without delay for a new clerk to take my place, and that very morning were intending to draw up the advertisement and send it to the papers.

Under these circumstances I appeared unexpectedly and just as usual on the Hawk Street horizon. No, not just as usual. Had I appeared just as usual, it might have been easier for the company generally to believe that I was really sound, but when my face presented a brilliant combination of most of the colours of the rainbow, the effect was rather sensational.

"Why, if it's not Batchelor," exclaimed Doubleday; not, however, advancing open-armed to meet me, but edging towards the far end of the desk, and dexterously insinuating Crow and Wallop between me and his precious person. "Why, we heard you had smallpox."

"So we thought yesterday," said I, gravely, half aggravated still that I had been defrauded of that distinction.

"Oh, you did, did you?" said Doubleday, gradually working back to his own seat. "Well, you *have* got something on your face to show for it; hasn't he, Wallop?"

"Looks as if he'd been painting up for the South Sea Islands," observed Wallop.

"That's rather a showy tint of yellow down his left cheek," said Crow. "Very fashionable colour just now."

"Did you lay it on yourself?" said Doubleday, "or did you get any one to help you?"

"Oh," I said, in as off-hand a manner as I could, "I was having a little box with Whipcord up at the Field-marshal's. You weren't there, by the way, Doubleday. Whipcord's rather a good hand."

"Is he?" said Doubleday, laughing exuberantly, with Wallop and Crow as chorus. "I would never have supposed that by your face, now; would you, you fellows? It strikes me you got a big box instead of smallpox, eh? Ha, ha!"

"I wonder at Whipcord standing up to you," said Crow. "He's such a quiet fellow, and doesn't know in the least what to do with his hands."

"He had the best of me," I said.

"Well, I don't know. It doesn't do to trust to appearances. If it did one might suppose he had—rather. I hope you'll ask me up when you have the return match."

I didn't see much fun in those witticisms, which, however, appeared to afford great merriment to the company generally, so much so that when Mr Barnacle presently opened the door he caught the whole counting-house laughing.

"What tomfoolery is this?" he demanded, looking angrily round. "You seem to forget, all of you, that you come here to work, and not to play. If you want to play you can go somewhere else. There!" So saying he passed into his private room, slamming the door ill-temperedly behind him.

This was not encouraging for me, who, of course, had to report myself, and contradict the rumours regarding my illness.

I gave him a quartet of an hour or so to quiet down, partly in the hope that Mr Merrett might meanwhile arrive. But as that event did not happen, and as Doubleday informed me that the advertisements for a new clerk were to be sent out that morning, I made up my mind there was nothing to be gained by further delay, and therefore made the venture.

I found myself anything but comfortable as I stood before Mr Barnacle's desk, and stammeringly began my statement.

"Please, sir—"

"Why, what is this, sir?" demanded Mr Barnacle, sternly. "We were told yesterday you were ill."

"So I was, sir, and I believed I was going to have smallpox, but the doctor says I'm not."

"And does that account for your face being in that state, pray?"

"No, sir, I got that boxing—that is fighting."

"Most discreditable conduct! Is that all you have to say?"

"Yes, sir. I'm sorry I was away yesterday."

"Well, now, listen to what I have to say," said Mr Barnacle, laying down his pen, and leaning forward in his chair. "You've not been doing well lately, Batchelor. I've watched you and I've watched your work, and I don't like it. I was mistaken in you, sir. You're idle, sir, and unless you improve I sha'n't keep you another week, mind that."

"Indeed, sir—" I began.

"Hold your tongue, sir," said Mr Barnacle. "We've no room in this office for boys of your kind, and unless you change you must go somewhere else. You've played the fool quite enough here."

I would fain have replied to justify myself, but in the junior partner's present temper the attempt would have been hazardous.

So I said nothing and returned to my work, determined for my own credit, as well as in my own interest, to show Mr Barnacle that he had judged me harshly.

How I worked that week! I refused invitation after invitation, and stayed late after every one else had gone to get ahead with my work. During office hours I steadily abstracted myself from what was going on all round, and determined that nothing should draw me from my tasks. I even volunteered for and undertook work not strictly my own, greatly to the amazement of everybody, especially Wallop, who began to think there really must be something in the rumour that I was not well. And all the while I most assiduously doctored my face, which gradually came to resume its normal complexion.

I could see that this burst of industry was having its due effect in high quarters. Mr Barnacle, who after his lecture had treated me gruffly and abruptly for some days, began again to treat me civilly, and Mr Merrett bestowed once or twice a special commendation on my industry.

In due time, so far from feeling myself a repentant idler, I had grown to consider myself one of the most virtuous, industrious, and well-principled clerks in London, and in proportion as this conviction got hold of me my application to work relaxed. One event especially completed my self-satisfaction. About three weeks after my interview with Mr Barnacle I was summoned into the partners' room, and there informed that, having now been eight months in their service, and proving myself useful in my situation, my salary would henceforth be twelve shillings a week!

I could hardly believe my ears! Why, it was just half as much again as what I had been receiving. On eight shillings a week I had lived economically, but not so badly. And now, what might I not do with twelve shillings a week?

Doubleday insisted on my coming up to his lodgings that evening to celebrate the joyful event with a quiet supper. This invitation I accepted, the first for nearly a month, and in view of the occasion spent my first extra four shillings in anticipation on a coloured Oxford-shirt, which I grandly requested, with the air of a moneyed man, to be put down to my account. I found myself quite the hero of the party that evening. Every one was there. I had an affecting reconciliation with Whipcord, and forgot all about Flanagan's desertion and Daly's indifference in my hour of tribulation; I discoursed condescendingly with the Field-Marshal about his hopeless attachment, and promised to go for a row up the river one Saturday with the twins. And all the time of supper I was mentally calculating the cost of Doubleday's entertainment, and wondering whether I could venture to give a party myself!

In fact, I was so much taken up with my own good fortune and my new rise in life, that I could think of nothing else. I forgot my former warnings and humiliations. I forgot that even with twelve shillings a week I had barely enough to clothe me respectably; I forgot that every one of these fellows was in the habit of laughing at me behind my back, and I forgot all my good resolutions to live steadily till Jack came back.

And I forgot all about poor Jack—(now, so the letters had told me), convalescent and slowly recovering health, but still lying lonely and weary in the Packworth Hospital. Indeed, that evening his name only twice crossed my mind—once when Doubleday and Crow were laughing over the prospect of "Bull's-eye" turning up with a face deeply marked with his late disease; and once when, walking back to Beadle Square, full of my new plans of extravagance, I chanced to pass a small boy, curled up on a doorstep, with his head resting on a shoeblack box, and the light of a neighbouring lamp shining full on his sleeping face. Then I remembered how, not very long ago, I had seen that same head lying side by side with Jack's head on the pillow at Mrs Nash's. And as I stood for a moment to look, I could almost have believed that the sleeping figure there, with all his vulgarity and dishonesty, had as good a title to call himself Jack Smith's friend as I had.

Chapter Seventeen
How I gave a Little Supper to some of my Friends

The idea of giving a party of my own to my new friends, in return for their hospitality to me, was not by any means a new one. It had been simmering in my mind for some weeks past. Indeed, ever since I began to be invited out, the thought that I could not return the compliment had always been a drawback to my pleasure.

But there had always been two obstacles in the way of carrying out my wish. The first was lack of funds, the second was Mrs Nash. On eight shillings a week I had come to the conclusion it was out of the question to dream of giving a party to eight persons. By the most modest calculation I couldn't possibly do the thing decently under a shilling a head. It was true I had my uncle's half-sovereign in my pocket still. I might, I reflected, borrow that, and pay it back by weekly instalments. But somehow I didn't like the idea quite, and never brought myself to the point of carrying it into effect. Now, however, with the sudden rise in my fortunes recorded in the last chapter, the financial obstacle to my hospitality was quite swept away. I had only to take the extra four shillings a week for two weeks—and the thing was done!

So the idea no longer simmered in my mind—it boiled; and I was determined for once in a way to astonish my friends.

But though one obstacle had vanished, the other remained. What would Mrs Nash say? For, much as I disliked it, I was forced to face the fact that my party, if I gave it, would have to come off in Beadle Square. I had half thought of borrowing Flanagan's room for the occasion, but didn't like to ask him; besides, if I did, it would have to be half his party and half mine, which wasn't at all my idea. Then it occurred to me, should I take lodgings for a week and give it there? No, it would cost too much even for twelve shillings a week; and my uncle, if he heard of it, might stop my keep at Mrs Nash's. Suppose I hired a room at an hotel for the evening, and asked the fellows there? It wasn't a bad idea, and would probably only cost me half a week's wages. But the worst of it is, if you ask fellows to dine with you at an hotel, they are sure to come expecting a grand turn out; and I doubted my talents to provide anything grand; besides, the hotel people would be sure to want to supply the things themselves, and ask for the money in advance. Or if I didn't humour them they would to a certainty turn crusty and critical, and spoil my party for me.

No, the only thing was to make the best of Beadle Square, and to that end I determined to tackle Mrs Nash at once.

You may fancy the good woman's surprise and scorn when I propounded to her my ambitious scheme.

"You give a party! Fiddlesticks! You'll do nothing of the sort."

"Please, Mrs Nash," pleaded I, "it will be a very quiet one, I promise."

"And where do you expect to have it, I wonder?" said she. "In the coal-cellar, I suppose? That's the only spot in the house that ain't occupied."

"Oh," replied I, thinking it judicious to laugh at this facetious suggestion, "I'd like the parlour for that evening, if you could manage it, Mrs Nash."

"What! are you going to ask all the fellows here to your party, then?"

"Oh, no. Couldn't you let them know the parlour's engaged for that evening?—just for once? You know I'd pay you something—"

"I dare say you would!—you'd pay anything, you would! And what are you going to give them all to eat, eh?"

"Oh, I'll see to that," said I.

This was an unfortunate reply of mine. Mrs Nash, as it happened, was inclined to enter into my scheme, and, had I only known it, would have offered to take some trouble to help me. But this answer of mine offended her sorely.

"Oh, very well," said she, loftily; "you don't want me, I can see, and I'm just as glad."

In vain I protested, and implored her not to be vexed. I hadn't meant it at all. I couldn't possibly do without her. I was a beast to say what I had, and so on. The most I could get out of her was a vague promise that I might have the room on the evening in question. As for the entertainment, she washed her hands of the whole affair.

I was inclined to give it up. Not that I had ever imagined she would help me; but to have her downright unfriendly at such a time would, I knew, ruin the thing totally.

For some days she would listen to nothing at all on the subject.

"It's your look-out," she said to every appeal. "Let's see what sort of a hand you'll make of it, my beauty."

I was in despair. I longed to issue my invitations, but till Mrs Nash was "squared" it was out of the question to name the happy day. It was evidently useless to argue the matter. The best thing I could do was to let it alone, and allow her to imagine the scheme had been abandoned.

In this calculation I was correct. Some days afterwards, happening to be in the parlour with her after breakfast, she said, "And when's your grand party, as you call it, coming off, Mr Batchelor?"

I started up in rapture at the question.

"Then you *will* help me, Mrs Nash?" I cried, running up to her, and taking it all for granted.

She first looked amazed, then angry, and finally she smiled.

"I never said so. You're a sight too independent for my taste, you are. *I* ain't a-goin' to put my fingers into where I ain't wanted."

"But you *are* wanted, and you will be a brick, I know!" cried I, almost hugging her in my eagerness.

The battle was won, and that morning I went down to the office positively jubilant. My party was fixed for Thursday!

I felt particularly important when the time came for inviting Doubleday and Crow to the festive assembly. I had rehearsed as I walked along the very words and tones I would use. On no account must they suppose the giving of a party was the momentous event it really proved itself.

"By the way, Doubleday," said I, in as off-hand a manner as I could assume, after some preliminary talk on different matters—"by the way, could you come up to supper on Thursday? Just the usual lot, you know."

I could have kicked myself for the way I blushed and stammered as I was delivering this short oration.

Doubleday gazed at me half curiously, half perplexed.

"Eh—supper? Oh, rather! Where's it to be? Mansion House or Guildhall?"

I didn't like this. It wasn't what I had expected.

"Oh, up at my place, you know—Beadle Square," I said.

At this Doubleday fairly laughed.

My Friend Smith | 159

"Supper at your place at Black Beadle Square? Oh, rather! I'll come. You'll come too, Crow, eh? The young un's got a supper on on Thursday. Oh, rather. Put me down for that, old man."

Could anything have been more mortifying? Most invitations are received politely and graciously. What there was to laugh at about mine I couldn't understand.

"Oh, yes, Crow's coming," I said, meekly. "At least I hope so."

"Oh, rather!" said Crow, beaming. "I wouldn't miss it for a lot. Is it evening dress or what?"

I was too much disconcerted and crestfallen to answer the question, and avoided my two prospective guests for the rest of the day.

Already I was half repenting my venture. But there was no drawing back now. Letters or messages came from the rest of the "usual lot"—the Twins, Flanagan, the Field-Marshal, Daly, and Whipcord, every one of them saying they'd be there. Yes, there was nothing left but to go through with it.

The next two days were two of the most anxious days I ever spent. I was running about all one afternoon (when I ought to have been delivering bills of lading), inquiring the prices of lobsters, pork-pies, oranges, and other delicacies, arranging for the hire of cups and saucers, ordering butter and eggs, and jam, and other such arduous and delicate duties. Then I spent the evening in discussing with myself the momentous questions whether I should lay in tea-cakes or penny buns, whether I need have brown bread as well as white, whether Mrs Nash's tea would be good enough, whether I should help my great dish—the eel-pie—myself, or trust it to one of the company to do.

These and similar momentous matters engaged my thoughts. And it began to dawn on me further that my financial estimates had been greatly out, and that my supper would cost me nearer a pound than ten shillings. Never mind. After all, was I not worth twelve shillings a week? I needn't trouble about the expense. Besides, the pastrycook had agreed to give me credit, so that really I should have comparatively little to pay down.

A far more serious anxiety was Mrs Nash. It required constant and most assiduous attention to keep her in good temper. And the nearer the time came the more touchy she got. If I suggested anything, she took it as a personal slight to herself; if I was bold enough to differ from her, she was mortally offended; if I ventured to express the slightest impatience, she turned crusty and threatened to let me shift for myself. The affair, too, naturally got wind amongst my fellow-lodgers, who one and all avowed that they would not give up their right to the parlour, and indulged in all manner of witticisms at my cost and the cost of my party. I pacified them as best I could by promising them the reversion of the feast, and took meekly all their gibes and jests when they begged to be allowed to come in to dessert and hear the speeches, or volunteered to come and hand round the champagne, or clear away the "turtle-soup," and so on.

But the nearer the fatal day came the more dejected and nervous I got. Mrs Nash's parlour was really a disreputable sort of room, and after all I had had no experience of suppers, and was positive I should not know what to do when the time came. I had neither the flow of conversation of Doubleday, nor the store of stories of Daly, nor Whipcord's sporting gossip, nor the Twins' self-possessed humour. And if my guests should turn critical I was a lost man; that I knew. How I wished I were safe on the other side of that awful Thursday!

The day came at last, and I hurried home as hard as I could after business to make my final preparations. The eel-pie was arriving as I got there, and my heart was comforted by the sight. Something, at least, was ready. But my joy was short-lived, for Mrs Nash was in a temper. The fact is, I had unconsciously neglected a piece of advice of hers in the matter of this very eel-pie. She had said, have it hot. I had told the pastrycook to deliver it cold. Therefore Mrs Nash, just at the critical moment, deserted me!

With a feeling of desperation I laid my own tablecloth—not a very good one—and arranged as best I could the plates and dishes. Time was getting short, and it was no use wasting time on my crabby landlady. Yet what could I do without her? Who was to lend me a kettle, or a saucepan for the eggs, or a toasting-fork, or, for the matter of that, any of the material of war? It was clear I must at all hazards regain Mrs Nash, and the next half-hour was spent in frantic appeals to every emotion she possessed, to the drawing of abject pictures of my own helplessness, to profuse apologies, and compliments and coaxings. I never worked so hard in my life as I did that half-hour.

Happily it was not all in vain. She consented, at any rate, to look after one or two of the matters in which I was most helpless, and I was duly and infinitely thankful.

In due time all was ready, and the hour arrived. All my terrors returned. I felt tempted to bolt from the house and leave my guests to entertain themselves. I *hated* Beadle Square. And there, of course, just when I should have liked things to be at their best, there were three or four cats setting up a most hideous concert in the yard, and the chimney in the parlour beginning to smoke. I could have torn my hair with rage and vexation.

I seized the tongs, and was kneeling down and vigorously pushing them up the chimney, to ascertain the cause of this last misfortune, when a loud double-knock at the door startled me nearly out of my senses. I had never realised what I was in for till now!

Horror of horrors! Who was to open the door, Mrs Nash, or I? We had never settled that. And while I stood trembling amid my smoke and eel-pie and half-boiled eggs, the knock was repeated—this time so long and loud that it must have been heard all over the square. I could hear voices and laughter outside. Some one asked, "Is this the shop?" and another voice said, "Don't see his name on the door."

Then, terrified lest they should perpetrate another solo on the knocker, I rushed out and opened the door myself, just as Mrs Nash, with her face scarlet and her sleeves tucked up above the elbows, also appeared in the passage.

They were all there; they had come down in a body. Oh, how shabby I felt as I saw them there with their fine clothes and free-and-easy manners!

"Hullo! here you are!" said Doubleday. "Found you out, then, at last. Haven't been this way for an age, but knew it at once by the cats. Hullo, is this your mother? How do, Mrs Batchelor. Glad to see you. Allow me to introduce—"

"It's not my mother!" I cried, with a suppressed groan, pulling his arm.

"Eh, not your mother?—your aunt, perhaps? How do you—"

"No, no," I whispered; "no relation."

"Not? That's a pity! She's a tidy-looking old body, too. I say, where do you stick your hats, eh? I bag the door-handle; you hang yours on the key, Crow. Come on in, you fellows. Here's a spree!"

Could anything be more distressing or humiliating? Mrs Nash, too indignant for words, had vanished to her own kitchen, shutting the door behind her with an ominous slam, and here was the hall chock-full of staring, giggling fellows, with not a place to hang their hats, and Doubleday already the self-constituted master of the ceremonies!

I mildly suggested they had better bring their hats inside, but they insisted on "stacking" them, as the Field-marshal called it, in pyramid form on the hall floor; and I let them have their way.

"Come in," I faltered presently, when this little diversion appeared to be ended. As I led the way into the parlour my heart was in my boots and no mistake.

They entered, all coughing very much at the smoke. What a seedy, disreputable hole Mrs Nash's parlour appeared at that moment!

"I'm sorry the chimney's smoking," I said, "a—a—won't you sit down?"

This invitation, I don't know why, seemed only to add to the amusement of the party. Daly proceeded to sit down on the floor, no chair being near, and the Twins solemnly established themselves on the top of him. The others sat down all round the room in silence. What could I do? In my cool moments I had thought of one or two topics of conversation, but of course they ah deserted me now. All except the weather.

"Turned rather cold," I observed to Whipcord.

"Who?" exclaimed that worthy, with an alarmed face.

"I mean the weather's turned rather cold."

"Poor chap, pity he don't wear a top-coat."

"I say," said Doubleday, who had, to my great discomfort, been making a tour of discovery round the room, "rather nice pictures some of these, this one of Peace and Plenty's not half bad, is it, Whip?"

"Why you old ass, that's not Peace and Plenty, it's a Storm at Sea."

"Well, I don't care who it is, it's rattling good likenesses of them. Hullo, Twins, don't you be going to sleep, do you hear?"

This was addressed to the two brothers, from under whom, at that moment, Daly contrived suddenly to remove himself, leaving them to fall all of a heap.

In the midst of the confusion caused by this accident, it occurred to me we might as well begin supper; so I called the company to attention.

"We may as well begin," I said, "there's no one else to wait for. Will you take that end, Doubleday?"

"I'm game," said Doubleday. "Now then, you fellows, tumble into your seats, do you hear? We're jist a-going to begin, as the conjurer says. I can tell you all I'm pretty peckish, too."

"So am I, rather," said Crow, winking at the company generally, who all laughed.

Awful thought! Suppose there's not enough for them to eat after all!

I began to pour out the coffee wildly, hardly venturing to look round. At last, however, I recollected my duties.

"That's an eel-pie in front of you, Doubleday," I said.

Now at all the parties I had been to I had never before seen an eel-pie. I therefore flattered myself I had a novelty to offer to my guests.

"Eel-pie, eh?" said Doubleday; "do you catch them about here, then? Eel-pie, who says eel-pie? Don't all speak at once. Bring forth the hot plates, my boy, and we'll lead off."

"It's cold," I faltered.

"Oh, goodness gracious! *Cold* eel-pie, gentlemen. You really must *not* all speak at once. Who says cold eel-pie? The Field-Marshal does!"

"No, he doesn't," replied the Field-Marshal, laughing.

"Flanagan does, then?"

"No, thank you," said Flanagan.

"Well, you Twins; you with the cut on your chin. I wish one of you'd always cut your chin shaving, one would know you from the other. Any cold eel-pie?"

"Rather not," said the Twin addressed.

"Have some lobster?" I said, despairingly. If no one was going to take eel-pie, it was certain my other provisions would not last round. Why hadn't I taken Mrs Nash's advice, and had that unlucky dish hot?

"What will you take?" I said to Flanagan.

"Oh, I don't mind," replied he, in a resigned manner; "I'll take a shrimp or two."

"Have something more than that. Have some lobster?" I said.

"No, thanks," he replied.

Evidently my good things were not in favour; why, I could not say. Nobody seemed to be taking anything, and Crow was most conspicuously *smelling* my lobster.

The meal dragged on heavily, with more talk than eating. Every dish came in for its share of criticism; the eel-pie remained uncut, the lobster had lost one claw, but more than half the contents of that was left on Abel's plate. My penny buns all vanished, that was one ray of comfort.

"Ring the bell for more buns," said Doubleday, as if he was presiding at his own table.

What was I to do? There were no more, and it was hardly likely Mrs Nash would go for more. Before I could make up my mind, Whipcord had rung a loud peal on the bell, and Mrs Nash in due time appeared.

"More buns, and look sharp, old woman," said Doubleday.

"I'll old woman you if I've much of your imperence, my young dandy!" was the somewhat startling rejoinder. "I'll bundle the pack of you out of the house, that I will, if you can't keep a civil tongue in your heads."

"I say, Batchelor," said Doubleday, laughing, "your aunt has got a temper, I fancy. I'm always sorry to see it in one so young. What will it be when—"

"Oh, please don't, Doubleday," I said; "you can see she doesn't like it. It doesn't matter, Mrs Nash, thank you," I added.

"Oh, don't it matter?" retorted the irate Mrs Nash, "that's all; we'll settle that pretty soon, my beauty. I'll teach you if it don't matter that a pack of puppies comes into my house, and drinks tea out of my cups, and calls me names before my face and behind my back; I'll teach you!" And she bounced from the room.

I thought that meal would never end, although no one took anything. In time even the fun and laughter, which had at first helped to keep the thing going, died away, and the fellows lolled back in the chairs in a listless, bored way. It was vain for me to try to lead the talk; I could not have done it even if I had had the spirit, and there was precious little spirit left now!

Doubleday began to look at his watch.

"Half-past seven. I say," said he, "time I was going. I've a particular engagement at eight."

"Well, I'll go with you," said Whipcord; "I want to get something to eat, and we can have supper together."

"Sorry we've got to go," said Doubleday. "Jolly evening, wasn't it, Crow?"

I was too much humiliated and disgusted to notice their departure. To have my grand entertainment sneered at and made fun of was bad enough, but for two of my guests to leave my table for the avowed purpose of getting something to eat was a little too much. I could barely be civil to the rest and ask them to remain, and it was a real relief when they one and all began to make some excuse for leaving.

So ended my famous supper-party, after which, for a season, I prudently retired into private life.

Chapter Eighteen
How my Friend Smith came back, and told me a Great Secret

My grand evening party was over, but I had still my accounts for that entertainment to square. And the result of that operation was appalling. It was a fortnight since my salary had been raised, but so far I had not a penny saved. The extra money had gone, I couldn't exactly say how, in sundry "trifling expenditures," such as pomatum, a scarf-pin, and a steel chain for my waistcoat, all of which it had seemed no harm to indulge in, especially as they were very cheap, under my altered circumstances.

On the strength of my new riches also I was already six shillings in debt to the Oxford-shirt man, and four shillings in debt to the Twins, who had paid my share in the boating expedition up the river. And now, when I came to reckon up my liabilities for the supper, I found I owed as much as eight shillings to the pastrycook and five shillings to the grocer, besides having already paid two shillings for the unlucky lobster (which to my horror and shame I found out after every one had left had *not* been fresh), one shilling for eggs, sixpence for shrimps, and one-and-sixpence for the hire of the cups and saucers.

The ingenious reader will be able to arrive at a true estimate of my financial position from these figures, and will see that so far, at any rate, my increase of riches had not made me a wealthier man than when I had lived within my income on eight shillings a week.

Nor had it made me either better or happier I made a few more good resolutions after the party to be a fool no longer. I could see plainly enough that all my so-called friends had been amusing themselves at my expense, and were certainly not worth my running myself head over ears in debt to retain. I could see too, when I came to reflect, that all my efforts to pass myself off as "one of them" had ended pitifully for me, if not ridiculously. Yes, it was time I gave it up. Alas! for the vanity of youth! The very day that witnessed the forming of my resolutions witnessed also the breaking of them.

"Hullo, young 'un!" cried Doubleday, as I put in my appearance at the office; "here you are! How are you after it all?"

"I'm quite well," said I, in what I intended to be a chilly voice.

"That's right. Very brickish of you to have us up. We all thought so, didn't we, Crow?"

"Rather," replied Crow.

"I'm afraid some of the fellows were rather rude," continued Doubleday. "Those Twins are awfully underbred beggars. I believe, you know, their mother never knew which of the two it was that wanted whopping, and so she let them both grow up anyhow. If I'd been her, I'd have licked them both regularly, wouldn't you, Crow?"

Without setting much store by Doubleday's moral disquisition on the duty of the parents of Twins, I felt mollified by the half apology implied in his reference to yesterday's entertainment, and to the manner of his behaviour towards me now. It was clear he felt rather ashamed of himself and his cronies for their behaviour. Who could tell whether, if they had given me a fair chance, my supper might not have been a success after all? At any rate, I didn't feel quite so downhearted about it as I had done.

"How's that festive old lady," proceeded Doubleday, "this morning? I pity you with an old dragon like her to look after you. That's the worst of those boarding-houses. A fellow can't do the civil to his friends but he's sure to be interfered with by somebody or other."

He was actually making excuses for me!

Yes; if it hadn't been for the rudeness of some of the fellows and the aggravating behaviour of Mrs Nash, my supper would have gone off quite well. I was quite thankful to Doubleday for the comfort he gave me, and cheerfully accepted an invitation to go up to his lodgings "to meet just the usual lot" next evening.

Which I did, and found the "usual lot" in their usual good spirits. No one seemed to bear a grudge against me for that cold eel-pie, and one or two assured me that they had enjoyed themselves immensely.

Nothing could speak more for my greenness and vanity than the fact that I believed what they said, and felt more convinced than ever that my party, however it had *seemed* to go off, had really been a success.

On my return to Beadle Square that evening I found a letter waiting for me, and to my joy and surprise it was in Jack Smith's own handwriting. It said:

"Dear Fred,—You'll be glad to hear I'm off the sick list at last, and have been turned out a perfect cure. Mrs Shield, my sister's nurse and friend, insists on my taking it easy another week, and then I shall come up to town, and mean to work like a nigger to make up for lost time. I'll tell you all the news when I come. I'm afraid you've been having a slow time.—Yours ever, Jack.

"P.S.—I've written to M., B., and Company, to tell them I'll be up on Monday next."

It seemed almost too good to be true that I should so soon see my friend again. Ah! how different it would all be when he came back! For the next week I could think of nothing else. What a lot I should have to tell him! How he would laugh over my adventures and misfortunes, and how he would scold me for my extravagances and follies! Well, these would be over at last, that was a comfort.

So, during the week, in view of giving up my extravagances, I bought a new suit of ready-made clothes that only half fitted me, and went on the Saturday afternoon with Whipcord and the Twins to see a steeplechase, where I was tempted to put two half-crowns, which I borrowed from the Twins, into a sweepstake, and lost them both. This was a good finish up to my little "fling" and no mistake; so much so that I began to think it was a pity Jack had not come last Monday instead of next.

"He would have kept me out of all this mischief," said I to myself. Ah! I had yet to learn that if one wants to keep out of mischief one must not depend altogether upon one's friends, or even oneself, for the blessing. Strength must be sought from a higher Power and a better Friend!

At last the long-looked-for Monday arrived, and I went down to the station in the evening to meet Jack's train.

I could scarcely have said what feeling it was which prompted me to wear, not my new stripe suit, but my old clothes, shabby as they were, or why, instead of wearing my coloured Oxford-shirt, I preferred to array myself in one of the old flannel shirts with its time-honoured paper collar.

Somehow I had no ambition to "make an impression" on my friend Smith.

There was his head out of the window and his hand waving long before the train pulled up. The face was the same I had always known, pale and solemn, with its big black eyes and clusters of black hair. His illness had left neither mark nor change on him; still less had it altered his tone and manner, as he sprang from the carriage and seizing me by the arm, said, "Well, old fellow, here we are again, at last!"

What a happy evening that was! We walked to Beadle Square, carrying Jack's bag between us, and talking all the way. The dull old place appeared quite bright now he was back; and the meal we had together in the parlour that evening before the other fellows came home seemed positively sumptuous, although it consisted only of weak tea and bread-and-butter.

Then we turned out for a long walk, anywhere, and having no bag to catch hold of this time, we caught hold of one another's arms, which was quite as comfortable.

"Well, old man," began Jack, "what have you been up to all the time? You never told me in your letters."

"There wasn't much to tell," I said. "It was awfully slow when you left, I can assure you."

"But you soon got over that?" said Jack, laughing.

He wasn't far wrong, as the reader knows, but somehow I would have preferred him to believe otherwise. I replied, "There would have been simply nothing to do of an evening if Doubleday—who is a very decent fellow at bottom, Jack—hadn't asked me up to his lodgings once or twice to supper."

I said this in as off-hand a way as I could. I don't know why I had fancied Jack would not be pleased with the intelligence, for Doubleday had never been very friendly to him.

"Did he?" said Jack. "That was rather brickish of him."

"Yes; he knew it would be dull while you were away, and I was very glad to go."

"Rather! I expect he gave you rather better suppers than we get up at Beadle Square, eh?"

"Yes. And then, you know, when I was there I heard where Flanagan was living, and found him out. Do you remember our hunt after him that night, Jack?"

"Don't I! By the way, Fred, has there been any news of the boy?"

"The young thief? I should fancy you'd had enough of him, old man, for a good while to come. But I have seen him."

"Where?" asked Jack, with an interest that quite amused me.

"One would think that after giving you smallpox, and robbing you of your money, you were really under an obligation to the young beggar, and wanted to thank him personally. If you are so very anxious to pay your respects, it's ten to one we shall run across him at the top of Style Street—that's where his place of business is."

"Place of business? What do you mean?"

"I mean that he has spent the money he stole from us in buying a shoeblack's apparatus, and seems to think it's something to be proud of, too," I replied.

Jack laughed. "He might have done worse. My boots want blacking, Fred; let's go round by Style Street."

The young vagabond was there, engaged, as we approached him, in walking round and round his box on the palms of his hands with his feet in the air.

At the sight of us he dropped suddenly into a human posture, and, with a very broad grin on his face, said, "Shine 'e boots, governor? Why, if it ain't t'other flat come back? Shine 'e boots?"

"Yes; I want my boots cleaned," said Jack, solemnly, planting one foot on the box.

The boy dropped briskly on his knees and went to work, making Jack's boot shine as it had never shone before. In the middle of the operation he stopped short, and, looking up, said, "You *was* a flat that there night, you was!"

I could only laugh at this frank piece of information.

"I think you were the flat!" said Jack, putting up his other foot on the box.

"Me? *I* ain't no flat, no error!" replied the boy, with a grin. "I'm a sharp 'un, that's what I are!"

"I think you were worse than a flat to steal my money, and my friend's."

The boy looked perplexed. "Ga on!" said he.

"What's your name?" asked Jack, changing the subject.

"Billy," replied the boy.

"Billy what?"

"Ga on! What do you mean by 'what'? Ain't Billy enough?"

"Where do you live?"

"Live? where I can; that's where I live!"

"Then you don't live with your mother in that court any longer?"

"The old gal—she ain't no concern of yourn!" said the youth, firing up.

"I know that," said Jack, evidently at a loss, as I had been, how to pursue the conversation with this queer boy. "I say, Billy," he added, "where are you going to sleep to-night?"

"Ain't a-goin' to sleep nowheres!" was the prompt reply.

"Would you like to come and sleep with me?"

"No fear!" was the complimentary reply.

"What are you going to do, then?"

"'Tain't no concern o' yourn; so it ain't."

"Will you be here to-morrow?"

"In corse I shall!"

"Well, I expect I'll want my boots done again to-morrow evening. Here's a penny for this time."

The boy took the penny and held it in the palm of his hand.

"Isn't it enough?" asked Jack.

"You're 'avin' a lark with me," said the boy. "This 'ere brown—"

"What's wrong? It's a good one, isn't it?"

"Oh, ain't you funny? I don't want yer brown!" and to my amazement he tossed the coin back.

Jack solemnly picked it up and put it back into his pocket. "Good-night, Billy," said he. "Mind you are here to-morrow."

"No fear!" said Billy, who was once more resuming his gymnastic exercises.

And so we left him.

My friend Smith was certainly a queer fellow. He seemed more interested during the remainder of our walk with the little dishonest shoeblack we had just left than with my half-candid story of my life in London during his absence.

"Depend upon it, that's his way of making amends," said he; "there's some good in the young scamp after all."

"It's precious hard to discover," said I. "He appears to me to be a graceless young reprobate, who knows well enough that it's wicked to steal, and seems rather proud of it than otherwise. I say, Jack, I'd advise you not to have too much to do with him. He's done you harm enough as it is."

When we returned to Beadle Square we found our amiable fellow-lodgers evidently expecting our arrival. It was so long since I had taken supper at Mrs Nash's that I seemed quite as much a stranger as Jack.

"Here they come," said Horncastle, who always shone on occasions like this. "Here comes the two smallpoxes. Hold your noses, you fellows."

In this flattering manner we were received as we proceeded to seat ourselves in our accustomed place at the table.

"They seem as cheerful and merry as ever," said Jack, solemnly, to me, looking round him.

"I say, Jones," cried Horncastle, in an audible voice to a friend, "wonderful how Batchelor turns up here now the other's come home! Got to stop going out every night now, and coming home drunk at two in the morning, eh? Going to behave now, eh? But he does go it, don't he, when his keeper's back's turned, eh?"

All this, ridiculous as it was, was not very pleasant for me. To Jack, however, it was highly amusing.

"I suppose they mean that for you," said he. "I feel quite flattered to be called your keeper."

"It's all a lie," I said angrily, "about my coming home drunk, and all that."

"I should rather hope it was," said my friend with a smile.

I was sufficiently uncomfortable, however, by the turn my fellow-lodgers' wit was taking. Without meaning to deceive, I had somehow, in my story to Jack, omitted all reference to my own extravagances, and represented my dissipations more as contrivances to pass the time in my friend's absence than congenial pleasures.

"Rum thing, too," continued Horncastle, who evidently saw I was not liking it—"rum thing he's dropped those new ready-made togs of his and his flash watch-chain. I wonder why—"

"Because they're not paid for," said another. "I know that, because I was in Shoddy's shop to-day, and he asked me to tell Batchelor the things were sold for ready money and no tick. Do you hear that, Batchelor? that's what he says, and you'd better attend to it, I can tell you."

Why need I have got myself into a rage over a suit of ready-made clothes? It was surely no crime to possess them; and if I was owing the amount it didn't follow I had anything to be ashamed of, as long as I paid in the end. But I flushed up dreadfully, in a manner which Jack could not help noticing, and replied, "You mind your own business—I'll mind mine!"

"You'd better, my boy," was the reply. "Pyman, the pastrycook, was asking most affectionately after you too. He says he hopes you won't move without letting him know, as he'd like to call and—"

"Come on, Jack!" I cried, taking Jack's arm; "it's enough to make one sick the way they talk."

And amid much laughter, and in no very amiable frame of mind, I quitted my persecutors.

I made sure Jack would read me a lecture, or at any rate refer to the subject which had caused me so much annoyance. He did neither.

"Lively lot they are," said he. "It's a wonder where they pick up all their notions."

"They want to make you believe I've been up to all sorts of mischief since you went away," I said.

Jack laughed.

"And they expect me to believe it," said he. "The best way with them is to let them say what they like, and take no notice."

We went upstairs to bed, as the only place where we could enjoy one another's society undisturbed.

As we were undressing. Jack took from his pocket a photograph, which he showed to me.

"Fred," said he, "would you like to see a portrait of Mary?"

"Your sister?" said I, taking the picture. "Yes."

It was a pretty little girl of about twelve or thirteen, with dark eyes and hair like Jack's; but, unlike him, with a merry, sunny face, which even under the eye of a photographer could not be made to look solemn.

"How jolly!" was my exclamation.

Jack looked as delighted with this unsentimental comment as if I had broken out into all sorts of poetic raptures, and replied, in his peculiar, solemn way, "Yes, she is jolly."

"Is she your only sister?" I asked, giving him back the portrait.

"Yes," said he.

"Was she very ill when you got down?"

"Yes; we hardly thought she was going to live," he replied.

"I heard how you were both getting on now and then from Mrs Shield. She seems a very kind person."

"She's our old nurse, you know," Jack said, "and like a mother to Mary and me."

He had never spoken like this about home before. Whenever we had approached the topic he had nervously changed the conversation. Now, however, he seemed almost glad to talk to some one, and there was quite a tremble in his voice as he spoke of his sister and Mrs Shield.

"Then your own mother's not alive?" I asked. I had asked the same question once at Stonebridge House, I remembered, and then he had almost resented it.

"No, she died when Mary was born, fourteen years ago. I cannot remember her at all."

"Just like me," I said. "I never saw my mother that I know of. I say, Jack, let's look at that portrait again."

He was delighted to show it to me, and I was glad once more to get a glimpse of that merry face.

"And your father," I inquired, presently, "is he dead too?"

"No!" said Jack, with a sudden return of his old abruptness.

I was perplexed, but it was no use, evidently, pumping my friend with further questions in that direction. So we proceeded to undress in silence, and were soon in bed.

Presently the other lodgers came up, and then there was no chance of renewing our talk, even if Jack had been so inclined. But he seemed evidently in no humour for pursuing it.

In due time all was quiet once more, and then, just as I was beginning to feel drowsy, and was lying half awake, half asleep, fancying myself back again at Stonebridge House in the old dormitory, I felt a hand on my arm and heard Jack's voice whisper, "Fred, are you asleep?"

"No," I replied, moving over to make room for him as he slipped in beside me.

"Fred," he whispered, "I'm afraid you think me a brute."

"No, I don't," replied I, astonished; "why ever should I?"

"Why, I offended you just now, when you meant to be kind."

"No you didn't," said I. "I know there are some things you don't like to talk about, and I—I've no right to ask you about them."

Jack lay silent for some minutes. Then he whispered—

"Old man, you can keep a secret, can't you?"

"Yes," I said, wondering what was coming.

"I've never told it to anybody yet; but somehow it's awful having no one to talk to," he said.

"What is it, Jack?" I asked. "I won't tell a soul."

He crept closer to me, and his voice dropped to a lower whisper as he said, "Fred—*my father is a convict!*"

I was too bewildered and shocked to speak. All I could do was to take the hand which lay on my arm and hold it in mine. This then was Jack's mystery. This explained his nervous avoidance of all references to home, his sudden changes of manner both at Stonebridge House and in London. Poor Jack!

We neither of us spoke for some time; then, as if in answer to the questions I longed to ask, he continued, "I hardly ever saw him. When mother died he went nearly mad and took to drinking, so Mrs Shield told me, and left home. No one heard of him again till it was discovered he had forged on his employers. I remember their coming and looking for him at M—, where we then lived. He wasn't there, but they found him in London, and,"—here Jack groaned—"he was transported."

"Poor Jack!" was all I could say. "How dreadful for you all!"

We said no more that night, but as we lay arm in arm, and presently fell asleep, I think we both felt we were bound together that night by a stronger tie than ever.

Yet, had I known what was to come, I would sooner have rushed from that house than allow my friend Smith to tell me his secret.

Chapter Nineteen
How Hawkesbury put in an Appearance at Hawk Street

When I woke in the morning and called to mind Jack's confidence of the night before, I could hardly believe I had not dreamt it.

I had always guessed, and I dare say the reader has guessed too, that there was some mystery attached to my friend's home. But I had never thought of this. No wonder now, when other boys had tormented him and called him "gaol-bird," he had flared up with unwonted fire. No wonder he had always shrunk from any reference to that unhappy home. But why had he told me all about it now? I could almost guess the reason. For the last month or two he had been back at the nearest approach to a home that he possessed, at his old nurse's cottage at Packworth, with her and his sister. And now, leaving them, and coming back once more to work in London, a home-sickness had seized him, and an irresistible craving for sympathy had prompted him to tell me his secret.

"And it shall be safe with me," I said to myself.

We did not refer to the subject again that day, or for several days. Indeed, I almost suspected he repented already of what he had done, for his manner was more reserved and shy than I had ever known it. He seemed to be in a constant fright lest I should return to the subject, while his almost deferential manner to me was quite distressing. However, we had our work to occupy our minds during most of the day.

"Slap bang, here we are again!" cried Doubleday, as we entered the office together that morning. "What cheer, Bulls'-eye? Awfully sorry we haven't got the decorations up, but we're out of flags at present. We're going to illuminate this evening, though, in your honour—when we light the gas."

"Awfully glad you're back," said Crow. "The governors have been in an awful way without you to advise them. We've positively done nothing since you went, have we, Wallop?"

"No—except read his life in the Newgate Calendar," said Wallop, who had not forgotten his knock down on the day Jack left.

All this Jack, like a sensible man, took quietly, though I could see, or fancied I saw, he winced at the last reference.

He quietly took his old place, and proceeded to resume his work just as if he had never been absent, wholly regardless of the witticisms of his comrades.

"We've drunk his health now and then in his absence, haven't we, Batch, old man?" said Doubleday again, addressing me.

I did not at all like to be thus drawn into the conversation, but I was forced to answer. "Yes, now and then."

"Let's see, what was the last sentiment—the other night up at Daly's, you know; what was it, Crow?"

"Oh, Doubleday!" cried I, suddenly, in terror at the turn the talk was taking, "would you look at this invoice, please? Only twelve cases are entered, and I'm certain thirteen were shipped."

"Eh, what?" exclaimed Doubleday, who in business matters was always prompt and serious; "only twelve entered? how's that? Why, you young idiot!" said he, taking up the paper; "can't you read what's straight in front of your nose? 'A set of samples, not invoiced, in case Number 13.'"

"So it is, to be sure," exclaimed I, who, of course, knew it all along, and had only raised the alarm in order to interrupt Doubleday's awkward talk. "Thanks."

This expedient of mine, disingenuous as it was, was successful. Before Doubleday could get back to his desk and take up the thread of his conversation where he left it, Mr Merrett entered the office. He walked straight up to Jack's desk, and said, heartily, "Well, Smith, my man, we're glad to see you back. Are you quite well again?"

"Quite well, thank you, sir," said Smith, rising to his feet, and flushing with pleasure at this unexpected attention from the head of the firm.

I felt quite as proud as he did, and still more so when presently Mr Barnacle arrived, and after first looking over his letters and glancing at his *Times*, touched the bell and said he wished to speak to Smith.

"They're going to make a partner of you," said Doubleday, mockingly, as he delivered the message. "Never mind; you won't forget your old servants, I know."

"Talking of partners," said Harris, of the Imports, over the screen, when Jack had gone in obedience to the summons, "we're to have the new chap here next week."

"What's his name?" asked Doubleday.

"Don't know. He's a nephew, I believe, of old Merrett's. The old boy told me the other day he was to come into my department to learn the business. He says I'm to teach him all I know, as he wants him to get on."

"That's pleasant. I suppose he's to be shoved over our heads, and tell us all what to do."

"Never fear," said Harris; "I sha'n't teach him too much. But the governor says he's a 'youth of good principles and fair attainments,' and thinks I shall like him."

Crow whistled.

"'Good principles and fair attainments!' That's a good un. I guess he's come to the wrong shop with those goods. Nobody deals in them here that *I* know of."

"Speak for yourself," retorted Doubleday, sententiously. "No one suspected you of going in for either, but Batchelor and I flatter ourselves we *are* a little in that line."

"Well, if you are," said Wallop, breaking in, "all I can say is, young Batchelor had better show his principle by stepping round to Shoddy's and paying his bill there, or he may 'attain' to something he doesn't expect."

"What do you mean?" I said. "I've only had the things a fortnight, and he said I needn't pay for them for a month."

"No doubt he did," said Wallop, not observing that Jack had by this time returned from the partners' room, and was seated once more at his desk. "No doubt he'd have let you go on tick for a twelve month, but when he finds you owe all round to the butcher and baker and candlestick maker, no wonder he gets a bit shy. Why, only yesterday—"

"Will you mind your own business?" I exclaimed, desperately, not knowing how to turn the talk.

"Only yesterday," continued Wallop, complacently, evidently noticing and enjoying my confusion, "he was asking me what I thought of your credit. Shoddy and I are chummy you know, Crow."

"Will you shut up and let me get on with my work?" I cried, despairingly.

"I told him," continued Wallop, deliberately, "I knew you only had twelve bob a week, and that, though you were a very nice boy, I would advise him to proceed with caution, as I knew for a fact—"

I sprang from my seat, determined, if I could not silence him by persuasion, I would do it by force. However, he adroitly fortified himself behind his desk, and proceeded, greatly to the amusement of every one but Jack, "I knew for a fact you owed a pot of money at the tuck shop—"

Here the speaker had to pause for the laughter which this announcement had elicited.

"And that the Twins had advanced you getting on for half-a-sov., besides—"

There was no escape. I sank down in my seat and let him go on as he liked.

I had the satisfaction of hearing a full, true, and particular account of my debts and delinquencies, which every one—I could not for the world tell how—seemed to know all about, and I had the still greater satisfaction of knowing that my friend Smith was hearing of my extravagances now for the first time, and not from my lips.

What would he think of me? How strange he must think it in me not to have trusted in him when he had confided to me his own far more important secret. I felt utterly ashamed. And yet, when I came to think of it, if I had acted foolishly, I had not committed a crime. Why should I be ashamed?

"I say," I began, when that evening we were walking home, rather moodily, side by side—"I say, you must have been astonished by what those fellows were saying to-day, Jack."

"Eh? Well, I couldn't quite make it out."

"They are always chaffing me about something," I said.

"Then it was all a make-up of Wallop's about what you owed?"

"Well, no—not exactly. The fact is, I do owe one or two little accounts."

"Do you?" said Jack. "It's a pity."

I did not quite like the tone in which he said this. It may have been that my conscience was not quite clear as to my own straightforwardness in this matter. I was not obliged to tell him everything, to be sure; but then, no more was I obliged to try to deceive him when I did tell him. At any rate, I felt a trifle irritated, and the rest of our walk proceeded in silence till we reached Style Street. Here we found Billy at his old sport, but evidently expecting us.

"Shine 'e boots, governor!" cried he, with a profound grin.

Jack put his foot upon the box, and the young artist fell-to work instantly.

"I'll stroll on," I said, out of humour, and anxious to be alone.

"All serene!" replied Jack, solemnly as usual.

By the time he turned up at Beadle Square I had somewhat recovered my equanimity, and the rest of the evening was spent in talking about indifferent matters, and avoiding all serious topics. Among other things, I told Jack of the expected addition to the staff at Hawk Street, which interested him greatly, especially as the new-comer was to work in the Import department.

"I hope he'll be a nice fellow," he said. "What's his name?"

"I don't know. He's a nephew of Merrett's, they say, and a good fellow. He's coming in as a clerk at first, but Harris says he's to be taken in as a partner in time."

"Then he's only a boy yet?"

"I suppose so—seventeen or eighteen."

Of course there was a considerable amount of speculation and curiosity as to the new arrival during the week which followed. I think most of us were a little jealous, and Doubleday was especially indignant at the fellow's meanness in being the governor's nephew.

"Of course, he'll peach about all we do," growled he, "and give his precious uncle a full, true, and particular account every evening of everything every one of us has been up to during the day. And the worst of it is, one can't even lick the beggar now and then, like any other fellow."

It undoubtedly was hard lines, and we all sympathised not a little with the chief clerk's grievance.

Our suspense was not protracted. On the appointed day Mr Merrett arrived, accompanied by a slender youth of about eighteen, at sight of whom Jack and I started as though we had been shot. The new-comer was no other than our former schoolfellow, Hawkesbury.

If a skeleton had walked into the office we could not have been more taken aback. Of all persons in the world, who would have guessed that this fellow whom we had last seen at Stonebridge House, and had never even heard of since should turn up now as the nephew of our employer, and as one of our own future chiefs at the office?

"Gentlemen," said Mr Merrett, "this is my nephew, Mr Hawkesbury. I trust you will all be good friends. Eh! what!"

This last exclamation was occasioned by Hawkesbury's advancing first to me and then to Smith, and shaking our hands, much to the surprise of everybody.

"These two gentlemen were at school with me, uncle," he said, by way of explanation. "It is quite a pleasant surprise to me to see them again."

"Very singular," said Mr Merrett; "I'm glad of it. You'll get on all the better. Harris; perhaps you will allow Mr Hawkesbury to assist you for a day or two, just while he is learning the work."

So saying, the senior partner vanished into his own room, leaving Hawkesbury in the midst of his new comrades.

I did not know whether to be glad or sorry. For myself, though I never quite liked Hawkesbury, I had always got on well with him, and been disposed to believe him a well-meaning fellow.

But on Jack Smith's account I felt very sorry, and not a little uneasy, for they had never "hit" it, and from what I could judge never would.

However, for the present at any rate, such apprehensions seemed to be groundless, for Hawkesbury, naturally a little ill at ease among so many strangers, appeared to be glad to claim the acquaintance of one of them, and sat down beside him and began to talk in quite a cordial manner.

"This is a pleasant surprise," he said again; "who would have thought of seeing you and Batchelor in Uncle Merrett's office?"

"We've been here several months," replied Jack, not quite as cordially, I could see, as his old schoolfellow.

"Have you? I'm afraid I shall never learn as much as you have," he said, with his old smile.

"Now then, young governor," said Harris, "when it's *quite* convenient to you we'll get to work. Don't put yourself out, pray; but if you can spare the time from your friend, I should like you to add up this column."

Hawkesbury looked a little astonished at this speech, but at once replied, with a smile, "You are Mr Harris, I suppose? I shall be glad to learn what you can teach me."

If Harris had expected to put the new-comer down by his witticisms he was sorely mistaken. Hawkesbury coolly seated himself at the desk beside him, and, with the air more of a man inspecting the work of another than of a learner seeking information, he examined the papers and books handed to him and catechised Harris as to their contents.

It was evident that he was fully aware from the beginning of his own position at the office, and that he wished us all to be aware of it also. He adopted a patronising air towards me and Jack and the other clerks, as if we were already in his employment and doing his work.

"A jolly cool hand," growled Doubleday to Crow, in an undertone most unusual to him when the principals were out of hearing. "I'm glad I'm not Harris."

"Now then, Harris," said Crow, "mind how you dot your p's and q's, old man—I mean your i's."

Hawkesbury looked up from his work and said, smiling, "I think Mr Harris dots his i's very well. What did you say is entered in this column, Harris?"

This was nothing short of a snub to Crow, who was quiet for the rest of the day.

After business, as Jack and I were proceeding to walk home, Hawkesbury came up and joined our party.

"Which way are you going?" inquired he. "I'll join you, if I may."

We could hardly say no, and yet we neither of us relished the offer. However, he did not appear to notice our reluctance, and walked along with us, conversing in his usual pleasant way.

"I hope we shall be good friends at the office," he said, after a long uncomfortable pause.

"I hope so," said I, who knew it was not much use to rely on Jack Smith to keep up the conversation.

"I dare say you know," said he, "that my uncle's idea is for me some day to join him and Mr Barnacle, but of course that depends on how I get on."

"Yes," said I, as there was a pause here.

"In any case I hope that won't make any difference between us old schoolfellows," he continued. "I hope not," again I replied.

"Where are you living in London?" he presently asked. I told him, and he thereupon proceeded to make further kind inquiries as to how we liked our quarters, if we had nice friends, what we did with ourselves, and so on. All of which it fell-to my lot to answer, as Jack Smith showed no inclination to assist me.

At length we reached the top of Style Street, where, as usual, the athletic Billy was at his sports. I really believe he spent the entire time he was not blacking boots in walking round and round his box on the palms of his hands with his feet up in the air.

At the sight of his patron he dropped promptly to attention.

"Well, Billy," said Smith, "are you ready for me?" Billy grinned all over his face, as he replied, "Yaas," and at once fell-to work.

Hawkesbury watched the incident with interest, not quite sure what to make of it, and rather taken aback to have our walk thus abruptly stopped.

"Old gal's bolted agin," observed Billy, in the middle of his task. "'Ave any of you blokes saw her?"

"No," said Smith, "when did she go?"

"Last night," said Billy. "She give me a dose fust, and when I came round, if she ain't sloped along of all my browns. She's a rum un."

Poor Billy, what a picture of his domestic life was this!

"Bless you, though," continued he, breathing hard on to the toes of Jack's boot, "she'll turn up. When she's done them browns she'll step round for more. Bless her old soul!"

"You ought to keep your money where she can't find it," suggested Jack.

"'Tain't no concern of yourn where I keep my brass. Oh, my eye, there's a nob!" cried he, suddenly perceiving Hawkesbury, who all this time had been looking on and listening in bewilderment. "Shin'e boots next, cap'n? Oh my, ain't he a topper?"

This last appeal was made to Jack, whose boots were now clean, and who, of course, did not reply.

"Who's your friend?" said Hawkesbury to him, with a smile.

"My friend's a shoeblack," drily replied Smith.

"Ah, a curious little fellow. Well, as I dare say you've plenty to say to one another, I'll be going. Good-bye," and he shook hands with us both and departed.

That evening Jack and I had a long and painful discussion about Hawkesbury. As usual, he had not a good word to say for him, while I, on the contrary, thought that at any rate he might be well-meaning.

"All I can say is," said Jack, "it wouldn't take much to make me leave Hawk Street now."

"Oh, don't say that!" I cried, miserable at the bare idea.

"Don't be afraid," said he, bitterly. "A convict's son can't get taken on anywhere, and I shall just have to stay where I am as long as there are the people at home to depend on me."

He said this in such a sad tone that my heart bled for him. Alas! there seemed to be anything but happy days in store for my friend Smith.

Chapter Twenty
How I served my Friend Smith anything but a Good Turn

A week sufficed to put Hawkesbury quite at his ease at Hawk Street. And it sufficed also to reconcile most of the clerks to the new arrival. For Hawkesbury, although he proved plainly he was aware of his position and prospects, showed no inclination to be stiff or unfriendly with his new associates. On the contrary, he took a good deal of trouble to make himself agreeable, and succeeded so well that in less than a week Doubleday pronounced him "not such a cad as he might be," which was very great praise from him.

Jack Smith, however, was irreconcilable. He seemed to have an instinctive dislike to his old schoolfellow, and resented the least approach on his part to friendliness. It was in vain I argued with him and urged him.

"I'm sure he's civil enough," I said.

"I'm glad to hear it."

"Why ever are you so down on him? I'm sure he would only be too glad to be friendly."

"I don't like him," said Jack.

"At any rate," said I, "you need not take so much trouble to make an enemy of him. Some day you may be sorry for it."

Jack did not answer, and I saw it was no use pursuing the unpleasant topic. But I was vexed with him. Why should he consider himself better than all of us who had accepted the proffered friendship of our new comrade?

"Young Batch," said Doubleday one morning about a week after Hawkesbury's arrival, "come up to my diggings this evening. The other fellows are coming up, and the new boss too."

This was rather an awkward question, as since Jack's return I had not gone out, and I imagined every one would conclude it was no use inviting me without him.

"I know what you're going to say," said Doubleday, noticing my hesitation. "You'll ask Bull's-eye's leave, and then tell me. Here, Bull's-eye, Smith—whatever your name is—I want young Batch to come up to supper with me this evening, and like a dutiful boy he says he can't come till you give him leave. What do you say?"

"Don't be an ass, Doubleday!" I cried, quite ashamed and confused to stand by and hear Smith thus appealed to. "I—I'm afraid I can't come this evening."

"Previous engagement?" said Doubleday, with a wink.

"No," I said; "I'm going for a walk with Smith."

"I'm going to stay here late to-night," said Jack, quietly, "I want to catch up some work." I wished I knew what he meant by it. "All serene! then the young 'un can come to us, can't he?" said Doubleday.

"Thanks," said I, not appearing to notice that the question was addressed to Smith.

My decision appeared to afford much amusement to the other clerks.

"Landed at last!" said Doubleday, mopping his face with his handkerchief and puffing like a man who had just gone through some great exertion.

I did not join in the laughter that followed, and spent the rest of the day rather uncomfortably. In the evening I left Jack at his desk.

"I hope you don't mind my going," I said. He looked up, half vexed, half astonished. "What do you mean?" he replied. "Surely it's nothing to do with me?"

"Oh, I know. But I wouldn't care to do it if you didn't like it. Besides, I feel rather low going when you're not asked too."

"I shouldn't go if I was asked," replied Jack.

"Why not?" I inquired.

"I've something better to do with my time and my money than that sort of thing," he replied, quietly.

I went up to Doubleday's that evening more uneasy in my mind than I had been for a long time. I was angry with him for asking me; I was angry with myself for going; and I was angry with Smith because I felt his rebuke was a just one.

"Hullo, young un!" cried my host as I entered his now familiar lodgings; "all waiting for you. Why, how glum you look! Has the Lantern been lecturing you? or have you been having a dose of cold eel-pie on the road? or what? Come on. You know all these fellows. By the way, my boy, glorious news for you! Don't know what we've all done to deserve it, upon my honour, but Abel here has knocked out one of his front teeth, so there'll be no more trouble about spotting him now."

Abel grinned and exhibited the gap in his jaw which had called forth this song of thankfulness from our host.

"How ever did you do it?" I asked, glad to turn the conversation from myself.

"Ran against a lamp-post," replied the mutilated Twin.

This simple explanation caused much merriment, for every one chose to believe that Abel had been intoxicated at the time, and as Abel himself joined in the laugh, it was easy to see that if that had been the cause of the accident, neither he nor any one else would be greatly ashamed of it.

"What would Jack think?" I could not help saying to myself.

Hawkesbury walked over to where I was and shook hands. "I'm glad you've come," said he, sweetly smiling; "I was afraid you would be prevented."

"No, I'd nothing to prevent me," replied I, colouring up.

"I fancied you would prefer staying with your friend Smith, or that he might not like you to come."

"Smith is working late at the office to-night," I replied, shortly.

"Now you fellows!" cried Doubleday, "if you want any grub, sit down. Batch, old man, will you take that end of the table? you're used to lobsters, I know."

Once more I blushed to the roots of my hair, as I obeyed in as unconcerned a manner as I could.

"What's the joke about the lobster?" asked Hawkesbury, innocently.

I wished the ground would open and swallow me. Was that unlucky lobster, then, to haunt me all the days of my life?

"There was no joke about it, I can tell you that!" said Whipcord, with a significant grimace; "was there, Daly?"

"Well, I don't know," said Daly, looking mysterious; "there was one rather good joke about it, if what I was told is true."

"What's that?" demanded the company.

"It was paid for!"

Don't you pity me, reader? I was obliged to join in the laugh, and appear to enjoy it.

"They're rather down on you," said Hawkesbury, amiably.

"Oh, they like their little joke," said I.

"So they do—who's got the butter?" said Doubleday—"so does everybody—hang it, the milk's burnt; don't you taste it burnt, Field-Marshal? I'll give my old woman notice—so does everybody, except—the muffins, please, Crow—except your precious friend Smith. I don't suppose he ever enjoyed a joke in his life now, or—help yourself, Hawkesbury—or saw one either, for the matter of that, notwithstanding his bull's-eyes."

"I don't know," said I, relieved again to divert the talk from myself, and glad at the same time to put in a mild word for my friend, "I think Smith has a good deal of fun in him."

"I'd like to know where he keeps it," said Crow; "I never saw it."

"Oh! I did," said Hawkesbury, "at school. He was a very amusing fellow at school, wasn't he, Batchelor? Did Batchelor ever tell you of the great rebellion that he and Smith got up there?"

I had not told the story, and was there and then called upon to do so—which I did, much to the gratification of the company.

"Why don't you bring this mysterious Mr Smith down to show to us one evening?" asked Whipcord. "We're always hearing about him. I'd like to see him, wouldn't you, Twins?"

"Very," replied Abel, who evidently had been thinking of something else.

"I'm not sure," said I, "whether he'd come out. I don't think he cares much about visiting."

"I hope he doesn't think it's wrong to visit," said the Field-Marshal.

"No, not that," said I, sorry I had embarked on the subject; "but somehow he doesn't get on, I think, in company."

"I should rather say he doesn't!" said Crow—"at any rate, at Hawk Street, for a more stuck-up, disagreeable, self-righteous prig I never saw."

"I think," said Hawkesbury, mildly, "you judge him rather hardly, Crow. Some of us thought the same at school; but I really think he means well."

"Yes," said I, ready to follow up this lead, "his manner's against him, perhaps, but he's a very good fellow at bottom."

"Besides," said Hawkesbury, "he really has had great disadvantages. He has no friend at all in London, except Batchelor."

This was flattering, certainly, and naturally enough I looked sheepish.

"I beg your pardon," said Hawkesbury, suddenly perceiving his error, "I meant that he has very few friends at all; isn't that so, Batchelor?"

"Yes," said I, "very few."

"Wasn't he in a grocer's shop, or some place of the kind, before he came to us?" asked Doubleday.

"Yes," I answered.

"No wonder he's a rough lot," said Whipcord. "I should have thought his governor might have done better for him than that."

"But," I said, feeling flurried by all this, and hardly knowing what I said, "he hasn't got a father—that is—I mean—"

"What do you mean?" asked Flanagan.

I was in a dreadful plight. Every one must have seen by my confusion that I was in a fix, and how was I to get out of it?

"Eh, what about his father?" demanded Doubleday.

"Oh," said I, "he's living abroad."

"Where, Botany Bay?" asked Daly, with a laugh.

I felt my face grow scarlet, and my whole manner utterly confused and guilty-looking, as I pretended not to hear the question, and turned to speak to Crow about some other matter. But my assailants were too quick for me. My manner had roused their curiosity and excited their suspicions, and I was not to be let off.

"Eh? Is that where he resides?" again demanded Daly.

"I really can't say where he lives," I replied, abruptly, and in a tone so unlike my ordinary voice that I hardly recognised it myself.

I was conscious of a startled look on the faces of one or two of the company as I said this, and of a low whistle from Crow.

What had I done?

"I don't think," said Hawkesbury, with his usual smile, "your friend Smith would be grateful to you, Batchelor, for letting the cat out of the bag like this."

"What cat?" I exclaimed, in an agitated voice. "You are all mistaken, indeed you are. Smith's father is not a—I mean he's merely away for his health, I assure you."

"Rather a lingering illness," drily replied the Field-marshal, amid general laughter, "if it's kept him abroad all these years."

"If you will take my advice, Batchelor," said Hawkesbury, "you'll be careful how you tell everybody a thing like this. It's not a pleasant sort of thing to be known of a fellow."

"Indeed, indeed," I cried once more, almost beside myself with terror and rage, "you're all wrong. I wish I'd said nothing about it. Won't you believe me?"

"Delighted," said Whipcord, who with every one else had been enjoying my dismay, and laughing at my efforts to extricate myself. "You say Smith's governor is a—"

"No—it's false. I was telling a lie!" I cried, in tones of misery which any ordinary mortal would have pitied. "I don't know what he is. I never heard of him. Indeed, indeed, I was only speaking in fun."

Thus wildly did I hope by a shield of lies to hide the secret which I had—by my manner more than my words—betrayed.

"I'm afraid, Batchelor," said Hawkesbury, with a grave but sweet smile, "you either are not telling quite the truth, or you are speaking in fun about a very serious matter."

"Oh yes, you're right," I cried; "I've been telling lies; upon my honour I have."

"Upon his honour he's been telling lies," said Daly. "The fellow *will* have his joke. Never saw such a joker in all my days."

I would fain have rushed from the place, but I dared not. Every word I said involved me deeper, and yet I could not leave them all like this without one effort at least either to recover my secret—Jack's secret—or else to appeal to their confidence and generosity.

It was evident they were not disposed to believe anything I told them, except the one hideous fact. And that, though I had not uttered it in so many words, every one believed from my lips as if I had been inspired.

I sat in abject misery while the meal lasted, listening to the brutal jests made at the cost of my absent friend, and knowing that I was responsible for them all.

Directly supper was over I appealed to Doubleday.

"I do hope you won't say anything about this at the office, Doubleday," I said, imploringly. "It would be such a dreadful thing for it to get out."

"Then it is true?" demanded Doubleday.

"No—that is—I—I—don't know," responded I, "but oh! don't say anything about it."

"Bless me, if you don't know," said he, "why do you make such a fuss? Take my advice, young un, and don't say any more about it to any one. You've done very well so far, and if you want the fellows to forget all about it you'd better not remind them of it so much."

"But, Doubleday," I implored once more, "out of friendship for me—"

"Out of friendship for you let me offer you a cigar," said Doubleday. "Now you fellows, what's it to be—whist, nap, poker, or what?"

I turned in despair to Hawkesbury.

"Please, Hawkesbury," I said, "promise to say nothing about it at the office. I would be so grateful if you would."

"Then," said Hawkesbury, asking the same question as Doubleday had just asked, "it is true?"

I dared not say "Yes," and to say "No" would, I knew, be useless.

"Oh, please don't ask me," I said, only "promise—do, Hawkesbury."

Hawkesbury smiled most sweetly.

"Really," he said, "one would think it was such a nice subject that a fellow would like to talk about it!"

"Then you won't!" I cried, ready to jump at the least encouragement; "oh, thanks, Hawkesbury!"

This was the only comfort I could get. Crow laughed at me when I appealed to him; and the other fellows reminded me that as they had not the pleasure of knowing my pet gaol-bird they were afraid they couldn't tell him what I had done, much as they would like.

Flanagan alone treated it seriously.

"Batchelor," said he, "I never believed you were such a fool. Can't you see you're only making things worse by your fuss? Why can't you hold your tongue? Smith has little enough to thank you for as it is."

He had indeed! As I walked home that evening, I felt as if I would never dare to look him in the face again.

It was late when I reached Beadle Square. Jack had returned before me, and was fast asleep in bed. A candle burned beside him, and on the counterpane, as if dropped from his hand, lay a book—a Roman History.

I groaned as I looked at him, and envied him his quiet sleep, the reward of honest work and a good conscience. I crept into bed that night as silently as I could, for fear of waking him.

The next few days I was on thorns. I dreaded to be alone with Jack, and still more dreaded to be by when the fellows were—now an ordinary pastime—chaffing him at the office. It was like living on a volcano which might at any moment explode. However, the days went on, and my fears did not come to pass. The fellows had either forgotten all about it, or, more likely, their sense of honour prevented them from making it known. I was devoutly thankful, of course, and by every means in my power endeavoured to show it. I made myself as agreeable as possible to my comrades, and bore all their chaff and persecution with the utmost good-humour, and went out of my way to secure and retain their good graces.

Of course I could not do this without in a way defying Jack's influence. Though he had never once taken me to task in so many words, I knew well enough he considered I was wasting my time and money in this perpetual round of festivities. But I had to take the risk of that. After all, I was playing to shield him. If he only knew all, he would be grateful to me, I reflected, rather than offended.

He could not help noticing my altered manner, and of course put it down to anything but its true cause. He thought I was offended with him for not encouraging my extravagances, and that the great intimacy with Doubleday and Hawkesbury and Crow was meant to show him that I was independent of him.

However, he made one brave effort to pull me up.

"Fred," said he, thoughtfully, one evening, as we walked home—"Fred, what are you going to do about your debts?"

"Oh, pay them some day, I suppose," I said, shortly.

"When will that be?" he continued, quietly, not noticing my manner.

"I really can't say," I replied, not liking to be thus questioned.

"Do you know how much you owe?" he asked.

"Really, Jack, you take a great interest in my debts!"

"I do," he replied, solemnly, and with the air of a fellow who had made up his mind to go through with an unpleasant duty.

"Well," I said, warming up rather, "I fancy I can look after them quite as well by myself."

"I'm afraid I am offending you," said Jack, looking straight at me, "but I don't think you do look after them properly."

"What do you mean?" I demanded.

"I mean," said Jack, with his arm still in mine, "that you are head over ears in debt, and that, instead of paying off, you are spending your money in other ways. And I don't think it's right, Fred."

"Upon my word, Jack," I said, "it's quite new for you to lecture me like this, and I don't like it. What business is it of yours, I should like to know?"

"You are my friend," he said, quietly.

I drew my arm roughly from his.

"If you are mine," said I, "when I want your advice I'll ask it."

He looked at me a moment doubtfully with his big eyes. Then he said, "I was afraid of this; we never quarrelled before, Fred."

"And we shouldn't quarrel now," I cried, "if you'd mind your own business."

"It is my business," he persisted—doggedly, as I thought.

"What's your business?" I demanded, with rising rage.

"To beg you not to be a fool," he replied, steadily.

My temper had already gone. My self-control now deserted me as I stopped abruptly, and turned to him.

"Your business!" I exclaimed, bitterly.

"Yes, Fred, my business," he said, quietly, with a touch of sadness in his tone.

"Then let me tell you," I exclaimed, forgetting everything but my resentment, "I don't intend to be told my duty *by you of all people!*"

It was enough. He knew the meaning of those cowardly words. His face turned suddenly pale, and his eyes dropped, as with a half-groan he started to walk slowly on.

I would have given worlds to recall the words—worlds to be able to seize his arm and beg his forgiveness. But my wicked vanity kept me back, and I let him go on alone. Then I followed. It was the first of many, many sad, solitary walks for me.

Chapter Twenty One
How a Door closed between my Friend Smith and me

If any one had told me a month before that I should quarrel with my friend Smith, I should have laughed at the bare idea. But now the impossible thing had happened.

That night as I lay awake in my bed I felt that I had not a friend in the world. I had wounded, in the cruellest way, the only true friend I ever had, and now I was to suffer for it. The words had come hastily and thoughtlessly, but they had come; and Jack, I knew, regarded me as a coward and a brute.

The next day we scarcely spoke a word to one another, and when we did it was in so constrained a manner that it would have been more comfortable had we remained silent. We walked to and from the office by separate ways, and during the mid-day half-hour we lunched for the first time at different eating-houses.

I longed to explain—to beg his pardon. But he was so stiff and distant in his manner that I could not venture to approach him. Once I did try, but he saw me coming and, I fancied, turned on his heel before I got up.

What was I to do? If this was to last, I should be miserable for ever. Yet how could it end? Would I write him a letter, or would I get some one to plead my cause for me? Or would I let him see how wretched I was, and work on his feelings that way? It was all my fault, I knew. Yet he might have come out a little and made a reconciliation easy. Surely if he had really been my friend, thought I, he would not be so quick to cast me off, and judge me by one or two hasty words!

What between an evil conscience, vexation, and disappointment, I was that day about the most miserable fellow alive. The fellows at the office all noticed and added to my discomfort by ostentatiously condoling with me.

"Poor old chap!" said Doubleday; "he's been letting you have it, has he? Awful shame."

"As if a fellow mayn't get screwed without his interfering," laughed Crow.

"It's nothing of the sort," said I, as usual taking in earnest what was meant as a jest; "I was never screwed."

Crow's only answer was a whistle, which greatly amused all the others.

"Never mind," said Doubleday, "come along with us to-night, old man; we've got a little spree on, haven't we, Crow? We're going to get tea and shrimps at the Magpie, and then going in a body to the Serio-Comics, and finish up with a supper somewhere or other. Going to make a regular night of it. Come along."

"I don't want to," I said; "besides, I can't afford it."

"Afford your great-grandmother! Why, a fellow who can entertain the whole lot of us as you did can't be so very hard up, can he, Wallop? So come, none of your gammon. You're coming with us to-night, my boy, and old Bull's-eye can sit and scowl at himself in the looking-glass if he likes."

I went with them, glad enough to get anywhere out of Jack's sight. We had a "rollicking evening," as the fellows called it; which meant that after a noisy and extravagant tea at the Magpie we adjourned in a body to the performance, where we made quite as much noise as the rest of the audience put together, after which we finished up with a fish supper of Doubleday's ordering, at a restaurant, the bill for which came to two shillings a head.

I was not in a condition to enjoy myself. The thought of Jack haunted me all the evening and made me miserable. I fancied him walking back from Hawk Street alone. He would stop to talk to Billy, I knew, and then he would go on to Beadle Square and bury himself in his book till bedtime. Would he ever think of me? Why, even the little shoeblack was more to him now than I was.

I got home late—so late that Mrs Nash protested angrily, and threatened to stand my irregularities no longer. Jack was not asleep when I entered the room, but at sight of me he turned over in his bed and drew the clothes round him. I was angry and miserable and made no attempt to speak to him. But I could not sleep. The spirit seemed to have gone out of my life in London, and I dreaded to-morrow as much as ever I had hated to-day.

I rose early in the morning, and after a hurried breakfast started from the house before Jack came down. At least I could take refuge in my work at the office.

I had the place to myself for quite half an hour, when Hawkesbury arrived.

"Well, Batchelor," said he, "you are industrious. I thought I should be first to-day, but you are before me. Where's your friend Smith?"

"I don't know," I said, hurriedly.

"I'm afraid," said Hawkesbury, with his sweet smile, "you and Smith haven't been getting on well lately. I noticed yesterday you never spoke to one another."

"I'm not obliged to speak to him," I growled.

"Certainly not. In fact I think it's very kind indeed of you to make him your friend under the circumstances."

Of course I knew what these last words meant. A day or two ago they would have terrified me; but now in my mortified state of mind they didn't even offend me.

"Jack and I always got on well," I said, "until he began to interfere with my affairs. I didn't like that."

"Of course not; nobody does. But then you know he has always been a sort of guardian to you."

"He was never anything of the sort," I retorted.

"Well," said Hawkesbury, pleasantly, but with a touch of melancholy in his voice, "I never like to see old friends fall out. Would you like me to speak to him and try to make it up?"

"Certainly not," I exclaimed. "If I want it, I can do that myself."

"What can he do himself?" cried Doubleday, entering at this moment with Crow and Wallop, and one or two others of last night's party. "Was the young un saying he could find his way home by himself after that supper last night, eh? My eye, that's a good 'un, isn't it, Crow?"

"Nice gratitude," cried Crow, "after our carrying him home and propping him up against his own front door."

"I wonder what his friend Smith thought of it?" said Wallop; "he must have been shocked."

"When you fellows have done," I said, who had felt bound to submit to all this with the best grace I could, "I'll get on with my work."

"What a joker the fellow is!" said Doubleday. "One would think he was always at his work."

"I want to work now," I said. "I do indeed."

"Do you indeed?" said Doubleday, mocking my tones and making a low bow.

"Since when did you take a fancy for hard labour?"

"Hard labour?"

At that moment the door opened and Jack Smith entered.

I could notice the quick start he gave as the words fell suddenly on his ear. He gave one scared look round the office, and then went quietly to his desk.

At the sight of him there was an abrupt silence amongst us. Crow and Wallop stopped short in the middle of their exclamation. Hawkesbury and I buried ourselves in our work, and Doubleday, standing before the fire, began to whistle softly.

Could anything have happened more awkwardly and suspiciously? Jack must certainly believe we were all talking about him, and the ill-fated word he had overheard would naturally suggest to him—

"When you've done laughing, young Batchelor," said Doubleday, stopping short in his whistling, "we'll get to work."

This unexpected remark, which of course was a delicate way of calling everybody's attention to my rueful countenance, served to put all the rest of the company except myself at their ease, and Mr Barnacle's entrance a minute afterwards put an end for the time to any further conversation.

But the day dragged on miserably. What must Jack think of me? He would be sure to believe the worst of me, and it was impossible for me to explain.

"After all," I thought, "if he does choose to form wrong conclusions, why should I afflict myself? No one was even speaking of him when he entered the office. What business of mine is it to put him right?"

And then, as usual, I forgot all about the injury I had done him, all my treachery, all my meanness, and instead felt rather aggrieved, and persuaded myself it was I, not he, who was the injured person.

At dinner-time I ostentatiously went out arm-in-arm with Hawkesbury, and when on returning I met Smith on the stairs I brushed past him as if I had not seen him.

That afternoon I was called upon unexpectedly to go down to the docks to see after the shipment of some goods. I was relieved to have the excuse for being alone and getting away from the unpleasant surroundings of Hawk Street.

It was late in the afternoon when I returned, so late that I almost expected the fellows would some of them have left for the day. But as I entered the office I noticed they were all there, and became aware that something unusual was taking place. From the loud tones of the speakers I concluded the partners had left for the day.

At first I could not tell whether it was a joke or a quarrel that was being enacted; but it soon began to dawn on me. Jack Smith was being set on by the others.

What his offence had been I could not quite gather, though I believe it consisted in his insisting on using the ledger he was at work on till the actual hour for ceasing work arrived, while Harris, who was responsible for the locking-up of the books, and who wanted this evening to go half an hour earlier, was demanding that he should give it up now.

"I must finish these accounts to-night," said Jack.

"I tell you I'm not going to be kept here half an hour just to please you," replied Harris.

"We're not supposed to stop work till seven," said Jack; "that's the time we always work to when Mr Barnacle is here. And it's only half-past six now."

"What business of yours is it when we're supposed to work to, Mr Prig?" demanded Harris, savagely. "You're under my orders here, and you'll do what I tell you."

"I'm under Mr Barnacle's orders," said Jack, going on with his writing.

"You mean to say you're not going to do what I tell you?" asked Harris, in a rage.

"I'm going to do what's right—that's all," said Smith, quietly.

"Right! You humbug! You're a nice respectable fellow to talk about right to us, Mr Gaol-bird! As if we didn't know who you are! You son of a thief and swindler! Right, indeed! We don't want to hear about right from you!"

Jack gave one startled, scared, upward look as he spoke; but it was turned not to the speaker, but to me. I shall never forget that look. I could have sunk into the earth with shame and misery as I encountered it.

He closed the ledger, and with white face and quivering lips took his hat and walked silently from the office.

To me his manner was more terrible than if he had broken out into torrents of passion and abuse. At the sight of his face that moment my treachery and sin appeared suddenly in their true light before my eyes. I had been false to my best friend, and more than false.

Who could tell if I had not ruined him? Vain and selfish fool that I had been! Always thinking what others would think of me, and never how best I could help him in his gallant struggle against his evil destiny.

I rushed wildly from the office after him, and overtook him on the stairs.

"Oh, Jack," I cried, "it really wasn't my—oh! I'm so dreadfully sorry, Jack! If you'll only let me explain, I can—"

He was gone. The door shut-to suddenly in my face, leaving me alone with my misery, and shutting out my one hope of recovering my only friend.

I returned miserable to the office—miserable and savage. Though I knew I had only myself to blame for what had happened, I was fain to vent my anger on the cowardly set who had used my secret against my friend. But when I tried to speak the words would not come. I locked up my desk dejectedly, and without a word to any one, and heedless of the looks and titters that followed me, walked from the place.

Half way down the street I became aware of a footstep following hurriedly, as if to overtake me. Could it be Jack? Was there yet a chance? No, it was Hawkesbury.

"Oh, Batchelor," he said, "I am so sorry. It's most unfortunate the way it came out, isn't it?"

I made no answer, and drew my arm out of his.

"Harris is such a short-tempered fellow," he went on, not noticing my manner, "but I never thought he would go as far as he did. I assure you, Batchelor, when I heard it, I felt quite as sorry as you did."

"I should like to know who told Harris about it," I said. "I didn't."

"Didn't you? Wasn't he there that evening you told all the rest of us? To be sure he wasn't. He must have heard the others speaking about it."

"They all promised—that is, I begged them all—not to tell any one," I said, with a groan.

"Yes, I remember your asking me that evening. It's a great shame if the fellows have told Harris. But he may have heard some other way."

"How could he?" said I.

"Well, I suppose it was all in the papers at the time," said Hawkesbury.

"Harris would hardly be in the habit of reading newspapers thirteen or fourteen years old," I said, bitterly.

"Was it so long ago as that?" said Hawkesbury. "No, it hardly does seem likely. Somebody must have told him."

"It was a blackguard thing of him to do," I said, "and I'll take good care never to speak to him again."

"Well, you'd be quite justified in cutting him dead," replied Hawkesbury. "I'd do the same if he'd done as much to a friend of mine."

I did not reply to this. After all, had Harris been much more to blame than I had been in the first instance?

"Well," said Hawkesbury, "I hope it will soon blow over. One never likes unpleasant things like this coming up. You must tell Smith how angry I am with Harris."

"I don't suppose Smith will ever speak to me again," I said.

"Really? Oh, I hope it's not so bad as that. After all, you know," said Hawkesbury, "it would have been much more straightforward of him to tell the fellows what he was at first. They don't like being taken by surprise in a matter like this. I really don't see that *he* has so much to complain of."

"But it was so low of Harris to fling it in his teeth like that," I said.

"Well, yes, it was," said Hawkesbury; "but it was not as bad as if he had said something about him that wasn't true. Well, good-night, Batchelor. I hope it will be all right in time."

I was not much comforted by this conversation; and yet I was not altogether displeased to find that Hawkesbury agreed with me in condemning Harris's conduct, and his last argument, though it took away nothing from my unkindness, certainly did strike me. However unpleasant and cruel Jack's treatment had been, one must remember that the story told about him was true. Yes, it was a great consolation to feel that, whatever else had happened, no one had told a lie!

As I passed the top of Style Street, meditating on these things, I became aware that Billy was striding across my path with a face full of grimy concern.

"I say, master," he cried, "where's t'other bloke?"

"I don't know," I said, walking on.

"What, ain't you saw him?" he demanded, trotting along, blacking-brush in hand, by my side.

"Yes—go away, do you hear? I don't want you walking beside me."

"That there clock," said Billy, pointing up to a clock just over his usual place of business—"that there clock's been gone seving a lump, and he ain't been."

"It's nothing to do with me," I cried angrily. "Come, get away, unless you want your ears boxed."

"Won't he's boots be in a muck, though," continued the boy, wholly regardless of my wrath, "without no shine."

"Do you hear what I say?" cried I, stopping short threateningly.

Billy slunk off more disconsolately than I had ever seen him, leaving me to pursue my way unmolested.

I do not know where I wandered to that evening, or what I thought of as I walked. My mind was too confused and miserable to take in anything clearly, except that I had lost my friend.

Fellows passed me arm-in-arm, in earnest talk or with beaming faces, and only reminded me of what I had lost. Memories of the past crowded in upon me—of Stonebridge House, where his friendship had been my one comfort and hope; of our early days in London, when it seemed as if, with one another for company, nothing could come amiss, and no hardship could be quite intolerable; of his illness and absence, and my gradual yielding to frivolity and extravagance; then of his return and confidence in me. Would that he had never told me that wretched secret! If he had only known to whom he was telling it, to what a pitiful, weak, vain nature he was confiding it, he would have bitten his tongue off before he did it, and I should have yet been comparatively happy!

But the evil was done now, and what power on earth could undo it?

I slunk home to Beadle Square when I imagined every one else would be in bed.

Mrs Nash met me at the door.

"Your friend Smith's gone," she said.

"Gone!" I exclaimed. "Where?"

"How should I know? He paid his bill and took off his traps two hours ago, and says he's not coming back!"

You may guess, reader, whether I slept that night.

Chapter Twenty Two
How I tried to forget my Friend Smith, and failed

When I rose next morning I was nearly ill with misery and remorse. The thought of Jack had haunted me all night long. I entertained all sorts of forebodings as to what had become of him and what was to be the result of my treachery to him. I pictured him gone forth alone and friendless into the world, hoping to lose himself in London, giving up all hope of a successful career, with his name gone and his prospects blighted, and all my fault. Poor Jack! I might never see him again, never even hear of him again!

As to hearing of him, however, I soon found that in one sense I was likely to hear a good deal of him, now he was gone from Beadle Square. Horncastle and his particular friends appeared that morning at breakfast in a state of the greatest jubilation.

"Well, that's what I call a jolly good riddance of bad rubbish," Horncastle was saying as I entered the room. "I thought we'd make the place too hot for him at last!"

"Yes, it was a job, though, to get rid of him."

"Bless you," said Horncastle, with the air of a hero, "a man doesn't like hurting a fellow's feelings, you know, or we could have told him straight off he was a beast. It was much better to let him see we didn't fancy him, and let him clear out of his own accord."

"Yes, much better," answered a toady friend; "you managed it very well, Horn, so you did."

"You see, when a fellow's a sneak and a cad he's sure to be uncomfortable among a lot of gentlemen," said Horncastle, by way of enlarging on the interesting topic.

If I had not been so miserable I should have felt amused at this edifying conversation. As it was I was rather tempted to break into it more than once, but I remembered with a pang that, though I had a friend to stand up for yesterday, I had none to-day.

"I suppose now he's gone," sneered some one of the same set, "his precious chum will be going too."

"I don't know," said Horncastle, pretending not to be aware that I was in the room. "Batchelor's got some good points about him, and now the other's gone he might improve if he stayed with us."

"Besides, he's got his lodgings paid for him, so I've heard," said another.

"Yes, there's something in that. And on the whole he's a pretty decent—hullo, Batchelor, I never knew you were here. So you've lost your chum, eh?"

"You seem to know all about it," I growled, by no means won over by the vague compliments bestowed on me.

"Oh, yes, I know all about it," cried Horncastle, mounting his high horse, and offended at my tones. "We were too respectable for him here. But we ain't going into mourning for him. And if you go too we shan't blub. Shall we, you fellows?"

"Not exactly," replied the chorus, with much laughter.

I ate a miserable breakfast, and sallied forth disconsolately to my now solitary walk to the office.

Would Jack Smith turn up at Hawk Street? That was a question which exercised not only me but the other fellows who had witnessed yesterday's catastrophe.

I hardly knew what to hope for. If he did come, I didn't know what I should do, or how I should meet him. If he did not come, then I should know I had driven him not only from me but from his very prospects in life.

The general impression at Hawk Street was that he would not come. Doubleday and Harris had a bet of a shilling on the event.

"If he does turn up," said Crow, "it'll show he means to brazen it out before us all."

"Then you may be sure he'll come," said Wallop, "It was all very well when we weren't supposed to know," said Harris, "but now it's all out he doesn't expect us to treat him like an ordinary gentleman."

"It's certainly not anything to be proud of," remarked Hawkesbury, pleasantly; "but—"

At that moment the door opened and Smith entered—solemn as ever, and to all appearances perfectly composed and unconscious of the curiosity his appearance occasioned.

But I who watched him narrowly could detect a quick, doubtful glance round as he entered and took his usual place.

He never looked at me. On the contrary, he appeared to guess where I was, and purposely avoided turning in that direction.

The fellows were evidently perplexed, and not quite pleased.

"You've won your bet," said Harris across the screen to Doubleday.

"Never mind, you've got your man," replied Doubleday.

"He seems awfully pleased with himself," said Crow.

"I wish my governor was a yellow-jacket, so I do," growled Wallop, "then I could hold up my head like a gentleman. But he's only a merchant!"

All this was said in a loud voice, evidently for the benefit of Smith. He, however, heeded it not, but quietly took his pen and blotting-paper from his desk, and turning to Harris said, "I want that ledger to go on with, if you'll unlock the safe, please."

Harris stared in astonishment. It had passed his comprehension how the fellow could have the face to show up at the office at all, but for him to have the audacity to address a fellow-clerk, and that fellow-clerk Harris, of all people, seemed fairly to stun that worthy.

It took him fully half a minute to recover his speech. Then he stammered out in white heat, "Eh? Do you know who you're speaking to—you cad?"

"I'm speaking to you," said Smith, calmly.

"Then what do you mean by it, you son of a thief?" demanded Harris. "When I want you to speak to me I'll ask you—there."

Smith looked up with a slight flush on his face.

"You seem to want to quarrel," he said. "I don't intend to quarrel. I'll wait till you choose to unlock the safe."

This mild reply seemed to exasperate Harris far more than an angry retort would have done. He was naturally short-tempered, and when conscious that he was being worsted in an argument before his fellow-clerks he was always particularly savage.

He walked up to Smith and demanded furiously, "Didn't I tell you I'm not going to be spoken to by a low gaol-bird like you? If you don't hold your tongue I'll give you such a thrashing as will make you remember it."

"Come now, you fellows," said Doubleday, "if you must have a row, keep it to yourselves. The governor will be here in a second. Plenty of time for a shindy in the evening."

Even this interposition failed to put the irate Harris off his purpose.

Seizing a ruler, he struck Smith a blow on the shoulder with it that resounded all through the office.

"There, you cowardly dog, take that for daring to speak to a gentleman!"

Smith sprang to his feet, his face flushed with sudden pain and anger. At the same moment I, who had been a silent and miserable spectator of the scene hitherto, could bear it no longer, and rushed forward to help my old friend. He had clenched his fist and seemed about to return the blow, when, catching sight of me, his face changed suddenly to one of misery and scorn, as letting fall his arm he dropped again on to his seat heedless of the second blow of his cowardly assailant.

Was ever misfortune like mine? Not only had I done my friend the worst injury one fellow could do to another, but at the very moment when, at least, he was about to show his comrades that all spirit had not been crushed out of him, I had by my hateful presence baulked him of his purpose, and made him appear before every one a coward!

And what a scorn his must be when he would rather submit tamely to a cowardly blow than have me suppose that for a moment anything *I* could do would be of service to him!

However, Mr Merrett's arrival put an end to further altercation for the present, and during the next few hours no one would have guessed what fires were smouldering under the peaceful surface of the Hawk Street counting-house.

As the evening approached I became more and more nervous and restless. For, come what would of it, I had determined I *would* speak to Jack Smith.

He seemed to guess my intention, for he delayed leaving the office unusually long, in the hope that I would leave before him. At last, however, when it seemed probable we should be left alone together in the counting-house, he took his hat and hurriedly left the office. I followed him, but so stealthily and nervously that I might have been a highwayman dogging his victim, rather than a friend trying to overtake a friend.

Despite all my caution, he soon became aware of my intention. At first with a half-glance back he started to walk rapidly away, but then, seeing that I still followed, he stopped short and waited till I came up with him.

Already I was repenting of my determination, and this attitude of his quite disheartened me.

Still I could not draw back now — speak to him I must.

"Oh, Jack," I cried, as I came up. "It really wasn't my fault—indeed it wasn't. I only—"

He put up his hand to stop me and said, his eyes blazing with indignation as he did so, "You've been a liar and a coward!"

He may have been right. He was right! But the words were ill-judged and rash. I had followed him ready to do anything to show my contrition, ready to make any atonement in my power for the wrong I had done him. One gentle word from him, one encouraging look, would have made the task easy. But this angry taunt, deserved as it was—nay, just because it was so fully deserved—stirred up in me a sudden sense of disappointment and resentment which choked all other feelings.

This was my reward for the effort I had made! This was the friend I had striven so desperately to recover!

He gave me no time to retort, even if I could have found the words to do so, but turned on his heel and left me, humbled and smarting, to find out that it would have been better far for me had I never tried to make matters right with Jack Smith.

But I was too angry to be dispirited that night. His bitter words rang in my ears at every step I took, and though my conscience cried out they were just, my pride cried out louder they were cruel. I longed to get out of their sound and forget the speaker. Who was he, a convict's son, to accuse me as he had? Half an hour ago it had been I who had wronged him. Now, to my smarting mind, it seemed as if it was he who was the wronger, and I the wronged.

"Hullo, old fly-by-night," suddenly exclaimed a voice beside me, as I walked slowly on my way; "what's the joke? Never saw such a fellow for grinning, upon my honour. Why can't you look glum for once in a way, eh, my mouldy lobster?"

I looked up and saw Doubleday, Crow, Wallop, and Whipcord, arm-in-arm across the pavement, and Hawkesbury and Harris following on behind.

"Still weeping for his lost Jemima, I mean Bull's-eye," said Wallop, "like what's his name in the Latin grammar."

It wasn't often Wallop indulged in classical quotations, but when he did they were always effective, as was the case now.

My recent adventure had left me just in an hysterical mood; and try all I would, I could not resist laughing at the very learned allusion.

"Bull's-eye be hanged!" I exclaimed, recklessly. "Hear, hear," was the general chorus. "Come along," cried Doubleday. "Now you are sober you can come along with us. Hook on to Whip. There's just room for five on the pavement comfortably. Plenty of room in the road for anybody else. Come on, we're on the spree, my boy, and no mistake. Hullo, old party," cried he to a stout old lady who was approaching, and innocently proposing to pass us; "extremely sorry—no thoroughfare this way, is there, Wallop? Must trouble you to go along by the roofs of the houses. Now, now, don't flourish your umbrella at me, or I shall call the police. My mother says I'm not to be worried, doesn't she, Crow?"

"You ought to be ashamed of yourselves, a set of young fellows like you," said the old lady, with great and very natural indignation, "insulting respectable people. I suppose you call yourselves gentlemen. I'm ashamed of you, that I am!"

"Oh, don't apologise," said Whipcord; "it's of no consequence."

"There's one of you," said the old lady, looking at me, "that looks as if he ought to know better. A nice man you're making of him among you!"

I blushed, half with shame, half with bashfulness, to be thus singled out, but considering it my duty to be as great a blackguard as my companions, I joined in the chorus of ridicule and insult in a manner which effectually disabused the poor lady of her suspicion that I was any better than the others.

In the end she was forced to go out into the road to let us pass, and we rollicked on rejoicing, as if we had achieved a great victory, and speculating as to who next would be our victim.

I mention this incident to show in what frame of mind the troubles of the day had left me. At any other time the idea of insulting a lady would have horrified me. Now I cared for nothing if only I could forget about Jack Smith.

We spent the remainder of the evening in the same rollicking way, getting up rows here and there with what we were pleased to call the "cads," and at other times indulging in practical jokes of all kinds, to the annoyance of some passers-by and the injury of others.

More than once we adjourned to drink, and returned thence to our sport more and more unsteady. As the evening grew later we grew more daring and outrageous. Hawkesbury and Harris left the rest of us presently, and, unrestrained even by their more sober demeanour, we chose the most crowded thoroughfares and the most harmless victims for our operations. Once we all of us trooped into a poor old man's shop who was too infirm to come from behind the counter to prevent our turning his whole stock upside down. Another time we considered it gentlemanly sport to upset an orange barrow, or to capture a mild-looking doctor's boy and hustle him along in front of us for a quarter of a mile.

In the course of our pilgrimage we came across the street in which Daly and the Field-Marshal lodged, and forthwith invaded their house and dragged them forth with such hideous uproar, that all the neighbours thought the house must be on fire, and one or two actually went for the engines.

About eleven we made a halt at a restaurant for supper, at the end of which, I say it now with bitter shame, I scarcely knew what I was doing.

I remember mildly suggesting that it was time for me to be going home, and being laughed to scorn and told the fun was only just beginning. Then presently, though how long afterwards I can't say, I remember being out in the road and hearing some one propose to ring all the bells down a certain street, and joining in the assent which greeted the proposition.

Whether I actually took part in the escapade I was too confused to know, but I became conscious of Doubleday's voice close beside me crying, "Look-out, there's a bobby. Run!"

Suddenly called back to myself by the exclamation, I ran as fast as my legs could carry me. My conscience had reproached me little enough during the evening's folly, but now in the presence of danger and the prospect of disgrace, my one idea was what a *fool* I had been.

Ah! greatest fool of all, that I had never discovered it till now, when disgrace and ruin stared me in the face. It is easy enough to be contrite with the policeman at your heels. But I was yet to discover that real repentance is made of sterner stuff, and needs a hand that is stronger to save and steadier to direct than any which I, poor blunderer that I was, had as yet reached out to.

If I could but escape—this once—how I vowed I would never fall into such folly again!

I ran as if for my life. The streets were empty, and my footsteps echoed all round till it sounded as if a whole regiment of police were pursuing me. My companions had all vanished, some one way, some another. They were used to this sport, but it was new—horribly new to me. I never thought I *could* run as I ran that night. I cared not where I went, provided only I could elude my pursuers. I dared not look behind me. I fancied I heard shouts and footsteps, and my heart sank as I listened. Still I bounded forward, along one street, across another, dodging this way and that way, diving through courts and down alleys, till at last, breathless and exhausted, I was compelled, if only for one moment, to halt.

I must have run a mile at the very least. I had never run a mile before that I knew of, and can safely say I have never run a mile since. But, remembering that night, I have sometimes thought a fellow can never possibly know how quickly he can get over the distance till some day he has to run it with a policeman behind him.

When I pulled up and looked round me, my pursuers, if ever I had had any, had disappeared. There was the steady tread of a policeman on the opposite side of the road, but he, I knew, was not after me. And there was the distant rumble of a cab, but that was ahead of me and not behind me. I had escaped after all! In my thankfulness I renewed with all fervour and sincerity my resolve to avoid all such foolish escapades for the future, and to devote myself to more profitable and less discreditable occupations.

As it was I dared not yet feel quite sure I was safe. I might have been seen, my name and address might have been discovered, and the policeman might be lying in wait for me yet, somewhere.

I slunk home that night down the darkest streets and along the shadiest sides of them, like a burglar. I trembled whenever I saw a policeman or heard a footfall on the road.

But my fears did not come to pass. I regained the City safely, and was soon on the familiar track leading to Beadle Square.

As I crossed the top of Style Street the place seemed as deserted as the grave. But my heart gave a leap to my mouth as suddenly I heard a voice at my side and a bound, as of some one springing upon me from a place of hiding.

It was only Billy, who had been curled up on a doorstep, but whose cat-like vigilance had discovered me even in this light and at this hour.

"Well, you are a-doin' it neat, you are," said he, grinning profusely; "where 'ave you been to, gov'nor?"

"What's that to do with you?" demanded I, to whom by this time the small ragamuffin's impudence had ceased to be astonishing.

"On'y 'cos t'other bloke he was 'ere four hour ago, and I ain't see'd you go by. I say, you're a-doin' it, you are."

"Has my fr— has Smith been here this evening?" I asked.

"He are so; and I give 'im a shine to-rights, I did. But, bless you, he was glum about the mazard, he was."

"What do you mean?" I asked.

"Ga on! As if you didn't know. 'Wot's up, governor?' says I. 'Things is a-going wrong with me, Billy,' says he—so he does. 'T'other bloke been givin' you any jaw?' says I, meaning you, says I. 'Never mind, Billy,' says he—'you give me a good shine,' says he, 'and I won't mind the rest.' And there, I *did* give he a proper shine. He's a gentleman, he is!"

Jack Smith had still a friend. I had sacrificed him, but he had yet another, more faithful and honest than ever I had been, ready to champion his cause, and rejoicing to do him service.

I slunk home to Mrs Nash's that evening more disgusted and discontented with myself than ever. My conscience, no longer to be kept down, was reproaching me right and left. I had been a false friend, a vain, self-righteous puppy, a weak, discreditable roysterer, without the courage to utter one protest on the side of chivalry and right. And at last, at a hint of danger, behold me a pitiful, abject coward, ready to vow anything if only I might escape the threatened catastrophe.

Reader, as I curled myself up in bed that night you may imagine I had little enough cause to be proud of myself!

Chapter Twenty Three
How I began to discover that I was not a very Nice Boy after all

If I had flattered myself I had ceased to care about my friend Smith, the events of the evening just described served to cure me of any delusion. I had thrown myself recklessly into dissipation and riot, so as to forget him; but now, as I lay on my bed and thought over what had befallen me, my misery at losing him returned tenfold, aggravated by the consciousness that now I deserved his friendship even less than ever.

"He's a gentleman, he is!" The words of the little shoeblack rang in my ears all night long, echoed by another voice from within, "What are *you*?" After all, had I not been doing my very best the last few days to prove Jack's own description of me as a liar and a coward to be true?

The fellows at the office next morning were in a high state of glee over the adventures of the previous evening.

"Wasn't it just about a spree?" said Wallop. "I never saw such a fellow as young Batch for leading one into mischief. I used to think *I* was a pretty wild hand, but I'm a perfect sheep to him, ain't I, Dubbs?"

"You are so," replied Doubleday. "Batch, my boy, if you go on at the rate you did last night, you'll overdo it. Take my word for that."

I had come to the office that morning determined to let every one see I was ashamed of my conduct; but these insinuations, and the half flattery implied in them, tempted me to join the conversation.

"It was you, not I, proposed ringing the bells," I said.

They all laughed, as if this were a joke.

"Well, that's a cool one if you like," replied Doubleday. "Why, it was all we could do to keep you from wrenching off the knockers as well, wasn't it, Crow?"

"Never thought we'd keep him from it," said Crow. "If the bobby hadn't turned up, I do believe he'd have wanted to smash the windows also."

"You're making all this up," I said, half amused, half angry, and almost beginning to wonder whether all that was being said of me was true.

"Not likely," said Doubleday; "the fact is, I couldn't have believed it of you if I hadn't seen it. By the way, Wallop, is it true the Field-Marshal was run in?"

"No, was he?" exclaimed Wallop, and Crow, and I, all in a breath.

"Well, I passed by Daly's this morning, and he told me he hadn't been home all night, and he supposed he'd have to go and bail him out."

"What a game!" cried Wallop.

"You'd call it a game if you had to hand out forty shillings, or take a week," replied Doubleday. "A nice expensive game this of yours, Master Batchelor. It'll cost you more than all your eel-pies, and lobsters, and flash toggery put together."

Fancy, reader, my amazement and horror at all this! It might be a joke to all the rest, but it was anything but a joke to me. Instead of the Field-Marshal it might have been I who was caught last night and locked up in a police cell, and what then would have become of me? My "friends" would all have laughed at it as a joke; but to me, I knew full well, it would have been disgrace and ruin!

I was in no humour to pursue the conversation, particularly as Jack Smith entered at that moment, composed and solemn as ever, without even a glance at me.

My only escape from wretched memories and uncomfortable reflections was in hard work, and that day I worked desperately. I was engaged in checking some very elaborate accounts under Doubleday's direction the whole day. It was a task which Wallop, to whom it fell by rights, shirked and passed on to me, greatly to my indignation, a week ago. But now it proved a very relief. The harder I worked, the easier my mind became, and the more difficult the work appeared, the more I rejoiced to have the tackling of it.

Our firm had received over a large cargo of miscellaneous goods from India, which they were about to trans-ship to South America; and what I had to do was first of all to reduce the value of the goods as they appeared in Indian currency to their exact English value, and after adding certain charges and profits, invoice them again in Spanish money.

"A nice spicy little bit of conjuring," as Doubleday described it, who, rackety fellow as he was, always warmed up to business difficulties.

He and I agreed to stay and finish the thing off after the others had gone, an arrangement I was very glad for all reasons to fall in with.

We worked away hammer-and-tongs for two hours (for it was a very lengthy and intricate operation), exchanging no words except such as had reference to our common task.

At last it was completed. The calculations and additions had all been doubly checked, and the fair copies and their duplicates written out, and then, for the first time, we were at leisure to think and speak of other topics.

Few things tend to draw two fellows together like hard work in common, and Doubleday and I, with the consciousness of our task well and honestly accomplished, found ourselves on specially friendly terms with one another.

Despite his extravagance and mischief, there had always been a good-nature and a frankness about the head clerk which had made me like him better than most of his companions either in or out of the office. Although he had never been backward to lead others into trouble, he had usually stopped short before any harm was done. Even in the persecutions of Jack Smith, many of which he had instigated himself, there was never any of the spite on his side which characterised the conduct of Crow, Wallop, and Harris. And although he never professed to admire my friend, he never denied him fair play when he was roused to resistance.

"Well," said he, shutting up the inkpot, and throwing our rough copies of the invoice into the waste-paper basket, "that's a good job done. You're not a bad hand at a big grind, young Batchelor. Crow or Wallop would have left me to do it all by myself."

Of course I was pleased at the compliment. I replied, "I rather enjoyed it."

"Well, there's not another fellow in the office would do the same," said he.

Wasn't there? I thought I knew better. "I think there's one other fellow," I said, hesitatingly. "Eh—oh, Bull's-eye! Yes, you're right there, and he'd have knocked it off smarter than you've done too, my boy." There was a pause after this. We had both accidentally got on to an awkward topic. Doubleday was the first to speak.

"I say, Batchelor," he went on, quite nervously for him, "excuse my saying it, but it's my opinion you're a bit of a fool, do you know!"

This unexpected announcement, coming from this unexpected quarter, naturally astonished me. "What do you mean?"

"Oh," said he, still rather embarrassed, "it's no concern of mine at all, but when you came here about a year ago you were rather a nice boy."

"Well," said I, not knowing exactly whether to be pleased or vexed.

"Well, you're not a nice boy now, you know!" I said nothing. I knew he was right, and his abrupt words struck home harder than he thought for. When Jack Smith, the night before, had called me a liar and a coward, I had fired up angrily. But when the rackety Doubleday now told me I wasn't a nice boy, I somehow felt a sudden pang of shame and humility that was quite new to me.

"I suppose you're going to flare up," continued Doubleday, noticing my silence, "when you've pumped up the words. I'll wait."

"No, no," said I, not looking up. "Go on."

"It doesn't concern me a bit how you and your precious friend get on," pursued my companion, cutting a quill pen, "and I see you're not in the same boat now by any means. But that's no reason why you should make a regular all-round ass of yourself in the way you're doing."

I looked up inquiringly. "I don't quite understand," I said, meekly.

"Well, I suppose you don't exactly imagine you've anything to be proud of over last night's performances?" said he.

"No, I was ashamed of myself for that," I said.

"Humph! I suppose you'd come again to-night and do the same thing if I asked you?"

I hesitated. "I don't think—" I began, but there pulled up. I knew well enough I *would* go if he asked me.

"Of course you would," said he; "you'd go anywhere. Just because a fellow a peg above you asks you, *you'll* go and make a fool of yourself and risk every chance you've got, because you've not the pluck to make yourself disagreeable!"

How true it all was! Yet why had I never seen it before?

"I'm afraid—I'm sure you're right," I said.

"I don't flatter myself," went on Doubleday, beginning on a new quill, "I'm very particular. I dare say I'm about as rackety a lot as any you'd pick up near here. But somehow I've no fancy for seeing a fellow going to the dogs out of sheer folly. It spoils my pleasure, in fact."

"I have been a fool, I know," I said.

"Of course you have, and so you will be unless you kick. Well, I'm off now," added he, taking up his hat. "I dare say I've offended you, and you'll call me an officious humbug. I may be a fool for concerning myself about a young muff like you; but anyhow I've told you what I think of you. So good-night, young un."

He left abruptly, before even I could say good-night, or thank him.

That night, as I walked home solitary, I felt more humble and less satisfied with myself than I had done for many a month.

One good sign was that I was by no means disposed this time to launch out into the extravagant resolutions to turn over a new leaf which had marked my former repentances. In fact, I said to myself, I won't resolve to do anything; but, God helping me, do something I will. And the first thing to do would be to get back my old friend Smith. For since I lost him everything had gone wrong with me.

And yet, now, how was it possible for me even to speak to him?

In the midst of these reflections I reached Style Street, where I suddenly became aware that something unusual was taking place. A small crowd was collected round the spot where Billy was usually in the habit of pursuing his business, and loud voices proclaimed that the occasion was one of anything but peace.

Curiosity tempted me to draw near, and a strange sight met my view as I did so. The central figures of the group were Billy and his "old gal," whom I recognised at once as the woman who had so vehemently ill-used him in the court that memorable evening weeks ago. She was a sad spectacle, more than half drunk, with every trace of tenderness and womanliness stamped out of her features.

If I had not recognised her by her appearance I should probably have done so by her occupation at that moment, for she was engaged in chastising her offspring with all the vehemence and all the cruelty of her former performances. But in the present case there was a difference. Billy, instead of taking his castigation meekly, as before, was violently resisting by shout and kick the attentions of his relative. This it was which appeared to render the transaction so particularly interesting to the onlookers.

"Go it, young bantam-cock," some one was crying as I approached, "let her have it."

"Give it up, do you hear, or I'll murder you!" shrieked the woman.

Billy replied nothing, but continued fighting tooth and nail. I never saw a child of his age so desperately active. He struggled not so much to escape his mother's blows aimed at himself, as to elude the clutches she made at a necktie he wore round his throat, which I at first glance recognised as having formerly belonged to Jack Smith.

This article of toilet the woman seemed as determined on having as her son was resolved on keeping. She probably considered it of some value—enough, at any rate, to pawn for drink; and Billy's violent refusal to give it up only roused her the more to secure it.

It was a revolting spectacle to watch, this struggle between mother and child. The one sparing neither blow nor curse, the other silent and active as a cat, watching every movement of his adversary, and ready for the slightest chance of escape. The crowd, careless of the rights of the case, cheered on both, and only interfered when the woman, having secured the boy in her grip, bade fair to bring the interesting encounter to too abrupt an end.

I dared not interfere, even if I had been able, but was forced to stand wedged up in the crowd to watch the issue of the struggle. And it was not long in coming. Amid loud cheers from the onlookers, Billy contrived for the seventh or eighth time to wriggle himself free from the clutches of his well-nigh frantic assailant, dealing her at the same time a blow on the arm with the blacking-brush he had all along retained in his hand. The surprise and pain of the blow, the jeers of the bystanders, and the tipsy rage of the woman combined to drive her nearly mad. With a fearful yell and threat she literally flung herself in wild fury upon her little victim. But the wary Billy was too quick for her. Stepping lightly aside, he eluded her reach, and left her to fall forward with a heavy crash on the pavement amid the howls and cheers of the brutal crowd.

Quick as thought the boy snatched up his box and brushes, and dived head-first into the crowd just where I stood. There was a cry of "Stop him!" "Fetch him back!" on all hands, and one young fellow near me actually made a grab at the poor boy and caught him by the arm. It was no time for ceremony or parley. It had been all I could do to stand still and watch the sickening spectacle. Now it should not be my fault if, just to please a party of blackguards, the whole thing was to be repeated.

With an angry shout of "Let him go!" I sprang at the fellow and struck him full on the chest. He dropped Billy as if he had been red-hot iron, and turning with livid face to me, stared at me for a single moment, and then tearing off his coat and clenching his fists rushed at me.

For all I know he might have annihilated me, but at that moment arose a cry of "Police!" at the sound of which the crowd dispersed like beetles before a candle, my antagonist being among the first to go, leaving me and Billy alone on the scene, from which even the tipsy woman had vanished.

It was not till the coast was all clear that Billy deposited his box or noticed my presence. The exciting scene which was just over seemed in no way to have disturbed the young gentleman's equanimity. He favoured me with one of his most affable grins and saluted me with one of his habitual somersaults as he said, "Shine 'e boots, master? T'other bloke he was 'ere at ten past seving."

"Hadn't you better go somewhere else?" I said. "Your mother will be back after you."

"Well," said Billy, in his usual touchy way, "she ain't no concern of yourn."

"Aren't you afraid of her hurting you?"

"'Urting me!" cried the boy, in tones of the utmost contempt, as if he had not been half-murdered once a week for the last eight years. "No fear! Ain't you funny? But she ain't a-going to collar this 'ere choker; not if I knows it!" said he, taking off his new article of decoration with a flourish and holding it up.

The well-worn and used-up necktie did not certainly look worth the battle that had been waged over it.

"Why are you so particular about this?" I asked, half guessing beforehand what the reply would be.

"Pertikler!" he cried, "why, that there bloke give me this 'ere!"

Nothing evidently could have been more conclusive to Billy's mind. I felt almost jealous to find how much truer Jack's new friend was than his old one.

"Was he here long this evening?" I asked, presently.

"Yaas; he was jawing nigh on half a' hour, he was, while I gi'en him a shine. But, bless you, them boots of his is pretty nigh 'andy wore out, and I tell him so. 'Never mind, Billy,' says he; 'I'll be getting a new pair soon when I've got the money saved,' says he. 'I mean to get a good strong pair,' says he, 'double-soled and plates on the 'eels, my boy,' he says, 'and you shall polish them up every night for me.' 'That I *will*,' says I. Bless you, governor, that there bloke'll 'ave the shiniest pair of boots in town."

It was a sight to see the little grimy face glow as he expatiated on the grateful theme.

"I suppose he didn't—did he say anything about me?" I asked, hesitatingly.

"Yaas," said Billy. "Says I to him, 'So t'other bloke,' (meaning you), 'has lagged off,' I says. 'Yes,' says he, 'we don't live together no more?' says he. 'I know all about it,' says I; 'I seen the animal,' (meaning you), says I, 'o'

Toosday.' 'Did you?' says he. 'Yaas,' I says, 'and nice and boozy he was,' I says, 'at eleving o'clock o' night,' I says. 'Did he say anything about me?' he says; and I told him, and he says he must go off, he says, 'cos he didn't want to be 'ere, he says, when you come. He do talk beautiful, he does."

I went on my lonely way more humbled than ever, but more determined, if possible, to recover my lost friend; yet thinking little or nothing of the greater and ever-present Friend against whom I had sinned so grievously.

But it was not to be for many days yet.

Smith always avoided me at the office in the same marked way, so that it was utterly impossible to make any advances to a reconciliation. The idea of writing to him occurred to me more than once, but the thought that he might throw my letter into the fire unread deterred me. No, the only thing was to bear my humiliation and wait for a chance.

Doubleday's lecture had wrought a considerable change in my habits. Although I found it impossible all at once to give up consorting with "the usual lot," especially those of them (now not a few), to whom I owed money, I was yet a good deal more chary of my complaisance, and less influenced by their example in ordinary matters. I succeeded, greatly to my own satisfaction and much to every one else's surprise, in making myself distinctly disagreeable on more than one occasion, which Doubleday looked upon as a very healthy sign, and which, though it involved me in a good deal of persecution at the time, did not seriously affect my position as a member of their honourable society.

How I wished I might once more call Jack Smith my friend, and cast off once for all these other shallow acquaintances!

During these wretched weeks Billy became my chief comforter, for he of all people was the only one I could talk to about Jack.

I always arranged my walks by Style Street so as to pass his "place of business" after the time when I knew Jack would have left, and then eagerly drank in all the news I could hear of my lost friend.

One evening, a week after the adventure with Billy and his mother just recorded, the boy greeted me with most extraordinary and mysterious demonstrations of importance and glee. He walked at least half a dozen times round his box on his hands before he would say a word, and then indulged in such a series of winks and grimaces as almost drove me into impatience.

"Whatever's the matter with you?" I asked, when this performance had been going on for some time "Oh my!—ain't it a game?" he chuckled.

"What's a game?" I demanded.

"Why—oh, ain't you a flat, though?—why, them there boots!"

"What boots? Why can't you talk sense?"

"Why, that there bloke's boots. When I was a-shinin' of 'em, if the sole of one on 'em don't come clean off!" he cried, with a grin.

"I don't see anything so very amusing in that," I replied.

"He's gone off to get 'em sewed on," continued the boy, beaming all over; "and he's a-coming back this way to show me. Bless you, they'll never sew that there sole on. The upper wouldn't hold it—you see if it does."

"He will have to get a new pair," I said.

"Why, he ain't *got* the browns. He's a-saving up, but it'll be a month afore he's got the brass."

Here Billy positively laughed, so that I felt strongly inclined to give him a box on the ear for his levity.

"And it's been a-rainin' all day," continued he, jocularly "and the streets is all one marsh of muck."

"Poor fellow!" said I. "I wish I could lend him a pair of mine."

"Ga on!" cried Billy, scornfully, dropping on his knees before his box.

"I say, guv'nor," said he, in a sudden mysterious tone, "can you keep it mum?"

"Yes—what?" I asked.

He looked carefully up the street and then down, and then all round. No one was near. He moved so as to let the light of a neighbouring lamp-post shine full on the pavement, as with jubilant face he lifted up his box and disclosed—a pair of new double-soled lace boots!

"Them's for *him*," he said, in an excited whisper.

"For him? Why, Billy, wherever did they come from?"

His grimy face turned up to mine all aglow with pride and triumph as he answered, "Stole 'em!"

Chapter Twenty Four
How I found that Hope deferred makes the Heart sick

The reader may picture my horror and astonishment on discovering Billy's secret. And the strangest part of it was that the graceless youth appeared to be utterly unconscious that he had done anything wrong. On the contrary, his jubilant face and triumphant voice showed plainly that he considered he had done a fine—a splendid thing.

I endeavoured to reason with him; he flared up as if I were trying to defraud Jack Smith of his new boots. I warned him of the punishment that would follow if he were caught. He gloried in the risk he ran. I told him it was wicked to steal—even for other persons. He retorted, "It wasn't no concern of mine."

Altogether it seemed hopeless to disenchant him with his exploit, and I therefore left him, wholly at a loss to make out this strange puzzle of a boy.

I was still more perplexed when, next morning, Jack Smith appeared at the office wearing the identical new pair of boots which had been the cause of all my horror!

I waited impatiently for the hours to pass, when I should be at liberty to pay my usual visit to Billy.

He was sitting there grimly, unlike his usual manner, evidently expecting me.

"Well," said I, "what have you done with those boots?"

"'Tain't no concern of yourn!"

"But he was wearing them to-day."

"In course he was!" said Billy, brightening a little.

"Did you tell him you had—had stolen them?"

"Yaas," replied the boy, gruffly.

"And he took them?" said I, in astonishment.

"Ain't you saw them on 'im?" demanded he, evidently disliking this catechism.

"Billy," said I, "I can't understand it."

"You ain't no call to!" was the polite reply; "'tain't no concern or yourn."

"It is my concern if other people are robbed," I said. "Don't you know, if I chose, I could fetch a policeman and get you locked up?"

"In course you could! Why don't yer?"

Was there ever such a hopeless young scamp?

"Whose shop did you take them from?" I asked.

"Trotter's, aside of our court. Go and tell him!" replied he, scornfully.

"How would you like any one to steal away one of your brushes?"

"I'd give 'em a topper!"

"But that's just what you've done to Trotter," I argued.

"Well, why don't you fetch him to give me a topper?" he replied.

I gave it up. There was no arguing with a boy like this. If there had been, there would have been no further opportunity that night, for as I stood by, puzzling in my mind what to say to bring home to the graceless youth a sense of his iniquity, he began picking up his brushes and shouldering his box.

"Where are you going so early?" I asked.

"Don't you like to know?" retorted he.

"Yes, I would."

"Well, if you must know, I'm a-going to the racket school!"

"The what?" I exclaimed.

"Racket school."

"Oh! ragged school, you mean. Where is it? I didn't know you went. They ought to teach you better there than to steal, Billy," I said.

"Oh!" replied the boy, with a touch of scorn in his voice, "that there bloke's a-going to learn me, not you!"

"What! does Smith teach at the ragged school, then?"

"In course he do! Do you suppose I'd go else?"

And off he trotted, leaving me utterly bewildered.

Jack Smith teaching in a ragged school! Jack Smith wearing a pair of boots that he knew were stolen! What could I think?

At any rate, I was resolved to be no party to Billy's dishonesty. At any cost, since I had not the heart to deliver up the culprit to justice, I must see that the victim was repaid. He might never have noticed the theft; but whether or no, I should have no rest till his loss had been made good.

It was no time to mince matters. My own funds, as the reader knows, were in a bad state. I owed far more than I could save in half a year. But I had still my uncle's half-sovereign in my pocket, which I had hitherto, despite all my difficulties, kept untouched. An emergency had now arisen, thought I, when surely I should be justified in using it. As long as I remained a party to Billy's dishonesty I was, I felt, little better than a thief myself, and that I could not endure, however bad in other respects I might have been.

I went straight to Trotter's shop. A jovial, red-faced woman stood at the door, just about to shut up for the night.

"I want to see Mr Trotter," said I.

"Mrs Trotter, you mean, I suppose?" said the woman. "I'm the lady."

"Can I speak to you for a minute?" I said.

"Yes—half an hour if you like. What is it?"

"It's something private."

"Bless us, are you going to offer to marry me, or what?" exclaimed she; "come, what is it?"

"Have you—that is, did you—the fact is, I don't know whether you happen to have missed a pair of boots," I said, falteringly.

She made a grab at my arm.

"So you're the thief, are you? A nice trade you've started at, young master, so I can tell you!"

"Oh," I cried, in the utmost alarm and terror, "you're quite wrong, you are indeed. I never touched them—I only—I—I know who did, that's all."

Mrs Trotter still held me fast.

"Oh, you know who did, do you?"

"Yes—he's a—" I was going to say "shoeblack," but I stopped myself in time, and said, "a little boy."

She released her grasp, greatly to my relief, and waited for me to go on.

My Friend Smith | 221

"And I really don't think he knows any better," said I, recovering my confidence.

"Well," she said, eyeing me sharply.

"Well," I said, "I know the proper thing would be to give him up to the police."

"That's what I'd do to you in a minute, if you'd stolen them," she said.

"I've rather an interest in the little boy," I said nervously, "and I thought if you wouldn't mind telling me what the boots came to, I'd ask you to let me pay for them. I don't think he'll do it again."

"Well, it's a very queer thing," said the woman; "what a popular young thief your friend must be! Why, I had a young gentleman here yesterday evening asking the very same thing of me!"

"What!" I exclaimed, "was it Jack Smith?"

"I don't know his name, but he'd a pair of black eyes that would astonish you."

"That's him, that's him!" I cried. "And he wanted to pay for the boots?"

"He did pay for them. I shall make my fortune out of that pair of boots," added she, laughing.

This, then, explained his wearing the boots that morning. How quick I had been to suspect him of far different conduct!

"You'd better keep your money for the next time he steals something," observed Mrs Trotter, rather enjoying my astonishment; "he's likely to be a costly young treat to you at this rate. I hope the next party he robs will be as lazy about her rights as me."

I dropped my uncle's half-sovereign back into my purse, with the rather sad conviction that after all I was not the only honest and righteous person in the world.

The next morning, on my arrival at Hawk Street rather before the time (I had taken to being early at the office, partly to avoid arriving there at the same time as Smith, and partly to have the company of young Larkins, of postage-stamp celebrity, in my walk from Beadle Square), I found Doubleday already there in a state of great perturbation.

"What do you think," he cried, almost before I entered the office—"what do you think they've done? I knew that young puppy's coming was no good to us! Here have I been here twelve years next Michaelmas, and he not a year, and blest if I haven't got to hand over the petty cash to my lord, because old Merrett wants the dear child to get used to a sense of responsibility in the business! Sense of rot, I call it!"

It certainly did seem hard lines. Doubleday, as long as I had been at Hawk Street, had always been the custodian of all loose cash paid into the office, which he carefully guarded and accounted for, handing it over regularly week by week to be paid into the bank.

It is never pleasant when a fellow has held an office of trust to have it coolly taken from him and handed to another. In this case no one would suspect it meant any lack of confidence; for Doubleday, even his enemies admitted, was as honest as the Bank of England; but it meant elevating another at his expense, which did not seem exactly fair.

"If the darling's such a big pot in the office," growled Doubleday, "they'd better make him head clerk at once, and let me run his errands for him."

"Never mind," said I, "it'll be so much less work for you."

"Yes, and a pretty mess the accounts will get into, to make up for it."

Hawkesbury entered at this moment, smiling most beautifully.

"How punctual you two are!" said he.

"Need to be punctual," growled Doubleday, "when I've got to hand you over the petty cash."

"Oh!" said Hawkesbury; "the petty cash? My uncle was saying something about my keeping it. I think it's a pity he couldn't let it stay where it was; you're so much more used to it than I am. Besides, I've plenty of work to do without it."

"I suppose I shall get some of your work to do for you," said Doubleday—"that is, if I'm competent!"

Hawkesbury laughed softly, as if it were a joke, and Doubleday relapsed into surly silence.

It was still some minutes before the other clerks were due. Hawkesbury used the interval in conversing amiably with me in a whisper.

"I'm afraid Doubleday's put out," said he. "You know, he's a very good sort of fellow; but, between you and me, don't you think he's a trifle too unsteady?"

What could I say? I certainly could not call Doubleday steady, as a rule, and yet I disliked to have to assent to Hawkesbury's question. "He's very steady in business," I said.

"Yes; but at other times I'm afraid he's not," said Hawkesbury. "Not that I'm blaming him. But of course, when a fellow's extravagant, and all that, it *is* a temptation, isn't it?"

"Do you mean a temptation to be dishonest?"

"Well, it's rather a strong way of putting it. I don't suppose for a moment Doubleday is not perfectly trustworthy; no more does my uncle."

"I should think not," said I, rather warmly.

"Of course not," said he, sweetly; "but you know, Batchelor, prevention is better than cure, and it seems the kindest thing, doesn't it, to put temptation quite out of a fellow's reach when one can?"

"But," observed I, "it seems to me you are taking it out of Doubleday's reach and putting it into your own."

For an instant a shade of vexation crossed his face, but directly afterwards he laughed again in his usual amused manner.

"You forget," said he, "I live at home, and haven't the chance of following Doubleday's example, even if I wished to. In fact, I'm a domestic character."

He seemed to forget that he had frequently accepted Doubleday's hospitality and joined in the festivities of the "usual lot."

"I thought you lived at your uncle's?" said I.

"Oh, no! My father's rectory is in Lambeth. But we're just going to move into the City. I don't enjoy the prospect, I can assure you! But I say, how are you and your friend Smith getting on now?"

He was always asking me about my friend Smith.

"The same as usual," said I.

"That's a pity! He really seems very unreasonable, considering he has so little to be proud of."

"It's I that have got little to be proud of," replied I.

"Really, Batchelor, you are quite wrong there. I think it's very generous the way you have always stuck to him—with certainly not much encouragement."

"Well," said I, "I shall have another attempt to make it up with him."

Hawkesbury mused a bit, and then said, smilingly, "Of course, it's a very fine thing of you; but do you know, Batchelor, I'm not sure that you are wise in appearing to be in such a hurry?"

"What do you mean?" I said.

"I mean, I shall be as glad as any one to see you two friends again: but if you seem too eager about it, I fancy you would only be demeaning yourself, and giving him a fresh chance of repulsing you. My advice as a friend is, wait a bit. As long as he sees you unhappy about it he will have a crow over you. Let him see you aren't so greatly afflicted, and then, take my word for it, he'll come a good deal more than half way to meet you."

There seemed to be something in this specious advice. I might, after all, be defeating my own ends by seeming too anxious to make it up with Jack Smith, and so making a reconciliation more difficult in the end. I felt inclined, at any rate, to give it a trial.

But the weeks that followed were wretched weeks. I heard daily and regularly from Billy all the news I could gather of my friend, but before Smith himself I endeavoured to appear cheerful and easy in mind. It was a poor show. How could I seem cheerful when every day I was feeling my loss more and more?

My only friends at this time were Hawkesbury and Billy and young Larkins. The former continued to encourage me to persevere in my behaviour before Smith, predicting that it would be sure, sooner or later, to make our reconciliation certain. But at present it did not look much like it. If I appeared cheerful and easy-minded, so did Smith. The signs of relenting which I looked for were certainly not to be discovered, and, so far from meeting me half way, the more unconcerned about him I seemed, the more unconcerned he seemed about me.

"Of course he'll be like that at first," said Hawkesbury, when I confided my disappointment one day to him, "but it won't last long. He's not so many friends in the world that he can afford to throw you over."

And so I waited week after week. I saw him daily, but our eyes scarcely ever met. Only when I glanced at him furtively I thought him looking paler and thinner even than usual, and longed still more intensely to call him my friend and know why it was.

"Most likely he's fretting," said Hawkesbury, "and will soon give in. It's a wonder to me how he's held out so long."

"Unless he speaks to me soon, I'll risk everything and speak to him."

"I can quite understand your anxiety," said my counsellor, "but I really wouldn't be too impatient."

I tried to find out from Billy the reason of Jack's altered looks.

"Yaas," said he, in response to my inquiry whether he had heard if my friend was ill—"yaas, he do look dicky. 'Governor,' says I, 'what's up?' I says. 'Up,' says he, 'what do you mean by it?' says he. 'Go on,' says I, 'as if you didn't know you was queer!' 'I ain't queer,' says he. 'Oh, no, ain't you,' says I; 'what do you want to look so green about the mazard for, then?' says I. 'Oh, that's nothing,' says he; 'reading late at night, that's what that is,' says he. 'Turn it up,' says I. 'So I will,' says he, 'when my Sam's over,' says he. Bless you, governor, I'd like to give that there Sam a topper, so I would."

So, then, he was reading for an examination! This paleness, after all, did not come from fretting on my account, but because he had found an occupation which drove me from his thoughts evening after evening!

I felt more hopeless of recovering my friend than ever.

"Do you go to the ragged school still?" I asked.

"Yaas, a Fridays. I say, governor, look here."

He dipped his finger into his blacking-pot, and, after cleaning the flagstone on which he knelt with his old hat, proceeded laboriously and slowly to trace an S upon it.

"There," he cried, when the feat was accomplished, "what do you think of that? That's a ess for Mr Smith, and a proper bloke he is. He do teach you to-rights, so I let you know, he do."

"What else does he teach you besides your letters?"

"Oh, about a bloke called Cain as give 'is pal a topper, and—"

He stopped abruptly, as he noticed the smile I could not restrain, and then added, in his offended tone, "I ain't a-goin' to tell you. 'Tain't no concern of yourn."

I knew Billy well enough by this time to be sure it was no use, after once offending him, trying to cajole him back into a good-humour, so I left him.

So the wretched weeks passed on, and I almost wished myself back at Stonebridge House. There at least I had some society and some friends. Now, during those lonely evenings at Mrs Nash's I had positively no one—except young Larkins.

That cheery youth was a standing rebuke to me. He had come up to town a year ago, a fresh, innocent boy; and a fresh, innocent boy he remained still. He kept his diary regularly, and wrote home like clock-work, and chirruped over his postage-stamp album, and laughed over his storybooks in a way which it did one's heart good to see. And yet it made my heart sore. Why should he be so happy and I not? He wasn't, so I believe, a cleverer boy than

I was. Certainly he wasn't getting on better than I was, for I had now had my third rise in salary, and he still only got what he started with. And he possessed no more friends at Beadle Square than I did. Why ever should he always be so jolly?

I knew, though I was loth to admit it. His conscience was as easy as his spirits. There was no one he had ever wronged, and a great many to whom he had done kind actions. When any one suggested to him to do what he considered wrong, it was the easiest thing in the world for him to refuse flatly, and say boldly why. If everybody else went one way, and he thought it not the right way, it cost him not an effort to turn and go his own way, even if he went it alone. Fellows didn't like him. They called him a prig—a sanctimonious young puppy. What cared he? If to do what was right manfully in the face of wrong, to persevere in the right in the face of drawbacks, constituted a prig, then Larkins was a prig of the first water, and he didn't care what fellows thought of him, but chirruped away over his postage-stamp album as before, and read his books, as happy as a king.

It was in this boy's society that during those wretched weeks I found a painful consolation. He was constantly reminding me of what I was not; but for all that I felt he was a better companion than the heroes with whom I used to associate, and with whom I still occasionally consorted. He knew nothing of my trouble, and thought I was the crossest-grained, slowest growler in existence. But since I chose his company, and seemed glad to have him beside me, he was delighted.

"I say," said he suddenly one evening, as we were engaged in experimenting with a small steam-engine he had lately become the proud possessor of, "I saw your old friend Smith to-day!"

"Where?" I asked.

"Why, down Drury Lane. I heard of a new Russian stamp that was to be had cheap in a shop there, and while I was in buying it he came in."

"Was he buying stamps too?"

"No; he lives in a room over the shop. Not a nice hole, I should fancy. Didn't you know he was there?"

"No," I said.

"Oh, you should go and see the place. He'd much better come back here, tell him. But I thought you saw one another every day?" he added, in his simple way.

"Did he say anything to you?" I asked, avoiding the question.

"Yes. I asked him how he was getting on, and he said very well; and I asked him what he thought of the Russian stamp; and he said if I liked he could get me a better specimen at his office. Isn't he a brick? and he's promised me a jolly Turkish one, too, that I haven't got."

"Was that all?" I asked. "I mean all he said?"

"Yes—oh, and I asked if he'd got any message for you, and he said no. Look, there—it's going! I say, isn't it a stunning little engine? I mean to make it work a little pump I've got in the greenhouse at home. It's just big enough."

Any message for me? No! Was it worth trying for any longer? I thought, as once more I crept solitary and disappointed to bed.

But the answer was nearer than I thought for.

Chapter Twenty Five
How I took part in a not very successful Holiday Party

Several weeks elapsed, and I was beginning to doubt whether Hawkesbury's advice, after all, was good, when a general holiday occurred to break the monotony of my life both at Hawk Street and Beadle Square.

I had for some time meditated, if I had the funds, taking advantage of my next holiday to run down to my uncle's. Not that I expected any particular welcome from him, but I longed to see the old familiar haunts of my childhood after my long imprisonment in London; and, even if there were no more congenial friend than Cad Prog to hail me, it would at least be a change from this dreary city, with its noise and bustle, and disappointed hopes and lost friendships.

But my intention in this direction was upset by a double reason. One was that I had no money. Indeed, my debts had got so far ahead of my means that it was clear a crisis in my financial affairs must soon come. The other reason was an invitation to join in a grand day's excursion by road to Windsor.

It came from Hawkesbury.

"Are you doing anything particular on Monday?" he asked me, a day or two before the holiday.

"No; I half thought of going home, but I can't afford that, so I may go to the British Museum."

"Not a very cheerful place to spend a holiday," laughed Hawkesbury. "What do you say to coming a quiet drive with me?"

Had the invitation come from Crow or Daly, or even Doubleday, I should have regarded it shyly. But Hawkesbury was a steady fellow, I thought, and not likely to lead one into mischief.

"I should like it awfully!" I said, "only—that is—I don't think I can afford it."

"Oh!" said he, smiling affably, "you shan't be at any expense at all. It's my affair, and I should like to take you with me."

Of course my gratitude was as profuse as it was sincere.

"My idea was," continued Hawkesbury, "to get a dogcart for the day and go somewhere in the direction of Windsor, taking our own provender with us, and having a jolly healthy day in the open air."

Nothing could be more delightful or more in accordance with my own wishes.

"Will it be just you and I?" I asked.

"Well, these traps generally hold four. I thought perhaps Whipcord would come for one; he's a good driver, you know, and a steady enough fellow when he's by himself. And there's a friend of mine called Masham I mean to ask as well."

I would have preferred it if the expedition had been confined to Hawkesbury and myself, but I had no right to be discontented with the arrangements which had been made, and spent the next few days in eager anticipation.

I wondered what Jack Smith meant to do on his holiday; most likely he would be reading hard for his "Sam," as Billy called it. It seemed shabby of me to go off on a spree and leave him to drudge; but, as Hawkesbury said when I referred to the matter, it would just show him what he missed by holding aloof, and make him all the more ready to try to get back my friendship.

Doubleday, when I told him of my plan for the day, snuffed up at it in no very pleasant way. But then he had always been jealous of Hawkesbury since giving up the petty-cash to his charge.

"All I can say is," said he, "*I'd* think twice about going with that party, and I'm not so very particular. I suppose you never met Mr Masham, did you?"

"No," said I.

"Ah!" he replied, laughing, "you'll find him a very nice boy; just a little too strait-laced for me, but he'll suit you."

I could not make out whether this was in jest or earnest; in any case, I put it down to the petty-cash, and thought it a pity Doubleday should be so put out by a trifle.

"What are you going to do?" I asked him.

"Oh! I'm going to do my best to be cheerful in a mild way," said he, "down the river. It's a good job Hawkesbury's booked you, my boy, for I meant to ask you to join us, and that would have done you out of your quiet day with Petty-Cash and his friends, which would be a pity."

The Monday came at last, and opened perfectly. My spirits rose as I looked out and saw the blue cloudless sky overhead, and thought of the trees, and birds, and flowers, and country air I was so soon to be among.

I was to meet my party at the Horseshoe stables in the City, and thither I repaired in good time, in my smartest get-up, and with a shilling plum-cake under my arm, which I had made up my mind to take as my contribution to the commissariat of the expedition. I passed Style Street on my way, and came in for hilarious greeting from Billy.

"Hi! shine 'e boots, governor? My eye, there's a nob! Shine 'e all over, governor. Ain't you got 'em on, though? What's up, mister?"

"See you again soon, Billy," said I, bustling on. I was angry with him for the way he laughed, and for the description of me I knew quite well he would presently give to Jack Smith.

Early as I was at the rendezvous, Hawkesbury was before me, and with him his friend Masham. The latter was a queer-looking fellow of about thirty. He was pale and dark round the eyes, like a person who hadn't slept for a week. His lips were large and red, and the lower part of his face a good deal too big for the upper. Altogether Mr Masham was neither a very healthy nor a very prepossessing-looking specimen; but Hawkesbury had told me he was clever and very amusing, so I supposed I oughtn't to judge by appearances.

"Punctual as usual," said Hawkesbury, as I approached. "Phil, this is my friend Batchelor I was telling you of."

I wished secretly I knew exactly what he had been telling him of me.

"Oh," said Masham, eyeing me all over, as he lit a cigar, and then held out his cigar-case to me. "What do you smoke, Batchelor?"

"I don't smoke, thank you," said I.

"Have you given it up, then?" said Hawkesbury. "You used to smoke at Doubleday's parties."

"Ah! I thought he looked like a chap that smoked," said Masham, holding out his case again. "Don't be modest, Batchelor. We're all friends here."

I didn't like the style of this Masham. Indeed, I was a trifle afraid of him already, and half repented coming.

"I gave up smoking some weeks ago," said I, determined not to give in if I could help. "I found I couldn't afford it."

"The very reason you should take a cigar now when you've a chance of getting one for nothing," replied Masham, digging me pleasantly in the ribs.

"Thanks, I'd rather not, if you'll excuse me," I replied again.

"Can't excuse you, my dear fellow. We're all bound to be sociable to-day. At least, so I fancy."

"Come, Batchelor," said Hawkesbury. "We may as well humour him. I'd advise you to take a cigar. I'll take one, too, to keep you company, though I hate them. They always make me feel sick."

So saying, he took a cigar and lit it. I felt bound to do the same, not only to relieve myself of Masham's importunity, but to avoid disturbing the harmony of our party at the very beginning of the day.

At this moment Whipcord arrived on the scene, as stylish as ever, with his hat all on one side of his head and his straw all on one side of his mouth.

"What cheer, my venerable chums?" he cried, as he approached. "Ah! Masham. You turned up again! I thought we'd lost—"

"That'll do," said Masham, with a significant jerk of his head towards me. "Have a weed?"

"Thanks, we'll see about that later on. I'm off my smoke just now. Ah! young Batchelor, you there? Brought your boxing-gloves with you, I hope? Hot fellow with the gloves is Batchelor, Phil. Well, where's your trap, Hawkesbury?"

"There it is coming out."

Whipcord eyed it professionally and critically. He liked the dogcart, but didn't think much of the horse.

"Do all right for a water-cart, I dare say," observed he, "or cat's meat. But I don't see how we're to get to Windsor and back with such a rheumatic old screw."

"You're out there, mister," said the ostler, who was harnessing the animal. "You'll find he ain't such a screw as you think. You'll need to keep a steady hand on him all the way, pertikler on the road home, or he'll screw you a way you don't fancy."

Whipcord laughed.

"I'll do my best," he said. "He does look a sort of beast to be nervous of, certainly."

The ostler grinned cynically, and we meanwhile mounted to our seats, Hawkesbury and Whipcord being in front, and I, much to my disgust, being placed beside Masham on the back seat.

Despite Whipcord's desponding prophecies, our charger stepped out at a pretty fair pace, and in due time we began to shake off the dust of London from our wheels and meet the first traces of country.

For a considerable time my companion absorbed himself in his cigar—much to my satisfaction—and I, for fear of appearing anxious for conversation, betook myself to mine.

At length, however, after about half an hour thus occupied, Masham broke the silence.

"Know Hawkesbury well?" he asked.

"Pretty well," I answered; "we were at school together first, and now we're in the same office."

"Nice boy at school?"

"Yes; I think so."

"Not quite sure, eh?"

"I always got on well with him."

"Yes, you would. Sort of a nest for bad eggs, that school, wasn't it?"

"Yes—that is, a good many of the boys were a bad sort," said I, not very comfortable to be undergoing this cross-examination.

"I understand. You weren't, of course, eh?" said he, digging me in the ribs with his knuckles.

His manner was most offensive. I felt strongly inclined to resent it, and yet somehow I felt that to be civil to him would be the less of two evils.

"Hawkesbury doing well at the office, eh?"

"Certainly!" said I. "Why not?"

"See no reason at all. Worthy chap, Hawkesbury. Nice boy at home; great comfort to the old people."

"Really," said I, "you know him much better than I do."

"Ah! should get to know Hawkesbury all you can. Moral chap—like you and me, eh?" and here followed another dig in the ribs.

This was getting intolerable. However, at this point Whipcord pulled up at a wayside inn, much to my relief. Anything was better than Masham's conversation.

We halted a quarter of an hour, to give our horse time to get breath, as Whipcord explained, but, as it really seemed, to allow that gentleman and Masham to refresh themselves also.

When we started again my companion began almost immediately to resume the conversation, but this time it was of a less personal nature, though disagreeable enough.

For he made no secret at all that he was a youth of depraved tastes and habits, and insisted on addressing me as though I resembled him in these respects. He gave me what he doubtless intended to be a highly entertaining and spicy account of many of his escapades and exploits in town and country, appealing to me every few sentences as to what I should have said or done or thought in similar circumstances.

And when he had exhausted his stories of himself he told me stories of his friends, some of which were disgusting, some horrifying, and some stupid. But with it all he had an air as if he believed everybody at heart was bad, and as if morality and sobriety and unselfishness were mere affectation and cant.

Has any of my readers ever met such a one as Masham? I hope not. If he should, let him beware of him as the worst enemy a boy could encounter. For no poison is more deadly than that which strives to make one man lose all faith in his fellow-man.

I was so far infected by his manner that, though I felt ashamed to be sitting and listening to his bad talk, I dared not protest, for fear of appearing (what he would be sure to consider me), a hypocrite.

And so, unprofitably, the journey was beguiled, not without frequent stoppings and refreshings, each of which had the effect of exhilarating Whipcord's spirits and making Masham's tongue looser and looser.

At length Windsor was reached, and I looked forward to exchanging my undesirable companion for more interesting occupation in seeing over the town with its grand old castle.

But in this I was woefully disappointed. Whipcord drove straight up to an inn in the town, where he ordered the horse and trap to be put up, while we all entered the smoky coffee-room and discussed the desirability of having dinner.

"I thought we were going to picnic out of doors?" I said, mildly, in answer to Masham's appeal whether we should not order dinner where we were.

"All very well if you could get your liquor laid on," said Whipcord. "I fancy we'd better stay where we are. What do you say, Hawkesbury?"

"I'm sorry to disappoint Batchelor," said Hawkesbury, smiling, "but I really think we shall get dinner more comfortably here. We've no plates or knives; and, as Whipcord says, there would be a difficulty about the beer."

I was outvoted, and had to give up my idea of a rustic meal in the open air.

It was not a very pleasant dinner. Masham, despite Hawkesbury's protests, persisted in interlarding it with his offensive stories, and Whipcord, who was taking very decided measures to excite his spirits, chimed in with his horsey slang, not unmixed with profanity.

"How are you getting on, Batchelor?" said the former presently to me. "Don't be afraid of that bottle, man, it's only whisky!"

"Don't you believe him; it's gin," laughed Whipcord.

"I thought you said it was brandy," said Hawkesbury.

"There you are!" said Masham. "One says one thing, one another, and one another. Now I tell you what, Batchelor shall be umpire, and we'll each put five shillings on it, eh? What do you say to that?"

"I'd rather not bet," replied Hawkesbury, "but I'd like to know what Batchelor says it is."

"I'll go half-sovs. with you on it," said Whipcord.

"Done with you!" said Masham; "but Hawkesbury must go too, for if it's brandy we both lose."

"I'd rather not bet," said Hawkesbury, "but if it will spoil your fun if I don't I'll join."

"Thanks. Now, Batchelor, fill up, old toper, and give us your verdict."

"I really am no judge of spirits," said I. "Innocent babe," said Masham, "how well he does it! But he doesn't seem to know the rule in these cases," added he, winking at the other two. "What rule?" I asked.

"Why, about hanging back. Half a tumbler for every twenty seconds, isn't that it, Whipcord?"

"I thought it was a whole tumbler!"

"Ah, wouldn't you take your time to decide, eh? Come now," said Masham, taking out his watch, "we'll start now."

"Hold hard," said Whipcord. "Surely we are to have glasses too, to see if he guesses right."

"Very well, fill all round. Now, Batchelor."

"I really can't do it," I said, faintly. "Five seconds gone!" bawled Masham, laughing. "Please, don't be so foolish," I cried, getting alarmed. "Hawkesbury, please stop them!"

"Ten seconds gone, eleven, twelve!"

"I tell you, I—"

"Seventeen, eighteen," said Masham, rising and reaching out his arm for the bottle.

There was no help for it. I seized my glass and gulped down its contents. It made me cough and sputter, and my eyes watered, greatly to the amusement of my persecutors.

"What is it?" they all cried.

I could scarcely speak for anger and the burning in my throat.

"It's a shame!" I began.

"That's not what it is," cried Whipcord. "Come, give it a name, or you'll have to drink another!"

"Oh, brandy," I almost shrieked, willing to do anything rather than that. "I say, Hawkesbury," I said, reproachfully, "I didn't expect you were bringing me to this sort of thing."

"It is a shame," he said to me aside. "I would have stopped it if I could; but don't you see they were eager about their bet, and it was the only way of quieting them. Never mind."

The rest of the afternoon passed away much as it had begun. After dinner we went down to the river and took a boat, in which Masham and Whipcord lay and slept all the time, while Hawkesbury and I rowed them about. It was with difficulty, about five o'clock, that we got them ashore again, and half led, half dragged them back to the inn.

"Come," said Hawkesbury to Whipcord, "it's time to be getting the trap ready for the start back, isn't it?"

"Is it? Go and tell the fellow, some of you," replied our driver. "I'll be ready pretty soon," said he, moving once more towards the bar.

"You surely aren't going to drink any more," cried I, taking his arm and trying gently to stop him.

He wrenched his arm loose and gave me a push back, saying, "Young prig! what's it to do with you?"

"I think he wants to come too," said Masham. "Come along, Batchelor."

I had positively to run away to elude them, and made the pretext of going to the stable to see after the harnessing of the horse.

When this was done I sought for Hawkesbury.

"Do you think it's safe for Whipcord to drive in the state he's in?"

"Oh, yes. With a horse like that too. He's pretending to be a great deal worse than he is, just to horrify you."

It seemed ages before we actually started. Whipcord, in a most quarrelsome humour, had to be dragged almost by force from the bar. Hawkesbury, at the last moment, discovered that he was going without paying the bill; while Masham, having once made himself comfortable in the bar parlour, flatly refused to be moved, and had finally to be left behind.

The only consolation in this was that I had the tail of the dogcart to myself, which was infinitely preferable to the odious society of Masham.

It was nearly six when we finally started from Windsor and turned our horse's head homeward. And this had been my day's enjoyment!

Chapter Twenty Six
How I fell badly, and was picked up in a way I little expected

The delightful picnic to which I had looked forward with such satisfaction had certainly not come off as I expected. And it was not *yet* over, for the drive home under the conduct of Mr Whipcord promised to be the most exciting portion of the whole day.

As long as we were in the country roads the unsteadiness of our Jehu did not so much matter, for he was sober enough to keep the horse upon the road, though hardly fit to steer him past other vehicles. However, it was marvellous how we did get on. What hairbreadth escapes we had! It was useless attempting to remonstrate with the fellow. He was in that quarrelsome and mischievous humour which would brook no protest. Once, very soon after starting, in passing a country cart we as nearly as possible upset against it, a misadventure which Whipcord immediately set down as a deliberate insult intended for himself, and which nothing would satisfy him but to avenge then and there.

He leaped down off the dogcart, heedless of what became of the horse, and, throwing off his coat, shouted to the countryman to "Come on!" an invitation which the countryman answered with a crack of his whip which made the doughty hero leap as high into the air as he had ever done in his life.

As might be expected, this incident did not tend to pacify the outraged feelings of the tipsy Whipcord, who, disappointed of his vengeance on the countryman, was most pressing in his invitations to Hawkesbury or me or both of us to dismount and "have it out." Indeed, he was so eager for satisfaction that he all but pulled me off my seat on to the road, and would have done so quite had not the horse given a start at the moment, which put me out of his reach, and nearly upset him in the dust.

Things certainly did not look promising for a nice quiet drive home. With difficulty we coaxed him back into the trap, where he at once began to vent his spleen on the horse in a manner which put that animal's temper to a grand test.

He further insisted on pulling up at every wayside inn for refreshment, until it became quite evident, if we ever reached London at all, we should certainly not do so till nearly midnight.

I held a hurried consultation with Hawkesbury as to what ought to be done.

"Don't you think," suggested I, "we had almost better go on by ourselves and leave him behind?"

"Oh no," said Hawkesbury; "that would never do. It wouldn't be honourable."

It occurred to me it would not be much less honourable than inviting a fellow to a quiet picnic and letting him in for an expedition like this.

"Well," said I, "suppose we let him drive home, and you and I go back some other way?"

"You forget I'm responsible for the trap. No, we'd better go on as we are. We've not come to grief so far. Perhaps, though," said he, "you'd sooner drive?"

"What's that about sooner drive?" shouted Whipcord, coming up at this moment. "Who'd sooner drive? You, young Batchelor? All right; off with your coat!" And he threw himself on me in a pugilistic attitude.

After a long delay we got once more under way, the vehicle travelling more unsteadily than ever, and my misgivings as to ever reaching London becoming momentarily more numerous.

How we ever got back I can't imagine, unless it was that after a time Whipcord finally dropped the reins and allowed the horse to find its own way home. He certainly thought he was driving, but I fancy the truth was that one of the ostlers on the road, seeing his condition, had cunningly looped the reins round the front rail of the trap, so that, drive all he would, he could not do much more harm than if he was sitting idle.

At length the lateness of the hour and the frequent lights announced that London must be near. It was fortunate it was so late, or we should certainly have come to grief in the first crowded street. As it was, Whipcord had already got command of the reins again, as the sudden jerks and shies of the horse testified.

My impulse was to avoid the danger by quietly jumping down from my seat and leaving the other two to proceed alone. But somehow it seemed a shabby proceeding to leave Hawkesbury in the lurch, besides which, even if I had overcome that scruple, the seat was so high that at the unsteady rate we were going I would run considerable risk by jumping. So I determined to hold on and hope for the best.

We got safely down Oxford Street, thanks to its emptiness, and were just proceeding towards Holborn, when Whipcord gave his horse a sudden turn down a side street to the right.

"Where are you going?" I cried; "it's straight on."

He pulled up immediately, and bidding Hawkesbury hold the reins, pulled off his coat for the twentieth time, and invited me to come and have it out on the pavement.

"Don't be a fool," said Hawkesbury; "drive on now, there's a good fellow."

"What does he want to tell me which way to drive for?" demanded the outraged charioteer.

"He didn't mean to offend you—did you, Batchelor? Drive on now, Whipcord, and get out of this narrow street."

With much persuasion Whipcord resumed his coat and seized the reins.

"Thinks I don't know the way to drive," he growled. "I'll teach him!"

I had been standing up, adding my endeavours to Hawkesbury's to pacify our companion, when he suddenly lashed furiously at the horse. The wretched animal, already irritated beyond endurance, gave a wild bound forward, which threw me off my feet, and before I could put out a hand to save myself pitched me backwards into the road.

I was conscious of falling with a heavy crash against the kerb with my arm under me, and of seeing the dogcart tearing down the street. Then everything seemed dark, and I remember nothing more.

When I did recover consciousness I was lying in a strange room on a strange bed. It took an effort to remember what had occurred. But a dull pain all over reminded me, and gradually a more acute and intense pain on my left side. I tried to move my arm, but it was powerless, and the exertion almost drove back my half-returning senses.

"Lie quiet," said a voice at my side, "the doctor will be here directly."

The voice was somehow familiar; but in my weak state I could not remember where I had heard it. And the exertion of turning my head to look was more than I could manage.

I lay there, I don't know how long, with half-closed eyes, seeing nothing, hearing nothing, and feeling only the pain and an occasional grateful passing of a wet sponge across my forehead.

Then I became aware of more people in the room and a man's voice saying—

"How was it?"

"I found him lying on the pavement. I think he must have been thrown out of a vehicle."

That voice I had certainly heard, but where?

"It's the arm—broken!" said the voice.

"Ah," said the doctor, leaning over me and touching me lightly near the elbow.

I groaned with agony as he did so.

"Go round to the other side," said he, hurriedly. "I must examine where the fracture is. I'm afraid, from what you say, it must be rather a bad one."

I just remembered catching sight of a well-known face bending over me, and a familiar voice whispering—

"Steady, old man, try to bear it."

The next moment I had fainted.

It may have been minutes or it may have been hours before I next came to myself, and then my arm lay bandaged by my side, and the sharpness of the pain had gone.

"Fred, old man," was the first thing I heard as I opened my eyes. I knew the voice now, and the face with its two great eyes which bent over me.

I had found my friend at last!

"Hush, don't talk now," he said, as I tried to speak; "lie quiet now, there's a dear fellow."

"Jack!" I said. I could not resist uttering his name, his old familiar long-lost name.

"Yes, it's Jack," he whispered, "but don't talk now."

"You forgive me, Jack?" I murmured, heedless of his injunction.

"Yes, a hundred times!" he said, brushing back the hair from my forehead, and putting his finger to my lips.

Then I obeyed him, and lay silent and happy all day. Happier with all my pain than I had been for months.

The doctor came later on and looked at my arm.

"He'll do now, I think," said he, "but he will very likely be feverish after it. You should have him taken to the hospital."

"Oh no," cried Jack. "He must stay here, please. I can look after him quite well."

"If it was only the arm," said the doctor. "But he's had a bad fall and is a good deal bruised and shaken besides. He would get better attention, I think, at the hospital."

"I would so much sooner he stayed here," said Jack; "but if he'd really be better at the hospital, I suppose I ought to let him go."

"I won't go to the hospital!" exclaimed I, making the longest speech I had yet made since my accident, with a vehemence that positively startled the two speakers.

This protest settled the question. If only a sick person threatens to get excited about anything, he is pretty sure to have his own way. And so it proved in my case.

"But will you be able to stay at home all day from business to look after him?" asked the doctor.

"No, I'm afraid not," said Jack, "but I think I know some one who will. He sha'n't be left alone, and I can always just run home in the dinner-hour to see how he's getting on."

The doctor left, only half satisfied with this arrangement, and repeating that it would have been far better to move me to the hospital.

When he was gone Jack came and smoothed my pillow. "I am glad you're to stay," he said. "Now, for fear you should begin to talk, I'm going out to Billy to get my boots blacked. So good-bye for a bit, old boy."

"But, Jack—" I began, trying to keep him.

"Not a word now," said he, going to the door. "Presently."

I was too contented and comfortable to fret myself about anything, still more to puzzle my brains about what I couldn't understand. So I lay still thinking of nothing, and knowing nothing except that I had found my friend once more, and that he was more to me than ever.

Nothing makes one so sleepy as thinking of nothing at all; and long before Jack returned from his visit to Billy I was asleep, and slept soundly all through the night.

Next morning I woke invigorated in body and mind. Jack was up and about before I opened my eyes. He was at my side in a moment as I moved.

"Well, you have had a sleep," he said, cheerily. "I have," replied I. "But, Jack, where am I?"

"Oh, this is my lodgings," said he. "I'm pretty comfortable here."

I looked round the room. It was a poor, bare apartment, with only two beds, a chair, a small table, and a washstand to furnish it. The table was covered with papers and books.

"You've got a sitting-room too, I suppose?" I said, after taking the room in.

He laughed.

"I find this quite as good a room to sit in as to lie in," said he, "for the matter of that. But I have got the use of another room belonging to a fellow-lodger. He's a literary man, and writes for the papers; but in his spare moments he coaches me in Latin and Greek, in consideration of which I give him half my room to sleep in."

"Whatever's he to do now when I'm here?" I asked.

"Oh, he's going to have a shake-down in his own room. You'll like him, Fred; he's a very good-natured, clever man."

"How old?" I asked.

"About fifty, I should think. And I fancy he's seen a good deal of trouble in his time, though I don't like to ask him."

"I say, Jack," I began in an embarrassed manner, "ever since that time—"

"Shut up, now," said Jack, briskly. "The doctor says unless you obey me in everything you're to go straight to the hospital. And one of my rules is, you're to talk about nothing I don't approve of."

"I was only going to say—"

"There you go. I don't approve of what you were going to say. I suppose you'll be interested to hear I reported your case to the firm yesterday, and they were very sorry to hear of it, and told me there were other fellows in the office they could have spared better. There's a compliment!"

"Was Hawkesbury at the office?" I asked.

Jack's face clouded for a moment.

"Yes, Hawkesbury was there."

"You know he was with me when the accident happened?" I said, by way of explanation.

"Oh," said Jack. "Hullo! here comes Billy. I hope, you won't be horrified to have him to look after you while I'm at the office. He's the only person I could think of."

"Billy and I are very good friends," I said, somewhat taken aback, however, by the prospect of being consigned to that young gentleman's charge for several hours every day.

"Here you are, Billy," said Jack, as the boy entered. "You needn't have brought your blacking-box with you, though."

"What, ain't none of the blokes here got no boots, then?" remarked the youth, depositing his burden.

"The bloke, as you call him, who lies there," said Jack, pointing to me, "won't be putting on his boots for a good many days yet."

Billy approached my bed with his most profuse grin.

"I say, ain't you been and done it? Do you hear? you've broke your arm!"

This piece of news being so remarkably unexpected visibly affected me.

"Yes," said Jack, "and I want you to sit here while I'm away, and see nobody breaks it again."

"I'll give the fust bloke that tries it on a topper, so I will," said Billy, fiercely, sitting down on his box and preparing to mount guard.

"I quite believe you," said Jack, laughing. "But mind, Billy, you mustn't make a noise or disturb him when he's resting. And if anything special happens and I'm badly wanted, you must run to my office and fetch me. You know where it is?"

"Yaas, I know," said Billy.

"If Mr Smith comes up, you may let him in and make yourself scarce till he goes away again."

"What Mr Smith?" I asked.

"Oh, my fellow-lodger. Isn't it funny his name's Smith? At least, wouldn't it be funny if every other person weren't called Smith?"

"It is rather a large family," said I, laughing.

Billy having received his full instructions, including the serving of certain provisions out of a cupboard in a corner of the room, made himself comfortable on his perch, and sat eyeing me, after Jack had gone, as if I were a criminal of some sort whom it was his duty to prevent from escaping.

It was a queer situation to be in, certainly. Left alone in a friend's lodging with a broken arm and other contusions, and a small shoeblack to look after me, who had once robbed me of my penknife and a sixpence!

I was rather doubtful whether his new employment was quite as congenial to him as his old. Indeed, I rather pitied him as he sat there silent and motionless like a watch-dog on guard.

"You may stand on your hands if you like, Billy," I said, presently.

He eyed me sharply and doubtfully.

"You're 'avin' a lark with me," he said.

"No, I'm not. You really may do it."

"Ain't a-goin' to do it," replied he, decisively.

"Why not?" I asked.

"T'other bloke ain't said I'm to do it," replied he.

"Well," said I, "if you don't think he'd like it, don't do it. For I'm sure he's very good to you, Billy, isn't he?"

"'Tain't no concern of yourn," responded my genial guardian.

After this there was a long silence, and I was getting drowsy, when Billy said, "That there 'orse was a-goin' it."

"What horse?"

"Why, as if you didn't know! That there 'orse as was drivin' you blokes a' Monday night."

"What, did you see us, then?" I asked.

"In corse I did. I seen you as I was a-comin' back from the racket school. My eye, wasn't you tidy and screwed though! You don't ought to be trusted with 'orses, you don't."

"I wasn't screwed, Billy," said I, "and I wasn't driving."

"No, that you wasn't driving. But I knows the bloke as was."

"Do you know Mr Whipcord?"

"Yaas, I knows the animal," he replied, with a grin. "He gave me a doin' with his stick once, he did."

"But did you see me pitched out?" I asked, not feeling particularly interested in the last reminiscence.

"In corse I did. I seen you. Thought you was dead, and I fetches the bloke to yer, and the bloke sends me for the doctor, and the doctor—"

At this moment the door opened and a stranger entered.

Chapter Twenty Seven
How I suffered a Relapse, which did me good

The gentleman who entered the room was a middle-aged man, of striking appearance. In face and person he seemed worn and feeble. He walked with a slight stoop; his cheeks were hollow and slightly flushed, and his brow was furrowed by lines which would have appeared deep even in a much older man. But as soon as he began to talk his face lit up, his eyes sparkled, and there was a ring in his voice which was more like Jack Smith himself than his older and more sedate namesake.

For this stranger, I guessed at once, must be the other Mr Smith with whom Jack lodged.

At sight of him Billy stopped abruptly in the middle of his sentence, and, putting his hand up to his forelock, saluted him with his usual familiar grin.

"Ah, William, my worthy friend, you here?" the gentleman said, almost gaily, as he entered. "I heard I should find you on duty. You must introduce me to this sick gentleman, and ask him if I shall disturb him."

Billy grinned in a confused sort of way, not knowing exactly how to do the honours. Then, looking at me and jerking his thumb in the direction of the stranger, he said, "This here's the cove from downstairs!"

The gentleman approached my bedside and said, gently, "Am I disturbing you? I found a note from my fellow-lodger when I got in just now, asking me to call up and see how you were getting on."

"It's very kind of you," said I. "I hope you can stay a bit."

"Certainly; I've nothing to do."

Billy, however, did not apparently favour this suggestion.

"This 'ere cove," said he, pointing to me, "ain't to jaw, mister!"

"Quite right, William," said the gentleman; "I'll see he doesn't. I'll do all the talking and he shall do the listening. You can go down to my room and make my bed ready for me and tidy up."

The boy looked dubiously first at the speaker, then at me, as if he was not quite sure about the propriety of allowing me out of his sight, but finally obeyed.

"There's a trusty youngster for you!" said the gentleman, laughing, as he disappeared. "Young Smith couldn't have found a safer nurse for you anywhere."

"I believe you are right," said I.

"And how are you feeling? You're looking better than when I saw you last, anyhow."

"I never saw you before, did I?" I asked.

"No, you didn't; but I saw you when you were brought in here the other evening. However, as Billy says, you mustn't talk now. I suppose you heard me order him to make my bed. I always go to bed every morning at eleven. Young Smith and I are like Box and Cox, you know; he's away all day, I'm away all night. Just when he's finishing up work I'm beginning."

"I wonder you can keep awake all the night," I said.

"Not more wonderful than you keeping awake all day, my boy. In fact, there's not much chance of a poor literary hack sleeping over his work. Now I wonder, when you read your newspaper in the morning, if you ever think of what has to be done to produce it. If you only did, I dare say you would find it more interesting than it often seems."

And then my companion launched out into a lively description of the work of a newspaper office, and of the various stages in the production of a paper, from the pen and ink in the sub-editor's room to the printed, folded, and delivered newspaper which lies on one's breakfast-table every morning. I wish I could repeat it all for the benefit of the reader, for few subjects are more interesting; but it would take more time than we have to spare to do so.

Of course Mr Smith the elder—for so I had to call him to distinguish him from my friend his namesake—rattled on in this strain, more for the sake of keeping me interested and amused than any other reason. Still, his talk was something better than idle chatter, and I began to feel that here at last, among all my miscellaneous acquaintance, was a man worth knowing.

He gave me no chance of talking myself, but rattled on from one topic to another in a way which left me quite free to listen or not as I liked, and finally rose, much to my regret, to go.

"Now I must be off, or I shall have Billy up to hunt me off. Good-bye, my boy; glad to see you doing so well. You've a lot to be thankful for, and of course you are."

"Will you come again?" I asked.

"Gladly; that is, if Billy allows me," said he, laughing, and nodding kindly as he left the room.

"No wonder," thought I, as I listened to his footsteps going down stairs—"no wonder Jack Smith found these lodgings pleasanter than Beadle Square."

I saw Mr Smith frequently during the next few days. He usually came up to sit with me for half an hour or so in the morning, and was always the same cheery and interesting companion.

And yet I could not quite make him out. For when not talking or smiling his face used to wear a look of habitual trouble and restlessness, which made me suspect he was either making an effort to be cheery before me, or else that he was the victim of a constant battle between good spirits and bad.

However, just as I was getting to feel intimate with him, and looking forward to hear more about him than I had yet learned, my recovery came to a sudden and rather serious halt.

I was lying one evening propped up in my bed, with my damaged arm feeling comparatively comfortable, and myself in a particularly jovial frame of mind as I listened to Jack Smith attempting to instil into the mind of the volatile Billy the art of spelling d-o-g—dog.

"Now, Billy," said the instructor, "you'll never get on at this rate. That letter you're pointing at is a B for Billy, and not a D."

"That there B's a caution," growled the boy; "he's always a-turnin' up."

"Time you knew him, then," said Smith. "Now show us the D."

Billy cocked his head a little to one side and took a critical survey of the alphabet before him. His eye passed once down and once up the procession, then looking up at Jack with a grin, he said, "He's 'iding, I reckon, governor. That there dorg'll have to start with a B after all."

Our laughter at this philosophic observation was interrupted by an unwonted footstep on the stairs outside. It certainly was not Mr Smith, for he was out at his work; nor was it the doctor, our only other visitor, for he always came up two steps at a time, and his boots always squeaked. Who could our visitor be?

"Come in," called Smith, as a knock sounded on the door.

To my utter astonishment and concern, Hawkesbury, with his sweetest smile, entered the room.

How had he found out my retreat? What did he want here? What would Jack Smith say? These were the questions which rushed through my mind as he closed the door behind him and walked into the room.

I glanced round at Jack. There was written anything but peace in his countenance, while Billy glared like a young bulldog ready to spring on the intruder.

"Well, Batchelor," said Hawkesbury, in his blandest voice, addressing me and ignoring everybody else; "you'll be surprised to see me here. The fact is, I couldn't feel happy till I came to see you and tell you how sorry I was for your accident."

My few days' confinement and the opportunity for meditation they had afforded had served to give me an insight into Hawkesbury's character which made me treat this speech suspiciously. I replied nothing, and felt very uncomfortable.

"It was most unfortunate," proceeded Hawkesbury, helping himself to the chair. "You know—"

"Excuse me," interrupted Smith at this point, in a tone which made me start; "this is my room, Hawkesbury, and I must ask you to go."

The visitor's face clouded with a quick shade of vexation, but immediately regained its chronic smile, as he said, "Ah, Smith! I should have said it was my friend Batchelor I came to see, not you."

"You're no friend of his," retorted Smith, with rising wrath.

"Do you hear, nob," broke in Billy, unable to restrain himself any longer; "you ain't a-wanted here."

Hawkesbury looked round with an amused smile.

"Really," said he, "a most gratifying reception, and from a most unexpected quarter. Er—excuse me, Smith, I'm afraid it's rather a strange request—would you mind allowing me to have a little private conversation with my friend?"

"No," replied Smith, firmly.

"Really," said Hawkesbury. "I must appeal to Batchelor himself."

"I shall answer for Batchelor," said Smith, not giving me time to reply. "Leave my room, please."

"Do you hear? You leave the bloke's room," cried Billy. "Ef you don't you'll get a topper."

Hawkesbury, whose colour had been rising during the last few moments, and whose assurance had gradually been deserting him, now turned round with a ceremonious smile to the last speaker as he rose to his feet and said, "If *you* desire it, I'll go. I can submit to be ordered off by a shoeblack, but the son of a convict is—"

With clenched fist and crimson face Jack gave a sudden bound towards the speaker. But as suddenly he checked himself and walked gently to my bed, where I had started up ready to spring to my feet and back up my friend in what seemed a certain quarrel.

"What a cad I am!" he murmured, as he bent over me, and motioned me gently back to my pillow, "but the fellow nearly drives me mad."

I was too exhausted by my effort to say anything.

Jack remained by my side while the unwelcome visitor slowly walked to the door. But if one of Hawkesbury's enemies was disposed of, another remained. Billy, who had been a fuming and speechless witness of this last scene, now boiled over completely, and was to be kept in check no longer.

Wasting no words, he made a wild dash at the retreating intruder and closed with him. He would have closed with a lion, I firmly believe, if a lion had made himself obnoxious to Jack Smith.

Hawkesbury turned suddenly to receive the assault; an angry flush overspread his face, his hands clenched, and next moment Billy reeled back bleeding and almost senseless into the middle of the room, and the visitor had gone.

This was the event which put a check on my recovery.

To lie helpless and see Jack Smith insulted before my face would have been bad enough, but to hear him taunted with the very secret I had so miserably and treacherously let out was more than I could endure.

I don't know what I did that evening, I was so weak and so excited. I have vague recollections of breaking out into passionate self-reproaches and wild entreaties for forgiveness; and of Jack Smith with pale and troubled face bending over me trying to soothe me, imploring me to be still, telling me twenty times there was nothing left to forgive. And then in the middle of the scene the doctor arrived, with serious face and hushed voice. He felt my pulse more carefully than ever, and took my temperature not once only, but several times. There was a hurried consultation in the corner of the room, of which all I heard were the words "most unfortunate" and "fever." My usual supper of bread-and-butter and an *egg* gave place to a cup of beef-tea, which I could scarcely taste, and after that some medicine. Jack, with a face more solemn than ever, made his bed at the foot of mine, and smoothed my pillow for me and whispered—

"Be sure and call if you want anything."

Then everything was silent and dark, and I began to realise that I was ill. I shall never forget that night. I tossed restlessly and ceaselessly all through it. In whatever position I lay I found no relief. My arm seemed to pain me more than ever before, my head ached, I was nearly suffocated with heat. And my mind was as restless as my body. One after another the follies and meannesses, the failures and sins of my life in London, rose up before me and stared me in the face. Try all I would, I could not get rid of them. I tried to think of other things—of books I had read, of stories I had heard, of places I had seen, of Stonebridge House, of Brownstroke—but no, the thought of my pitiful career in London, my debts, my evil acquaintances, my treachery to my friend, would come and come and come, and drive out all else. And all the while I seemed to see Jack's solemn face looking reproachfully at me from the bottom of the bed, just as it had looked at me that morning weeks ago at Hawk Street. Once, instead of being at the bottom of the bed, I found it close beside me, saying—

"What is it, old boy?"

"Eh? nothing. I didn't call."

"Yes you did. Do try and lie still and get some rest."

Lie still! As soon tell the waves to lie still in the storm as expect me, with my fever-tossed body and mind, to rest!

So the night wore on, and when the morning light struggled through the window it found me in a raging fever and delirious.

I must pass over the weeks that followed. I was very ill—as ill, so they told me afterwards, as I well could be, and live.

Jack watched me incessantly. I don't know what arrangement he came to at Hawk Street, but while I was at my worst he never left my bedside day or night.

No one else was allowed up, except occasionally Billy, to relieve guard. With these two nurses to tend me—and never a patient had two such guardian angels!—I battled with my fever, and came through it.

I came through it an altered being.

Surely—this was the thought with which I returned to health—we boys, sent up to rough it in London, are not, after all, mere slung stones. There *is* One who cares for us, some One who comes after us when we go astray, some One who saves us when we are at the point of falling, if we will but cry, in true penitence, to Him!

I had had many and grievous lessons before I had found it out; but now I had, life seemed a new thing to me!

As my convalescence advanced and my bodily strength returned, my spirits rose within me, and I felt eager to be back at my post at Hawk Street. However, I had to exercise some patience yet. Meanwhile, with Billy (and occasionally Mr Smith), as my companion by day, and Jack by night, the time could hardly hang heavily.

"Well, Billy," I said one morning when the doctor had been and told me that next week I might be allowed to sit up for an hour or so a day, "I shall soon be rid of this bed. I don't know what would have become of me if it hadn't been for you and Jack Smith."

"Ga on," said Billy, who, with his tongue in one cheek and his face twisting into all sorts of contortions, was sitting writing an exercise in a copy-book, "you don't know what you're torkin' about."

"Oh yes, I do, though," I replied, understanding that this was Billy's modest way of disclaiming any merit.

"More'n you didn't when you was 'avin' the fever!" observed the boy.

"What?" I inquired. "Was I talking much when I was ill?"

"You was so," said Billy, "a-joring and a-joring and a-joring same as you never heard a bloke."

"What was I saying?" I asked, feeling a little uneasy as to what I might have said in my delirium.

"You was a swearin' tremenjus," said the boy.

"Was I?" Alas! Jack would have heard it all.

"Yes, and you was a-torkin' about your Crowses, and Wollopses, and Doubledaisies, and sich like. And you was a-tellin' that there 'Orksbury (which I'd like to do for, the animal, so I would), as you was a convex son, and he wasn't to tell no one for fear Mashing should 'ear of it. And you was a-crying out for your friend Smith to shine your boots, and tellin' him you wouldn't do it never no more. And you was a-singin' out that there was a little gal a-bein' run away with on a pony, and you must go and stop 'im. You was a-jawin', rather."

I could hardly help laughing at his description, though its details reminded me sadly of my old follies and their consequences.

The most extraordinary raving of all, however, was that which referred to my stopping the little girl's runaway pony at Packworth years ago—an incident I don't believe I had ever once thought of since.

It was curious, too, that, now it was called to memory, I thought of the adventure a good deal, and wished I knew what had become of the owner of that restive little pony. I determined to tell Jack about it when he came home.

"What do you think, Jack?" I said, as he was tucking me up for the night. "Billy has been telling me what I was talking about in my fever, and says one thing I discoursed about was a little girl who was being run away with by a pony."

"Yes," said Jack, laughing; "I heard that. It was quite a new light for you, old man, to be dreaming of that sort of romantic thing."

"But it really happened once," I said.

"No! where? I thought the Henniker and Mrs Nash were the only lady friends you ever had? Where was it?"

"At Packworth, of all places," I said. "It was that day I went over to try and find you out—just before we came up to London, you know. I was walking back to Brownstroke, and met the pony bolting down the road."

Jack seemed suddenly very much interested. "What sort of little girl was it?" he asked.

"I can't exactly tell you. She was so frightened I had hardly time to look at her. But—"

"What sort of pony?" asked Jack.

"A grey one—and a jolly little animal, too!" I said. "But why do you ask?"

"Only," said Jack, with a peculiar smile, "because it strikes me very forcibly the young person in question was my sister, that's all!"

"What!" I exclaimed, in amazement, "your sister!—the little girl of the photograph! Oh, Jack, how extraordinary!"

"It is queer," said Jack; "but it's a fact all the same. I heard about it when I was last home. The pony took fright, so they told me, and—wasn't there a nurse with her?"

"Yes, there was."

"Yes; that was Mrs Shield. The pony took fright as she was walking beside it, and Mary would have come to grief to a dead certainty, so they both say, if a young gentleman hadn't rushed up and stopped it. Why, Fred, old man," said he, taking my hand, "I little thought I owed you all that!"

I took his hand warmly, but humbly.

"Jack," I said, "I think it's almost time you and I gave up talking about what we owe to one another. But," I added, after a moment, "if you do want to do me a favour, just let us have a look at that photograph again, will you, old man?"

Chapter Twenty Eight
How I found myself once more at Hawk Street

In due time the doctor paid his final visit and gave me leave to return to Hawk Street.

I can't describe how strange it seemed to be walking out once more in the open air, leaning on Jack's arm, and feeling myself an active member of society.

The part of the town where Jack's lodgings were situated was new to me. It could not have been worse than Beadle Square, but it wasn't much better. This street was narrow and squalid and crowded, and presented no attractions either in the way of fresh air or convenience. Still, to me, any place that harboured Jack Smith would have been more homelike than the stateliest mansion.

"By the way," said Jack, as we walked down to the office the first morning, "I suppose you don't want to go back to Beadle Square."

"Not if I can help it," I said; "the only thing is, I suppose, I ought to tell my uncle. You know he paid my lodging there."

"Oh, that's all right," said Jack. "I went down one day and saw Mrs Nash and told her what had become of you, and said she might let your bed to any one else. And I wrote to your uncle (I thought it best not to bother you by telling you at the time), and told him where you were and how you were getting on. He wrote back a civil note to say he was glad to hear you were getting better; and with regard to the lodgings, he had been just about to write and say that as you had now a respectable income at the office he would not be continuing to pay for your lodging; so that when you got well you might consider yourself free to do as you liked in that respect."

"Awfully obliging of him," said I.

"Well, it struck me as rather a cordial way of putting it," remarked Jack, laughing.

"I had better look for quarters at once," said I.

"Do nothing of the kind. Stay where you are!"

"What?" I exclaimed, in pleased astonishment. The idea had never occurred to me before. "How ever could I? As it is I've been turning Mr Smith out long enough."

"He was talking to me about it the other day," said Jack. "He finds that all his time is now required at the office of the newspaper he writes for, and therefore he has really no use for his room except as a bedroom. So that our room up stairs is at our complete disposal."

"How jolly!" I exclaimed. "Nothing could have happened more delightfully."

"Nothing," said Jack, as pleased as I was; "and he says any time of an evening when he's away we can use the lower room as if it was our own. Isn't it brickish of him?"

I agreed heartily in the sentiment, and proceeded to Hawk Street with less weight on my mind than ever.

There, as was natural, I found myself an object of a good deal of interest and remark. Doubleday, who once during my illness had sent me a short note of sympathy by Smith, was the first to welcome me back to my old quarters.

"Here we are again, young 'un, alive and kicking," cried he, clapping me on the back as I entered. "How his whiskers have grown, haven't they, Wallop? Well, how's your game leg?"

"It was my arm, not my leg," I said.

"No! was it? I heard it was your off-leg and your spine and your skull that were smashed. That's what made me so surprised to see you. Never mind, I'm glad to see you, young 'un, for there's a ticklish bit of figure work to do. None of the others would look at it, so I've saved it up for you, my boy."

"And I'm ready for it," said I.

Crow and Wallop greeted me rather more shyly. I fancy they had had rather a fright when they heard how very ill I had been.

They shook hands rather sheepishly, and Wallop said something about the weather which had no actual bearing, on my recovery. I had come to the conclusion during my illness that Crow and Wallop had not been altogether profitable companions, and I was therefore glad they were not more demonstrative now.

But I had yet to meet Hawkesbury, and wished the operation well over; for however much I may once have believed in him, I now disliked him, and determined to have as little to do with him as possible.

"Ah, Batchelor," cried he, coming up with outstretched hand, and beaming as if the incident in my sick-room weeks ago had never happened. "So glad to see you back. We have missed you greatly. How do you feel? You're looking better than when I saw you last."

I just took his hand and said, "Thank you," as shortly as I could.

He appeared neither to notice my manner nor my tone.

"You've had a long spell of it," said he. "I'd no idea a broken arm was such a serious thing. But I dare say you'll be all the better for your long rest."

I set to work to open my desk and get together my papers and pens, ready for work.

"It was a bad fall you had," continued he, standing beside me as I was thus employed. "You have no idea how distressed I was when it happened. But Whipcord was really in such a shocking state that night that—"

"Can you give me a piece of blotting-paper?" I said to Doubleday across the desk.

He waited till I had got what I wanted, and proceeded, smiling as ever, "It really wasn't safe for any of us. Masham, by the way, was very sorry to hear of your accident, and asked me to tell you so. I meant to do so the evening I called, but your friend was really so polite that I forgot all about it."

I had stood it thus far, and kept to my resolve of saying as little as I could. But when he brought in Jack's name it was all I could do to hold my peace.

I made an excuse to leave my place and consult a Directory, in the hopes of shaking him off, but there he was when I returned, ready to go on as benignly as ever.

"I'm sure, Batchelor," said he, "it must have been greatly against you to be cooped up in that miserable lodging all the time, and in—what I should call—such uncongenial society. But when one is ill, of course one has just to put up with what one can get."

My patience had reached its limit at last.

"My friend's society is more congenial to me than yours is at present!" I said, colouring up and bending over my writing.

"I see," said he, "he has got you under this thumb again, and means to keep you there."

"Will you let me get on with my work?" I said.

"Oh, certainly!" said he, smiling blandly. "I merely wished to tell you how glad I was to see you back at last; but I dare say that doesn't interest you."

I made no answer, and, seeing that I was determined to hold no more conversation, he gently withdrew.

I felt quite relieved when he had done so, and still more to find that, for the first time in my life, I had been proof against his blandishments.

"What have you been doing to Petty-Cash?" whispered Doubleday to me, presently; "he looks so smiling and benevolent that I'm certain you must have given him mortal offence about something or other."

"I don't care if I have," I said.

Doubleday whistled softly. "I say, young 'un," said he, "your illness has smartened you up a bit, I reckon, eh?"

This, coming from the source it did, I felt to be a compliment. However, I had more calls upon my new resolutions before the day was over.

The partners arrived and received me—each in his own peculiar way—very kindly. Mr Merrett was good enough to say the work of the office had suffered a good deal in my absence, and Mr Barnacle said he hoped I had come back prepared to make up for lost time. To both which observations I listened respectfully, and returned once more to my desk.

The morning passed quickly and busily. I had made a plunge into the difficult task so considerately saved up for me by Doubleday, and felt quite refreshed by the array of figures to be dealt with. In fact, I was so engrossed with it that when Jack came and asked me if I was going out to lunch I said I really could not leave it now, but would take my lunch later on.

So he went, and several of the others, leaving me with Crow, Wallop, and Hawkesbury, in possession of the office.

The two former heroes had by this time somewhat recovered from their surprise at seeing me once more in the land of the living, and seemed disposed to wax facetious in proportion at my expense.

I dug my thumbs into my ears, in the hopes of getting on with my work, but it was not easy, and I had at last to give up the attempt.

"Jolly glad he's not kicked the bucket, for one thing," said Wallop.

"Why?" asked Crow, apparently surprised that there should be any reason for thankfulness in such an event.

"He owes me thirty bob, that's all," said Wallop.

It was true! It was one of the oldest of my debts, and one which had been greatly on my mind for many a day.

"Ah!" said I, feeling constrained to take some notice of the remark. "I'm afraid I've kept you out of that money a long time, Wallop."

"Don't mention it," said Wallop. "When I want it I'll drop on you for it, my boy."

"I'll try to pay it off as soon as ever I can," I said.

I disliked Wallop, as I have said, and the thought that I owed him money was not at all pleasant to me.

My creditor laughed.

"There's plenty more will be glad to hear you're better," said he. "There's Shoddy I met the other week in a regular blue funk because he thought you'd bolted. He wanted to come down and see the governors here about his little bill, but I managed to pacify him. But he says if you don't give him a call soon he'll wake you up."

"I'll go and see him at once," I said, feeling very uncomfortable.

"Then there's the Twins. It seems you're on their books for a matter of a sov. or so advanced you at odd times. They've been most affectionate in their inquiries about you."

It wasn't pleasant to be reminded thus on my first morning back at work of the burden of debt which still pressed on me from the old, and I humbly hoped bygone, days of my extravagance. Not even a broken arm or a dangerous fever will wipe off old scores.

Wallop rather enjoyed going through the catalogue of my debts.

"Then there's Tucker, the pastrycook, wants half-a-sov. at the very least, and Weeden, the tobacconist, a florin for mild cigarettes, and—"

"Yes, yes," I said; "I know all about it, and I'm going to pay them all."

"That's a good job," remarked Wallop, "and the sooner you tell them all so the better. They'd all like to have your present address."

"I'm not sure that that would console them much," said Crow. "It's rather a shadier place than the old one."

"Yes, when you come to think of it, a fellow would get a bit shy when he read the address, 'care of Tom Jailbird, Esquire, Up a Slum, Drury Lane.'"

"Look here!" cried I, suddenly starting up; "don't you call my friend names, please."

Nothing could have delighted the genial pair more than my excitement. They greeted my protest with laughter, and winking at one another, continued to talk among themselves.

"Good practice, I should think. Crow, living with a chap like that—get used to prison fare. Come all the easier later on."

"Wonder if they practise picking one another's pockets to keep their hands in, of an evening."

"I'm told that jailbird has got an album full of tickets-of-leave."

"Ah! His father must have travelled a good bit in his time."

It was pitiful, paltry jesting, but it was more than I could stand.

"Will you stop?" I shouted.

"Nobody was speaking to you," said Wallop.

"You were speaking of my friend!" I exclaimed.

"More shame to you for chumming up with such disreputable lot," said Crow.

"Do you hear? stop it!" I shouted.

"We'll stop it," said Wallop, "when—"

I did not wait to hear more, but rushed upon the speaker.

The upshot might have been serious for me in my present weak condition, and being one against two. But before my blow could be returned Hawkesbury, who had so far been a silent witness to the scene, sprang from his place and pulled me away. I struggled to get free, but he held me firm, as he said, "Batchelor, don't be foolish. You two, be quiet, will you, or I must report you to my uncle. Fighting is not allowed in here."

"I didn't want to fight," said Wallop, putting up his hand to his smarting cheek, "but I'll have it out with him."

"Young prig!" growled Crow, savagely.

"You hear what I say," said Hawkesbury. "I won't allow it to go any further. Here, Batchelor, go to your seat, and don't be absurd."

This tone of authority and his unasked-for interference irritated me as much as ever the language of my two adversaries had done. Hawkesbury was always getting the pull of me in ways like this.

I retired sulkily to my seat, saying I would thrash any one who insulted Smith in my presence, at which the others sneered.

"All I can say is," said Wallop, with his hand still up to his face, "if I don't get that thirty shillings he owes me to-morrow, I'll show him up in a way that will astonish him—that's all."

With which threat he took up his hat and went out, leaving me in a very agitated and uncomfortable frame of mind, as the reader may guess.

I would far sooner have been thrashed out and out by Wallop than be left thus under what Hawkesbury would certainly consider an obligation to him.

"I thought it best," said he, in his insinuating way, "to interfere. You are really not well enough for that sort of thing, Batchelor."

During the rest of the day my mind was too uneasy to permit me to make much progress with my work, and I was glad when evening came and I could escape with my friend.

"You look fagged," said he, as I took his arm.

"I am rather," said I, "and worried too, Jack."

"What about?" he asked.

Then I told him all about my debts; and we spent the rest of the evening in a sort of committee of ways and means.

Taken separately my debts were none of them very large, but added all together their total was something appalling. Ten pounds would scarcely cover them, and that did not include what I owed the doctor.

It was a serious business, without doubt.

Wallop's threat to insist on immediate payment, or else "show me up" before the partners and my other creditors, may have been mere bounce; but it may equally well have been in earnest, in which case I was ruined.

Jack's one solicitude that evening was to keep me from fretting too much. But it is all very well to say, "Don't fret," and another thing to remove the cause of fretting. And that we could neither of us do.

Jack had no money. What little he had saved he had spent on books or sent home to Mrs Shield. As for Mr Smith, senior, even if I had cared to ask him to help me, I knew he had barely enough to keep body and soul together. The idea of borrowing from Doubleday occurred to me, but Smith promptly discouraged it. Besides, I had once asked him for a loan, and he had refused it, on the ground he never lent money to anybody.

"The only thing," said Jack, "is to write home to your uncle."

I could scarcely help smiling at the idea. I knew my uncle better than Jack Smith did, and I might as well hope to get blood out of a stone as expect him to pay for my extravagances in London.

However, Jack was so sure it was the right and only thing to do that I finally consented to sit down and make a clean breast of it, which I did in the following note:—

"Dear Uncle,—I am better now, and back at work. I am sorry to say, however, I am in a good deal of difficulty about money. Before my illness I had got into extravagant ways and run into debt. I enclose a list of what I believe I owe at the present moment. You will see—not including the doctor's bill—it comes to £10 2 shillings 4 pence. The names marked with a star are clerks at the office who have lent me money, I am sorry to say, for gambling and other purposes. I don't know what to do about paying them back. I thought if you wouldn't mind advancing the amount I could pay you back so much a week out of my salary. I hope and trust you will help me in my difficulty. I need hardly say I have seen the folly of my old ways, and am determined to live carefully and economically in future. Do please write by return and help me.

"Your affect. nephew,—

"Fred. Batchelor."

Jack approved of this effusion as businesslike and to the point.

"You haven't gone out of the way to excuse yourself," said he, "and I dare say it will go down all the better for that. If he doesn't write and send up the money I shall be surprised."

Poor Jack! A lot he knew about uncles of my sort!

However, I felt more comfortable to have written the letter, and if I could only have been sure Wallop's threat was mere idle bluster I should have slept easily.

As it was, I had had rather a stirring day for my first one out, and at the end of it felt a good deal less game for work than at the beginning. Nothing could exceed Jack's tenderness and anxiety to relieve me of as much worry as possible. When I was in bed he came and read aloud to me. It was Virgil he read—which he was working at for his examination. And I remember that evening lying half awake, half asleep, listening now to him, thinking now of my debts, mixing up Aeneas with Wallop, and Mr Shoddy with Laocoön, and poor old Priam with my uncle.

The following morning I rose only half refreshed, and made my way anxiously to the office. One of the first fellows I met was Wallop, who greeted my approach with a surly grin.

I felt sure at that moment he had meant what he threatened yesterday, and my heart quailed within me at the prospect.

"Well, young prig," said he, "I suppose you've brought my money?"

"No," said I; "I'm afraid I must ask you to wait a little longer. I hope you won't do anything for a day or two, at any rate. I will do my best to get it by then."

He laughed in my face, and evidently enjoyed my distress.

"You sung a different tune yesterday, my boy, when you hit me. Do you remember? That wasn't the payment I wanted!"

"I'm sorry I lost my temper," said I.

"Well, I mean to show you I pay my debts more punctually than you do," said he; and with that he gave me a cuff on my head which sent me reeling half across the office.

I could not—I dare not—return it, and he knew it.

"There," said he, laughing brutally; "now we're quits! As to that thirty shillings, I'll let you off, as it has been paid me."

"Paid you!" I exclaimed, in utter bewilderment. "Who by?"

"Hawkesbury!"

Chapter Twenty Nine
How I began to see Daylight through my Troubles

Those of my readers who have read their Virgil will most likely remember an observation made by one of the gentlemen who figure conspicuously in the story of the *Aeneid*. He dreaded his hereditary enemies, the Greeks, under any circumstances; but he never dreaded them so much as when they came and offered him presents!

This was pretty much my feeling when I was told that my debt to Wallop had been paid for me by Hawkesbury.

There had been a time in my life when I almost liked Hawkesbury. More recently I had suspected him of being not quite the angel I once believed him. Later still I had felt my suspicion grow to very decided dislike. And now, at the moment when he made me his debtor for thirty shillings, I positively loathed him.

I could not guess his motive. I was certain it was not out of pure love for me or pity for Wallop. Indeed, I was pretty certain there was far more mischief than good in the action. I would sooner have owed Wallop thirty pounds than Hawkesbury thirty shillings. He knew it, too, and for that very reason paid my debt to Wallop.

"Whatever business of Hawkesbury's is it?" I demanded of Wallop, as soon as I could find words to express myself.

"Goodness knows," replied Wallop, with a laugh.

"But I won't let him do it. I don't want him to pay my debts. You must give him the money back, Wallop." Wallop grinned delightedly.

"Oh, quite so. It's rather likely, when I've been waiting for my money the best part of a year, I should decline to receive it when I've got the chance! No, my boy, you can settle with Hawkesbury now. You owe him the thirty bob, not me!"

What was I to do? I demanded an explanation of Hawkesbury as soon as he appeared.

"Wallop tells me you've paid him the thirty shillings I owed him," said I.

"Oh, he shouldn't have told you," said Hawkesbury, with the meek air of a benevolent man who doesn't like to hear his own good deeds talked about.

"I wish you hadn't done it," said I.

"Oh, you mustn't think of it," said he, blandly. "It was only because I heard him threaten to get you into trouble if you didn't pay him, and I should have been so sorry if that had happened."

"Thank you, but really I prefer to pay my own debts!"

He laughed as if it was a joke.

"I'm sure you do; but as I knew you couldn't do it, I thought it would be a relief to you if I did it for you."

Could he be in earnest? He talked as if I ought to be grateful to him instead of in a rage, as I was. Certainly it was a queer position to be in—storming at a fellow who has just saved you from debt, perhaps disgrace, possibly ruin, I *couldn't* make out what to think of it.

"I daresay you thought you were doing me a good turn," I said as civilly as I could, "but as it happens I wish you had let the thing alone."

He sighed forgivingly and went to his desk.

The moment Jack and I got outside at dinner-time I unburdened my woes to him.

He was in as great if not a greater commotion than I was.

"What does he mean by it?" he exclaimed. "Fred, you must pay him back at once, whatever it costs you!"

"All very well," said I, "but you know I've nothing."

"Can't you pawn anything? can't you get a job of some sort to do? anything to pay him off. I shall be miserable as long as you owe him a farthing!"

He spoke with a vehemence that quite astonished me.—"You don't mean to say you're going to let yourself stop in his debt?" he exclaimed, when I did not answer.

"Not a second after I can get the money."

"When will you hear from your uncle?"

"To-morrow morning if he writes by return. But I've no hopes from him."

"I suppose it would not do to ask the partners," said Jack.

I was thunderstruck at the very idea. For Jack to entertain it for a moment only showed how desperately in earnest he was.

We could get no light on the subject, and I had the pleasure of being reminded by Hawkesbury's smile all day long that I was in his power, and saw no way out.

That whole evening Jack and I sat and discussed the situation. We even rose early, to consult Mr Smith the elder on his return to the lodgings. He soon appreciated our difficulty; but he could suggest no relief. For he was as poor as either of us, and had as few friends.

My uncle's letter did not come that day or the next.

Meanwhile I knew no peace. Hawkesbury's manner was more suave and condescending than ever.

To the rest of my fellow-clerks during those two days I was the most cross-grained and obnoxious comrade conceivable. My only relief seemed to be in quarrelling with somebody, and as they all laid themselves out to bait and tease me one way or another I had a pretty lively time of it.

My chief hope was (and Jack shared in it), that if my uncle had been determined not to help me at all he would probably have written by return. The delay might mean he was at least considering the matter.

At last, on the third day of my waiting, the postman knocked at our door. With beating heart I rushed to receive the letter which I knew must be for me.

It was, but it was not from my uncle, it was from Hawkesbury.

"My Dear Batchelor," he wrote, "I am very sorry to see that I have given you offence by settling your debt with Wallop. I really meant it for the best, because I knew you could not pay, and I was afraid if it came to my uncle's or Mr Barnacle's knowledge it might be awkward for you, for I happen to know my uncle feels very strongly about clerks getting into debt, especially through gambling. I'm afraid I can't undo what has been done, for Wallop will hardly give me back the money. So I write to tell you how sorry I am, and to say I hope you will forgive me. Please do not trouble about the repayment of the loan; you must take whatever time suits you. I trust this little matter will not make us worse friends than before.

"Yours sincerely, —

"E. Hawkesbury.

"P.S.—I write this as I shall be away from the office the next two days, while we are moving to our new house. When we are settled in I hope you will come and see us."

What was I to think of it? For the last three days I had been losing no opportunity of snubbing this fellow, and to demonstrate to him that, so far from feeling obliged to him, I disliked him all the more for what he had done. In return for which he now writes me this beautiful letter, breathing forgiveness and considerateness, and absolutely apologising for having paid thirty shillings to save me from ruin!

Either he must be a paragon of the first water, or else—

I gave it up, and handed the letter across to Jack Smith. He read it, with knit brows, from beginning to end, and then a second time; after which he tossed it back to me and said, "Well, what do you think of that?"

"What do you?"

"Rot, every bit of it!"

I expected he would say so. "But, Jack," I began.

"You don't mean to say," said Jack, "you're going to let yourself be taken in by that stuff?"

"But unless he means what he says, what possible motive can he have for writing a letter like that?"

Jack did not answer. We did not discuss the matter further, but I went down to the office that morning with the letter in my pocket, heartily wishing I could make up my mind what to think of it all as easily as Jack Smith.

One thing, at any rate, was a comfort—I should not see Hawkesbury for two days.

But if I was to be spared the sight of one unwelcome person, I had in store for me another which I little expected. I was coming with Jack out of the office on the second evening afterwards, after a hard day's work, wondering why my uncle did not write, and sighing inwardly at the prospect of seeing Hawkesbury back next day, when a stranger accosted me in the street.

At least, I thought him a stranger until, standing full in front of him, I saw his face and heard him speak.

"Oh, good evening, Mr Batchelor, sir! The governor's compliments, sir—Mr Shoddy's compliments—and he'll be particularly glad if you'll step round now, sir."

I owed Shoddy three pounds, and this summons fell on my ear like a knell.

"Better go," said Jack.

How sick Jack must be of me, thought I, by this time. Ever since I had been back with him he had been for ever worried either with my health or my debts or my office rows. I was half tempted to ask him not to come, but I could not bring myself to be sufficiently self-denying.

"What does Mr Shoddy want me for?" I asked of the assistant as we walked along.

"I believe, sir, between ourselves, it's about your little account, sir. How do the clothes wear, sir? Nice stuff that tweed we made them of. Could do you a very nice suit of the same now, sir, dirt cheap. Two fifteen to you, and measure the coat. We should charge three guineas to any one else."

It occurred to me to wonder why so great exception should be made in my favour, especially as I had owed my present bill so long. However, we let the fellow rattle on at his shoppy talk, and soon arrived at Mr Shoddy's ready-made clothes establishment.

I felt rather like a criminal being brought up before a judge than a customer before the tailor of his patronage.

"Good evening, Mr Batchelor," said the tailor. "Take a seat, sir."

I did so, and Jack took another.

A long pause ensued.

"You wished to see me," observed I.

"Well, yes, I do," said the tailor. "The fact is, Mr Batchelor, you aren't treating me well. Those clothes were sold you for cash, sir—cash down!"

"Yes, I'm afraid I have been rather slow in paying, Mr Shoddy," said I.

"Quite so, sir! The question is, have you the amount with you now—three pounds plus six shillings for interest to date?"

"I certainly have not the money with me," said I.

"Ah! Then you are prepared to give me security, of course? Now what do you say to my drawing on Messrs Merrett, Barnacle, and Company, at one month, for the amount? I should be satisfied with their bill."

I nearly jumped off my seat with horror.

"Merrett, Barnacle, and Company pay my tailor's bill! Oh, no! quite out of the question!" I exclaimed.

"Ah, that's a pity! I should have liked their bill, and you could pay them by instalments."

"I wouldn't on any account have them spoken to on the subject," said I.

"Well, perhaps your friend here—"

"No," said Jack; "I've no money at all."

"Your uncle possibly—"

How had the man heard that I had an uncle? He seemed to know all about me, and I began to get uncomfortable.

"My uncle, I fear, would not advance the money. I have already asked him, and had no reply."

"This is rather awkward for you, sir," said Mr Shoddy, coolly. "I quite hoped you would have been prepared with a proposal."

"I might be able to pay you a shilling a week," I faltered.

Mr Shoddy shrugged his shoulders. "Three pounds six is sixty-six shillings, interest six and six; seventy-two shillings and sixpence—seventy-two and a half weeks—one year and four and a half months to pay off. Thank you, sir; can't do it."

"I don't know what to do if you won't accept that," I faltered.

"Three shillings a week, *secured*," said the tailor, "would meet the case, I think. What do you think?"

"I could never keep it up, I fear," said I; "but I'd try."

"Thank you, sir. You draw your salary weekly, I believe?"

"Yes," I said.

"Oh, then, if I just look in and see one of the principals and explain, he'll stop the three shillings a week for me, which will save all trouble. What time are they generally at home?"

The cool resolve of the man to make my employers a party to my debt positively terrified me. I begged him to give up the idea, promised wildly to do all sorts of things to pay him, and entreated him to give me more time.

He was politely inexorable. "Pleased to oblige you, but, after a year, we must look after our little accounts, mustn't we? Let's see, to-morrow I'm engaged. I'll look in on Friday and settle it."

No argument or entreaty of mine could make him understand such a step would be ruination to me. He was firmly convinced a guarantee from the firm would be the best security for his money, and so, simply disregarding all my protests and appeals, gaily promised to see me again on Friday.

What was I to do? My only hope was in my uncle's answer, and that, as the reader knows, was small enough.

The following morning it arrived. It was brief, and to the point:—

"Dear Nephew,—I hold that lads of your age cannot learn too soon that the people to pay debts are those who make them. I return your list, as it may be useful.

"Yours,—

"F. Jakeman."

It was what I had expected. My last hope of a respite now gone to the winds!

We walked down disconsolately to the office. Hawkesbury was back in his place, smiling as usual. But the dread of Shoddy's visit to-morrow drove away all thought for the present of resentment against Hawkesbury. I was even constrained to greet him civilly, and when he asked if I had received his letter, to say yes, I was much obliged.

On leaving the office that evening the tailor's assistant was hanging about outside as before. I imagined he had some fresh message, and went up to him eagerly. "Well," said I, "what is it?"

"Nothing that I know of," said he. "I was just passing this way, and thought I'd see how you were getting on. No orders, I suppose? None of your young gentlemen want a nice cheap suit? Pleased to make you a consideration for the introduction. If one or two of you joined together and took a piece, could do the lot very reasonably indeed."

So, not only was I to be exposed before my employers to-morrow, but meanwhile my movements were being watched, for fear I should run away, I suppose.

"Jack," said I, as we walked along, "I believe you are right after all."

"How?" said Jack.

"The only thing to do is to tell the partners all about it, before Shoddy comes to-morrow!"

"Well," said Jack, "I don't see it could be much worse than letting them hear all about it from him."

With which consoling but desperate resolution we proceeded.

To beguile the time, we went round by Style Street.

A youth was standing having his boots blacked as we came up. We thought we recognised the figure—though till he turned round we could not recall his name. Then to our surprise we saw it was Flanagan.

But such a swell as he was! He had alarmed me more than once by the grandeur of his attire when I had met him at the parties of the "usual lot." I had seen him rarely since. As for Jack, the two had scarcely met since they left Stonebridge House.

"Hullo, Batchelor," he cried, as we approached, "that you? I heard you'd been ill, and—why, Smith," he broke out, catching sight of my companion, "how are you? Haven't seen you for ages! And the rum thing is I was speaking about you this very moment—wasn't I, kid?"

"Yaas," said Billy, with a grin.

"You know, Batchelor, you once introduced me to this young gentleman when we were rolling home one night after a spree—fearfully slow parties some of those!—and I've given him a job pretty often since—and he was just telling me about you. Lodging Drury Lane way, I hear?"

"Yes," said I. There was something so genuine in the tone of my old schoolfellow that I could almost forgive him his grand clothes.

"I say, couldn't you come along to my rooms to-night? I'm all by myself. Jolly to talk over old days. Come on, Smith."

"Thanks," said Smith, who, I could see, felt half shy of this old comrade, "but I have to work for an exam., and it's coming off now in a week or two."

"Well, Batchelor, you come," said Flanagan.

I hesitated a moment, and then consented. The fact was, I suspected Flanagan might possibly get his clothes made at Shoddy's. In which case, as to all appearance he must be a good customer, he might, I thought, use his influence with the tailor to prevent the threatened visit to-morrow.

So I went with him, much to his satisfaction, and we had a pleasant evening together. He confided to me his troubles. How he was getting tired of the "usual lot," and of London altogether, and wanted his father to let him be a farmer. How he was always getting into trouble up here in town, living by himself, with far more money than he wanted, and no one "to pull him up," as he called it. How he often recalled Stonebridge House with all its hardships, and wished himself back there instead of in this unsatisfactory world of London.

"If I could only grind like Smith," said he, "it wouldn't be so bad; but what's the use of my grinding? In fact, what's the use of my being up here at all, when I only get into rows, and spend one half of my time going to the dogs and the other in pulling up?"

"Well," said I, "that's better than me, who spend all my time in going to the dogs."

"Oh, but you had Smith to keep you steady," said he. "You couldn't go far wrong with him. I've got no one of that sort. I really wish my father would put me to farming. A fellow couldn't go to the dogs, you know, all among the cows, and pigs, and horses—that is," added he, laughing, "not the sort of dogs I mean."

There was a great deal in Flanagan's troubles with which I could sympathise. He was a fellow with a kind nature at bottom, but too easy-going to withstand the temptations of London.

In return for his confidence I told him most of my troubles. He was greatly interested in the story, and especially reproached himself with his share in aiding and abetting my past extravagances.

When, however, I came to tell him of my financial troubles with Hawkesbury and Shoddy he brightened up suddenly.

"Why, why ever didn't you tell me of that before, Batchelor?" he exclaimed. "And this beggar Shoddy's going to show you up, is he? Ha, ha! we'll disappoint him for once in a way. I know him of old."

"I was wondering if you knew him," said I, suddenly feeling my spirits lightened, "and would mind asking him not to call up at the office."

"Of course I will," said Flanagan, jumping up and taking his hat. "Come along, old man, he won't be shut up yet, I expect. If he is we'll wake him up."

And off we went, my heart full of joy at this unexpected hope.

Shoddy's shop was still open, and its lord was at home. He greeted Flanagan obsequiously, as a good customer.

"Ah, Shoddy, how are you? Just make out my friend's bill here, will you—look sharp!"

Shoddy, in as much surprise as I was, promptly obeyed, adding the interest for the last year and the next.

"Knock off that last six-and-six," demanded my friend.

"But that's for—"

"Knock it off, do you hear?" shouted Flanagan, "and receipt it."

Fancy my astonishment! I had expected to see Shoddy persuaded to abandon his idea of calling at the office; but this was far more than I ever dreamt of.

"Oh, Flanagan," I began, "you really—"

"Shut up," said Flanagan. "May as well owe it to me as Shoddy. There," added he, putting down the money and giving me the receipt, "and look here, Mr Shoddy, the next time you try your sharp practice on us I change my tailor."

"And now," said he, putting a note into my hand, "this will help to square accounts with Hawkesbury and some of the others. Mind you pay it back, do you hear?"

Before I could even turn to speak to him he had bolted round the corner and vanished!

Chapter Thirty
How I paid off a Score, and made a rather Awkward Discovery

I stood staring at the five-pound note which Flanagan had left in my hand in a state of utter bewilderment.

My first impulse was to give chase to my benefactor and compel him to take back the money. My second was to do nothing of the sort, but rejoice with thankfulness over the help thus unexpectedly sent me.

It was little enough I had done to deserve any one's kindness, and it was only too reasonable to expect to have to get myself out of my own troubles. But here, like some good fairy, my old Irish schoolfellow had stepped on to the scene, and sent all those troubles to the right-about with a single turn of the hand.

What rejoicings Jack and I had that night over my good fortune! What careful plans we made for a systematic repayment of the loan! and how jubilantly I looked forward to handing Hawkesbury back his thirty shillings in the morning!

Since I had received that letter of his my wrath had somewhat abated towards him. Much as I disliked and suspected him, still I could not feel quite certain that he might not after all have meant well by what he did, however blundering and objectionable a way he had taken to show it. That, however, did not interfere with my satisfaction now at the prospect of being quits.

It was a positive luxury, as Jack and I entered the office next morning, to be able to meet his amiable, condescending smile in a straightforward way, and not by colouring up and looking confused and chafing inwardly.

I was anxious to get the ceremony over as soon as possible, and therefore walked straight up to his desk, and, placing the thirty shillings before him, said, in a voice which I did not trouble to conceal from the other clerks present.

"That's the thirty shillings you paid Wallop for me the other day, Hawkesbury. I'm much obliged for the loan of it."

If some one had informed him he was to start in five minutes for the North Pole, he could not have looked more amazed or taken aback. Nothing, evidently, had been farther from his thoughts than that I should be able to repay the loan, and to have it here returned into his hands before I had been his debtor a week fairly astonished him.

His face darkened suddenly into an expression very unusual with him, as he looked first at the money, then at me.

However, I gave him no time to say anything, but hurried off to my desk, feeling—for the first time since my return to Hawk Street—that there was not a man at the office I dared not look in the face.

As I expected, he sidled up to me at the first opportunity.

"Batchelor," said he, "you must really take the money back. I am sure you must want it. I should be quite uncomfortable to feel I was depriving you of it."

And so saying, he actually laid the two coins down on my desk.

"Thank you," I began; "but if—"

"Please don't talk so loud," said he; "I would rather everybody didn't hear."

"Then," said I, "kindly take the money off my desk. It's yours."

"But, really, Batchelor, I don't feel comfortable—"

"I do," I interrupted.

"I am sure you are not in a position to afford it," said he. "Excuse my asking, but—"

"I suppose you'd like to know where I got it from," said I, irritated at his persistency. "You may be surprised to hear I didn't steal it, and equally surprised to hear I have no notion of gratifying your curiosity."

I was perfectly amazed at my own hardihood in thus addressing him. But now I had paid him I was afraid of him no more. He was too much put out to keep up his chronic smile as he said. "I hardly expected to be spoken to in this way by you, Batchelor, after all that has happened. If you had been left to yourself, I'm sure you would not have spoken so, but your friend Smith appears to have a special spite against me."

I was tempted to retort, but did not, and he went back pensively to his desk, taking the money with him.

The remainder of the five-pound note served to discharge my debts to the Twins, and to Tucker, the pastrycook, and Weeden, the tobacconist. The last two I paid myself; the first I sent by Doubleday, not wishing to encounter again the familiar heroes of the "usual lot."

It was with a light heart and a sense of burden removed from my life that I returned that evening to the lodgings, whither jack had preceded me.

On my arrival I found him in a state of uneasiness.

"Very queer," said he, "Billy's not turned up. He was to be here at seven, and it's now half-past; I never knew him late before."

"Very likely he's had some unexpected customers to detain him," I said.

"Not likely. Billy wouldn't be late for an appointment here if the Prince of Wales himself came to get his boots blacked."

"What can have become of him, then?" I said.

"I wish I knew. I am afraid he's got into trouble."

We waited another half-hour, and no Billy appeared. Smith looked more and more anxious.

"I think," said he, "we'd better go and look for him, Fred; what do you say?"

"I'll come, certainly," said I; "but where do you expect to find him?"

"If there is no sign of him in Style Street, I expect he'll be in the court where his mother lives."

I had a lively recollection of my last visit to that aristocratic thoroughfare. But I did not wish to seem unwilling to accompany Jack in his quest. Only I rather hoped we should find our man—or boy—in Style Street.

But that we did not do. The flagstone on which he was wont to establish his box was there, bare and unoccupied except for the scrawling letters and sums traced out with his finger-tip. High or low, he was not to be found in Style Street.

We went on in the growing dark towards the court.

"Do you know the house he lives at?"

"I'm not sure," said Jack.

"Do you know what name to inquire for?"

"No, only Billy," said Jack.

"Don't you think," said I, "it's rather unlikely we shall come across him in a crowded court like that, knowing neither the name nor the house where he lives?"

"Let us try, anyhow," said Jack.

We went on, and soon reached the well-known "slum." I must confess honestly I would rather not have entered. Last time we had been there one of us had been struck by smallpox, and both had had to run for our lives, and it seemed to me—perhaps my illness had made me a coward—that we were running an unnecessary risk now by plunging into it just because Billy happened to be an hour late for an appointment.

However, Jack was determined, and I was determined to stick by Jack.

When we first entered, the court was as before, swarming with men and women and children, and in the crowd we passed some way unnoticed.

Presently, however, Jack stopped and asked a woman—

"Do you know in what house a little boy called Billy who black boots lives?"

The woman who was engaged in sewing a black sleeve on to an old grey coat, looked up sharply, and demanded—

"What do you want to know for?"

"I want to see him," said Jack.

"What do you want to see him for?"

"He didn't come to the ragged school to-night."

The woman flared up.

"We don't want none of your ragged schools! You go and teach yourselves manners—that's what you'd better do, and don't come nosing about here—as if we couldn't get on without a parcel of snuffing young prigs like you to tell us what to do. That's what I think of you."

And the honest British matron tossed her head in a huff, and went on with her patchwork.

"If everybody was as honest as you," said Jack—where the sly dog learned the art of flattery I can't imagine—"no one would interfere. But we are afraid Billy's mother is not very good to him."

The woman looked up again, as if not quite sure what to make of this speech. But Jack looked so much in earnest that she said, shortly—

"You're about right there. I'm a poor woman, but I hope I know better than to make a beast of myself to my own childer."

Then she knew Billy, and could tell us where he lived after all.

Jack began, almost confidentially—

"Do you think—"

But he got no farther just then, for we had not noticed a group of idlers who, attracted by our presence in the court, and curious to know our business, had gathered round, and now began, half in jest, half in earnest, to hustle us, crying—

"Go on home. Go and teach yourselves. We don't want none of your ABC."

We thought it wise to walk slowly on, without appearing to be running away.

About half way up the court, however, a further stoppage occurred.

This was occasioned by the appearance of another stranger in the court besides ourselves—a clergyman, who, with a small but offence-less crowd at his heels, was making a grand tour of the various houses and flats.

He was a tall, kindly-looking man, with hair just turning white, who looked like a man who did not spare himself or live for himself. He had a pleasant word for everybody, however unpleasant and unpromising they might seem, and bore all the remarks and jests of unfriendly loafers with great good-humour and composure.

The sight of him in the midst of our difficulties was most welcome. We quickened our steps to meet him. The knot of roughs who were following us looked on this as a rout, and set up a yell of defiance. Others, seeing us walking rapidly away, joined in the demonstration, and one or two, not content with following us with their voices, followed us with stones.

Just as we came up to the clergyman a stone intended for one of us whizzed past my ear, and struck him on the cheek. He never moved a muscle, or even looked to see where it came from, but walked on to meet us.

"Oh! sir," said Jack, stepping forward, "we're so glad to meet you. We're looking for a little boy called Billy, who lives in this court, who generally comes to our ragged school, but wasn't there this evening. He's a shoeblack. Do you know where he lives?"

"I wish I could tell you," said the clergyman, "but this is my first visit here. Where is your school?"

"Oh, it's not properly a school, but Billy and sometimes one or two others come to our lodgings, and learn to write and read. He has never missed before. That's what makes me fear something is wrong."

At that moment the object of our search stood before us, with his usual grin wider than ever.

"What cheer, blokes?" was his greeting. "Oh, 'ere, governor, I reckon you're a-goin' to turn me up 'cos I wasn't at the racket school. But my old gal, she's a-missin'. She's always a-skylarkin' somewheres, she is, and I was a-lookin' for her."

"Have you found her?" asked Jack, whose pleasure at finding his young *protégé* was unconcealed.

"Found 'er! No; but I knows where she is."

"Where?"

"In the station, for smashin' winders. Ain't she a wonner?"

"My poor boy!" said the clergyman, sympathisingly.

"Ga on! I ain't your boy. Don't know yer; I'm this 'ere bloke's chap, and I ain't a-goin' to be larned by no one else."

It was impossible to avoid smiling at this frank declaration, seriously as it was uttered.

"When did your mother get into trouble?" asked Jack.

"This very afternoon, bless 'er old 'art. She was on the fly all yesterday, a-goin' on any'ow. So I comes round afore the racket school, to see if she was a-coolin' down, and, there! if she 'adn't hooked it! I 'as a good look up and down the court, but she'd walked. So I cuts to the nighest station, and sees a pal o' mine outside. 'It's all right,' says he; 'she's in there,' meaning the lock-up. 'Wot was she up to?' says I. 'Winders agin,' he says. So she's all safe, she is."

"I tell you what it is, Billy," said Smith. "I'm afraid you let her spend the money you get for blacking boots on drink. That's what gets her into trouble."

"That ain't no concern of yourn," said Billy. Then, suddenly correcting himself, he added, "Leastways it ain't no concern of these here two blokes. Mister, I say, governor, is it too late for to learn me to-night?"

"Yes, it's too late to-night; but we'll have the school to-morrow instead. Where will you live while your mother's away?"

"Oh, ain't you funny!" said the boy, with a grin. "As if a chap liked me lived anywheres!"

"Well," said Jack, taking my arm, and not desirous to prolong the discussion, "mind you turn up to-morrow, Billy."

"No fears," cried Billy, with a grin, accompanying us for a step or two, walking on his hands.

"That's a most extraordinary lad," said the clergyman.

"There's a lot of good in him," responded Smith.

"And you are doing your best to bring it out," said the clergyman.

"Which way are you going?" said he, when presently with no further adventure we had got through the court.

"To Drury Lane," said I.

"Ah, down this street. That's my way too. Will you just come into my house and have a bit of supper?"

Jack never liked accepting invitations, but there was something so friendly and simple-minded about this clergyman that it would almost have seemed rude to say no.

"This is quite a new part of the town to me," said he, as we walked along. "I suppose you know it well?"

"Yes," said I, "we lived close here for some months."

"I wished you lived here still," he said. "I want workers of your sort in my new parish."

He insisted on including *me* in his compliments, not knowing how little I deserved them.

"My walk this evening," said he, "is really the first serious voyage of discovery I have made in my parish, and the result is not very encouraging. It seems a very low neighbourhood, worse a good deal than I expected. However, there will be all the more to do."

There was something so modest and yet so resolute in the way he spoke that we both liked him.

His house, a dull-looking City rectory, was at the end of the street, and here we halted.

"We're rather in a state of confusion here," said he, as he rang the bell, "we only moved in this week. So you must take us as you find us."

We entered, and were ushered into a pleasant parlour, which appeared to be the only completely furnished room at present.

"Is Mr Edward at home?" asked our host of the servant.

"Yes, sir, he's upstairs."

"Ask him to come down," said he, "and bring in supper."

He explained to us that Edward was his son, whom he would like us to know.

"I'm often sorry for him," said the father; "he has no mother, and I am too much occupied to be much with him. I wish he had some *good* friends in London."

He emphasised the word "good," as much as to say that some of his son's friends were not very desirable.

The servant brought in supper, and said that Master Edward would be down presently.

Meanwhile our host chatted pleasantly, chiefly about his parish and his plans for improving it. I could not help admiring him more and more as he went on. He was not, to all appearance, a very clever man, but there was an honest ring about all he said which made me feel that, had I only known him in the months past I might have been spared many of my follies and troubles.

At last there was a step in the hall outside, and the door opened. What was our amazement and consternation when we beheld in Edward, the good clergyman's son—Hawkesbury!

Our consternation, however, hardly exceeded his, on seeing who his father's visitors were. And as for the clergyman himself, the sight of our mutual astonishment fairly took him aback.

It was half a minute at least before any one could sufficiently recover his surprise to speak. During the interval my great fear was how Smith would act. I knew he detested Hawkesbury, and believed him to be a hypocrite and a deceiver, and I knew too that he was rarely able to contain himself when face to face with the fellow. How he would behave now, a guest in the father's house, I could not imagine. Fool that I was! I was always doubting my friend!

"Why, how is this," said Mr Hawkesbury, "you seem to know one another?"

"Yes," said I, "Hawkesbury here is at Merrett, Barnacle, and Company's with Smith and me."

"How very curious!" said the clergyman; "and, to be sure, I neither knew your names, nor you mine. Well, as you all know one another, I needn't introduce you."

"Father," said Hawkesbury, standing still at the door, "I want to speak to you a moment, please."

"Yes, presently; but come in now, Edward, we are waiting to begin supper. Now, what an odd coincidence to come across you in this way!"

"I want to speak to you, father," again said Hawkesbury.

The father looked vexed as he turned towards his son.

Smith rose at the same moment and said, holding out his hand to Mr Hawkesbury, "I think, if you will excuse us, we had better go, sir."

"What, before supper! why, how is this?"

"I think your son would rather not have us here," said Jack, solemnly.

The father looked in amazement, first at us, then at his son, who once more asked to speak to his father.

The good man, in evident bewilderment, begged us to excuse him for a moment. But Jack, taking my arm once more, said, before our host could leave the room, "Good-night, sir. Thank you very much for your kindness."

And before I well knew where I was, we were standing out in the street.

Chapter Thirty One
How I made a still more Important Discovery

A few evenings after the awkward discovery recorded in the last chapter Mr Hawkesbury himself called at our lodgings. He looked troubled and constrained, but as kind as usual.

He came to tell us how sorry he was to have been deprived of our company that evening, and to offer a sort of apology for his son's conduct.

"I fear from what he tells me that you do not all get on very happily together at the office. I am so sorry, for I would have liked you all to be friends."

It was hardly possible to tell the father frankly what we thought of his son, so I replied, vaguely, "No, we don't get on very well, I'm sorry to say."

"The fact is," said Jack, "we never have been friends."

"He told me so, greatly to my sorrow."

"I suppose he also told you why?" asked Jack, glancing sharply at the clergyman.

The latter looked disturbed and a trifle confused as he replied, "Yes, he did tell me something which—"

"He told you I was a convict's son," said Jack, quietly.

"What!" exclaimed the clergyman, with an involuntary start—"what! No, he didn't tell me that, my poor boy: he never told me that!"

"I am," quietly said Jack.

I was amazed at the composure with which he said it, and looked the visitor in the face as he did so.

The face was full of pity and sympathy. Not a shade of horror crossed it, and for all he was Hawkesbury's father, I liked him more than ever.

"Do you mind telling me what he did say about me?" asked Jack, presently.

"We will not talk about that," said the clergyman.

Jack looked disposed for a moment to persevere in his demand, but the father's troubled face disarmed him.

"Poor Edward has had great disadvantages," he began, in a half-apologetic, half-melancholy way, "and I often fear I am to blame. I have thought too much of my work out of doors, and too little of my duty to him. I have not been to him all that a father should be."

He said this more in the way of talking to himself than of addressing us. But I saw Jack colour up at the last reference, and hastened to change the subject.

We felt quite sorry for him when he rose to go. He evidently knew his son's failings only too well, and with a father's love tried to cover them. And I could see how in all he said he was almost pleading with us to befriend his boy.

To me it was more than painful to hear him talk thus—to speak to me as if I was a paragon of virtue, and to apologise to *me* for the defects of his own son. It was more than I could endure; and when he started to go I asked if I might walk with him.

He gladly assented, and then I poured into his ears the whole story of my follies and struggles and troubles in London.

I shall never forget the kind way in which he listened and the still kinder way in which he talked when he had heard all.

I am not going to repeat that talk here; the reader may guess for himself what a simple Christian minister would have to say to one in my case, and how he would say it. He neither preached nor lectured, and he broke out into no exclamations. Had he done so, I should probably have been flurried and frightened away. But he talked to me as a father to his son—or rather as a big brother to a young one—entering into all my troubles and difficulties, and even claiming a share in them himself.

It was a long time since I had had such a talk with any one, and it did me good.

An uneventful week or two followed. We occasionally saw Mr Hawkesbury at our lodgings, for Smith could never bring himself to the point of again visiting the rectory. Indeed, he was now so busily engaged in the evenings preparing for his coming examination that he had time for nothing, and even the education of the lively Billy temporarily devolved on me.

It was not till after a regular battle royal that that young gentleman could be brought to submit to be "larned" by any one but his own special "bloke," and even when he did yield, under threats of actual expulsion from the school, he made such a point of comparing everything I did and said with the far superior manner in which Smith did and said it, that for a time it was rather uphill work. At length, however, he quieted down, and displayed no small aptitude for instruction, which was decidedly encouraging.

At the office Hawkesbury, ever since the uncomfortable meeting at his father's, had been very constrained in his manner to Jack and me, attempting no longer to force his society on us, and, indeed, relapsing into an almost mysterious reserve, which surprised more of those who knew him than our two selves.

As Doubleday said — who had never quite got over his sense of injury — "he had shut himself up with his petty-cash, and left us to get on the best we could without him."

Smith and I would both, for his father's sake, have liked if possible to befriend him or do him a good turn. But he seemed studiously to avoid giving us the opportunity, and was now as distant to us as we had once been to him.

However, in other respects our life at Hawk Street proceeded pleasantly enough, not the least pleasant thing being a further rise in both our salaries, an event which enabled me to set aside so much more every week to repay Flanagan his generous loan, as well as to clear myself finally of debt.

Things were going on thus smoothly, and it was beginning to seem as if the tide of life was set calm for both of us, when an event happened which once more suddenly stirred us to excitement and perturbation.

It was a Sunday evening, the evening preceding Jack's examination. He had been working hard, too hard, night after night for weeks past, and was now taking a literal day of rest before his ordeal. We were in our room with Mr Smith the elder, who was a regular Sunday visitor. He had devoted whatever spare time he could give of late to Jack's preparations, "coaching" him in Latin and Greek, and reading with him Ancient History. And now he was almost as excited and anxious about the result as either of us two.

Indeed, Jack himself took the whole matter so coolly that it seemed he must either have been perfectly confident of success, or perfectly indifferent to it, and this evening he was doing quite as much to keep up our spirits as we his.

The examination, which was to last two days, was to begin at nine next morning, and Jack had received a gratifying permission from the partners to absent himself for those two days accordingly.

"It will be a pretty hard grind while it lasts," Jack said, "for the examination goes on eight hours each day."

"When is the *viva-voce* portion?" asked Mr Smith.

"To-morrow. They begin with it, and I shall be glad when it is over. I don't mind the writing nearly so much."

"Hadn't you better go to bed now," suggested I, "and get a good-night?"

"So I will," said he, "presently. But I must first write to Mrs Shield."

I happened to be looking towards Mr Smith the elder as Jack said this. He gave a quick involuntary start, which, however, he instantly turned off into a fit of coughing as his eyes met mine.

Mr Smith had had a racking cough ever since I had known him, but I don't think I ever remembered his having a spasm of this kind before.

"The fact is," said Jack, whose back was turned, as he looked for some note-paper on the shelf, "I ought to have written last week, but I was so busy. And if I put it off any longer they will both think something is wrong."

I only heard what he said mechanically, for my eyes were fixed on Mr Smith.

His face had turned deadly white, and the old frightened look about his eyes came out now with startling intensity. He certainly must be ill or in pain.

"Are you—" I began.

But with a sudden effort he rose to his feet, and with a glance at Jack motioned to me to be silent, and leave the question unasked.

"What?" said Jack, turning round to me.

"Are you—going to write a long letter?" I asked.

"I can't say till I begin," said Jack, laughing, and sitting down to write.

"I'll say good-night," said Mr Smith, in a hoarse but otherwise composed voice.

"Good-night," said Jack. "I wish you'd get rid of your cold. All that night work must be bad for you."

Mr Smith shook hands with me in silence and quitted the room. I heard his footsteps go strangely down the stairs, and his door shut behind him in the room below.

I didn't feel comfortable. I was afraid he was ill—more ill than he wished either of us to suspect. It was the only way in which I could account for the spasm which preluded that last fit of coughing.

If it was so, he would be naturally anxious to conceal the fact from Jack on the eve of his examination, and that would account for his abrupt interruption of my question.

However, I had no examination to-morrow, and I was determined if possible to know the truth about our friend that very evening.

I sat by while Jack wrote his letter, thinking it interminable, and wondering what he could have to say to fill two sheets. When it was done I insisted on taking it to the post.

"It's after ten now," said I, "and you really ought to be in bed."

"You're precious careful of me, old boy," he said. "However, you shall have your own way for once."

I saw him safe in bed before I started, and then hastened out.

To post the letter was the work of a minute or two, for there was a pillar-box a little way down the road. This done, I returned eagerly and with some trepidation to the lodgings, and knocked at Mr Smith's door.

He made no answer, so I entered without leave.

He was sitting on a chair by the tireless hearth with his head on his hands, either asleep or buried in thought.

It was not till I touched him that he became aware of my presence, and then he did so with a start, as if I had been a ghost.

"Ah, Batchelor," said he, recovering himself and leaning back in his chair.

"Are you ill, Mr Smith?" I asked.

"No, my boy, no," said he; "not ill."

"I thought you were—upstairs just now."

"Did you? Ah! you saw me jump; I had a twinge. But don't let's talk of that. Sit down and let's talk of something else."

I sat down, very perplexed and uneasy, and more convinced than ever that Mr Smith was not himself.

"How do you think he'll get on in his examination?" asked he, after a pause.

"Jack? Oh, I have very little doubts about it," said I.

"No more have I; he's well and carefully prepared."

"Thanks a great deal to you," said I. "Well, I did get him on a little with the Greek, I believe," said Mr Smith.

Another pause ensued, during which Mr Smith sat looking hard into the empty grate. Then he asked, "You have known him a long time, Batchelor?"

"Yes; we were at school together."

"Do you know his parents at all?"

"No," I replied, feeling uncomfortable to be once more on this dangerous ground, although on my guard, and prepared to bite my tongue off rather than play my friend false again.

Mr Smith assumed as complete an air of unconcern as he could as he asked, "It's a strange question, but do you know anything about them?"

I would have given a good deal to be out of that room. There was something in Mr Smith's voice and manner and frightened eyes which made the question, coming from him, very different from the same inquiry flippantly thrown out by one of my old comrades. And yet I would not—I could not—answer it.

"I can't say," I replied, as shortly as possible, and rising at the same time to leave the room.

He prevented me by a quick gesture, which almost ordered me not to go, and I resumed my seat.

"You wonder why I ask the question?" said he, slowly.

"I think," said I, "it would be best to ask it of Jack himself."

Mr Smith said nothing, but sat brooding silently for a minute. Then he said, in a tone which sounded as if he was asking the question of himself rather than me, "Who is the Mrs Shield he writes to?"

He spoke so queerly and looked so strangely that I half wondered whether he was not wandering in his mind.

"Please," said I, "do not ask me these questions. What is the matter with you, Mr Smith?"

"Matter, my boy!" said he, with a bitter laugh; "it's a big question you ask. But I'll tell you if you'll listen."

I repented of having asked the question, he looked so haggard and excited. However, there was nothing for it but to sit still while he, pacing to and fro in the room, told me his story in his own way.

"This is not the first time you have been curious about me, Batchelor. You have suspected I was or had been something different from the poor literary hack you see me, and you have been right, my boy."

He stopped short in his walk as he said this, and his eyes flashed, just as I had sometimes seen Jack's eyes flash in the old days.

"Sixteen—no, seventeen—years ago I was the happiest man alive. I can see the little cottage where we lived, my wife and child and I, with its ivy-covered porch and tiny balcony, and the garden which she so prided in behind. It seemed as if nothing could come and disturb our little paradise. I was not rich, but I had all I wanted, and some to spare. I used to walk daily across the field to—where the bank of which I was manager was situated, and they—she and the boy—came to meet me every evening on my return. I felt as if my life was set fair. I could picture no happiness greater than our quiet evenings, and no hope brighter than a future like the present."

Here Mr Smith paused. This picture of a happy home he had drawn with a dreamy voice, as one would describe a fancy rather than a reality. After a pause he went on:

"The thing I thought impossible happened suddenly, fearfully, while I was even hugging myself in my prosperity and happiness. She died. A week before she had given me a sister for my boy. Our cup of joy seemed full to overflowing. The mother and child throve as well as any one could expect. She was to get up next day, and I was to carry her down stairs, and set her for a little amongst her flowers in the little drawing-room. I wished her good-bye gaily that morning as I went off to my work, and bade her be ready for me when I returned.

"Ah! what a return that was! At mid-day a messenger rushed into the bank and called to me to come at once to my wife. I flew to her on the wings of terror, and found her—dead!"

Here the speaker paused again. His voice had trembled at the last word, but his face was almost fierce as he turned his eyes to me.

I said nothing, but my heart bled for him. "The hope had gone from my life. I had no ballast, nothing to steady me in the tempest. My hope had been all in the present, and it perished with her. I cared for nothing, my little children were a misery to me, the old home was unendurable. I got leave of absence from my employers, and came up here—desperate. I dashed into every sort of dissipation and extravagance; I tried one excitement after another, if only I could drown every memory I had. I abandoned myself to so-called 'friends' of the worst sort, who degraded me to their own level, then forsook me. Still I plunged deeper—I was mad. My one dread was to have a moment to myself—a moment to think of my home, my children, my wife. How I lived through it all I cannot think—and I did not care.

"At last a letter reached me from my employers, requiring my presence at business. My money had long gone, my creditors pressed me on every hand, my friends one and all mocked at my destitution. I returned to —, hiding before my employers the traces of my madness, and letting them wonder how grief had changed me. My home I could not go near—the sight of it and of the children would have driven me utterly mad. I lived in the town. For a week or so I tried hard to keep up appearances—but the evil spirit was on me, and I could not withstand him. I had not then learnt to look to a Greater for strength. I must fly once more from one misery to another tenfold worse.

"But I had no money. My savings were exhausted. My salary was not due. I dared not beg it in advance. I was manager of the bank, and had control over all that was in it. The devil within me tempted me, and I yielded. I falsified the accounts, and tampered with the books of the bank. My very desperation made me ingenious, and it was not till I had been away a month with my ill-gotten booty that the frauds were discovered."

Again he stopped, and I waited with strangely perturbed feelings till he resumed.

"At first I tried to hide myself, and spent some weeks abroad. But though I escaped justice, my misery followed me. During those weeks, I, who till then had been upright and honest, knew not a moment's peace. At night I never slept an hour together, by day I trembled at every face I met. The new torture was worse than the old, and at last in sheer despair I returned to London and courted detection. It seemed as if they would never find me. The less I hid myself, the more secure I seemed. At last, however, they found me—it was a relief when they did.

"I acknowledged all, and was sentenced to penal servitude for fourteen years."

"What!" I exclaimed, springing from my seat. "You are—"

"Hush!" said Mr Smith, pointing up to the ceiling, "you'll wake him. Yes, I am, or I was, a convict. Listen to the little more I have to say."

I restrained myself with a mighty effort and resumed my seat.

"I was transported, and for ten years lived the life of a convicted felon. It was a rough school, my boy, but in it I learned lessons an eternity of happiness might never have taught me. Christ is very pitiful. They brought me out of madness into sense, and out of storm into calm. As I sat at night in my cell I could bear once more to think of the little ivy-covered cottage, of the green grave in the churchyard, and of the two helpless children who might still live to call me father. What had become of them? They were perhaps growing up into boyhood and girlhood, beginning to discover for themselves the snares and sorrows of the world which had overcome me. Need I tell you I prayed for those two night and day? A convict's prayer it was—a forger's prayer, a thief's prayer; but a father's prayer to a pitiful Father for his children.

"After ten years I received a 'ticket-of-leave,' and was free to return home. But I could not do it yet. I preferred to remain where I was, in Australia, till the full term of my disgrace was ended, and I was at liberty as a free and unfettered man to show my face once more in England. It is not two years since I returned. No one knew me. Even in — my name had been forgotten. The ivy-covered cottage belonged to a stranger, and no one could tell me what had become of the forger's children who once lived there. It was part of my punishment, and it may be my long waiting is not yet over."

Here once more he paused, looking hard at me with his frightened eyes. I was going to speak, but he stopped me.

"No; let me finish. I came here, sought work, and found it; and found more than work—I found your friend. When I first met him he was unhappy and friendless. You know why better than I do. I watched him, and saw his gallant struggle against poverty and discouragement and perhaps unkindness. I found in him the first congenial companion I had met since she died. I shared his studies, and—and the rest you know. But now," said he, as once more I was about to speak, "you will wonder what all this has to do with the questions I asked you just now. You may guess or you may not; I don't know. This is why. When she died, and I madly deserted all the scenes of my old happiness, my two orphan children were left in the charge of a nurse, a young married woman then, whose name was Shield. Now do you wonder at my questions?"

Chapter Thirty Two
How I came to have several Important Cares upon me

I scarcely knew whether I was awake or dreaming as Mr Smith closed his strange story with the inquiry—

"Now do you wonder at my questions?"

Little had I thought when that evening I knocked at his door and entered, that before I left the room I should have found Jack's father.

It was some time before I could talk coherently or rationally, I was so excited, so wild at the discovery. My impulse was to rush to Jack at once, and tell him what I had found, to run for Mr Hawkesbury, to telegraph to Mrs Shield—to *do* something.

"Don't be foolish," said he, who was now as composed as he had lately been wild and excited. "We may be wrong after all."

"But there can be no doubt," I said. "This Mrs Shield is his old nurse and his sister's—he has told me so himself—who took care of them when their father—went away."

Mr Smith sighed.

"Surely," I cried, "you will come and tell Jack all about it?"

"Not yet," said he, quietly. "I have waited all these years; I can wait two days more—till his examinations are over—and then you must do it for me, my boy."

It was late before I left him and went up to my bed in Jack's room.

There he lay sound asleep, with pale, untroubled face, dreaming perhaps of his examination to-morrow, but little dreaming of what was in store when that was over.

It was little enough I could sleep during the night. As I lay and tossed and thought over the events of the evening, I did not know whether to be happy or afraid. Supposing Jack should refuse to own his father! Suppose, when he heard that story of sin and shame, he should turn and repudiate the father who had so cruelly wronged him and his sister!

What a story it was! And yet, as I went over its details and pictured to myself the tragedy of that ruined life, I trembled to think how nearly a similar story might have been mine, had I not by God's grace been mercifully arrested in time.

Who was I, to think ill of him? He had been driven to his ruin by a shock which had nearly robbed him of reason. I had fallen through sheer vanity and folly, and who was to say I might not have fallen as low as he, had there been no hand to save me, no friend to recall me, by God's mercy, to myself?

I was thankful when I heard Jack stir, and had an excuse for getting up.

"Hullo!" said he, as I did so; "you were a jolly long time posting that letter last night, or else I must have gone to sleep pretty quickly."

"I just looked in to talk to Mr Smith," I said, "on my way back."

"Ah, do you know, I think he's working too hard. He didn't look well last night."

"He seemed a little out of sorts," I said, "but I'm afraid that's nothing very unusual. Well, old boy, how do you feel in prospect of your exam.?"

"Oh, all right," said Jack, complacently. "I suppose I ought to feel in mortal terror and nervousness and despondency. I believe that's what's expected of a fellow before an exam. If so, I'm unorthodox. Perhaps it's a sign I shall be plucked."

"I'm not afraid of that," said I.

"Well, I have a notion I may pull through."

"If you pass," said I, struck with a thought that had not before occurred to me, "shall you go to college, Jack?"

He laughed at the question.

"I should have to come out first of all," said he, "to get what would keep me at college. And even so, I'm not cut out for that sort of life."

"If you mean living by your brains, I say you are."

"Of course you say so. You're always stuffing me up. But, apart from that, you know there are other reasons why I should not be likely to get on well at a university."

I knew what his meaning was only too well.

"But what rubbish we are talking!" said he. "We've made up our minds I'm going to come out first, when it's more likely all I shall do will be to scrape through with a pass, and not take honours at all."

At this point Mr Smith looked in to wish Jack joy before he started, and greatly to my relief Billy entered at the same time.

The latter visitor was quite unexpected.

"Well, Billy, what's up?" I inquired.

"Ga on! As if you didn't know," replied the grinning youth.

"I don't know."

"What," said Billy, jerking his head towards Jack, "ain't he goin' to 'is 'sam, then?"

"Yes, he's going to his examination this morning."

"And I are a-goin' to give him a proper shine afore he goes," replied the boy, almost fiercely.

"Of course you are, Billy," said Jack. "I believe I should come to grief altogether if I went without having my boots polished."

"In corse you would," said the delighted Billy, commencing operations forthwith.

"I say, governor," said he, looking up, halfway through his task, "I give the animal a topper last night."

"What animal?" inquired Jack.

"That there 'Orksbury, so I did. Him and 'is pal comes along and twigs me a-sottin' on my box. 'That's the kid. Mashing,' says 'Orksbury. Mashing he up to me, and says he, 'Would you like a shillin', my boy?' says he. 'You're 'avin' a lark with me,' says I. 'No, I ain't,' says 'e, 'oldin' it out. 'What do yer want?' says I. 'You know Smith?' says 'Orksbury. 'That ain't no concern of yourn,' says I. 'You ain't got no concern with my governor,' says I. 'Oh, then you don't want the shillin'?' says he. 'No, I don't,' says I, seein' they was up to games. 'What do you mean by it?' says Mashing, a-pullin' my ear. (Bless you, 'e don't know the way to pull a cove's ear; my old gal can do it proper.) 'No one is going to do anything to Smith,' says 'e. 'We only want you to give him this,' says he, pullin' out a bit of paper. 'Don't give it 'im,' says 'Orksbury; 'he's a young thief,' says 'e, 'and 'e'll only spoil it all.' 'I will so,' says I, 'and I'll spoil you too,' says I, aimin' a brush at his 'ed. They gives me a wipin' for it, but there, they can't 'arf do it. And they says if I want my shillin' I can go and get it from that cantin' son of a thief—meanin' you, governor—what kep' me. Bless you, they did jaw, them two, but I give that 'Orksbury a topper, which I owed 'im one afore."

This spirited address on the part of our young friend I need hardly say interested us all deeply. We all resented the outrage which had been offered to him, and admired the spirit with which he had stood to his colours during the interview.

This little episode served to smooth the way for Mr Smith's interview with Jack. It gave him time to compose himself, and get over the emotion which the first sight of his lost son since last night's discovery naturally roused.

When he did speak it was steadily and cheerily as ever.

"Just popped up," he said, "to wish you success, my boy. Keep your head during the *viva-voce*, and remember that rule about the second aorist."

"All serene," said Jack, laughing. "I say, Mr Smith," added he, "if I don't pass I shall feel myself the most ungrateful brute out."

"So you will be," replied Mr Smith, nodding pleasantly as he left the room.

I wondered at his nerve, and admired the self-control which could thus enable him to talk and even jest at such a time.

I had time to walk round with Jack to the place of examination before business, and give him my final benediction at the door.

Then I hurried off to Hawk Street.

It was a long, dull day there without him. Hawk Street had long since ceased to be exciting. The fellows I liked—and they were very few—did not obtrude their affections on me during business hours, and the fellows I disliked had given up the pastime of baiting me as a bad job. I had my own department of work to attend to, and very little communication with any one else in the doing of it, except with Doubleday, who, as the reader knows, usually favoured me when anything specially uninviting wanted doing.

Of Hawkesbury I now saw and heard less than any one. He had been promoted to a little glazed-in box of his own, where in stately solitude he managed the petty-cash, kept the correspondence, and generally worked as hard as one who is a cut above a clerk and a cut below a partner is expected to do.

On the day in question I was strongly tempted to break in upon his solitude and demand an explanation of his conduct to Billy on the preceding evening. But a moment's reflection convinced me of the folly of such a course. It was not likely, if I got any answer at all, I should get a satisfactory one, while to reopen communications at all after what had occurred might be unwise and mischievous. For ever since Hawkesbury and I had ceased to be on talking terms at the office I had been more comfortable there, and involved in fewer troubles than ever before.

So I let well alone.

During the day an important telegram arrived at the office, which kept the partners closeted together in the inner-room for an hour, in earnest conference, at the end of which time Hawkesbury was sent for.

Doubleday, who had seen the telegram, told me it was to say that a vessel reported lost had turned up, with a cargo which was now double the value in the market it would have been had she arrived when expected. However, there were points connected with the insurance and other matters which would require the presence of one of the firm at Liverpool, and this was evidently the object of the present confabulation.

"A year ago," said Doubleday, "they would have sent me. But now the darling comes in for all the trips."

Which proved to be the case now. Hawkesbury emerged from the inner-room with an important face, and told the junior clerk (I no longer held that distinguished post), to fetch a hansom immediately. Doubleday nudged me.

"If it was you or me, I fancy we'd fetch our own hansoms, eh! Never mind, we've neither of us got uncles."

"Haven't we?" said I, laughing. "I have."

"Ah—so have I, for the matter of that. Three—all as poor as church mice too. I mean we've not got uncles in the firm. But what puzzles me is, what is to become of the petty-cash? I suppose I'm to be favoured with that job during his lordship's absence. I shall certainly cover the book with crape."

"Batchelor," called Hawkesbury at that moment, just putting his head out of the door of his box, "will you step here, please?"

Doubleday nudged me again, harder than ever.

"I say," said he, with glee, "you're to be sent too to carry his bag—see if you aren't."

However, Doubleday was wrong for once. The honour he prophesied was not reserved for me. But another was, almost as surprising.

"Batchelor," said Hawkesbury, almost in his old wheedling tone, "I shall be away for three or four days. I'll get you to keep the petty-cash accounts till I return. I won't leave the regular book out, as I have not time to balance it. You can enter anything on a separate paper, which I will copy in when I return. There is £3 in the cash-box now. You had better keep it locked up in your desk."

I could not help being surprised that he should fix on me of all persons to undertake this responsibility for him during his absence. It seemed so much more naturally to devolve on its former guardian that I could not help asking, "Don't you think Doubleday had better—"

"I prefer you should do it, please," said Hawkesbury, decisively, bustling off to another desk at the same moment, and so cutting short further parley.

So I had nothing for it but to take up the cash-box, and, after making sure it contained exactly the £3 he had mentioned, transfer it to my own desk.

When I told Doubleday that afternoon what had happened he waxed very facetious on the head of it. He was undoubtedly a little hurt that I should be selected for the charge instead of him. But we were too good friends to misunderstand one another in the matter.

"I expect he's left it with you because you're a young hand, and he thinks you're sure to make a mess of it. That would just suit him."

"I'll do my best to deprive him of the luxury of putting me right," said I.

"If you do get up a tree," said Doubleday, "I'm your man. But I hope you won't, for I don't want to have anything to do with it."

After all it was not such very alarming work. A few people dropped in during the day and paid small amounts in cash, which I received, and carefully entered on my sheet. And a few demands came from various quarters for small disbursements in the way of postage-stamps, telegrams, cab fares, and the like, all which I also carefully entered on the other side of my account.

Before I left in the evening I balanced the two sides, and found the cash in my box tallying exactly with the amount that appeared on my sheet. Whereat I rejoiced exceedingly, and, locking-up my desk, thought the keeping of the petty-cash was ridiculously simple work.

That evening when I reached the lodgings I found Jack had arrived before me. I was eager to hear of his success or otherwise at the examination, and he was prepared to gratify my curiosity.

He had got on well, he thought. The *viva-voce* portion, which he had dreaded most, had been easy, or, at any rate, the questions which fell-to him had been such as he could readily answer. As for the written part, all he could say was that he had replied to all the questions, and he believed correctly, although time prevented him from doing one or two as full justice as they deserved. In fact, after talking it over, we both came to the conclusion that the day's effort had been a success, and if to-morrow turned out as well, all doubt as to the result might be dispensed with.

Then I told him of my adventures, which did not seem altogether to overjoy him.

"I don't know why it is," said he, "but Hawkesbury is a fellow I cannot but mistrust."

"But," said I, "I don't see what there can possibly be to suspect in his handing over this simple account to me to keep."

"All I can say is," said he, "I wish he hadn't done it. Why didn't he hand it over to Doubleday?"

"I wondered at that," said I, "but there's no love lost between those two. Doubleday says he thinks he did it because I am a bit of a fool, and he wants the pleasure of seeing me in a mess over the account."

Jack laughed.

"Doubleday is always flattering somebody," said he. "Never mind; it may be only fancy on my part after all."

Jack wanted to get to his books that evening, but I dissuaded him.

"It can do no good," said I, "and it may just muddle you for to-morrow. Take an easy evening now, and go to bed early. You'll be all the fresher for it to-morrow."

So, instead of study, we fell-to talking, and somehow got on to the subject of the home at Packworth.

"By the way, Fred," said Jack, "I got a letter from you the other day."

"From me?" I cried; "I haven't written to you for months."

"It *was* from you, though, but it had been a good time on the road, for it was written from Stonebridge House just after I had left."

"What! the letter you never called for at the post-office?"

"The letter you addressed to 'J.' instead of 'T.' my boy; But I'm glad to have it now. It is most interesting."

"But however did you come by it?" I asked.

"If you will stop runaway horses when your hands are full you must expect to lose things. This letter was picked up by Mrs Shield after that little adventure, and only came to light out of the lining of her bag last week. She remembered seeing it lying on the road, she says, and picking it up, along with Mary's shawl and handkerchief, which had also fallen. But she was too flurried to think anything of it, and until it mysteriously turned up the other day she had forgotten its existence. So there's a romantic story belonging to your letter."

I could not be satisfied till the interesting document was produced and conned over. We laughed a good deal in the reading, over the reminiscences it brought up, and the change that had come over both our lives since then.

"Mrs Shield says Mary insisted it belonging to her, and that she had no right to send it to me," said Jack, laughing. "What do you think of that?"

"It's very kind of her," said I, "to think anything about it. I say, Jack," I added, blushing a little, "got that photo about you?"

Jack handed out his treasure, and we fell-to talking a good deal about the original of the picture, which interested me quite as much as it did Jack.

"Do you know, Fred," said he, presently, "she doesn't know anything about—about father? She believes she is an orphan, and that I am the only relation she has."

"I'm sure," said I, "it's far better so."

"Yes," said Jack, sadly. "At present it is. But some day she ought to know."

"Why?" said I.

"If he ever—but we're not going to talk of that. What do you say to turning in? That's half-past ten striking by the church."

So ended the first day of suspense.

I regret to say that my last act that day was one of petty larceny!

During our talk about Mary I had held the photograph in my hand, looking at it occasionally, and occasionally laying it down on my knee. When Jack rose and proposed turning in for the night he gathered together the other papers he had taken from his pocket and replaced them. But, strangely enough, he forgot to look for the photograph, or else supposed it was with the other papers.

It wasn't, for it lay under my hand all the while, and presently, when his back was turned, it lay in my pocket.

Later on, when the lights were out and all was quiet, it lay under my pillow for greater security!

No wonder the reader is shocked! If ever there was a clear case of purloining this was. I know it, dear reader. I knew it at the time, and yet I did it.

For I had a motive, which perhaps the reader can guess.

The picture which had lain first under my hand, then in my pocket, then under my pillow, experienced yet another change of situation that night.

Just as the first streak of dawn struggled through the window I heard a door close and a footstep in the room below. Mr Smith had come home.

Lightly and silently I crept from my bed, and with my treasure in my hand sped down the stairs and slipped into his room.

And for an hour after that the picture lay in a hand which had never touched it before, and the bright laughing eyes looked up and met the tearful eyes of a father!

Chapter Thirty Three
How Several Visitors Called at our Lodgings

Billy arrived punctually as we were dressing next morning in great good-humour.

"What cheer, covies?" cried he before he was well in the room. "She's come back!"

"Who—your mother?" said Jack.

"Yaas," said Billy; "worn't she jolly neither? She give me a wipin' last night same as I never got."

And when we came to look at our queer visitor he bore about his face and person undoubted marks of the truth of this story.

"What a shame it is!" I said to Jack. "Can't anything be done to stop it? He'll be murdered right out one day."

"'Taint no concern of yourn!" said Billy. "But I say, governor," added he, turning to Jack, "she are a rum 'un, she are! She was a-sayin' you was makin' a idle young dorg of me, she says, and she'll wait upon you, she says, and know the reason why, she says. And she says ef she ketches me messin' about any more with my ABC, she says she'll knock the 'ed off me. But don't you mind 'er, she's on'y a-jawing!"

Jack looked a good deal troubled. He had taken upon himself the welfare of this happy family in the court, and it seemed likely to cost him many an uneasy moment. Only a short time before, he had told me, he had called with Mr Hawkesbury and seen Billy's mother, just after her release from prison, and tried to plead with her on Billy's behalf, but, he said, you might as well talk to a griffin.

Billy appeared to be oppressed with no cares on the subject. "It's that there penny bang," said he, "as she's got her back up agin. I told her as I was a shovin' my coppers in there, and she says she'll shove you in, governor, she says. She did swear at you, governor! It's a game to hear her."

"When you learn better, Billy," said Jack, quite sternly, "you won't talk like that of your mother."

Billy's face overclouded suddenly. He looked first at me, then at Jack, and finally at the boot in his hand, which he fell-to polishing till it dazzled. But Jack's tone and look had effectually damped his spirits, and when he spoke again it was with a half whine.

"I *are* a larning better, governor, do you hear? I knows my letters. You ask this 'ere bloke," pointing to me with his brush. "And them Aggers, too. I writ 'em all up on my slate, didn't I? You tell the governor if I didn't!"

"Yes," I said; "you did."

"There you are! Do you hear, governor? I'm larnin' better. I writ all them there Aggers, I did; and I can say my d-o-g, dorg, proper, can't I, pal? And I've shove my coppers in the bang, and I am larnin'."

"I know you are," said Jack, kindly. "Come, it's time I got on my boots. Are they done?"

Billy in the delight of his heart took one more furious turn at the boots. He breathed hard upon them till he was nearly black in the face, and polished them till it was a wonder any leather at all was left. And, to complete all, he polished up the tags of the laces with the sleeve of his own coat, and then deposited the boots with an air of utmost pride and jubilation.

"I shall be done the examination to-day," said Jack, as the boy started to go; "I'll come down and see you in the evening."

Billy's face was nearly as bright as the boots he had polished as he grinned his acknowledgments and went on his way rejoicing.

Mr Smith did not put in an appearance before it was time for Jack to start. He had told me he would not. He was afraid of betraying his secret prematurely, and deemed it wisest to stay away. And I was just as glad he did so, for it was all I could do not to show by my manner that something of serious moment was in the wind.

However, by an effort, I tried to appear as if nothing unusual had occurred.

"By the way, Jack," said I, as we walked down to the examination hall, "you're a nice fellow to take care of a photograph! Do you know you left this at my mercy all night?"

"What!" he exclaimed, "I thought I put it back in my pocket with the other papers. What a go if I'd lost it!"

"What a go if I'd kept it!" said I. "The next time I will."

"To prevent which," said Jack, "take your last look, for you shall never see it again! Good-bye, old man. It will be all over when I see you next."

"All over!" mused I, as I walked back to the office. "It will be only beginning."

I never made a more rash promise in all my life than when I undertook to Mr Smith to break the news of his discovery to Jack.

It had appeared so simple at the time, but when the moment came the task seemed to be one bristling with difficulties on every hand. All that day the sense of the coming ordeal haunted me, and even the custody of the petty-cash could not wholly divert my mind.

I was therefore quite relieved that evening, on returning to the lodgings, to hear as I ascended the stairs voices speaking in our room, and to find that Jack had a visitor. I should, at least, get some time to recover the wits which the near approach of my ordeal had scattered.

For a moment I wondered whether Jack's visitor could be Mr Smith himself. It was a man's voice, and unless it were Mr Smith or Mr Hawkesbury, I was at a loss to guess who it could be.

To my astonishment I found, on entering the room, that the visitor was no other than my uncle!

Whatever had brought him here?

Jack looked as if his *tête-à-tête* had not been a very cheerful one, for he jumped up at my arrival with evident joy, and cried, "Oh, here you are at last! Here's your uncle, Fred, come to see you. He was afraid he would have to go before you got back."

This, at least, was a comfort. My uncle was not going to stay all night.

I went up in a most dutiful manner to my relative, and hoped he was well.

"Yes," he replied, in his usual frigid way. "You seem surprised to see me. But as I had business in town I found out this place, and came to look you up."

"It was very kind of you," said I.

"You shouldn't say that when you don't mean it," said my uncle. "And as I am going in a few minutes you need not look so alarmed."

"I hope you will have a cup of tea before you go," said I, hoping to change the subject.

"No, thank you. Your friend here asked me that already. Now, what about your debts, Fred?"

"Oh," said I, "they are all paid by this time. An old schoolfellow advanced me the money, kindly, and I have all but repaid him out of my weekly allowance."

"Humph!" said my uncle. "That scrape will be a lesson to you, I hope. Boys who make fools of themselves like that must suffer the consequences."

"I had been very foolish I know," I replied, humbly.

"But Fred's as steady as a judge now," said Jack, interposing for my relief.

"It's nearly time he was," replied my uncle, "unless he has made up his mind to ruin himself. He's given up all his wild friends, I hope?"

"Oh yes, every one," said I; "haven't I, Jack?"

"Yes, he's nothing to do with them now," said Jack.

"And he spends his evenings in something better than drinking and gambling and that sort of thing?"

This was pleasant for me. As the question appeared to be addressed to Jack, I allowed him to answer it for me.

"Well," said my uncle, after a few more similar inquiries had been satisfactorily answered, "I hope what you tell me is true. It may seem as if I did not care much what became of you, Fred. And as long as you went on in the way you did, no more I did. You had chosen your friends, and you might get on the best you could with them. But now, if you have done what you say you have and given them up—"

At that moment there was a sudden tumult on the stairs outside, which made us all start. It was a sound of scuffling and laughter and shouting, in the midst of which my uncle's voice was drowned. Whoever the visitors were, they appeared not to be quite sure of their quarters, for they were trying every door they came to on their way up. At length they came nearer, and a voice, the tones of which were only too familiar, shouted, "Come on, you fellows. We'll smoke him out. Batchelor ahoy there! Wonder if he lives on the roof."

It was Whipcord's voice, whom I had not seen since my accident, and who now had fixed on this evening of all others to come with his friends and pay me a visit!

"It's Whipcord," I said to Jack; "he mustn't come in! Let's barricade the door, anything to keep them out."

Jack, who looked fully as alarmed as I did, was quite ready to agree, but my uncle, who had hitherto been an astounded witness of the interruption, interfered, and said, "No—they shall come in. These are some of your reformed friends, I suppose, Mr Fred. I'd like to see them. Let them come in."

"Oh no, uncle," I cried, in agitation, "they mustn't come in, indeed they mustn't, they are—"

As I spoke the shouting outside increased twofold, and at the same moment the door was flung open, and Whipcord, Crow, the Field-Marshal, the Twins, Daly, and Masham, burst into the room!

Is it any wonder if, as I looked first at them, then at my uncle, a feeling of utter despair took possession of me?

They were all, evidently, in a highly festive state of mind and ready for any diversion.

"Here he is," cried Whipcord, who appeared to be leader of the party. "Here you are, Batch, my boy—we got your address at the police-station and came to look you up, and oh, I say, what a glorious old codger!"

This last note of admiration was directed to my uncle, who sat sternly back in his chair, gazing at the intruders with mingled wrath and astonishment.

"I say, introduce us, Batch," said the Field-Marshal, "and to the other aristocrat, too, will you?"

"Why, that's Bull's-eye," cried Crow. "You know, Twins, the fellow I told you about who's—"

"Oh, that's the Botany Bay hero, is it?" cried Masham. "I must shake hands with him. One doesn't get the chance of saying how d'ye do to a real gaol-bird every day. How are you, Treadmill?"

Jack, whose face was very pale, and whose eyes flashed fiercely, remained motionless, and with an evident effort, as Masham held out his hand.

"What—thinks we aren't good enough for him, does he?" said Masham.

"So used to the handcuffs," said Abel, "doesn't know how to use his hands, that's it."

"But we don't know yet who this old weathercock is," cried Whipcord, turning again to my uncle. "What do they call you at home, old Stick-in-the-mud?" and he nudged him in the ribs by way of emphasis.

It was time I interposed. Hitherto, in sheer helplessness, I had stood by and watched the invasion with silent despair. Now, however, that my uncle seemed to be in danger of rough handling, something must be done.

"If you fellows have any pretence to be called gentlemen," I shouted, in tones choked with mingled shame and anger, "you will leave Jack's room and mine."

"Jack's! who's Jack? Is the old pawnbroker called Jack, then? Oh, I say, you fellows," cried Whipcord, dropping on a chair, and nearly choking himself with a fit of laughter. "Oh, you fellows, I've got it at last. I've got it. Jack! I know who it is."

"Who is it?" cried the others.

"Why, can't you guess?" yelled Whipcord.

"No! Who?"

"Jack Ketch!"

This new idea was taken up with the utmost rapture, and my uncle was forthwith dubbed with his fresh title.

"Three cheers for Uncle Ketch, you fellows!" shouted Whipcord.

The cheers were given with great hubbub. Then my uncle was called upon for a speech, and, as he declined, a proposal was made to compel him.

Up to this time, protest as well as resistance had seemed worse than useless. Jack and I were only two against seven, and our visitors were hardly in a condition to give us fair play, even if we did come to blows. But our wrath had been gradually approaching boiling-point, and now the time seemed to have come to brave all consequences and assert ourselves.

Whipcord and Masham had each seized one of my uncle's arms, with a view to carry out their threat, when by a mutual impulse Jack, and I assumed the defensive and rushed into the fray. Both our adversaries were, of course, utterly unprepared for such a demonstration, and in consequence, and before they could either of them take in the state of affairs, they were sprawling at full length on the floor. The whole action was so rapidly executed that it was not for a moment or two that the rest of the party took in the fact that the affair was something more than a joke. When, however, they did so, a general engagement ensued, in which Jack and I, even with the unlooked-for and gallant aid of my uncle, could do very little against superior numbers.

What the upshot might have been—whether we should have been eventually ejected from our own lodgings, or whether the invaders would presently have wearied of their sport and made off of their own accord—I cannot say, but just as things were looking at their worst for us an opportune diversion occurred which turned the tide of battle.

This was none other than the simultaneous arrival of Billy and Flanagan. The latter, I recollected, had promised to look in during the evening, to see how Jack had fared at the examination.

In the general confusion the new-comers entered the room almost unnoticed. The unexpected scene which met their eyes in our usually quiet quarters naturally alarmed them, and it was a second or more before, in the midst of all the riot, they could make out what was the matter.

Billy was the first to recover himself. The sight of Jack Smith being attacked by Masham was quite enough for him, and, with a cry of, "Do you hear, you let him be!" he sprang upon his patron's assailant like a young tiger.

Poor, gallant Billy! Masham, taken aback to find himself thus attacked by a small boy who seemed to come from nowhere, recoiled for an instant before his vigorous onslaught. But it was only for an instant. Stepping back, and leaving the others to engage Jack and me, he seized the boy by the arm, and, dealing him a blow on the side of the head, flung him savagely to the floor, adding a brutal kick as he lay there, stunned and senseless at his feet.

The sight of this outrage was all that was wanted to rouse us to one desperate effort to rid ourselves of our cowardly invaders. Jack closed in an instant with Masham, and by sheer force carried him to the door and literally flung him from the room. The others, one by one, followed. Some, half ashamed at the whole proceeding, slunk away of their own accord; the others, seeing themselves worsted, lost spirit, and made but a slight resistance to our united assault, now vigorously reinforced by Flanagan.

The last to leave was Whipcord, who endeavoured to carry the thing off with his usual swagger to the last. "Well, ta, ta, Batch," he said; "we just looked in to see how you were, that's all. Thanks for the jolly evening. By-bye, old Jack Ketch, and—"

And here, in consequence of a sudden forward movement from Flanagan, he hurriedly withdrew, and left us for the first time that evening with leisure to look about us.

It was no time, however, for asking questions or giving explanations. An exclamation from Jack turned all attention to Billy, who lay still unconscious and as white as a sheet where he had fallen. Jack gently raised him and laid him on the bed. "Open the window, somebody," said he.

The air seemed to revive the boy somewhat, for he opened his eyes and looked vacantly round. But a fit of sickness followed this partial recovery, and again he swooned.

Jack's face was nearly as pale as the boy's as he looked up and said, "Fetch the doctor! Quick!"

Flanagan darted off almost before the words were out of his lips.

There was nothing for us who were left behind to do but to watch with painful anxiety the poor little sufferer, who lay mostly unconscious, and still at intervals violently sick.

Masham's ruffianly blow and kick had evidently done far more damage than he or any one supposed. As we waited in silence for the doctor to come our alarm increased, and it even seemed doubtful whether, as we stood there, we were not destined to see a terrible end to that evening's proceedings.

"Has the boy a father or mother?" whispered my uncle to me.

Jack who sat with the sufferer's head on his arm, heard the question, and said hurriedly, "Yes. You must fetch his mother, Fred!"

There was such a tone of alarm in his voice that had Billy's mother been a wild beast I could hardly have disobeyed.

I darted off on my unenviable quest, meeting the doctor on the stairs. I knew the house in the court by this time, and was myself well-known to its inmates.

The woman was not at home; she had not been home since the morning, and no one knew where she was. I left a message apprising her of what had happened, and telling her to come at once to the lodgings. Then with much foreboding I hastened back to Drury Lane.

The evening had been a strangely different one from what I had expected. I was to have broken the news to Jack of his father's discovery, instead of which, here was I rushing frantically about trying to find an unhappy woman and summon her to what, for all I knew, might be the death-bed of her son!

I found when I returned that Billy had somewhat revived. He was lying back, very white still, and apparently unconscious, but they told me the doctor had given some hope of his recovery, and that the fits of sickness had stopped and left him stronger.

My uncle, whose concern for the poor boy was scarcely less than ours, had relieved Jack at the patient's bedside. Jack, who, now that the imminent anxiety was over, had given way to a natural reaction, was, I could see, in a terrible state of misery and rage.

"If he dies," muttered he to me, "I'll—"

What he meant to say I do not know. He stopped short and flung himself in the empty seat by the window, trembling all over. I had never known before how fond he was of the poor boy.

"What about his mother?" he said presently, turning to me.

"I couldn't find her, or hear of her anywhere," I said. "But I left a message for her."

Just then my uncle beckoned with his hand.

Billy had opened his eyes, and was looking about him. He had done so once or twice before, but always in a vacant, stupid sort of way. Now, to our intense joy, there was a glimmer of something like the old life in his pale face, especially when, catching sight of Jack, who sprang to his side in a moment, his features broke into a faint smile.

My uncle came quietly to me across the room.

"I'll go now," said he—more kindly than I had ever heard him speak. "I shall stay in town to-night, and will look in in the morning;" and so saying he went.

Mr Smith and I accompanied him to the door. As we were returning up the stairs some one called after us. I turned, and saw that the new-comer was Billy's mother.

Chapter Thirty Four
How I got rid of the Petty-Cash, and of Mr Smith's Secret

Billy's mother was, for the first time in my experience, sober. I stayed behind for her on the stairs, while Mr Smith retired to his own room, saying he would come up and see us all in the morning. I wished he would have stayed and countenanced me in my interview with the unhappy woman.

"What's all this, mister?" she said, as she came up.

Once, possibly, Billy's mother might have been a handsome and even attractive woman, but drink had defaced whatever beauty she once had, and had degraded her terribly, as it always does, both in body and mind.

"Billy has been badly hurt," I said, "and we thought you ought to come."

"Who hurt him?" she demanded.

There was no sympathy or even concern in her tone. She spoke like a person to whom all the world is an enemy, in league to do her wrong.

"There was a struggle," I said. "A man was hitting Mr Smith—"

"Mr Smith!" she exclaimed, fiercely; "who's he—who's Mr Smith?"

"Why, my friend who sometimes goes to see you in the court."

"Oh!" said she, with a contemptuous laugh, "that fool!"

"Some one was striking him, and Billy put himself between them, and was badly hurt."

"Well, what's come to him? Is he dead, or what?" demanded the woman.

"No, he's not, mercifully," said I. "He's getting better, we hope."

"And you mean to say," said the woman, with her wrath rising, "you've got that child among you, and you're not content with robbing him and keeping him away from me, but here you've half-murdered him into the bargain, you— Where is he, mister? I'll take him back along with me; I've had enough of this tomfoolery, I tell you."

"Oh!" I exclaimed, "it would kill him to move him! You mustn't think of it."

"Get out of the way!" she exclaimed, fiercely, trying to push past me. "I'll take him out of this. I'll teach you all whose child the boy is! Get out of my way! Let me go to him."

What could I do? I had no right to keep a mother from her son; and yet, were she to carry out her threat, no one could say what the result to the boy might not be.

In my dilemma I thought of Mr Smith, and conducted my intractable visitor to his room, in the hopes that he might be able to dissuade her from carrying out her threat.

But nothing he could do or say could bring her to reason. She appeared to be persuaded in her own mind that the whole affair was a conspiracy to do her some wrong, and that being so, entreaties, threats, and even bribes would not put her off her idea of taking Billy away with her.

"Come now," said she, after this ineffectual parley had gone on for some time, "I'm not going to be made a fool of by you two any more. Where's Billy? where are you hiding him? It's no use you trying to impose on me with your gammon!"

"He's upstairs," said I, feeling that further resistance was worse than useless. "I'll run up and tell Jack you're coming. Billy may be asleep."

But the woman caught me roughly by the arm. "No, no!" said she, "I don't want none of your schemes and plots; I can go up without your help, mister."

So saying, she broke away from us and went up the stairs.

"Don't follow her," said Mr Smith; "the fewer up there the better. Jack will manage."

So we spent an anxious half-hour, listening to the voices and sound of feet above, and wondering how the interview was going on. Evidently it began with an altercation, and once Billy's shrill treble joined in in a way which sounded very familiar. Eventually the angry tones of the woman ceased, and presently she returned to us, quiet in her manner, though still hunted-looking and mistrustful.

To our relief she was alone.

"I'm coming for him in the morning," said she as she passed us.

We could never make out how Jack had subdued her and put her off. When we asked him, he said simply he begged her to wait a little, at any rate, till the boy was better, and had then promised to bring him home himself.

That night I shared Mr Smith's room—or rather I occupied it during his absence, leaving Jack and Billy in possession upstairs.

My reflections during the night were not pleasant. If it had not been for my folly, my sin, in times past, the calamity of this evening would never have happened. These "friends" of former days were not to be shaken off as easily as they had been picked up, and meanwhile it was not I who was made to suffer, but Jack and Billy, who had never been guilty of my follies and sins. And, more than this, I felt the burden of Mr Smith's secret still hanging unrelieved on my mind. And how was I to get rid of it and tell Jack all, while this anxiety about Billy lasted?

In the early morning Mr Smith returned, and I confided to him all my troubles. He was very sympathetic, and agreed with me that the present was hardly the time to tell Jack his secret. And yet it was plain to see he was in terrible suspense till it should be all over.

We did not sleep much that night, and in the morning hastened to the room above. To our relief, we found Billy much better. He was even grinning as usual as we entered, and greeted us both in very like his old familiar way.

"What cheer!" said he, feebly but cheerily. "I *are* got a dose off that there Mashing! He do give yer toppers!"

"Come, hush, Billy!" said Jack, pleasantly; "didn't I tell you not to talk?"

"Yaas," said the boy, relapsing abruptly into silence.

His mother, as we rather anticipated, did not put in an appearance. My uncle did, and, after ascertaining that all was going on well, went off, leaving, greatly to my astonishment and not a little to my gratification, a sovereign in my hand as he said good-bye.

There was something kindly about my uncle, after all!

Leaving Mr Smith in charge, Jack and I went down to the office that morning with lighter hearts than we had expected to have.

Crow was waiting for us outside the office, with an anxious face.

"I say," said he, as he came up, and not heeding Jack's wrathful looks, "is it true what I hear, that that boy was killed last night?"

"Who told you so?" demanded Jack.

"I heard it from Daly. And Masham has bolted. Is it true, then?"

"No!" said Jack, "and no thanks to you it isn't, you coward!"

Crow had evidently been too much frightened by the news he had heard to resent this hard name. He answered, meekly, "I'm glad it's not true. I'm ashamed of that affair last night, and there's no harm in telling you so."

This was a good deal to come from a fellow like Crow. We did not reply, but entered the office.

There, for a few hours at least, hard work drove away all other cares. At dinner-time Jack rushed home, and brought back a further good report of the patient, whom the doctor had seen, and pronounced to be making satisfactory progress.

As for me, I stayed at the office and made up for the lost time of the evening before. Part of my work was a grand balancing up of the petty-cash, which, as Hawkesbury was due back next morning, I would then have to be prepared to hand over. It was no small satisfaction to find that my accounts were right to a penny, and to know that in the fair copy of those accounts which I drew up no ingenuity or patience would be able to discover an error. Indeed, I was so particular, that, having made a minute blot in my first fair copy, I went to the trouble of writing out another, absolutely faultless, preserving the other in my desk, as an occasional feast to my own eyes in my self-satisfied moments.

That evening I was strongly tempted to unburden my secret to Jack as we walked home. But I could not bring myself up to the point. At least, I could not do so till we got to the door of our lodgings, and then it was too late, for Jack had rushed to Billy's bedside, and it was hopeless to get him to think of anything else. So I had to wait on, and once more to endure the sight of Mr Smith's anxious, frightened face.

The following morning brought a letter from my uncle, addressed, not to me, but to Jack Smith. It contained a five-pound note, which he said might be useful when Billy's doctor's bill had to be paid, and anything that was over might go to buy the boy a suit of clothes! My uncle was certainly coming out in a new light! It was like him writing to Jack instead of me, and I thought nothing of that. But for him to send a five-pound note for the benefit of a little stranger was certainly a novelty, which surprised as much as it encouraged me about my relative.

The money, as it happened, was very opportune, for neither of us was very flush of cash at the time.

Billy, who was now steadily recovering from the shock of his blow, pleaded very hard to be allowed to get up, and only Jack's express command could keep him in bed.

"Ga on, governor," said he, "let's get up. I ain't a-getting no coppers for that there penny bang, no more I ain't; and I ain't a-larnin' nothink, and she," (we knew only too well whom he meant), "may be up to all manner of larks, and me not know nothink about it."

"You shall get up soon, when you're better," was Jack's reply.

"I are better, governor."

"Yes, but you won't be unless you lie still for a day or two more, and do what you're told," said Jack, firmly.

Whereat the boy subsided.

Hawkesbury turned up at his place at the office in a benevolent frame of mind, and received over my petty-cash and the beautiful copy of accounts which accompanied it with the utmost condescension.

He was extremely obliged to me, he said, for taking charge of the accounts during his absence, and had no doubt he would find everything correct when he went through the figures. He hoped it had not given me much extra work, and that during his absence I had been in the enjoyment of good health and spirits.

All which "gush" I accepted with due gratitude, wondering inwardly whether he had been actually made a partner since I last saw him—he was so very gracious.

"By the way," said I, when the ceremony was at an end, and feeling a little mischievously inclined, as well as being anxious to vent my feelings on the point—"by the way, your particular friend Masham came to our lodging the other evening."

"Ah, did he?" said Hawkesbury, blandly; "I'm glad he called. He wanted to see you again. He took rather a fancy to you that day, you know."

"Did he?" said I. "I think he was rather sorry he called, though."

"Why?"

"Why, because Smith gave him the thrashing he deserved, and the thrashing he's not likely to forget in a hurry either!"

"I don't understand," said Hawkesbury. "What has Smith to do with my friend Masham?"

"Just what he has to do with any other blackguard," retorted I, warming up.

"Batchelor, you are forgetting yourself, I think," said Hawkesbury. "I hope what you are saying is not true."

"If you mean about Masham being a blackguard," said I, "it's as true as that he is your friend."

"I really don't know what all this means," said Hawkesbury, haughtily. "I must ask Masham himself."

"I'm afraid you won't find him," I said. "He nearly murdered the boy who was with us at the time. And as the report went out that the child was actually dead, he is prudently keeping out of the way for the present. I'm sure he will be—"

"Excuse me, Batchelor," said Hawkesbury, interrupting. "I really haven't time to talk now. Kindly get on with your work, and I will do the same."

I may not have derived much good by this edifying conversation, but I had at least the satisfaction of feeling that Hawkesbury now knew what I thought of his friend.

Jack said that evening he thought it was a pity I had said as much as I had, and further reflection made me think the same. However, it couldn't be helped now, and anything that made clear the estimation in which I held Masham was on the whole no bad thing.

That evening when we got back we found Mr Smith at home. He had come, he said, to insist on taking Jack's place with Billy for the night. Jack protested in vain that he felt quite fresh, that he was not in the least sleepy, and so on. Mr Smith was inexorable for once, so we had finally to retire together to the room downstairs, and leave him in possession.

As we said good-night he gave me a look which I well understood.

"It's awful nonsense," said Jack, "making out I want sleep. Why, I've slept most of every night I've been up there. I'm sure more than he has."

"He thinks a good deal about you, Jack, I fancy," said I, anxious to steer the talk round in the required direction. Jack nodded and went and opened the window.

"It's awfully close to-night," said he.

We stood leaning out of the window for some minutes, watching the few passengers in the street below and saying nothing. What Jack was thinking about I could not tell. What was passing through my mind I knew well enough.

"How do you think he seems?" asked I, after a long pause.

"Who, Billy? He's getting on wonderfully."

"I didn't mean Billy," said I. "I meant Mr Smith."

"Oh, you ought to know better than I do. I really have hardly seen him the last few days. I've not heard him cough so much, though."

"He's not been himself at all the last few days," I said.

"No wonder," said Jack. "That night's work was enough to upset anybody."

"Oh, I don't mean in that way," I said, feeling hopeless as to ever getting out my secret. "Though I am sure he was very much concerned about Billy. But he seems to have other things on his mind too."

"Has he? He works too hard, that's what it is; and not content with that," added he, "he insists on sitting up all night with Billy."

There was another pause. I was no nearer than before, and for any hint I had given Jack of what was coming he knew as little of it as he did of the North Pole.

I must be more explicit, or I should never get out with it.

"Do you know, Jack," said I presently, "he's been telling me a good deal of his history lately?"

"Oh," said Jack, "you two have got to be quite chummy. By the way, we ought to hear the result of the exam, on Tuesday, certainly."

"It is very strange and sad," said I, thinking more of what was in my mind than of what he was saying.

"What *do* you mean? They oughtn't to take more than a week surely to go through the papers."

"Oh, I wasn't talking about that," I said. "I was thinking of Mr Smith's story."

"Why, what's up with you, Fred? You've gone daft about Mr Smith, surely. What's strange and sad?"

"The story of his life, Jack. He was once—"

"Stop," said Jack, firmly. "I dare say it's all you say, Fred, but I'd rather you didn't tell it me."

"Why not?" I said.

"He told it to you, but not to me. If he wants me to know it, he will tell me himself."

I could not but feel the rebuke. Had I but been as careful of another secret, half my troubles would never have come upon me.

"You are quite right, Jack," I said. "I know by this time that I should have no business to tell other people's secrets. But, as it happens, Mr Smith is anxious for me to tell you his story; and that is the reason, I believe, why he has insisted on leaving us together to-night."

I had launched my ship now!

Jack looked at me in a puzzled way.

"Wants you to tell me his story?" he repeated.

"Yes."

"Why?"

"He has a reason. I think you had better hear it, Jack."

Jack was no fool. He had wits enough to tell him by this time that in all this mysterious blundering talk of mine there was after all something more serious than commonplace tittle-tattle. My face and tone must have proved it, if nothing else did.

He remained leaning out of the window by my side as I told him that story in words as near those of Mr Smith himself as I could recall.

He interrupted me by no starts or exclamations, but remained silent, with his head on his hands, till the very end.

Indeed, he was so still after it was all told that for a moment I felt uneasy, lest he was taken ill.

But presently he looked up, with his face very pale, and said, "I can scarcely believe it, Fred."

There was nothing in his tone or look to say whether the disclosure came to him as good news or bad. I longed to know, but I dared not ask. A long silence followed. He sat down on a chair with his face turned from me. I felt that to say another word would be a rude disturbance.

After a while he rose and said, in a voice very low and trembling, "I'll go up stairs, Fred."

"No," said I, taking his arm and gently leading him back to his chair. "I'll go up, old boy, and look after Billy to-night."

He did not resist, and I hastened up.

Mr Smith met me at the door with anxious face.

"Well?" he inquired, in a voice which trembled as much as Jack's had done.

"He knows all," I said.

"Yes? and—"

"And he is downstairs, expecting you," I said.

With a sigh very like a sob, Mr Smith left me and went down the stairs. All that long night, as I sat beside Billy and watched his fitful sleep, I could hear the sound of voices in the room below.

What they said to one another I never knew, and never inquired.

But next morning, when Jack came and summoned me to breakfast, his happy face and Mr Smith's quiet smile answered far more eloquently than words every question I could possibly have asked about that strange and sacred meeting between a lost father and a lost son.

Chapter Thirty Five
How Jack and I talked louder than we need have done

About a week after the experiences narrated in the last chapter, my friend Smith and I went down one morning early to Hawk Street.

We usually took a short walk on our way when we happened to be early, and I don't exactly know why we did not do so this time. But certain it is that instead of reaching the office at half-past nine, we found ourselves there a few minutes before nine.

The housekeeper was sweeping the stairs and shaking the mats on the pavement as we arrived.

She naturally looked surprised to see us, and said she had the office yet to sweep out, and we had better take a walk.

But, being lazily disposed, we declined the invitation, and determined to brave the dust and go up.

The office was certainly not very tempting for work. The windows were wide open, and the din of omnibuses and other traffic from the street below was almost deafening. Stools and chairs were stacked together in the middle of the floor, and the waste-paper of yesterday littered the whole place. Even our own desks were thick with dust.

Under these depressing circumstances we were forced to admit that possibly the housekeeper was right, and that we had better take a walk.

"It's a nuisance," said I, "for I had to leave one or two things unfinished yesterday."

"I've a good mind to try," said Jack. "Unless I can catch up my work I shall have to stay late to-night, and I don't want to do that, as father is going to try to get away early."

So we dusted our desks as best we could, shut the windows to keep out the noise, recovered our stools from the assortment in the middle, and prepared to make the best of it.

"Do you know, Jack," said I, as I was getting out my papers, "it is so queer to hear you talking of Mr Smith as father? I can hardly realise it yet."

"No more can I, often," said Jack, "though I am getting more used to the idea."

"When are you going to take him to Packworth?" I asked.

"I'm not quite sure. He thinks he can get a week at the end of this month, and I shall try to get the partners to let me take my holiday at the same time."

"I hope you'll be able to manage it."

"So do I. Poor father is in very low spirits at the prospect of meeting Mary, I think. You know we shall have to tell her everything."

"Will you? Is it necessary?"

"Oh, yes. At least father says it is. If she were to hear of his story from any other source, he says he would never dare see her again. It will be far better to tell her. But I wish it was over."

"So do I," I said. "Poor Mary!"

I had got quite into the way of talking of her to Jack by her Christian name, as if she were my sister as well as his.

"I suppose," said I, "she will still live with Mrs Shield at Packworth?"

"Oh, yes, for the present. There's no place to bring her to in London till we get a little better off."

"I hope that won't be very long," said I.

"I'm afraid father's situation on the staff of the *Banner* is not a very—"

"Hush!" I exclaimed, suddenly.

We had remained, so far, in undisturbed possession of the office, and there was no chance of any new-comer entering without our knowing. But while Jack was speaking I thought I heard a sound, not on the stairs outside, but in the partners' room, which opened out of the counting-house.

Suppose one of the partners had been there all the while, and heard all we had said.

Jack stopped dead in his talk, and with pale face looked inquiringly at me.

"I thought I heard a noise in there," said I, pointing to the door.

"What?" said Jack, with a gasp. The same thought was evidently crossing his mind which had crossed mine.

"It can't be either of the partners," whispered he, "at this hour."

"We'd better see," said I; "it may be a thief."

We went quietly to the door. All was silent as we listened; and yet I felt I could not have been mistaken about the noise. The door was closed to, but not fastened. Jack opened it softly.

There, sitting at the partners' table, with his head on his hands, apparently absorbed in work, and unconscious of everything else, sat—Hawkesbury!

A spectre could not have startled and horrified us more!

At first he did not seem to be aware of our presence, and it was not till Jack advanced a step, and involuntarily exclaimed "Hawkesbury!" that he looked up in a flurried way.

"Why, Smith!" he exclaimed, "and Batchelor! What a start you gave me! What are you doing here at this hour, and in this room?"

"We've been here a quarter of an hour," said Jack, solemnly.

"Have you? How quiet you've been!"

This, at any rate, was a relief. He could hardly have heard our conversation.

"But what are you doing in here?" he added, in an important voice. "You must know this room is private, and not for the clerks."

"We heard a noise," said I, "and did not know who was here."

Hawkesbury smiled incredulously.

"All I can say is," said he, "I hope you are not in the habit of coming in here when you are by yourselves in the office. But kindly leave me now—I am busy."

He had a lot of papers spread out on the table before him, which he was gathering together in his hand while he spoke. Whether they were accounts, or letters, or what, we could not tell; but as there was nothing more to be said we withdrew to the counting-house. He followed us out in about five minutes, carrying the papers to his desk. Then, informing the housekeeper in an audible voice that he would just go and get breakfast, he left us to ourselves.

"What a mercy," said I, "he doesn't seem to have heard what we were talking about!"

Jack smiled bitterly.

"Unless I'm mistaken, he's heard every word!"

"Surely, Jack," I exclaimed, stunned by the very idea, "you don't mean that?"

"I'm sure of it."

Our feelings during the remainder of that day may be more easily imagined than expressed. If there was one person in the world more than another we would have wished not to hear what had been said, it was Hawkesbury. Thanks to my folly and meanness, he had known far too much as it was, before, and trouble had fallen on Jack in consequence. Now, if Jack's surmise was true, to what use might he not put the knowledge just obtained?

No one quite understood Hawkesbury. But I knew enough of him to see that jealousy of my friend Smith mixed up with all the motives for his conduct at Hawk Street. His tone of superiority, his favouring one clerk above another, his efforts to assert his influence over me had all been part of a purpose to triumph over Jack Smith. And yet, in spite of it all, Jack had held on his way, rising meanwhile daily in favour and confidence with his employers, and even with some of his formerly hostile fellow-clerks.

But now, with this new secret in his hand, Hawkesbury once more had my friend in his power, and how he would use it there was no knowing.

All that day he was particularly bland and condescending in his manner to me, and particularly pompous and exacting in his manner to Jack, and this, more than anything else, convinced me the latter was right in his suspicion.

Our discussion as we walked home that night was dismal enough. The brighter prospects which had seemed to dawn on Jack and his father appeared somehow suddenly clouded, and a sense of trouble hung over both our minds.

"One thing is certain," said Jack, "I must tell the partners everything now."

"Perhaps you are right—if there is any chance of his telling them. But he could surely hardly act so shamefully."

"It may be too late, even now," said Jack. "You know, when I was taken on at Hawk Street, and they asked me about my father, I said simply he was abroad. I've thought since it was hardly straightforward, and yet it didn't seem necessary to tell them all about it."

"Certainly not. Why should your prospects be ruined because your father—"

"Because my father," said Jack, taking me up quietly, "had lost his? That's what I thought. But perhaps they will think differently. At any rate, I will tell them."

"If you do," said I, "and they take it kindly, as I expect they will, I don't see what more harm he can do you."

"Unless," said Jack, "he thinks it his duty to tell the proprietors of the *Banner*."

"What possible good could that do him?" I asked.

"Why, he might as well think it his duty to tell Mary."

Jack said nothing, and we walked on, very uneasy and depressed.

When we arrived at our lodgings we found Billy, whose recovery was now almost complete, sitting up in the bed with a jubilant face.

"You're a-done it, governor," cried he, as we entered. "You are a-done it."

"Done what?" said Jack.

"Why, that there sam."

"What about it?" we cried, eagerly.

"Oh, that there flashy bloke, Flanikin, 'e comes up, and says 'e, 'Jack Smith in?' says he—meanin' you, governor. 'Ain't no concern of yourn,' says I—not 'olding with them animals as comes to see yer. 'Yes it is,' says 'e, a blowin' with the run he'd 'ad. 'Tell 'im the moment 'e comes in that 'e's fust in the sam,' says he."

"Hurrah!" I cried, forgetting everything in this good news. "Old man, how splendid!"

Jack too for a moment relaxed his grave face as he answered my greeting.

"I can hardly believe it," said he.

"Oh, there ain't no error, so I tells you," cried Billy, "the cove 'ad been up to the shop, he says, and copied it down. He was nigh off 'is 'ead, was that there Flanikin, and 'e's a-comin' in to see you 'imself, he says, afore eight o'clock."

And before eight Flanagan turned up and confirmed the glorious news with a printed list, in which sure enough "Smith" stood out distinctly in the first place.

"You know, I thought it might be another Smith," said Flanagan, laughing; "there are one or two of the same name in the world, I know. But there's not another in the list, so it's all right. I say, wouldn't old Henniker be proud of you now, my boy—eh, Fred? She'd let you sneeze without pulling you up for it, I do believe."

A letter by the evening post to Jack brought the official confirmation of the news from the examiners, and announced further that the distinction carried with it a scholarship worth £50 a year for three years.

In the midst of our jubilation, Mr Smith came in, and that evening, but for the morning's cloud which still hung over us, our happiness would have been complete.

The next day Jack took an early opportunity of seeking an interview with the partners, and making a clean breast to them of his birth and position. He gave me an account of the interview afterwards, and said that while Mr Merrett, as usual, took everything kindly and even sympathetically, Mr Barnacle was disposed to regard Jack's representation of himself on first coming to the office as not candid, and so blameworthy. However, they both agreed that he had done the proper thing in speaking out now, and willingly agreed to let him take his holiday at the time proposed, so as to accompany his father to Packworth.

So a great weight was taken off our minds, and the consciousness that now nothing remained concealed from our employers enabled us to bear Hawkesbury's lofty manner with comparative indifference.

I even yet had my doubts whether he could really have overheard our talk that morning. Nothing certainly that he said or did gave colour to the suspicion; only his almost deferential manner to me, and his almost scornful manner to Jack, seemed to hint that it might be so.

Jack's opinion, however, on the point was unshaken.

An uneventful fortnight passed. Billy was up again and back at his work as usual, except that he was strictly forbidden to walk about on his hands any more—a terrible hardship for the lad.

The first half-year's cheque of Jack's scholarship had come, and had been proudly deposited in the bank, as a nucleus of a fund in which father, son, and daughter were some day to participate.

And now the long-looked-for time had arrived when Jack and his father were to pay their promised visit to Packworth. I had seen them both half rejoicing in, half dreading the prospect; and now that I saw them actually start, I scarcely knew whether most to pity or envy them.

It was a lonely evening for me, the evening after I had seem them off. They had promised to write and tell me how they fared; but meanwhile I felt very desolate. Even Billy's company failed altogether to raise my spirits.

However, as it happened, that youth had some news to give me which at any rate tended to divert my mind for a time from my bereaved condition.

"I seen that Mashing agin," he said, abruptly.

"Did you? Where?"

"Down Trade Street. I was on a pal's beat there, for a change, and he comes and wants his boots blacked. I knows the animal, but he don't twig me, bein' off my beat. I would a-liked to give the beauty a topper, so I would; but, bless you, where's the use!"

"So you blacked his boots for him?"

"I did so. An' 'e got a pal along of him, and they was a-jawin' about a parson's son as owed Mashing fifteen pound, and saying as they'd crack him up if he didn't pay up. And then they was a-jawin' about the shine up here that night, and the pal was a-chaffin' Mashing cos of the wipin' my bloke give 'im, and Mashing he says he reckons he's quits with the prig—meaning the governor—by this time, he says. And t'other one say "Ow?" And Mashing says as the governor's a conwex son, and he knows who Mr Conwex is, he says, and he are writ a letter to Miss Conwex, he says, down in the country, that'll open 'er goggle eyes, he says."

"What!" I exclaimed, starting from my seat, "he's written to Mary, the brute!"

"Dunno so much about your Mary, but that's what he says," replied Billy, composedly.

"When—when did he write—eh?" I cried.

"'Ow do I know?" retorted Billy, who evidently misunderstood and failed to appreciate my agitated manner.

"I aren't arsked 'im. Arst 'im yourself if you want to know."

And he drew himself up in evident dudgeon.

I didn't know what to do. It was no time to denounce or lament. The thought of the poor innocent girl receiving such a letter as Masham would be likely to write was too much to endure. If only I could prevent her seeing it!

"When did you hear all this?" I said to Billy.

"Find out. 'Tain't no concern of yourn," said the offended hero.

"But, Billy," said I, "it's most important. Do you, know that what Masham has done will make your Mr Smith miserable?"

Billy started at this.

"If I'd a known that, I'd a wrung his leg off," said he.

"But when was it? This morning?"

"No, last night."

Last night! Then the letter would already have reached Packworth, and long before Jack and his father arrived the happiness of her life would have been dashed.

It seemed no use attempting anything. I determined, however, to send a telegram to meet Jack on his arrival, so as to warn him, in case the letter should still be undelivered. I worded it carefully, for fear it might be opened before Jack arrived.

"Hawkesbury did hear our talk. He told Masham, who has written a letter to some one we both care for."

This I flattered myself was sufficiently unintelligible to any one but Jack.

I spent the rest of the evening in fighting against the tumult of my own feelings. My impulse had been to rush at once to Hawkesbury and charge him with his infamy. But what good would that do? And who was I, to prefer such a charge against another? My next was to find out Masham, and take some desperate revenge on him. But, after all, my only authority was Billy's report of a conversation overheard by him; and, though it might be all true, I had no right, I felt, without further proof, even if then, to do anything.

On the whole, I came to the conclusion I had better go to bed, which I did. But whether I slept or not the reader may guess.

Chapter Thirty Six
How Hawkesbury and I came across one another rather seriously

It took a great effort to appear before Hawkesbury next morning as if I was not aware of his meanness. Now Jack was away, he once again put on an air of friendliness towards me which was particularly aggravating. Had he only made himself disagreeable, and given me an opportunity of venting my wrath, I should have been positively grateful. But to stand by all day and be simpered to, and even cringed to, was galling in the extreme.

I did once venture on a mild protest.

He was speaking to me about the coming holidays, and begging me in a most humble manner to choose what time I should like to take mine, assuring me that any time would do for him.

I suggested, curtly, that as Doubleday had not yet had his holiday I considered he had first choice.

"Oh," he said, "I don't think so. Besides, Batchelor, Doubleday and I could both be away at the same time; but I really would hardly feel comfortable in going unless you could take charge of the petty-cash while I am away."

"Smith will be back," I said; "he could do that for you."

As I expected, his face clouded.

"I can't agree with you there, Batchelor. But don't let us talk of that. I hope you will choose the time you would like best. I can easily arrange for any time."

"I don't know what makes you so wonderfully civil," said I, losing patience at all this soft soap. "After all that has happened, Hawkesbury, I should have thought you might have spared yourself this gush, as far as I was concerned."

"I would like bygones to be bygones between us, Batchelor. I know quite well I have been to blame in many things! I am sorry for them now, if it prevents our being friends."

And he smiled sweetly.

I gave it up in disgust, and let him say what he liked. It was not worth the trouble of preventing him, unless I was prepared for an open rupture, which just then I felt would be unwise, both on Jack's account and my own.

So he had the satisfaction of believing his sweetness had made its due impression on my savage breast, and of scoring to himself a victory in consequence.

As I had found it before, hard work proved now to be the best specific for dull spirits, and during the next few days I gave the remedy a full trial.

It seemed ages before any letter came from Packworth, and I was dying to hear. For meanwhile all sorts of doubts and fears took hold of me. How had that strange family meeting gone off? Had it been marred by Masham's cruel letter? or was the poor lost father once more finding happiness in the sight of one whom he had last seen an infant beside his dead wife? Surely if sympathy and common interest were to count for kinship, I was as much a member of that little family as any of them!

At last the letter came. It was from Jack:

"Dear Fred,—We got down on Wednesday. Father went that night to the hotel, as his heart failed him at the last moment. I went on to Mrs Shield's, and found your telegram on my arrival. I was horrified, but hardly surprised at what it told me. Happily, Mary was in bed, as I had not been expected till the morning, so I was able to explain all to Mrs Shield. She knew all about it before I told her; for the enclosed letter had arrived by the post in the morning, addressed to Mary. Mercifully, seeing it was in a strange hand, and, as I have often told you, being most jealously careful of Mary, Mrs Shield took it into her head to open the letter and read it before giving it to Mary, and you may imagine her utter horror. She of course did not let her see it, and thus saved the child from what would have been a fearful shock; and I was able to break it all to her gradually. Father is to come this evening—I am thankful it is all so well over.

"How are you getting on? Anything fresh at Hawk Street? I don't envy Hawkesbury or his friend their feelings just now; but I am determined to take no notice of this last brutal plot. Good-bye now.

"Yours ever,—

"J.S."

The enclosure, written in an evidently disguised hand, was as follows:—

"An unknown admirer thinks it may interest Mary Smith to know that her father is a common thief and swindler, who has just come back from fourteen years' penal servitude among the convicts. He is now living in London with his son, Mary's brother, who, Mary may as well know, is following close in his dear father's footsteps, however pious he may seem to others. This is the truth, or the writer would not have taken the trouble to send it. The best thing, if Mary wants to prevent the whole affair being made public, is to make her brother leave his place in London at once, and go somewhere in the country where he will be a nuisance to nobody."

My first feeling on reading this was one of devout thankfulness for the Providence which had kept it from falling into the hands for which it was designed. But my wrath soon drove out every other feeling—wrath ten times the more fierce because it was helpless.

I could do nothing. I might go and attempt to thrash Masham, or I might thrash Hawkesbury, who was equally to blame, if not more. But what good would it do? It would only make bad worse. Jack's secret, instead of being the private property of a few, would become common talk. I should be unable to bring positive proof of my charges, and even if I could, I should only be putting myself in the wrong by using force to redress my wrongs. No, after all, the only punishment was to take no notice of the affair, to let the two blackguards flatter themselves their plot had succeeded, and to leave them to find out as best they could that they had failed.

So I kept my hands resolutely in my pockets when next I met Hawkesbury, and consoled myself by picturing what his feelings would have been, had he known that that letter of his and his friend's was in my pocket all the time.

However, my resolution to have nothing to do with him was upset very shortly, and in an unexpected manner.

Since the eventful morning when Jack and I had had that unlucky conversation at Hawk Street, I had not again put in an appearance there before the stated time. Now, however, that I was all by myself in town, with very few attractions towards a solitary walk, and a constant sense of work to catch up at Hawk Street, it occurred to me one fine morning—I should say one wet morning—when the streets were very uninviting, to seek shelter at the unearthly hour of half-past eight in Messrs Merrett, Barnacle, and Company's premises.

The housekeeper, greatly to my satisfaction, was engaged in clearing out the offices below ours, so that I was able to ascend without challenge and establish myself at my desk. I had not been there five minutes when another footstep sounded on the stairs and Hawkesbury entered.

I had thought it quite possible he might be there when I arrived, and was therefore not nearly so surprised to see him as he appeared to see me.

"What, Batchelor!" he exclaimed, "are you here?"

"Yes," I replied, "are you?"

Why should he express such surprise, I wondered, at my doing just what he was doing?

"What brings you here at this hour?" he demanded, dropping for a moment the coaxing tone with which I had become so familiar the last day or two.

"What brings you here, for the matter of that?" I retorted.

If he thought I was going to clear out to please him, he was mistaken.

"Don't address me like that," he replied, with as great a tone of authority as he could assume. "I have a right to be here. You have none."

"Until I am told so by some one better than yourself I sha'n't believe it," I replied.

I was losing my temper fast. Masham's letter burned in my pocket, and the sight of this fellow giving himself airs to me was as much as I could stand.

Fortunately for us both, however, he did not prolong the discussion, but went to his desk.

It was evident, despite his assumed displeasure, he was very much put out about something. That something, I could not help thinking, must be my presence. He fidgeted about uneasily, looking now at the clock, now at me, now opening his desk, now shutting it, now scribbling on the paper before him, now tearing it up.

All this I saw as I tried to proceed steadily with my work. At last he brought me an envelope he had just addressed, and said in a rather more persuasive manner than he had yet assumed—

"Batchelor, would you kindly take this note round to Hodge and Company's? It is very important; they should have had it yesterday."

"Hodge's are never open till ten," I said.

"Oh yes, indeed they are. At least they expect this letter by nine o'clock. It's a bill of lading for their goods."

"If that's so," replied I, "the mail went out yesterday—you know that—and there's not another till Monday."

"Oh, but there's a letter with it that has to be attended to immediately."

"It's not been copied," said I, who had charge of the letter-book, and was responsible for copying everything that went out.

"I've kept a copy. I'll see to that. It's only to ask them to call round," he said, with evident confusion.

I did not believe a word he said. And more than that, I strongly suspected all this was a device to get me out of the office—and that was what I had no intention of submitting to.

"If it's to ask them to call round," I said, "it will do when the commissionaire comes at half-past nine."

"But I tell you it must be there at *nine*," he exclaimed.

"Then," said I, "you had better take it yourself."

I had ceased to be afraid of Hawkesbury, or the look with which he returned to his desk might have made me uneasy.

I could see that as the time went on he became still more uneasy.

Once more he came to me.

"Will you go with the letter?" he demanded angrily.

"No, I won't go with the letter," I replied, in decided tones.

"You'll be sorry for it, Batchelor," he said, in a significant way.

"Shall I?"

"You would not like my uncle and Mr Barnacle to be told of your early visits here without leave."

"They are quite welcome to know it."

"And of my catching you and Smith going into their private room."

"Where we found *you*," I replied, laughing, "busy at nobody knows what?"

He looked at me hard as I drew this bow at a venture, and then said, "You must know, Batchelor, that I have a right to sit in that room when I choose. And," he added, dropping his voice to a whisper and looking at me in a most significant way—"and if the door happens to be open, and if you and Smith happen to talk secrets, there's every chance of their being overheard!"

This was his trump card! If anything was to settle the question of my obeying him and taking Hodge and Company's letter, this was to do it.

"Then you did hear what was said?" I asked.

"Yes, I did," he said.

"And you mean to say—"

"I mean to say," said he, with a glance up at the clock, "that you had better take this letter at once, Batchelor."

"And if I don't?"

"If you don't, your friend Smith shall smart for it."

Before I could make up my mind what to do—whether to feign alarm and take the letter, leaving him to suppose he still had the whip-hand over us, or whether to undeceive him at once, and defy him point-blank—before I could reply at all, the door suddenly opened, and Masham entered.

If anything was still wanted to decide me, this sufficed. I felt certain now that there was mischief on foot somewhere, and the appearance of this bird of ill-omen was sufficient to account for Hawkesbury's eagerness to get me out of the way.

What could have brought these two to arrange a meeting here, at the office, and at an hour when in the ordinary course of things no one else would be present?

I determined to stay where I was at all risks.

Masham on seeing me started, and looked inquiringly at Hawkesbury.

"What's he doing here?" he said. The very sound of his voice made my blood boil.

"He is going to take a letter to the Borough for me," said Hawkesbury, bestowing a meaning glance on me.

"I'm not going to take it," said I.

"What?" exclaimed Hawkesbury, in sudden fury.

"I'm not going to take it. I'm going to stay where I am."

"You know the consequences?" he muttered between his teeth.

"Yes."

"You know what it means for your friend Smith?"

"Yes."

He looked perplexed, as well he might. That I should defy him in the face of his threat against Jack Smith was the last thing he had expected, "Batchelor," said he, altering his tone suddenly to one of entreaty, "I have very important business to arrange with Masham. Would you mind leaving us for half an hour? I would not ask you, only I shall get into awful trouble if I can't talk to him alone for a little."

It passed my comprehension how, after threatening me with Jack's ruin, he should now turn round with such an appeal. And he put on such a beseeching manner that in the midst of my wrath I half pitied him. However, I was not to be moved. "If you want to see him so privately as all that," said I, "take him up to the sample-room. No one will disturb you there."

He gave me one look of hatred and menace, and then said to Masham, "We must fix another time, Masham; we can't go into the matter now."

"Eh?" said Masham, who had hitherto stood by in silence. "What do you say? If we can't do it now, we won't do it at all, my boy."

Hawkesbury went up to him and whispered something.

"Oh, we'll soon settle that!" said the other, laughing. "He won't go, won't he! We'll help him, that's all? Whereabouts is the coal-hole?"

So saying he made a grab at my arm, and before I could resist Hawkesbury had secured the other.

I struggled all I could, but unavailingly. Between them I was dragged up stairs to the sample-room, into which I were ignominiously thrust, and the door locked behind me. At first my rage and indignation were too great to allow me to think of anything but kicking at the door and shouting to my captors to release me. But this I soon discovered was fruitless, and in due time I gave it up, and resolved to wait my time and make the best of my lot.

That some mischief was afoot I now felt certain, and whatever it was, I felt equally sure it was being enacted during my imprisonment. Yet what could I do? I could only listen to the sound of voices below and speculate as to what was going on. Suddenly, however, it flashed across me that the room in which I was was not over the office, but over the partners' room, and that therefore the sounds I heard must proceed from thence.

What could they be up to? I heard a door open and shut, and a noise of what might have been keys, followed by a heavy slamming-to of something which, for the thud it gave, might have been the iron safe itself.

I felt very uncomfortable, but I was forced to remain chafing where I was for nearly half an hour, when the lock of my prison turned and the two entered the room. They both seized me as before.

"Now you can come down," said Masham.

"Not till he promises to say nothing about this," said Hawkesbury.

"He knows what to expect if he doesn't!" said Masham.

"After all," said Hawkesbury, "we didn't mean to hurt you; Masham and I only wanted to settle some horse-racing and other scores, and as the papers were all in my desk, we were bound to use the office, and of course I couldn't ask him round any other time. If you'd been half a gentleman, Batchelor, you would have left us at once."

"I don't believe you," I replied. "What did you want in the partners' room, I should like to know, eh?"

"What!" exclaimed Hawkesbury, in a rage. "We were never there, were we, Masham?"

"Never knew there was a partners' room," said Masham, "and if there had been, what if we had been in it?"

"We were in the counting-house all the time," said Hawkesbury. Then he added, "But come down now, and take my advice, Batchelor, and don't ruin yourself."

"Ruin myself!" cried I, with a scornful laugh; "I don't see how letting the partners know your goings on would ruin me."

"You'll see!" was the reply.

He doubtless considered the threat enough, but, knowing as I did that Jack had told the partners everything Hawkesbury could possibly tell, I could afford to treat it with contempt.

Masham took his departure, and I returned with Hawkesbury to the counting-house, where we were soon joined by our fellow-clerks.

I was very uncomfortable, and hardly knew how to act. That it was my duty to tell the partners what had happened I had no doubt; but how much to tell them, and when, I could not make up my mind. I determined to take Doubleday into my confidence, and get the advantage of his good advice and clear head.

But it was easier said than done. Almost as soon as he came in Doubleday had to go down to the docks, and the opportunity of consulting him was thus delayed. Every moment that passed I felt more and more uneasy. Mr Barnacle had already arrived, and Mr Merrett was due in a few minutes. What right had I to delay even for a moment a matter which affected the credit of the whole house?

Yet suppose, after all, I had found a mare's-nest! Suppose Hawkesbury's explanation of what had occurred should by any chance have been correct—suppose the sounds I heard during my confinement had not been caused by those two at all, but by the housekeeper sweeping out the room and putting it in order? If that was so, what a fool I should make of myself!

No; I resolved, for all the difference it would make, I would wait till I could consult Doubleday.

Hawkesbury was very busy that morning; he was constantly fidgeting in and out of his little box, giving vague directions to one clerk and another, and keeping a special eye on me and all I did.

When Mr Merrett arrived he went as usual to say good-morning to his uncle, and as usual followed him into the partners' room, to receive such letters as might require answering.

I wished Doubleday had not been called down to the docks this morning of all others. He would have told me in a moment what I ought to do, or, which came to the same thing, what he would have done in my place. Anything would be better than this suspense. I was tempted even then to break in upon the partners and tell them what had happened, and what my suspicions were. But I could not do it while Hawkesbury was there. When he came out—

By the way, what an unconscionable lot of letters there must be to keep him in there all this time! He was usually there about five minutes, but this morning he had been half an hour at the very least.

The thought suddenly occurred to me, could he be telling the partners about Jack Smith's antecedents? In the midst of all my uneasiness I almost smiled to think how sold he would be when he discovered they had heard it all already!

Ah! here he was at last.

No. It was Mr Merrett who appeared at the door with an extremely long face; and looking round the office, fixed his eyes on me, and said, "Batchelor—come in here!"

I obeyed.

Instead of going in as usual before me, he waited till I had entered, and then followed me, closing the door behind him.

What on earth does it all mean?

Mr Barnacle sat looking straight before him through his spectacles. Hawkesbury also sat at the table, twisting a quill pen backwards and forwards with his fingers.

"Hawkesbury," said Mr Merrett, as he re-entered, "you might leave us, please. I will call you when you are wanted."

Hawkesbury, without looking at me, rose to obey. As he reached the door, Mr Merrett stepped after him, and whispered something. At ordinary times I should not have heard what he whispered, or thought of listening for it. But there was such a silence in the room, and my nerves were strung up to such a pitch, that I distinctly caught the words.

What I heard was this—

"Fetch a policeman!"

Chapter Thirty Seven
How Hawkesbury and I spent a Morning in the Partners' Room

"Fetch a policeman!" The truth flashed across me as I heard the words. Instead of standing here an accuser, I stood the accused. Hawkesbury had been before me with a vengeance!

The very shock of the discovery called back the presence of mind, which, on my first summons, I had almost lost. I was determined at least that nothing I should do or say would lend colour to the false charge against me.

"Batchelor," said Mr Merrett, after Hawkesbury had gone and the door was locked—"Batchelor, we have sent for you here under very painful circumstances. You doubtless know why."

"I must ask you to tell me, sir," I replied, respectfully, but with a tremble in my voice which I would have given anything to conceal.

"I will tell you," said Mr Merrett, "when you have first told Mr Barnacle and me what you have been doing since eight o'clock this morning."

"And let me advise you," said Mr Barnacle, looking up, "to tell the truth."

"I certainly will tell the truth," I began.

What possessed that unlucky voice of mine to quaver in the way it did? Those few words, I was convinced, would tell more against me than the most circumstantial narrative. I clutched hold of the back of a chair near me, and made a desperate effort to steady myself as I proceeded. I gave an exact account of everything that had happened since I entered the office that morning, omitting nothing, glossing over nothing, shirking nothing. They both listened attentively, eyeing me keenly all the time, and betraying no sign in their faces whether they believed me or not.

"Then you mean to say," said Mr Merrett, when it was done, "that you were not in this room at all?"

"Yes, I never entered it."

"Were you ever in this room without our knowledge?"

"Yes, a fortnight ago. Smith and I were here early, and hearing a noise inside, we opened the door and came in to see what it was."

"What did you find?"

"Hawkesbury, working at the table where Mr Barnacle is now sitting."

"What occurred?"

I related precisely what had occurred, repeating as nearly as I could the very words that had been used.

There was a silence, and then Mr Merrett, in his most solemn tones, said, "Now, Batchelor, answer this question. You say you were here before any one else arrived this morning?"

"Yes, sir. I had been here about five minutes before Hawkesbury came."

"What were you doing during that time?"

"I was working at my desk."

"You are quite sure?"

"Perfectly," said I, my cheeks burning and my heart swelling within me to be thus spoken to by those whom, with all my faults, I had never once so much as dreamt of deceiving.

"You did not enter this room?"

"No."

Mr Merrett touched his bell, and Hawkesbury appeared. I scarcely wondered he should try to avoid my eye as he stood at the table waiting.

"Hawkesbury, repeat once more, in Batchelor's hearing, what you have already told us."

He kept his head down and his face averted from me as he said, "I arrived here at a quarter to nine this morning, and noticed the door of this room open, and when I came to see who was there I saw Batchelor in the act of shutting the safe. He did not notice me at first, not until he was coming out of the room. I asked him what he was doing here. He seemed very much disconcerted, and said he had been looking for some papers he had left on Mr Barnacle's table the day before. I asked him what he had been doing with the safe, and where he had got the key to open it. He got into a great state, and begged me to say nothing about it. I said I was bound to tell you what I had seen. Then he flew into a rage, and told me he'd serve me out. I told him that wouldn't prevent me doing what was right. Then he left the office, and didn't come back till a quarter to ten."

All this Hawkesbury repeated glibly and hurriedly in a low voice. To me, who stood by and heard it, it was a cowardly lie from beginning to end. But to my employers, I felt, it must sound both businesslike and straightforward; quite as straightforward, I feared, as my own equally exact but tremblingly-spoken story.

"You hear what Hawkesbury says?" said Mr Merrett, turning to me.

I roused myself with an effort, and answered quietly, "Yes, sir."

"What have you to say to it?"

"That it is false from beginning to end."

"You deny, in fact, ever having been at this safe, or in this room?"

"Most certainly."

They all looked grave, and Mr Merrett said, solemnly, "I am sorry to hear you deny it, Batchelor. If you had made a full confession we should have been disposed to deal more leniently with you."

"I never did it—it's all false!" I cried, suddenly losing all self-control. "You know it's false; it's a plot to ruin me and Jack."

"Silence, sir!" said Mr Merrett, sternly.

"I won't be silent," I shouted; "I never deceived you, and yet you go and believe what this miserable—"

Mr Merrett touched his bell angrily; but before any one answered it Mr Barnacle had looked up.

The junior partner had been silent all this time, an attentive but impassive listener to all that had passed. Once or twice during Hawkesbury's story he had darted a quick glance at the speaker, and once or twice during my indignant protest his brows had knit, as it seemed, in anger. Mr Barnacle had always had the reputation of being the sterner of the two partners, and now, as he abruptly joined in the conversation, I felt as if it boded very little good for me.

"One moment," said he to Mr Merrett; "there are a few more questions we should ask, I think. Batchelor, you are doing yourself no good by this noise," he added, turning to me.

He was right, and I saw it. I quieted down with an effort, and wondered what was coming next.

Wallop appeared at the door in answer to the bell, and was told he was not wanted. Then Mr Barnacle turned to Hawkesbury and asked, "What brought you here so early as a quarter to nine, Hawkesbury?"

This question surprised Hawkesbury as much as it delighted me. I hardly expected to have a cross-examination in my favour conducted by Mr Barnacle.

"I came to do some work," said Hawkesbury.

"What work?"

"I had several things to catch up."

"What? Invoices, or letters, or accounts, or what?"

"I had the petty-cash to balance."

"That is supposed to be done every day, is it not?"

"Yes; but I had got rather behind."

"How many days behind?" said Mr Barnacle.

"Really I can't quite say," said Hawkesbury, who did not seem used to being driven into a corner. "My journey North threw me out of it."

"Then you have not balanced the petty-cash since before you went North, nearly three weeks ago? Am I to understand that?"

"Yes," said Hawkesbury.

"Is this the first morning you have come here early?"

"No. I have been once or twice."

"This is the only time you found Batchelor here?"

"No; about a fortnight ago he was here with Smith. I found them both in this room."

"What were they doing?"

"They were writing something at the table. They were in a great rage with me when I came in."

"Was the safe open at the time?"

Hawkesbury had got past the stage of sticking at trifles.

"Yes," he said; "when I came in it was. But they made a rush and turned me out of the room and locked the door. And then when I came in again it was shut."

"And did you mention this to anybody?"

"No."

"And why, pray?"

Hawkesbury was taken aback by the sudden question. It was evident he could not make his story square at all four corners.

"I—I—hoped I might be mistaken," said he, uncomfortably. "In fact, I meant to mention the affair, but—but I forgot."

"Oh," said Mr Barnacle, in a way that made the witness writhe.

"I hope you don't doubt my word," said Hawkesbury, attempting to assume a lofty air of virtuous indignation.

Mr Barnacle vouchsafed no reply.

"What we desire," said Mr Merrett, "is to come at the truth of the matter, and I can only say that it would be much better if the culprit were to make a full confession here now."

He looked hard at me as he spoke, and I did my best to stand the look as an innocent man should.

"A cheque for eight pounds has been missed," continued Mr Merrett, "which was only drawn yesterday, and left in the safe. I ask you, Batchelor, do you know anything of it?"

"No, sir," I replied.

"Do you?" said Mr Barnacle to Hawkesbury.

Hawkesbury flushed as he replied, "I never expected to be asked such a question, Mr Barnacle. I know nothing about it."

Mr Merrett evidently disliked his partner's persistency in putting to Hawkesbury the same questions as had been put to me, but he could hardly complain. He turned to his nephew and said, "Did you fetch a policeman, Hawkesbury?"

"No; I was just going when you called me in here."

Mr Merrett touched his bell, and Crow appeared.

"Is Doubleday in?" asked the senior partner.

"No, sir."

"As soon as he comes in, tell him he is wanted."

Crow took an eyeful of us as we stood there, evidently dying of curiosity to know what it all meant, and then retired.

"You two had better go to your work for the present," said Mr Barnacle; "but understand that you are neither of you at liberty to leave the office. Merrett, I will go down to the bank."

"Do," said Mr Merrett.

And so this first painful interview ended. My feelings on finding myself once more at my desk among my fellow-clerks may be more easily imagined than described.

My indignation and sense of injury would scarcely allow me to think calmly on my position. That my employers should be ready, on the testimony of such a fellow as Hawkesbury, to believe a charge like this against me, was simply unbearable, and my own helplessness to prove my innocence only added tenfold to my trouble. Oh! if Jack were only here, I might get some light.

I hurriedly dashed off a note to him, telling him all, and begging him to come. Yet what was the use of writing when I was not allowed to leave the office to post the letter?

I only wished Mr Barnacle would come back from the bank, and that I might know the worst.

As for Hawkesbury, he had shut himself up in his glass box, and was invisible.

Presently, not a little to my comfort, Doubleday returned. Fortunately, Crow was in another part of the office at the time, so that before he delivered his message I had time for a hurried consultation.

"Doubleday," said I, in a whisper, "I am accused of stealing a cheque; can you help me out?"

"Guilty, or not guilty?" inquired Doubleday, taking a practical view of the case at once. This was pleasant, but it was no time to be particular.

"It is a lie from beginning to end, invented by Hawkesbury to shield himself from a similar charge."

"Oh, that's it? He's been coming out in that line has he?"

I hurriedly narrated the morning's adventures, greatly to his astonishment and wrath. He took in the situation at once.

"Jolly awkward fix," said he. "Seen the cheque?"

"No; Mr Barnacle is down at the bank now."

"Doubleday," said Crow, entering at this moment, "the governors want you—sharp."

"They are going to send you for a policeman," I said. "If anything happens, Doubleday, will you please telegraph to Smith, at Mrs Shield's, Packworth, and tell him to come to me, and also find out Billy, the shoeblack, and say I want to see him."

Doubleday looked at me with something like amazement as I made this request, which, however, he promised to fulfil, and then waited on Mr Merrett in the partners' room.

However, he returned almost immediately, and said he was to wait until Mr Barnacle came back.

It seemed ages before that event happened. Meanwhile Doubleday advised me not to be seen talking to him, or anybody, but to go to my desk and keep my own counsel. It was good advice, and I took it. Mr Barnacle returned presently, accompanied by a man who I fancied must be connected with the bank. The two partners and this stranger were closeted together for some time in the inner-room, and then Doubleday was summoned.

After what seemed a century he emerged and beckoned to me to go in. "You're wanted," he said.

I could gather neither comfort nor hope from his face as he stood to let me pass.

"Come when I ring," said Mr Merrett to him.

Once more I stood before my employers. The stranger was still in the room, and eyed me as I entered in a manner which made me feel as if, whatever I was, I ought to be the guilty person.

"This matter, Batchelor," began Mr Merrett, solemnly, "is more serious than we imagined. Not only has a cheque been stolen, but it has been tampered with. Look here!"

So saying he held out the cheque. It was dated the previous day, and payable to bearer. But the amount, instead of being eight pounds, was eighty. The alteration had been neatly made, and no one who did not know the original amount drawn for would have suspected that £80 was not the proper sum.

"This cheque," said Mr Merrett, "was presented at the bank this morning at ten o'clock and cashed."

I made no reply, being determined to say as little as I could.

"You were here at this hour, I believe," continued Mr Merrett, "but you had left the office between 9 and 9:45."

"No, sir. I have not left the office since I arrived at half-past eight."

Mr Merrett touched the bell.

"Send Hawkesbury here," he said to Doubleday.

Hawkesbury appeared, and at Mr Merrett's bidding, after being shown the cheque, repeated once more his story in the hearing of the stranger.

It did not vary from the former version, and included the statement that I had quitted the office at the time alleged.

"Did you leave the office at all?" inquired Mr Barnacle.

"No," said Hawkesbury.

"Not at all?"

"No, I said so," replied he.

"And no one came to see you here?"

"No."

"Your friend Masham did not?"

Hawkesbury, much offended to be thus catechised, made no reply.

Mr Barnacle coolly repeated the question.

"No—he did not!"

"What were you doing all the time?"

"I was working."

"Yes, what particular work were you engaged in?"

"I told you—I was balancing the petty-cash."

"Did you finish it?"

"Nearly."

Mr Barnacle touched the bell, and Doubleday appeared.

"Doubleday, go to Hawkesbury's desk and bring me the petty-cash book and box."

Hawkesbury turned pale and broke out into a rage.

"What is this for, Mr Barnacle? I am not going to stand it! What right have you to suspect me?"

"Give Doubleday the key," repeated Mr Barnacle.

"No," exclaimed Hawkesbury, in a white heat. "I will not, I will fetch the book myself. He doesn't know where to find it. He has no business to go to my desk."

"Remain where you are, Hawkesbury," said Mr Barnacle.

"What right have you to search my desk? I have private things in it. Uncle Merrett, are you going to allow this?"

"Mr Barnacle has a perfect right to see the petty-cash account," said Mr Merrett, looking, however, by no means pleased.

"Why don't you examine his desk?" said Hawkesbury, pointing to me; "he is the one to suspect, not me. Why don't you search his desk?"

"I have no objection to my desk being searched," said I, feeling a good deal concerned, however, at the thought of the mess that receptacle was in.

"It is only fair," said Mr Barnacle. "This gentleman will search both, I dare say. Doubleday, show this gentleman both desks."

It was a long, uncomfortable interval which ensued, Hawkesbury breaking out in periodical protests against his desk being examined, and I wondering where and how to look for help. The partners meanwhile stood and talked together in a whisper at the window.

At length the gentleman, who, it had dawned on me, was not a bank official, but a detective, returned with Doubleday, who carried in his hands a few books and papers.

The petty-cash book and box were first delivered over, and without examination consigned to the safe.

"These letters were in the same desk," said the detective, laying down the papers on the table. They appeared to be letters, and in the address of the top one I instantly recognised the handwriting of the letter sent to Mary Smith, which I still had in my pocket.

Hawkesbury made an angry grasp at the papers. "They are private letters," he exclaimed, "give them up! What right have you to touch them?"

"Hawkesbury," said Mr Barnacle, "in a case like this it is better for you to submit quietly to what has been done. Nothing in these papers that does not concern the matter in hand is likely to tell against you. Is that all, officer?"

"That's all in that desk," said the detective. "In the other young gentleman's desk the only thing besides business papers and litter was this key."

A key? What key could it be? It was the first I had seen of it!

"Let me look at it," said Mr Merrett, suddenly, as the detective laid it on the table.

It was handed to him, and his face changed as he took it. He turned for a moment to show it to Mr Barnacle and whisper something. Then he said, "This is my key of the safe, which I left last night in the pocket of my office coat in this room!"

Chapter Thirty Eight
How I ended the Day more comfortably than I had expected

My misfortunes had now fairly reached a climax, and it seemed useless to struggle against circumstances any more.

Of course, I could see, as soon as my stunned senses recovered sufficiently to enable me to perceive anything, that the same false hand which had pointed me out as a thief had also placed that key in my desk as part of his wicked plot. I remembered that when I was conveyed up to the sample-room that morning my desk had been open. Nothing, therefore, could have been more simple than to secrete the key there during my absence, and so lay up against me a silent accuser which it would be far harder to gainsay than a talking one.

But what was the use of explaining all this when evidently fortune had decreed that I should become a victim? After all, was it not better to give in at once, and let fate do its worst?

"This is my key of the safe," said Mr Merrett, and all eyes turned on me.

Nothing I could say, it was clear, could do any good. I therefore gaped stupidly at the key and said nothing.

"How came it in your desk, Batchelor?" asked Mr Barnacle.

I didn't know, and therefore I couldn't say, and consequently said nothing.

"Have you any explanation to offer?" repeated Mr Barnacle.

"No," I replied.

"Then, officer," said Mr Merrett, "we must give him in charge."

The bare idea of being walked off to a police-station was enough to drive all my sullenness and reserve to the four winds.

Suddenly finding my tongue, I cried —

"Oh, please don't, please don't! I can explain it all. For mercy sake don't be cruel—don't send me to prison! I am innocent, Mr Merrett, Mr Barnacle; I can explain it all. Please don't have me locked up."

In my confusion and panic I turned round and addressed these last words to Hawkesbury, who received them with a smile in which there was more of triumph than pity.

"You false coward!" I exclaimed, suddenly seeing who it was, "you did this. You put the key in my desk while I was locked up stairs."

"Really, Batchelor," replied he, in his sweetest tones, "I'm afraid you hardly know what you're saying. I don't understand you."

"You do," said I, "and you understand how helpless I am to defend myself. You and Masham did your work well this morning."

"At any rate," retorted he, firing up, "we gave you a lesson for your impudence."

Mr Merrett had been speaking with the detective, and did not hear this dialogue; but Mr Barnacle did, happily for me.

"Then," he said, turning short round to Hawkesbury, "Masham *was* here this morning?"

Hawkesbury, thus suddenly cornered, turned first red, then white, and tried to mumble out some evasion. But Mr Barnacle was not the man to be put off in that way.

"Then he *was* here this morning?" he demanded again.

Hawkesbury had no retreat, and he saw it.

"He just called in for a moment," he said, sullenly; "that's all."

"Oh," said Mr Barnacle, "you can go to your desk, Hawkesbury, for the present."

Hawkesbury, looking anything but triumphant, obeyed, and Mr Barnacle, who evidently suspected the real truth more than his partner did, turned to me.

"Batchelor, do you still decline to offer any explanation of the discovery of this key in your desk?"

"I can only say," I replied, "that it must have been put there, for I never touched it."

"Who would put it there?"

"Hawkesbury, I suppose. When he and his friend dragged me up stairs my desk was left open."

"Can you describe this Masham?"

I could, and did.

"The description," said the detective, "tallies exactly with that given at the bank of the person who presented the cheque."

"Do you know his writing?"

"I know what I believe to be his writing," said I.

"Is that it?" inquired Mr Barnacle, showing me an envelope addressed to Hawkesbury.

"No, that is not the handwriting I believe to be his."

"Is that?" showing another.

"No."

"Is that?" This time it was the envelope I had already recognised.

"Yes, that is it."

"How are you able to recognise it?"

"By this," said I, producing the letter to Mary Smith from my pocket. The handwriting on the two envelopes was compared and found to be alike, and further to correspond with a signature at the back of the cheque. The clerk, it seemed, being a little doubtful of the person who presented the cheque, had required him to write his name on the back; and the fictitious signature "A. Robinson" was accordingly given in Masham's hand.

"That seems clear," said the detective.

"I see," said Mr Barnacle, looking again at the envelope I had given him, "this letter is addressed to the place where Smith lives. Is Masham a friend of Smith or his family?"

"Would you mind reading the letter, sir?" I said; "that will answer the question better than I can."

Mr Barnacle did so, and Mr Merrett also.

In the midst of my trouble it was at least a satisfaction to see the look of disgust which came into both their faces as they perused its contents.

"A dastardly letter!" said Mr Merrett. "How came Masham to know of Smith's private affairs?"

"Hawkesbury overheard Smith and me talking of them on the first occasion that we found him here, and must have told Masham, who had a grudge against Smith."

"You heard, of course, that Hawkesbury included Smith as well as yourself in his accusation?"

"Yes, I did. And I wish he was here to confirm my denial of it. What happened was—"

"Yes," said Mr Barnacle, "you need not go into that again. But answer one more question, Batchelor. Are you acquainted with Masham?"

"Slightly. I once was introduced to him by Hawkesbury and spent a day with him."

"Have you any reason to believe he is a swindler?"

"I know of nothing which would warrant me in saying so," replied I.

"Do you know whether Hawkesbury owes him money?"

"Yes—at least I have been told so."

"By whom?"

"By a boy—a shoeblack who—"

"A shoeblack!" exclaimed Mr Merrett. "Is that your only authority?"

"I believe he is honest," I said; "he overheard a conversation between Masham and a friend, in which Masham mentioned that Hawkesbury owed him £15."

"Really," said Mr Merrett, "this is almost absurd to take such testimony as that."

"It wouldn't be amiss to see the boy, though," said Mr Barnacle; "a great deal depends on whether or no Hawkesbury owed money to Masham. Where is this boy to be found?"

"Oh, I could fetch him at once. I know where he works," I said.

"No," said Mr Barnacle, "you must stay here. Doubleday can go." And he touched the bell.

"Doubleday," he said, when that youth entered, "we want you to bring here a shoeblack."

"Yes, sir," said Doubleday, artlessly: "will any one do?"

"No, no," said Mr Barnacle, "the boy we wish to see is—where is he, Batchelor?"

"He works at the top of Style Street," I said; "you will know the place by the writing all over the flagstones on either side."

With this lucid direction Doubleday started, and I in the meanwhile was left to go on with my usual work. Most of the fellows were away at dinner, and Hawkesbury as before was invisible, so I had the place pretty much to myself, and was spared, for a time, at any rate, a good deal of unwelcome questioning.

In due time there was a sound of scuffling and protest on the stairs outside, and Doubleday reappeared dragging in Billy. That youthful hero, evidently doubting the import of this strange summons, was in a highly indignant frame of mind at being thus hauled along by the mischievous Doubleday, who, vouchsafing no explanation and heeding no protest, had simply made a grab at his unlucky young victim, and then led him away, box, brushes, and all, to Hawk Street.

"Do you hear? turn it up—do you hear?" he cried, as they entered. "Oh, go on, you let my arm be—let me go, do you hear?"

At this point he recognised me, who thought it well to interpose.

"Don't alarm yourself, Billy," said I, "no one's going to hurt you."

"This cove do—and he *are*!"

"Well, he didn't mean. The gentlemen here want to ask you some questions, that's all."

"I ain't a-goin' to be arsted no questions. They ain't my governors, so I let them know. I ain't a-goin' to be arsted questions by any one 'sep my governor."

"But what they want to ask you, Billy," said I, "has something to do with Mr Smith's happiness and mine. All you have to do is to tell the truth."

This explanation mollified the ruffled Billy somewhat.

"Come, young cock-sparrow," said Doubleday, returning from announcing the distinguished visitor, "you're wanted inside. They want you, too, Batch."

We entered. Billy, as usual, was more at his ease than any one else. "What cheer? Well, what do you want to arst me?" he cried, jauntily.

The partners, thus encouraged, looked rather amused, and Mr Barnacle said, "You're the little shoeblack, are you?"

"In corse I are!"

"And you know this gentleman?"

"Yaas; I knows the animal!"

"And you know Mr Smith?"

"What! my governor? He ain't no concern of yourn," retorted the boy, firing up a little at this liberty taken with his "governor's" name.

Mr Barnacle gazed curiously at the strange urchin through his spectacles, and then resumed, in as coaxing a tone as he could assume, "You know a person called Masham, do you?"

"Yaas; I knows 'im."

"What sort of person is he?"

"What sort? Why, he are a beauty, so I tell you!"

"Yes; but I mean, what sort of looking man? Is he tall or short? Has he dark hair or light? Would you know him if you saw him?"

"Know him? Oh no—no fear—I know the beauty!"

"Well, what sort of looking man is he?" asked Mr Barnacle.

"He's a ugly bloke with a mug like yourn, and a 'orseshoe pin in 'is weskit."

"Yes? And what colour is his hair?"

"Carrots!"

That was quite enough. This unromantic portrait corresponded sufficiently nearly with the description already given.

"Now," said Mr Barnacle, "will you tell us when you last blacked his boots?"

"A Toosdy."

"Do you remember whether he was alone?"

"Ain't you arstin' me questions, though!" exclaimed Billy. "Of course he 'ad a bloke along of him, and, says he, 'That there parson's son,' says he, 'is a cuttin' it fat?' says he. 'He do owe me a fifteen pun,' says 'e, 'and ef 'e don't hand it over sharp,' says he, 'I'll wake 'im up!' And then—"

"Yes," said Mr Barnacle; "that's enough, my man, thank you."

When Billy had gone, Mr Merrett turned to me and said, "Go to your work, Batchelor, and tell Doubleday to send Hawkesbury here."

I obeyed, feeling that, after all, as far as I was concerned, the storm had blown over.

Doubleday went to Hawkesbury's glass box and opened the door. "You're wanted, Hawkes— Hullo!"

This exclamation was caused by the discovery that Hawkesbury was not there!

"Where's Hawkesbury?" he inquired of the office generally.

"He's not come back," said Crow.

"When did he go out?"

"Why, the usual time, to be sure."

Doubleday gave a low whistle, and exclaimed, "Bolted!" And so it was. That afternoon Hawkesbury did not appear again at Hawk Street, or the next day, or the next week, or the next month. And when inquiry was made at the rectory, all that could be ascertained was that he had left home, and that not even his father knew where he had gone.

Chapter Thirty Nine
Which parts me from the Reader, but not from my Friend Smith

And now, reader, my story is all but done. One short scene more, and then my friend Smith and I must retire out of sight.

It was on a Christmas day, three years after the event last narrated, that a little party assembled in a tiny house in Hackney to spend a very quiet evening.

It was, I daresay, as modest a party in as modest a house as could have been found that Christmas-time in all London.

The house had hardly yet lost the smell of paint and varnish which had greeted its occupants when they first moved into it a week ago. To-day, however, that savour is seriously interfered with by another which proceeds from the little kitchen behind, and which dispenses a wonderfully homelike influence through the small establishment. In fact, the dinner now in course of preparation will be the first regular meal which that household has celebrated, and the occasion being more or less of a state one, the two ladies of the house are in a considerable state of flutter over the preparations.

While they are absorbed in the mysterious orgies of the kitchen, the four gentlemen are sitting round the cheery little parlour fire with their feet on the fender, talking about a great many things.

One of the gentlemen is middle-aged, with hair turning white, and a face which looks as if it had seen stormy weather in its journey through life. He is the quietest of the party, the talk being chiefly sustained by two younger men of about twenty-one years, considerably assisted by a boy who appears to be very much at home on every subject, especially boots and mothers. Indeed, this boy (who might be ten, or might be fifteen, there is nothing in his figure or face or voice to say which), is the liveliest member of the party, and keeps the others, even occasionally the older gentleman, amused.

In due time the ladies appear, as trim and unconcerned as if they had never put their foot in a kitchen all their lives, and the circle round the fire widens to admit them. The elder of these ladies is a careworn but pleasant, motherly-looking body, who calls the elder gentleman "sir" when she speaks to him, and invariably addresses one of the two young men—the one with the black eyes—as Mister Johnny. As for the younger lady, whose likeness to Mister Johnny is very apparent, she is all sunshine and smiles, and one wonders how the little parlour was lighted at all before she entered it.

At least the other young man—he without the black eyes—wonders thus as he looks towards where she sits with the elder gentleman's hand in her own, and her smiles putting even the hearth to shame.

"So, Billy," says she, addressing the boy, "you've been made office-boy at Hawk Street, I hear?"

"I are so—leastways I ham so," replies Billy, who appears to be in some difficulty just now with his mother tongue.

"You mustn't stand on your head in the office, you know," says the young lady, with a mischievous smile, "or the junior partner would be horrified."

The young lady's brother smiles, as if this observation referred to him, and the elderly lady looks particularly proud, for some reason or other.

"That there bloke—" begins the boy.

"Order, sir," exclaims the young lady; "haven't I told you, Billy, that 'bloke' is not a nice word? It's all very well for a shoeblack, but it won't do for an office-boy."

"You do jaw me—" again began the boy.

"I what you?"

"Jaw—leastways you tork, you do," said Billy, who appeared to be as much in awe of the young lady as he was hopeless of attaining the classical English.

"I say, Mary," laughed the brother, "you might give Billy a holiday to-day, as it's Christmas Day. You can't expect him to master the Queen's English all at once."

So Billy is allowed to express himself for the rest of the evening in the way most natural to him, and shows his gratitude by making ample use of his liberty.

Presently the elder lady disappears, and returns in a minute or two with the information that dinner is ready, an announcement which Billy greets with the laconic ejaculation, "Proper!"

It is a cheery Christmas dinner that. The elderly gentleman is rather quiet, and so is the young gentleman called Fred, who looks a great deal oftener at the young lady than he does at the plate before him. But the others make up in fun and chatter for the silence of these two, and as the meal goes on the good spirits of the party rise all round.

"This is rather better than Drury Lane, eh, Jack?" says Fred.

"Rather," says Jack. "The only fear is about its being too far away for father."

"Not at all," says the elder gentleman. "I'm better already for the walk every day. You've no idea how agreeable the streets are at three o'clock every morning."

"Do you remember our first walk out this way, Fred," says Jack, "when we tried to find out Flanagan?"

"Yes, I do, indeed. We missed him, but we found Billy instead."

"Yaas, and you was a nice pair of flats, you was, when I fust comed across you," observes Billy, who, I regret to say, has not quite finished his mouthful of plum-pudding before he speaks.

"They're pulling down the court, I see, Billy," says Fred.

"They are so. 'Tain't no concern of mine, though, now she's hooked it."

Billy says this with a grave face, and means no irreverence in thus speaking of his dead mother.

"Mr Hawkesbury will be almost sorry to see it pulled down," says Jack, "for he had done so much good there."

"Poor Mr Hawkesbury!" says Mary. "I wish he would have come to us to-day. But he says he would be happier at his regular work, and we hadn't the heart to urge him."

"He's good deal happier now, though," says Fred, "since he heard from his son. In fact, he's had one or two letters, and Hawkesbury really seems to be turning over a new leaf; so the father is quite hopeful."

There is a pause, and then Jack changes the subject.

"Talking of pulling down places," says he, "I saw an advertisement to-day, Fred, of the sale of that valuable and desirable place, Stonebridge House."

"Did you?" says Fred.

And then follows a talk about old school days in which more present are interested than the two who actually take part.

"It seems a long while since we were there," says Jack.

"It's seven years six months and a week to-day since I left," says Fred.

"Why, how exact you are in your dates!" smiles the young lady.

"It was on the eighteenth of June," replies Fred. "I recollect it because it was on the twenty-first that I first met you."

He had not meant to say this, and blushes when it escapes him, and for the next minute or two he occupies himself with his plate. So does the young lady with hers.

Then the talk drifts off to other subjects, and the party fall to sketching out the programme of their new life in London. Jack is to be home to tea every evening at seven, and as Jack's father has not to leave for his newspaper office till eight, the little family will at any rate get one hour a day together. And as soon as the spring comes Miss Mary is going to convert the little strip of garden behind into a second paradise, and Mr Fred, if he pleases, may come and help her. Indeed, it is taken for granted that, although his lodging is away in a street hard by, he is to be considered as free of this house and one of the family; as also is Billy, provided he does not call Jack "bloke," and attends diligently to the instructions Miss Mary promises to give him two evenings a week.

In due time dinner is ended, and the little party once more congregate round the parlour fire. Scarcely have they assembled when there is a ring at the door, and next moment a cheery gentleman called Doubleday is announced. Every one welcomes the visitor warmly, and room is made for him in the magic circle.

"Thought I'd call and pay my respects," says Mr Doubleday, bobbing to the ladies. "Jolly snug little box you've got here, too."

"Yes, it is snug," says Jack.

"Glad to see you settled down before I go," says the other. "Settled down both here and at Hawk Street too, eh?"

"I'm awfully sorry you're going abroad," says Jack, "we shall miss you badly."

"Oh, I'll soon be back. You see, it's rather a good offer, this Bombay agency, and I'm bound to have to hop over to the old country every now and then to look you up."

"The oftener the better," says every one.

Mr Doubleday fidgets a bit in his chair, and then remarks, "I say, Smith, excuse my saying it, but I'm very glad you ever came to Hawk Street, and I may as well tell you so."

Jack is about to say something, but Doubleday is before him.

"I know what you're going to say, but it's a fact. Batch here thinks so too."

Mr Fred assents warmly.

"Fact is," says Doubleday, "I don't know how you did the trick, but you've drawn more than one of us out of Queer Street."

"What do you—" begins Jack, but Doubleday continues, "Of course you'll deny it, but no one believes you; do they, Batch? Why, even Crow was saying yesterday—"

"That's Flanikin," exclaimed Billy at this point, as another ring sounded at the door.

This interruption, though it cuts short Mr Doubleday's speech, is a decidedly pleasant one; and when a burly, rosy-faced Irish gentleman enters and joins the party the magic circle seems finally complete.

I need not recount all the talk of that happy Christmas evening. It was a merry Christmas, without doubt, though not a boisterous one. No one seemed to want any better enjoyment than chatting over old times, or sitting and listening while others chatted; and when Mary's sweet voice rang out presently in the words of some of the grand old Christmas hymns, the joy that lit up more than one face in the happy group spoke more eloquently than words of the true happiness which this season of peace and goodwill brought to their hearts.

In due time the hands of the little clock crawl round to eleven, and the two visitors rise to leave.

When they are gone the rest of the party once more draw in round the fire. By some accident, I suppose, Mr Fred's chair finds itself next to Miss Mary's, which, as it turns out, is convenient, for these two young people happen to have a good deal to say to one another which can only be spoken in whispers.

What they say, or most of what they say, is doubtless silly enough. But one or two sentences have some truth in them, and seem to express what is in the hearts of all that little party.

"Yes," says Mary, "it really does seem as if this was the beginning of a happy time for us all."

"I hope and trust it may be," Fred responds.

"Dear father seems better in health and spirits already, doesn't he? And Jack—Well, I dare say you are jealous of our taking him away from you?"

"Jealous, no!" says Fred. "He deserves all the happiness he has found, and far more."

"Yes," responds Mary. "He has always been a good brother."

"This one thing I know," says Fred. "If there is any good in me—and there's precious little—I owe it all, under God, to my friend Smith."

And, reader, I owe it still.